Praise for *Sweet Offerings, Bitte*
New Beginnings

Chan Ling Yap's third novel *New Beginnings* has all the
assurance of her first two successes – and more. A strong story
line, deftly rendered in brief and readable instalments, takes us
from the turbulence of a China unmercifully exploited with
opium by the western powers in Victorian times, to the race
and clan rivalries of an emerging Singapore and Malaya. The
beautiful and tragic figure of Hua might serve as a metaphor
for the suffering sub-continent; and that of her husband Ngao
for the resilience of the Chinese themselves.

The refinement and the thuggery of China alike, the
bustle of Singapore and the tropical potential of Malaya in
those days are all made to feel familiar rather than foreign, the
high emotions to be shared rather than differentiate us. The
characters are entirely believable, the degree of background
'colour' is perfectly judged, and the pace seductive: don't be
surprised if you find you read this book at a sitting.

—Bill Jackson,
Editor of *The Corporal and the Celestial*

Bitter-Sweet Harvest is one of "4 Books you Won't Want to
Put Down". A controversial page-turner ... heart breaking and
thought provoking.

—Review from *Cosmopolitan* (Singapore, January 2012)

Bitter-Sweet Harvest is a love story beautifully and engagingly told. It reflects the complex ethnic, religious and social tensions of Malaysia and beyond—all made vivid through the experience of characters, movingly depicted, and the exciting action, which carries the reader briskly from page to page.

—Dato' (Dr) Erik Jensen,
Author of *Where Hornbills Fly*

Tautly written, Chan Ling Yap's second novel is a powerful story of the problems of intercultural marriage that can arise from family interference. With a superbly woven plot, *Bitter-Sweet Harvest* leads the reader through a minefield of cultural, ethnic and religious conflicts. Compelling and gripping, I found I could not put down this tragic saga of missed opportunities for the lovers. A poignant love story that is highly recommended!

—Professor Bill Edeson,
Professorial Fellow, University of Wollongong

Sweet Offerings is a great read with real emotion and such detail as one can almost smell the atmosphere coming from the pages. Also I cannot recall ever reading a book where the very last word carried so much meaning for the future.

—Chris Allen

A FLASH
of WATER

mc **Marshall Cavendish**
Editions

Cover designed by Cover Kitchen Pte Ltd

Published by Marshall Cavendish Editions
An imprint of Marshall Cavendish International (Asia) Pte Ltd
1 New Industrial Road, Singapore 536196

Other Marshall Cavendish Offices:
Marshall Cavendish Corporation. 99 White Plains Road, Tarrytown NY 10591-
9001, USA • Marshall Cavendish International (Thailand) Co Ltd. 253 Asoke,
12th Flr, Sukhumvit 21 Road, Klongtoey Nua, Wattana, Bangkok 10110, Thailand
• Marshall Cavendish (Malaysia) Sdn Bhd, Times Subang, Lot 46, Subang Hi-Tech
Industrial Park, Batu Tiga, 40000 Shah Alam, Selangor Darul Ehsan, Malaysia

Marshall Cavendish is a trademark of Times Publishing Limited

National Library Board Singapore Cataloguing in Publication Data
Yap, Chan Ling, author.
A Flash of Water. – Singapore : Marshall Cavendish Editions, [2015]
pages cm

ISBN : 978-981-4677-76-9 (paperback)
1. Malaya – History – Fiction. 2. China – Social conditions – 19th century – Fiction.
I. Title.

PR6125.A35
M823.92 – dc23   OCN919288742

Printed in Singapore by Markono Print Media Pte Ltd

Dedication

In loving memory of my husband Tony Loftas.

Acknowledgements

I would like to thank Ann Smith, Gabriel Anderson and Marian Gosling for reading my draft manuscript and their commitment to the book.

Thanks also go to my son, Lee Loftas, for his comments.

Author's Note

A Flash of Water follows *New Beginnings* and together with *Sweet Offerings* and *Bitter-Sweet Harvest* forms a quadrilogy, which traces the lives of one family against the turbulent political, economic and social changes in China and Malaya. The stories are complete in themselves and could be read on their own.

Part One

Guandong, China

1883

Chapter 1

THE PEDALS WERE rough under her bare feet. Li Ling could feel the uneven texture of the wood grate into her soles. She pushed hard shifting her weight from side to side. The wheel groaned. Water gushed through, rippling down the narrow channels into the land all round her.

Li Ling looked up with a triumphant smile on her face. Her cheeks were flushed from the effort of working the water wheel. She could see her mother standing in the glistening paddy field with her cotton trousers rolled up high on her calves. She raised a hand to wave at the diminutive figure but her mother was too busy to notice. Over and over again, Ah Lan retrieved green shoots from the basket she carried on one hip and pushed them into the wet soil. Under the sweltering midday sun, the flooded ground glimmered black, like a still pond.

On the other side of the field, beyond the raised bund that separated it from another plot, her father was pulling a wooden plough, his back bent under its weight. Ribbons of turned-up soil followed him as he trundled forward in the soft mud. His feet sank deep with each step, the strain on his shoulders seen in the tendons bunched tight on his neck. It would take the whole day to plough that part of the field; and then it too would have to be flooded.

Li Ling grinned at her little brother pedalling beside her. Although he was still small for the work, his weight provided a useful balance. Once the momentum of the pedals was set, she could manage. Moreover she could hardly leave him alone at home for she could not look after him there and work the waterwheel at the same time.

"Shall we sing a song?" she asked.

"*Bu yao!* No! I don't want to. I am tired. You sing." Bao stuck out his lower lip in petulant rebellion. Suddenly his eyes brightened with excitement. "Look!" He pointed to a group of men coming towards them. There were five of them. They walked with an exaggerated swagger; their unbuttoned tunics flapped open with the breeze to reveal smooth muscular torsos. Their shaven foreheads glinted with the sun's glaring heat. With a quick practised flick of their heads, they swung back their long queues, thick braids of black hair like oiled ropes, and yelled. Their voices resonated across the field.

"*Hush!*" Li Ling said to her brother. "Don't attract their attention."

She saw the men heading towards her father. He must have seen their approach. He had already dropped the yoke and was hastening towards them. Even from where she was, she could sense the fear in her father's movements.

Ah Lan ran towards her children gesturing all the while towards the north. She flung both her arms out. "Go! Go!" she mouthed. In her haste she dropped her basket of seedlings. She stumbled; her feet sank deep into the soft mud; she picked herself up and lurched once more towards the children. She stumbled again, and as her knees connected with the earth, her hands made wide sweeping movements. "Move! Run!" the flailing arms seemed to say.

Li Ling jumped, dragging her brother along with her. They ran towards the dry bunds. From there they could move fast to the hedge and beyond. There was a little cave hidden behind the grove of trees. There they would wait for their mother. They had practised this drill before. Her parents had drummed into her over and over again that in times of emergency, she should run into the caves and wait till someone came to fetch her. She turned to look over her shoulder. Taken by surprise, the five men too were running, branching out to encircle the scattering figures when suddenly they seemed to change their minds. From the corner of her eye, she could see them regrouping and striding towards their father.

"Don't look back!" her mother shouted. She had seen her daughter hesitate.

Reluctantly, Li Ling continued. She pulled her brother along, her feet pummelling the dry path that verged round the wet fields until she reached grassland. She could feel her brother Bao lagging. She dropped to her knees and motioned him to climb on her back, "Hang on tight," she said. She hitched him up on her back. Her mother's words came to her. "Always take care of your brother; he is called Bao, precious, because he is our only son and you have to take care of him always. He comes first before all things. Remember! Bao carries our family name."

"And me?" Li Ling had asked.

"Ah my little daughter," said Ah Lan, brushing a strand of hair away from Li Ling's face. "You are a girl. When you marry you become part of another household. I love you dearly. However, as my own mother reminds me, we women are *fang jian shui*, just a flash of water to our own family. Once we marry, we disappear into the earth, soaked up with little signs of our earlier existence. When we are born, we have to obey our father; when we marry, we obey our husband, and when we are widowed, we obey our sons."

***

Ah Kang had seen the men coming. He recognised them, at least the two that stood with their feet planted wide and their arms akimbo. They were from their landlord, a warlord who owned all the fields in this valley. He had never spoken to his landlord before. He had only seen him on his horse with his retinue of men when they rode round the countryside. The two that were now glaring at him were his frequent companions. Ah Kang slowed his pace to buy time and to gather his thoughts. He glanced quickly in the direction of the big water wheel. It had ground to a stop. His wife and children could no longer be seen. He felt a quick rush of relief and quickened his footsteps once more to meet the men.

"So!" shouted one of the two men. "You have sent your family scattering. Are you scared of us? Do you have something to hide?"

Ah Kang bowed, his head and back bent so low that he was almost prostrating himself before them. "No! Please forgive my hasty actions. I shooed them away. I didn't wish you to look at their ugly faces. My wife is in the period of the moon that brings bad luck to all. I do not wish to offend you with bad fortune." He bowed humbly once more, his eyes averted to the ground.

Ah Gan the leader turned to the others and sneered. "This one has the mouth of a well-oiled pot."

"We come," he said glaring at Ah Kang, "to collect the rent due to our master. He is raising an army to defend our village from the foreign devils that have invaded our land. I am here to give you notice that we will be collecting our dues in two weeks."

"But ... but we have already paid for this year," spluttered Kang.

"Who is talking about this year? We are collecting the next year's rent now. Otherwise, forget about planting the crop. Since it will be harvested only after the spring festival, you will not be entitled to it."

"But ... but," stammered Kang.

"Forget the buts! *Fan su tow*!" said Gan gesturing and pointing a finger to his head to indicate that Kang had the brains of a potato. "Just think yourself lucky that we have bothered to give you notice. Unless of course, you have something else to offer." He threw a meaningful glance over Kang's shoulder. "My master is always happy to have a beautiful addition to his household." With that, Gan, with both hands on his hips, lifted one foot and kicked Kang, sending him sprawling on the ground.

"We will find them wherever they are. They cannot hide from us. Choose! The rent or the women! Don't worry!" His cackling laughter echoed across the fields. "We are not going to take your old woman. Who wants a used up bag like her? It is the girl we are looking for. I hear she is quite a beauty." He shook with laughter again. "You can spare her can't you? A mere girl! *Seet boon for*! A commodity that yields no profit. Hand her to us! You could then, at least, make some money. Think about it."

Kang scrambled to his knee. He prostrated himself before

them, his eyes fixed to the ground. How could he tell his wife? He kept silent maintaining his bow until the men's footsteps receded. Then he squatted down on his haunches and buried his head in his hands. He stayed still until his legs felt numb. Then he got up quickly and hurried towards the cave.

***

Ah Lan struck a match and held it against the wick. Immediately a flame spluttered to life in the oil lamp and light fell on the scattering of odd bowls and spoons on the table. The night air was heavy with the smell of the farmyard. It blew in through the opened door, which had been left slightly ajar. The stench infused every corner of the confined space. Outside in the fenced pen, chickens and ducks were settling in for the night. The family had just completed their evening meal. Ah Lan placed a protective hand on Li Ling's head. "Go to bed. Your father and I need to talk." Impulsively, she kissed her daughter's forehead, startling her by the intimacy.

Li Ling saw the distress in her mother's eyes and nodded. She slid down from the stool and made her way to the far corner of the room where a makeshift wooden bed stood. She climbed up the bed, taking care not to disturb her brother, and pulled the thin sheet over herself. She drew her knees to her chest and curled into a tight ball on her side. The wood planks grated hard against her hip. Holding her breath, she settled down quietly to listen. She knew she could hear her parents if she kept absolutely still. There was little privacy in the one room hut.

Ah Lan sat down on the stool and pushed the empty bowls to one side. "Did he specifically mean Li Ling?" she asked lowering her voice to a whisper.

At the other end of the room, Li Ling strained to hear. She clutched the thin sheets even more tightly and raised her head slightly.

"Who else could he mean? It was either you or her. He specifically said it was not you." He stared at Ah Lan's face, noting the furrowed forehead and the fine lines radiating from her eyes. Years of squinting against the bright sunshine had transformed the face to one that bore little resemblance to the girl he had married. He had not noticed until the man's rude comments.

"She is only thirteen. We have been very careful not to take her out beyond our patch of land. Few people have seen her. She has not even been to the market. Only the other day, she begged to accompany me to the village. I was on my way to deliver vegetables to the street vendor. I was tempted to take her with me. My shoulders were sore from carrying the pole with the heavy baskets hanging from each end of it. Even then, I resisted. I have never allowed her to wander out on her own. So how do they know if she is pretty or not?"

Ah Kang shrugged his shoulders. "Our neighbours?" he suggested.

Ah Lan fell silent. It could be, she thought. They might be directing the warlord's men to us to protect their own family. Would she not have done the same herself?

After a while, she let out a long sigh. While she had repeatedly told Li Ling that a woman should always conform and obey, inwardly she was praying that her daughter could be spared from such a life. She did not wish Li Ling to have a life of drudgery. Yet she did not wish her daughter to be taken as a concubine to a warlord. That too was not a life she wished for her. Her mind raced. She remembered a conversation she had overheard in the market place.

"There is a woman," she said, her words tripping out of her mouth in fits and starts. "She is a nun, not a temple nun. She is a nun from the foreign she-devil convent. She is a Chinese lady, may God forgive her soul for praying to a foreign god. Nevertheless I hear people say she is a good woman. She is helping women join their husbands and families in a place of opportunity in Southeast Asia. They call it Malaya. They say that women are now allowed to leave China and she is helping to arrange their travel."

"*Low poh*, old woman," he repeated emphasising the word old. "How could a woman do all this? Are you sure she is not a man disguised as a woman to lure young females into a life of corruption and decadence, to be sold to whoever can pay the price?"

"Quite the contrary, she is doing this to prevent women from falling into such a trap. She is here to visit her ailing aunt. See for yourself. Go to the market."

"Then what?" he asked. "What is the point of seeing this nun? Haven't we enough on our hands?"

"To see if she could help us of course," Ah Lan retorted, exasperated by her husband's slowness. She bowed her head to stop herself from flashing her steely eyes at Ah Kang. "Perhaps, we could all leave for Malaya," she muttered softly. "At the very least she might be able to help Li Ling."

"What about the crop? We are already late in our planting."

"I will stay back to finish off. Li Ling will help me."

"Don't place your hopes on foreign nuns. Remember it is the foreign devils that have made our lives miserable. If they had not built their monasteries and convents and taken land from the warlords, there would not be this incessant fighting and the warlords might not have to raise our tithe. They extract from our masters, our masters passed the burden to us."

"Try for me, for Li Ling at least," Ah Lan begged.

In the bed at the far side of the room, Li Ling held her breath.

"All right, all right," she heard her father say with gritted teeth. "In any case, it might not be a bad idea. I could see if we could borrow some money from your brother. He might know of this nun; I'll ask him.

Chapter 2

A SHAFT OF LIGHT seeped through the window slats turning the dormitory walls a buttery gold.

Mary sat by the bed with both hands clasped in front of her. Her head was bowed low and her knees were pressed close together beneath her rough woven skirt. She moved her lips silently in prayer. She felt a movement in the bed; just a slight rustling of starched sheets. It was sufficient to alert her that her aunt was awake.

Mary reached out and took her aunt's hand. It was limp and the skin dry and paper-thin. Dark blue veins like gnarled knots covered it. She saw a slight flutter of movement beneath the patient's closed eyelids and a tiny tremble at the corner of the parched lips.

"Shao Peng? You are still here?" Heong Yook's voice was barely a whisper.

"Yes," Mary answered still holding on to her aunt's hand, which lay light as a sparrow's wing in her own.

"Then, tell me again all about Malaya. How is your father? Is he still angry with me? Does he still blame me for your mother's death?"

"He is not angry with you. The past is the past. There is nothing to tell. I have told you all that I can about father." She leaned closer for her aunt's voice had grown even weaker and her breath laboured.

"Then tell me about you. Why have you not married? Why do you call yourself Mary? Why have you taken a foreign name?"

"It is a name given to me by..." Even while she spoke her aunt had drifted off. She tucked the bedclothes around her aunt's slight body. Then slowly she got up and went to the window.

It was quiet, so quiet, she could hear sparrows chirping in the courtyard. The building was previously a Chinese temple and the four core buildings of the Buddhist temple together with its central courtyard were still intact. It had been taken over by English missionaries. Dr Elizabeth Morrison headed the mission. Only four women, aided by a handful of village girls, manned the hospital she had set up for local Chinese women. So they were glad to welcome her, especially when she spoke English and Chinese to boot. That she came from a different Christian order did not seem to matter.

Shao Peng reached into the deep pockets of her pinafore and felt for her rosary. She needed it to remind her of what she was now. At times like this, she was torn. She leaned against the window pane. It felt cool against her forehead. Why had she not married? Wasn't that what she had wished and yearned for? She thought of him. Those deep blue eyes that had both startled and mesmerised her; the straight nose, the lock of hair that fell forward rebelliously even when he brushed it away, his lean, hard body.

Mary blushed. She was not a nun, not as yet. They call her Sister only to give her a title, which when translated into Chinese would just mean a female sibling. It was a title loosely used to give reverence to her position. She shook her head with impatience. Her thoughts of him had no right to intrude; they should be relegated to the past. She bowed her head in prayer, but to no avail. His image would not leave her. She remembered his touch. He had held her face close to him, willing her to change her mind, to defy her father and marry him. She could feel his touch even now; his scent and the hardness of his body when he held her. In desperation, she turned and walked quickly out of the dormitory towards the chapel. I must pray for forgiveness. I must not think of him, she chided herself. Then she remembered her promise to stay with her aunt. Abruptly she wheeled round and retraced her footsteps back to the bed. She couldn't leave her aunt alone. How could she be distracted by her own thoughts? She must be there for her in her last moments. Dr Elizabeth had said that there was little hope and that she must be prepared.

She hurried back to her aunt and drew the chair closer to the bed. Holding her aunt's hands in hers, she whispered, "Father is not angry with you. He does not blame you or uncle for my mother's death. He loves you; he wants you to know that he is grateful to you for bringing me up and sending me back to him. He is happy now with his new family. My brother Siew Loong is a fine young man, tall, good-looking, and everything father hoped for. Rohani, my stepmother has been wonderful to me.

All this is due to you. I love you aunt. Don't worry about me. I am not married because I chose not to be."

Her voice faltered. She felt a slight pressure of her aunt's hands and then the clasp of her fingers interlacing with her own.

"I chose not to marry because I do not wish to hurt father. The man I loved was an Englishman and I could not agree to the marriage father arranged for me. I ran to the Convent and they took me in."

She got up and leaned over her aunt. Her aunt's hands were ice cold and she was so still, that Mary feared she had passed away. She placed her cheek near her aunt's face and felt a slight breath. "He is called Jack, Jack Webster," she whispered in her aunt's ear.

Suddenly her aunt's fingers tightened with surprising strength. Her eyes fluttered open. She raised her head with difficulty and still holding on to Shao Peng's hands said, "Don't give up on yourself. Give yourself a chance for happiness. Shao Peng, you are not Sister Mary. It will not be fair for your Order, to the nuns that helped you. Be true to yourself. Promise me you will think again about taking vows; it is a life commitment and not just a means to escape."

She fell back on to her pillow. The effort had exhausted her. A tremor crossed her face and then she closed her eyes. Her body went limp; the flicker of life extinguished.

Shao Peng held on to her aunt's hands. Tears ran down her face. Unashamedly she wept.

Chapter 3

THE TWO-STOREY TEAHOUSE was situated in a cobbled narrow street leading to the market square. It was a place popular with merchants and the gentry. A narrow wooden stairway led to the upper level. Kang knew that his brother-in-law would be upstairs having *dim sum*. His mouth watered at the thought of the little steamed dumplings in bamboo caskets. He could imagine their succulence and aroma. He had never eaten in the teahouse. How could he afford it? Dumplings such as those served in the teahouse were not for people like him. He had breakfasted that morning on a boiled sweet potato and drank tea made from the acrid black remains of discarded tea shoots. To drink the green tea favoured by his brother-in-law would cost the same as several bowls of rice. He gulped again; his stomach rumbled with hunger.

He hesitated at the bottom of the stairway. Someone was strumming a harp in the room above. The music rippled down the stairs and he felt encompassed by it. It was beautiful in its simplicity. He knew the song. It told of the folklore in this part of the world, tales that his grandmother related, tales about the wistful aspirations and loves of beautiful court ladies. He went up the stairs and stood for a moment to locate his brother-in-law. He found him at a table overlooking the courtyard below. His brother-in-law did not notice his arrival. He was observing a small group of gentlemen with birdcages in their hands, engaged in a poetry session.

He hurried to the table. Huang looked up. A flash of annoyance appeared on his face. "You again. Can't it wait?" he asked with his chopsticks held aloft, poised to place a dumpling in his mouth. He deposited the morsel deftly and waved Kang to the seat before him.

"Brother Huang, we need your advice urgently. I would not take up your time if I could help it."

"All right, all right. Sit down. Tell me." A loud sigh of exasperation accompanied his invitation. Huang knew that his wife despised his poor relatives. Seeing Kang in the eatery would be better than having him in the house. He was fond of his sister Ah Lan, but he had married into wealth and his wife's wishes were important, more important than those of his sister. He sat back, folded his arms and listened while Kang recounted the threats of his landlord and Ah Lan's story about a Chinese Christian nun.

"First of all," Huang said with emphasis, rolling his tongue over the words, "I can't help you with money. You know how hard it is for me." He lowered his voice and looked round him to see if anyone was within earshot. He was embarrassed to have to explain his own situation. "I have to account for everything.

I can't just siphon out money. My wife will know. I have loaned you money earlier this year to help you buy seeds; last year I helped with your rent. I can't do it again."

"Big brother, I know, I know. We are grateful. We have nothing to defend ourselves against natural calamity. The crop failed last year because of drought. Please, we have no one to turn to."

"Why not take their suggestion and let them have Li Ling?"

"No! No! Ah Lan will not agree to it. Do you know this nun she spoke about, the one they call Sister Mary?"

"I have heard of her. She is a bold woman by all accounts. In my view, a woman who travels alone, who forsakes her own Chinese name and adopts a foreign one is an unworthy chattel. She has defied the teachings of Confucius. Can you trust such a person who has given her soul and her name to the foreign devils?"

Kang's mouth dropped. He had not thought of it this way and now felt the full impact of his brother-in-law's words. There had been increasing resentment against foreigners ever since the Opium Wars. He needed only to look across the street to know why. He looked out of the window to the building on the opposite side of the road. He had passed it many times and observed the people coming out of the den. Their eyes were inevitably glazed and their skin had an unhealthy glassy shine. He wondered how one could be lured into the depravity of opium smoking. Yet he had no doubt that there were many such people. Even in this tucked-away village in Guangdong, hundreds had fallen into the trap. His brother-in-law had told him that almost half the young men in China were imbibing opium. Foreigners brought the opiate freely into the country and the Emperor could not do anything having lost the war against it. He had been forced to accede to their demands to bring opium to China under the Treaty of Tientsin.

"This woman is not the only one who has gone over to the

foreign devils." Huang sat back and folded his arms before continuing.

"These *gwei loh* are buying people's souls by giving them food and shelter. Yet they do not care enough to learn their names, forcing them to take on foreign ones! *Huh!* Why do they call her Mary when she has a perfectly respectable name? Do you consider that kindness? Why does she allow them to defile her name? Far better to let Li Ling marry the warlord than recruit such a woman's help."

Kang got up. He knew that there was little use in pursuing the subject; his brother-in-law's attention was already elsewhere. He was once more gazing with rapt attention at the group of men and their songbirds. "I'll take my leave and talk this over with Ah Lan," Kang said, getting up. Huang did not hear him.

***

With a heavy heart, Kang made his way to the market square. It was crowded. To one side of the square were a couple of stalls that sold food. In one, steamed white buns stuffed with meat were stacked shoulder high on the stall. In the other, a man was dishing out scalding hot stew into rough china bowls. Kang sniffed, his mouth salivated. He recognised the aroma, pork ribs and intestines stewed in soya sauce with a hint of aniseed, cinnamon and cloves. His eyes followed a man holding a bowl. He was tucking into the dish with relish. He was seated on a rough wooden stool and, with a pair of chopsticks, was dunking batons of crispy fried *youtiao*, bread sticks, into the dark rich sauce. Kang felt his stomach rumble with hunger. He turned away and walked to the far end of the square to join a group of men. They too were staring at the two food stalls with eyes filled with longing.

"Maybe they will give us some if they can't sell all the food," said one in jest.

"*Huh!* Are you dreaming? Of course they won't," said another.

"Look, not many people are buying. Who can afford it? So there will be leftovers."

"If you want to eat, and don't care about who gives it to you, then you stand a better chance if you go to the old temple," said another. "Ever since the foreign women took over the building, they have been doling out food once a day around this time. Just thin gruel! Still, something to fill the stomach."

"My family would turn in their graves if I were to do that. My ancestral tablets were kept in the temple in the past. I do not know where they are now. How is it right that our place of worship has to be given up to foreigners?"

"Keep your voice down. These foreign devils have special powers. Under the treaties they extracted from the Imperial Government, the Missionary compound has special rights. Even the Imperial force cannot venture in to exert their control."

"Don't be too sure of that. The Imperial force might be bound to the treaties, but our brothers are not similarly constrained. They have fled to the mountains to train and prepare for the day we can expel foreigners from our land. Did you hear what happened to the foreign missionaries in the village to the north of us?" He paused for effect and looked around him. Then with a deliberate swift motion, he drew his index finger across his neck.

A hush fell over the crowd.

"Do you know who was responsible?" asked a man standing at the edge of the crowd. His question was received with stony silence. Everyone stared ahead. They pretended they had not heard. That is all except for a burly fellow. With a quick glance around, he held out his fist and punched the air. "That's who," he whispered in reply, leaning in to the ear of the questioner.

"Why do we need their food?" countered another, seemingly oblivious to the exchange. "Do you not remember that in this very village we had a similar system? Old Master Tao always gave food to the poor until he was bankrupted. He lost his family and business because of the wars waged on us by the foreigners. Are we to be grateful to the foreigners because now they feed us? Remember the previous missionary, the guy with the big nose—I mean the one that presided before the present lady doctor at the Mission? He helped the foreigners who invaded the village during the opium war."

Kang, squeezed in from all sides, looked from one angry face to the other. In a voice that was barely a whisper, he asked. "Has anyone heard of Sister Mary, a Chinese nun?"

His question was immediately greeted with derisive laughter.

"That turncoat! The one that brought her aunt from Beiliu to the Missionary?"

"No! No, that is not true. She is a good woman, at least she has been good to my family," protested one of the men. He had kept silent until then. Now all eyes were on him for his bold intervention. "My sister-in-law was able to join my brother in Singapore because of her," he explained. "The foreign missionaries are not bad people. They are doctors, here to help us." His eyes darted from one angry face to another. His voice wobbled and trailed off, drowned by the angry muttering that followed. Everyone, it seemed, had a view on Chinese women who take up the foreign religion.

Kang held his breath. So what his wife said was true. The Chinese nun was helping people leave China. He edged closer to the man who had just spoken and whispered in his ear. "Can you tell me how to reach Sister Mary?

Chapter 4

"Do you wish your aunt to be buried in the Mission's grounds? She is not of our faith and her family might object," said Dr Elizabeth Morrison. They were seated in Elizabeth's office, a little cubicle previously used as a store room.

Shao Peng pondered the question. It was one that had been troubling her. "I am all she has in China, " she replied after a while. "You are right. I don't think my aunt would wish to be buried in Christian ground. When I was a child in her care, she spoke to me of filial piety. She said it was important to give respect and reverence to our ancestors. She would wish this for herself. She has no immediate family in China to do that for her. Her husband and son have passed away. If she is cremated, I can then take her ashes along with those kept of my uncle back to Malaya. They can be placed in the ancestral hall. Although I am a Christian, I can still give her respect in death."

"Are you not staying on in China?" Until then, Elizabeth had refrained from asking too many questions of Shao Peng. She suspected that the young woman needed space. Nonetheless, she was intrigued. Not many Chinese women, in fact no one she knew, would take on such an arduous and dangerous task as travelling to and from China.

Shao Peng looked out of the window. The sun had almost disappeared behind the rooftop; just one errant ray struck the far corner of the inner courtyard to light up one of the pillars supporting the eastern building into a blaze of gold. She thought of her aunt's words and was overwhelmed by an unbearable sadness. She fought hard not to show it. "I'll leave after the funeral. I will finish what I have to do for the women that I am helping," she said quietly.

"Perhaps that is wise. It is not safe for you here. Feelings are running high against missionaries. I know that. What we do here is not sufficient to compensate for the harm done to your people." Elizabeth gestured to the beds that lined one side of the small room across the hallway. They were filled with women: some ill with fever or dysentery, common diseases that ravaged the countryside, others, however, were just bodies wasted from the smoking of opium.

"We are trying," she said with a wan smile, "and the London Missionary Society is doing its best. Our resources are limited. There are not many women doctors they can send. As you know, Chinese women only allow women doctors to attend them. Our male colleagues are not able to help. Moreover, it takes time to build up trust. Many do not trust us enough to bring their sick."

"You have worked so hard to help us. We are grateful. I am only sorry I cannot stay on to help."

"I work to repay the harm that we did to China. I know that there were some among us who turned a blind eye to the forced imports of opium into this country." She blushed as she recalled the words of a fellow missionary. "The opium wars were part of God's plan to make China a Christian country," he had said when she protested against its vileness.

"I am ashamed. I understand full well the Chinese people's distrust of us." Elizabeth fell silent, embarrassed by her own outburst. Then with a forced smile she clapped; a sharp gesture to underline that no more should be said.

"Enough about me! The Presbyterian Church of America is thinking of setting up a medical school to train women doctors here. It will be good if that can happen." She reached out to take Shao Peng's hand. "And you, what do you intend to do?"

"I don't know. I can only think of what I need to do now. And now, my task is to help women join their husbands in Malaya. They couldn't before because it was illegal, so the situation became dire over there. There were many more Chinese men than women. The imbalance has led women to be snatched from China. These poor creatures are smuggled into the country and enslaved by brothel owners." Her voice broke. "My mother would have been one of those women if she had not taken her own life."

"What happened?"

"We were both kidnapped. They tried to force her into prostitution, drugging her with opium. She killed herself. I was rescued by the brothel maid and returned to my aunt who brought me up. Later on an Englishman by the name of Edward Grime brought me to Malaya."

"Your father? Where was he?"

"He was abducted and sent off to Singapore to work. We did not know his whereabouts for years."

***

The sun broke through the heavy clouds. With it the shadows in the courtyard came alive. The women had been up early. By the time the night watchman sounded his first gong in the morning, the washing had been done and hung out on the clothesline. It billowed in the breeze—sheet after sheet of rough cotton suspended from high, their dye faded to only a previous hint of the colours they were.

"Come," said Shao Peng tucking the last of the pegs into the cloth bag slung low on her hip, "we have to clean out the dormitories. We will be going after lunch to Canton. We can't leave Dr Elizabeth with more work; she has enough on her hands."

"It's all right. You have cleaned enough," said Elizabeth coming into the courtyard. She waved the women away. "Breakfast is ready. If you hurry to the kitchen now, you might be able to help serve it to the sick and eat some as well."

She beckoned Shao Peng to her. "Come with me. A woman is here to see you. She has a young girl with her. They arrived very late at night. I put them up in my little office. I didn't want to wake you. They were so tired. I am afraid I could only give them some bedding and they had to sleep on the floor." She threw Shao Peng a puzzled look; her grey eyes were filled with concern. "She said it was a matter of life and death. I thought you said you had no kin remaining in China."

Who could it be, Shao Peng wondered. She too was mystified.

They arrived together outside the office, stopping only to catch their breath for they had hurried there. The door stood ajar. A woman's voice, low and urgent, could be heard from within. "Don't be frightened. This is our only way to save you. Do as they tell you. Don't answer back and you will be fine. They will look after you," she said.

A young voice, clear as a bell, answered, "Yes, mama."

Shao Peng and Dr Elizabeth pushed open the door. Both mother and child turned to face them. The woman, with a face wizened and lined by harsh hours under the sun, was burnt brown. Her hair was roughly coiled into a bun leaving strands of grey to escape and hang in defiance around her face. She stood with her mouth open. Taken by surprise, she was caught mid-sentence instructing her daughter. The child was slim and waif-like, a beauty with eyes like a doe, shy yet bright with curiosity and excitement that were hardly concealed.

"You wished to see me?" said Shao Peng, addressing the woman. "Do I know you?"

"You don't know me. We have heard of you and come to beg your help." The woman dropped to her knees, causing Shao Peng to immediately lower herself until her face was level with the woman.

"Please get up. Don't kneel. I am younger than you and am of no importance. Please aunty, come. Rise," she said drawing the woman to her feet.

Ah Lan threw an anxious glance at Elizabeth and turned quickly away. She had never seen grey eyes before; they looked soulless, like steel. How could such eyes see, she wondered. She avoided eye contact with Elizabeth. She had heard of the curse that could befall Chinese people if they locked eyes with the *gwei loh*. Wasn't that why China had fallen prey to this terrible poverty and despair, because of the curse of such eyes?

Elizabeth, sensing the woman's fear, retreated. "I will be outside if you need me." She went out, leaving the door half-opened.

Shao Peng drew Ah Lan to a stool. "Please tell me what brought you here."

Outside, Dr Elizabeth listened quietly to the story unfolded by the woman, a story that she had become familiar with in the three years she lived in China. The destitution of the poor; desperate families selling their female offsprings to repay debts; the untenable situation these girls found themselves in. Yet, should she be shocked? She reflected on her own experience as a member of the National Society for Woman's Suffrage in England. We were only better in some respects, she thought. We did not kill off baby girls nor did we sell our daughters to be concubines. However, women were still badly treated.

She leaned against the door. A wry smile appeared on her face as she recalled some of her fellow missionaries and their indignation about the plight of Chinese women. But were we really so much better off, she wondered. The words of the barrister Leone Levi came to her mind. He had insisted that a woman loses her personal identity on marriage. He believed that her person was completely subservient to that of her husband. Through marriage, a husband acquired an absolute mastery over a woman's person and effects. Why, until a decade or so ago, a married woman in England could not even engage in trade. Even among missionaries the attitude had remained undoubtedly biased. She recalled the words of one male colleague. "Women missionaries in foreign lands must be careful to recognise the headship of men," he had said. He had then paused and then enunciated slowly, his face patient as though he was explaining to a child, "the head of a woman is the man."

The sound of sobbing interrupted her thoughts. Elizabeth placed her ear close to the door.

"I do not know if I can help you," she heard Shao Peng say, distress in her voice. "I am mainly here to bring women to their families in Malaya. I come entrusted by their husbands to fetch them. I do not know if I could take Li Ling with me, seeing she has no kin there."

"Make her your kin," said Elizabeth pushing open the door. She spoke in Cantonese to make sure that the woman understood. They turned in surprise at her intervention. "You can say that she is your cousin. I'll help with the funds. I have some savings and I might be able to put in a good word with the ship's captain."

Shao Peng looked at Ah Lan then at Li Ling. The girl was holding on to her mother's tunic blouse, crushing the hemline into a tight ball, fear in her face. How could she not help them? She was glad of Elizabeth's intervention. It reminded her of her cause. "Yes, I'll do it. I'll take Li Ling with me," she said. "What about you, good aunty? What would you and your husband do?"

"Our main concern is for our daughter. She is the one in immediate danger. Once she is out of the way they could only threaten and extract money from us. They would beat us up. I don't think they would drive us out from the land immediately. I suspect we would be forced to work it without return. Who could pay the exorbitant rent and take over from us?" Ah Lan and Kang had discussed this at length and that was the conclusion they had reached. In a countryside ravaged by war, they could see only poor peasants like themselves.

Ah Lan turned to Elizabeth and was about to kneel again, when they caught her in time. "*Doh chei, doh chei,*" she said with both hands clasped in thanks. She was embarrassed and ashamed by her unkind thoughts about the Missionary lady.

"I am so sorry for coming so late last night," she said looking directly for the first time at Elizabeth. She felt the need to explain. She had to make amends for not looking at or speaking to her. She had not even thanked the lady properly when she let them in and gave them a place to sleep. She had been too terrified.

Even now she had to quell her fears and force herself to engage the eyes of the doctor.

"I couldn't leave the house with my daughter in daylight. I was frightened that someone might see us. That was why we came so late. Forgive me for disturbing your sleep." She remembered a flustered Elizabeth at the door, holding together her dressing gown when she opened it to let them in.

Shao Peng smiled. "Come," she said, "Dr Elizabeth is not offended or angry. Those thoughts never crossed her mind, I assure you. Come," she repeated, "let us have something to eat."

Chapter 5

THE OPEN CART rolled forward, creaking and bouncing over the rough terrain. Unaccustomed to the motion, the women held onto each other. They wore wide cone shaped straw hats, typical of those worn by local farmers. A kerchief was tied round Li Ling's head and it protruded like a hood to help obscure her face. Shao Peng thought it best that the girl was less visible.

The plan was that they would be in Canton by nightfall where they would stay in another Missionary house and then leave for Singapore the following day.

Lai Ma was the oldest. She had wept bitterly the night before. In the cramped dormitory she spoke of the four children she had left behind with her in-laws. The youngest was only five. She had wanted to take all of them with her. She could not. Her husband was only able to send her a ticket for just one passage.

Moreover, as her mother-in-law pointed out, she would not be able to work if she had the children and she needed to earn. "Any job, Miss Shao Peng," Lai Ma had pleaded, "so long as it pays and I can put aside enough to send for them. Meantime, I have to send money home for their upkeep. My in-laws are poor farmers eking out a living growing vegetables. They do not have enough to take on four additional mouths to feed."

Now seated in the open cart, Lai Ma looked resigned. The dark circles round her eyes and the swollen eyelids were all the traces left of last night's emotions. Sensing that she was being watched, her lips trembled into a semblance of a smile. "I'll be all right," she assured Shao Peng. A tear, bright like mercury, however, rolled down one cheek even while she professed she was fine. She brushed it away fiercely and turned her face quickly away.

Shao Peng leaned over and placed an arm around Lai Ma's shoulders. There was little she could say to console her.

Overhead, the sun that was shining brightly just minutes ago, disappeared behind dark clouds blowing in from the west. Streaks of lightning flashed through the sky and huge drops of rain pelted down fast and furious, drenching everyone in the cart. The women drew their feet up to huddle under their wide brimmed hats. They clutched their belongings close to them. The rain came sweeping down, angling straight into their faces. There was nothing to stop their onslaught for it was all flat land.

"Look," cried Jing-jing, with a broad grin on her face, "we are all crying." She was seventeen and the youngest of the three women. She tilted her face up to the sky, letting her hat slip behind her back, uncaring that it caused a stream of water to pour on to the other women. She stood up, swaying with the motion of the carriage. The cart continued to roll forward, its wheels squeaking in protest.

"I don't mind this. I'll be joining my husband. I'll be free from the incessant spiteful berating of my mother-in-law."

"Sit down!" Shao Peng shouted to make herself heard above the storm's uproar. "You will upset the cart." With her other arm, she gathered her charge Li Ling closer to her. She turned and whispered to Lai Ma, "Ignore Jing-jing. She is young and has her reasons.

Jing-jing heard. She squatted down and, shivering as the wind bit through her wet cotton top, yelled, "I can't help it. I am sorry if I upset you. This journey sets me free. For over two years, I suffered in my mother-in-law's household. She hated me. She said I was barren so she worked me hard. From morning to night I had not a minute to myself. Drawing water from the well, emptying the chamber pots, massaging her feet, those bound smelly feet which she was so proud of while all the time shaming me for what she called my big ugly ones. She made me kneel to serve her tea and it was never right for her taste. It was too hot; then it was too cold; or she would complain that it was weak or excessively strong. I cried myself to sleep every night, all eight hundred and twenty-six days since my husband left China. I want to celebrate this day!"

So saying, she leapt up again, her face glistening with the rain while her eyes shone with feverish fervour. Shao Peng pulled her down. "Stay still! We understand your feelings. Just stop rocking the cart or we'll crash. Look at the lightning." She pointed to a flash of silver hurtling through the sky. A roll of thunder followed. The horse wheeled suddenly to the right. It raised its forelegs and scrambled them in the air before landing back on the ground with a thud. The driver muttered a loud curse and the cart lurched to the right and into the ditch.

"Get out! Get out!" he yelled. "Get behind the cart. Push when I tell you."

The women jumped out of the cart. Their feet, shod in wooden clogs, were swallowed immediately by oozing mud.

"Push," he ordered.

They pushed shoulder to shoulder, some losing their footwear to the squelching mire. It took them several efforts before the wheels broke free and rolled once more out onto the road. They clambered wet and weary back onto the cart. Shao Peng counted quickly to make sure that everyone was on board and the cart rolled forward, continuing its ungainly journey towards Canton.

"Chun," Shao Peng said solicitously to the third woman in their group, "are you all right?" She had noticed that Chun was uncommonly quiet. She had barely spoken a word throughout the journey. Indeed, Shao Peng could not recall her saying anything during her entire stay at the Mission. Chun was just a year or two older than Jing-jing and was as serious and quiet as Jing-jing was exuberant and talkative. While the other women exchanged stories, Chun kept to herself. Only when Shao Peng asked her what her name meant so that she could write it correctly, did she venture to explain that it stood for spring. "My mother said that my name is to depict the start of life, when the cherry blossoms bloom." She had then blushed and relapsed into silence, making no further response to the questions and chatter of the other women.

"If you are not feeling well, perhaps you would like to take my seat. Lean against the side of the cart. It is more tiring seated in the middle with nothing to support your back." Shao Peng was eager to engage her into a conversation. It was important that the women got along. Jing-jing had grumbled that she found Chun unfriendly. "And look," she added, "it has almost stopped raining."

"Thank you. I am fine," Chun replied looking up to the sky. The dark clouds that had loomed like thick forests of black cotton wool had begun to disperse to reveal patches of clear blue.

Shao Peng searched into her bag and found a boiled sweet potato. She fished it out and broke the root into clumps to share amongst the women. "Can we not find some shelter to eat and rest?" she asked the driver.

He turned to cast her a cutting look. "What!" he said incredulously. "And risk being attacked by bandits? We have to reach Canton before nightfall. Eat and rest if you wish. No one is to get down from the cart until I finish delivering you to the Mission."

Jing-jing nudged Li Ling seated next to her. "He is cross. So beware!" When Li Ling did not reply, she addressed Shao Peng with a toss of her head. "You have another silent one over here."

Shao Peng's heart went out to Li Ling sitting in silence with eyes cast down. She remembered her own first journey at seven years old and the wrench she felt when she had to leave all that were dear and familiar to her. "Here, have my share. I am not hungry," pushing the clump of soft golden tuberous root into Li Ling's hand. Rummaging in her bag she fished out five lengths of sugar cane. Their green skin gleamed invitingly. "Your mother gave us these for our journey. They would help us quench our thirst."

Li Ling took the cane and bit down on to the hard fibrous root, tearing the outer skin with her little white teeth. Then closing her eyes she sucked the fibrous stalk and for the first time in the journey, she smiled. "We grow these in our backyard. My mother will squeeze the juice out and boil them in summer to sell in the market. I don't like it warm though, I much prefer eating it this way."

"My children like it too," said Lai Ma. "I give it to them if they have sore throats. It is supposed to be a cooling drink, a *yin* to balance out the *yang* in our body. They like it because it is sweet. She too smiled with her fond memories. The atmosphere visibly lightened and the cart settled to a steady roll towards Canton.

***

The Mission in Canton stood in a narrow street. The back of the building overlooked a canal, one of the many that formed a labyrinth connecting various sections of the city. The women got out of the cart and proceeded to the front door of the grey brick building. They knocked. An elderly woman opened the door and invited them in. Her hands were gnarled and their knuckles red and raw. "Let me take you to the waiting room. I am in the middle of helping out in the kitchen and will leave you there for a moment. Come, come, this way."

She led on. The long corridor was cool and dark. Rooms branched off on either side. From behind their closed doors, the smell of bleach and soap mingled with that of wax candles seeped through. "This is used mainly as a hospital," she explained. "A few rooms to the rear of the building are kept for fellow missionaries passing through and you will probably be put there for the night. The doctor will tell you more."

They turned a corner and entered a room. "Please wait here," she said and then she closed the door quietly behind her.

Left to themselves the women wandered around the confines of the room. They soon sat down for there was little to see. The room was clean and spartan. A few wooden chairs, a table and, on the wall, a cross, were all that was there. A beam of fading sunlight shone in through the window. They could hear swallows chirping outside, their little winged bodies swooping and rising to finally settle in a tight row on a wooden beam beneath the roof.

"Do we have to pray to the foreign God?" asked Lai Ma eyeing the cross. Despite her induction to Christianity, she was not sure of how she stood in terms of her belief. A life long practice of ancestor worship did not prepare her for a sudden shift in allegiance. She had observed the prayers, the devotion and kindness of the missionaries. It all seemed good. Yet, did she have to give up her worship of ancestors to become a Christian? How would the kitchen god who reports on each household, view her when he ascends to heaven, she wondered fearfully? Would the missionaries force her to accept a new religion?

"No, only if you wish," said Shao Peng breaking into her thoughts. "If you wish to learn more about Christ, we can learn together when we are on board the ship. Taking up Christianity is not a condition for my helping you."

"Sister Mary," cried Dr Fulton coming into the room, her arms outstretched in welcome."

Shao Peng blushed. "I am not a Sister, Dr Fulton. I am only at the very start of my journey. The term has been used very loosely here."

"No matter. Our Mission is set up by the London Missionary Society. We are non-denominational. What is important is here," she said, placing a fist on her heart, "and we welcome your work."

She spun round to look at the other women. She beamed at them, "*Huan ying, huan ying*. Welcome, welcome," she said before turning once more to Shao Peng. "I'll show you around our hospital and school later. With the help of our benefactors we are setting up a medical school to train doctors. We have taken in two women into our college. We are so proud; this is a tremendous achievement and would be so useful for our work.

Dr Elizabeth must have told you that Chinese women would only allow women doctor to examine them and hence training women doctors is..." Dr Fulton stopped. "What am I saying? Of course, you know, having been born here." She laughed a fulsome, hearty laugh that rang from her chest. "My apologies. I do get carried away. Come let me show you to your quarters for tonight. We can talk after supper. Tomorrow, as I understand, you will leave us."

***

The room was quiet. Chun pushed her blanket quietly to one side and swung both feet to the ground. Reaching down under the bed, she found her pair of shoes and her cloth bag of belongings. She rose to her feet and moved towards the door. She took each step slowly. A sudden loud sigh made her stop, feet mid-stride in a balletic trance. Then quiet returned and the soft sounds of sleep once more filled the room. Chun moved quickly towards the door. Her bare feet barely registered on the cold tiles. Gently she eased it open. She slipped out and almost tripped as her bag caught the door handle in her anxiety to make haste. With great care, she disentangled the bag and closed the door behind her. She hastened towards the kitchen. She knew the route. They had had supper last night in the dining room adjacent to the kitchen.

It was still dark; everyone was asleep. In an hour or so, the place would be bustling with activity. In the village she had seen the early hours that people keep in the Mission; they were all up and about before the cock crowed. She had to be quick. She made her way, still with bare feet, to the rear of the kitchen. There was a door opening out to a platform. The cook explained that supplies and groceries were delivered there by passing boat vendors. Once on the platform, she slipped on her shoes. She crouched down rolling her body into a tight ball, arms clasped around her knees, her chin on her knees. She could feel the thudding in her heart. She stayed still, her mouth dry with expectation, looking out to the stretch of water before her. It gleamed like a snake of black oil, rippling gently when the wind blew. Then she saw him, silhouetted against the moonlight, a lone figure standing tall in the narrow dinghy. He rowed towards her, his oar breaking the stillness of the water surface as he eased the boat forward.

Chun glanced quickly around and then stood up. She waved both her arms letting her cloth bag hang carelessly around one shoulder. The boat contacted the jetty with a slight wobble. She jumped in.

***

Bowls of steaming hot rice porridge were laid out on the long wooden trestle for breakfast. In the middle stood three small dishes, no bigger than the palm of one's hand. They contained different types of salted pickled vegetables. Nearer to where Shao Peng was seated with Li Ling stood a miniscule bowl of fermented *tofu*; its creamy white texture was speckled with red chillies. At the other end, lay a tiny plate of salted duck eggs. The eggs were peeled and cut into minute segments. "One egg for five people or we will run out of provisions very quickly," instructed the cook when Shao Peng offered to help peel them. "They are only to pep up your taste buds, and are far too salty to be taken in large quantities. Good job, or my housekeeping money would not extend to the mouths that keep turning up at this Mission."

Shao Peng looked down the table; several staff at the Mission had joined them. The table was now full but for one seat still empty. "Where is Chun?" she asked. "I looked for her this morning and couldn't find her."

Jing-jing shrugged. "I haven't seen her. She keeps to herself. I can't draw her into any conversation. So I just leave her be," she said tucking into her porridge and making quick forays into the dishes before her.

Shao Peng turned to Li Ling and Lai Ma. They too had not seen Chun. Shao Peng got up quickly leaving her food half eaten. "Perhaps she is not well," she said. She hurried out of the room and went to the kitchen. She was about to walk past the cook, when she hesitated. The cook saw her.

"Would you like a second helping?" the cook asked. She recognised Shao Peng who had helped her earlier in the morning. "I have still some in the pot. It is fast sticking to the base, so come and get it if you want more. Only be quick about it." She was stirring a pot of porridge as she spoke, her face a study of concentration. She was a small plump lady and the wood-burning stove came up to almost the level of her chest. Her face was flushed from the heat and the effort.

"No thank you but have you seen one of our ladies, Chun? She is the quiet one and is about this tall." Shao Peng demonstrated with her hand.

"*Ahhh!* I forgot. She said last night that I was to give you this after breakfast." Cook rummaged into her pocket and took out a piece of paper. "She specifically said to hold on to it until breakfast was over before giving it to you."

Shao Peng took the paper. How strange, she thought. "Did she say anything else? Did you see her this morning?"

"No! She said very little. I could see that she was jittery

and nervous though. Look, I have to carry this to the breakfast table before it gets cold. Once cold, it congeals and is not nice." Without waiting for a reply, the cook strode off with the pot.

Shao Peng unfolded the paper. It was very crumpled; someone had folded and refolded it many times, leaving creases upon creases on it. Smoothing it with the palm of her hand she read.

Sister Mary, I thank you for trying to help me leave China to go to my betrothed. I was engaged to him when I was a child. I was only thirteen when my parents made that decision for me. I would probably have been his child bride, if he had not gone to Malaya. But he left and I stayed with my parents. I am in love with another boy in the village. My parents do not know. Please, I do not wish to be found. By the time you read this letter I will have left with him. I thank you for giving us this opportunity to be together. I am ashamed and sorry to be so deceitful. There was no other way. Chun

Shao Peng clutched the piece of paper tightly. Her hand shook. She was shocked by her own naivety. How could she have been so blind? She had thought that Chun was like Jing-jing, eager to leave for Malaya. No wonder she had said so little. Perhaps she should have asked Chun what she wanted and not make assumptions. She would have been party to a forced marriage like the one she herself had fought so hard against.

Somehow, news of this turn of events must have reached Dr Fulton because she was striding purposefully towards her with Lai Ma, Li Ling and Jing-jing in tow.

"You don't have time to go after your charge," she cried even before she reached Shao Peng. "The boat leaves in less than two hours. Don't even think of trying. This is a big city teeming with people. Go! You have to leave now. Let her be."

Shao Peng agreed. She wanted no part in forcing Chun into a marriage she did not want. But what should she do? She had booked the berth for Chun and the money given by Chun's betrothed had been spent. Surely it would be too late to attempt to seek a refund. Suddenly a thought struck her and her eyes brightened as the thought took form. She need not retrieve it. She could use the ticket for Li Ling. Surely the ship captain would have no objection to this? Then she would use the money Elizabeth had given towards Li Ling's passage, add her own savings and recompense Chun's fiancée. In fact, it might make it easier to get Li Ling on board this way. Dr Fulton had warned her of the difficulties of getting a ticket for Li Ling.

"Yes! We will pack and leave now," she said. "I won't look for her; she does not wish to be found. If Chun comes to visit in the future, tell her we pray for her and wish her luck."

***

The ocean going junk loomed large before them. Shao Peng looked around the quay. It was heaving with people. People pressed in on all sides and the women found themselves swallowed into the mass of humanity surging forward. She was told that the junk would be full to capacity if not exceeding it. "It will not be a problem," a cynical bystander had remarked. "The boat might start the journey having too many passengers, it will not remain so. By the time it reaches its destination, it will have lost a significant proportion of its passengers. It only makes economical sense to pack the boat to the full. It costs the ship captain virtually nothing to take people on board. Indeed it makes him a lot of profit. Pigs in cages, that's what they think of the coolies."

Jing-jing tugged at Shao Peng's sleeves. She looked frightened for the first time. "What does he mean by that? Does it mean that we too might die?"

Shao Peng smiled and squeezed Jing-jing's hand reassuringly. "Unlike most of the men who are going out as coolies and owe their passage to the ship captain, we have paid for our tickets. Our travel conditions should be better. I have travelled on such boats twice. I survived. This does not mean that there is no risk at all. There is always the risk of death in any journey. We have talked about it before. Remember? We have to be careful about what we eat and drink, and we have to look out for one another."

She looked at her fellow passengers. When she left China disguised as a boy, every passenger on the boat was a man. No female passengers were allowed because women were banned from leaving China. Now, judging from her rough headcount, there were quite a few of them. She could see that the women were not from well-off families. They were peasants or from the town's poor. Their unbound feet were testament to their status. She saw the eagerness in their faces. Like Lai Ma and Jing-jing they were leaving to join their husbands. It would be a true reunion of families and heart when they reach Malaya. And for girls like Li Ling, running from forced marriages, it would be a new beginning, just like it had been for her when she left China those many years ago. She tightened her grip on Li Ling's hand and, bending down, whispered, "I shall look after you like a sister. You will stay with me, so do not fret. I too have to start my life all over again." She straightened her back. She recalled her aunt's last words to her. I must not run. I should take the example of Chun, to have her bravery to fight for what I want.

***

The women were segregated from the men and placed en masse below deck. About eighty of them were placed in a single compartment. They lay almost cheek by jowl in narrow confinement. A weak oil lamp cast a dim yellow light over the occupants. It was airless and stifling. The hot air suffused with the smell of human bodies soon grew rank. There was little to do. They had to resign themselves to the conditions. Nothing was achieved by protesting. Just as their men had survived before them, they too had to try.

At first, the women lay listless, surrendering themselves to the hard journey, their bodies racked with pain and discomfort with each roll of the ship. Sickness was rife. They tried to wash off the stench. Buckets upon buckets of seawater were doused on the floor. It was futile. The air remained suffused with the smell of vomit. They were warned that worse was to come were they to meet with bad weather. To survive they had to think of what could be gained at the end of the journey. "Imagine," they were told, "a new life with your loved ones and most importantly, the wealth that you could accumulate. For those who are unafraid to work, the streets in *Nanyang* are paved with gold for the taking." Thus the women were encouraged and gradually with the passing of the days, most adapted to life on board the junk.

There was little to entertain or occupy them. The days went by monotonously, broken here and there by the squabbles that inevitably broke out in the confined space of the cabin. Food was scarce and unchanging. They ate principally what they brought with them. For the most part the women had only brought rice, which they boiled and shared out amongst themselves. Exchanging stories about their previous lives and their aspirations for the future became their main source of entertainment. They listened to each other enthralled. Gradually a sense of comradeship grew between them.

Shao Peng sat with one arm around Li Ling. "The streets are not paved with gold," she whispered to her charges. "There is opportunity to earn and do well if you are willing to work hard. It will not be easy. Do not be duped by the ship captain. My father slaved for many years before he did well."

"I shall work all day and all night to make sure my boys have an education and we can pay for their passage to join us in Malaya," said Lai Ma. "I do not wish them to come as indentured labourers like my husband did. It took him years before he could repay his debt and to save enough for just one ticket."

"I'll see what I can do to find you a job. My father or brother might be able to help. I can't promise though," Shao Peng hastened to add. She thought of the circumstances of her departure and her father's anger at her decision to return to China.

"What would people say?" he had railed at her. "You are already an old maid with little prospects of a good marriage. You threw away your last chance with your infatuation for a *gwei loh*. Do you wish to add to this? People will inevitably gossip if you were to travel alone. It is not safe for a woman, not even a nun! I forbid it!"

"Don't you worry about me. I am sure my husband will take care of everything," said Jing-jing confidently breaking into Shao Peng's thoughts. "He might not want me to work. Maybe I can be a proper lady, a *siew nai*, a mistress of the house with maids to attend to me." She broke into a song, and her voice soared clear and sweet in the cabin.

"*Huh!*" exclaimed a woman who was sitting close by them. "More likely she would become a songstress, a singer to entertain men."

Jing-jing did not hear. She was carried away by her own exuberance.

"What about you?" Lai Ma asked Shao Peng. "Are you really going to become a nun?"

Shao Peng didn't know what to say. She didn't know herself. She pretended not to hear. She rose and pulled Li Ling with her for the girl had remained quiet and withdrawn. She had heard her sobbing in her sleep. "Let us walk a little; my legs are numb from sitting on my haunches. Lai Ma, Jing-jing, please look after our space. When we come back, perhaps you and Jing-jing might wish to take a turn on the deck. We'll guard your space for you."

***

The days merged from one to the next. For the women holed-in below deck in the dark, day and night were little different. Seasickness remained rampant as storms buffeted the boat, sending them rolling from one end of the compartment to the other. Outside on the deck the men slaved under the hot sun and slept in the open air under rough shelters. As predicted, some did not survive the journey. Their bodies, unceremoniously wrapped in sacking, were confined to the sea watched helplessly by those on board. Thus, the junk carrying its human cargo edged its way round the southern coast of China into the turbulent South China Sea towards Singapore and Malaya.

Chapter 6

Kuala Lumpur, Malaysia, 1883

EVEN FROM A DISTANCE Shao Peng could see that something was wrong. She held on to Li Ling as the rickshaw came to an abrupt stop. The street was packed with people, all moving towards her father's house. The gates were thrown open. Hanging from the top left gatepost was a white lantern. Her hand flew to her mouth. Shao Peng scrambled down from the rickshaw pulling Li Ling along with her. "Here, take this!" she said thrusting money into the rough worn hand of the bewildered rickshaw puller. Clutching her bag and Li Ling's arm, she half ran towards the gate. People parted to let her through. "The daughter," she could hear some of them say, "the one that went to China, the one who went against her father's wish and took up the foreign religion."

A crescendo of shrill cries pierced the air when she neared the house. It came in waves interrupted by sorrowful sobbing. Someone nudged her, digging an elbow into her side. "Professional mourners," the person explained without looking at her, "hired to express grief for an important man. They need to have such mourners to help them; he has only two children. One, I was told, is not here. How else can they broadcast their respect and sorrow with so few children on the ground? So rich, yet so few descendants! What could he have been thinking when he was alive! If it had been me, I would make sure that I had many children." He gave Shao Peng a lurid wink.

"Shut up, you stupid man," said another bystander in an exaggerated whisper that was meant to be heard. "Can't you see? You are talking to the very one you said is not here. She is the wayward daughter." He gave Shao Peng a spiteful look.

Shao Peng could feel a flush of heat in her cheeks. She ignored him and pushed her way forward, holding Li Ling's hand in hers.

"Is this where you live?" Li Ling asked, wide eyed. She hurried after Shao Peng. "Why are all these people lining up to go in?" She had not expected Shao Peng to live in such a grand house. She looked up at the tall gates. Garlands of white cloth hung suspended from it. The keening from within the compound became louder and louder. Startled, Li Ling drew back.

Shao Peng licked her lips. They were parched. She could feel her heart thumping. From the garlands of white, she knew that there had been a death and, judging from the unkind and vicious remarks of bystanders, it was her father's. But how could it be? She had been away for just three months. He had seemed in rude health when she left. They pushed through the throng of people. Ah Sook, her father's old retainer, saw them and came rushing out. He bobbed and bowed, his white skullcap stuck to his head. Sweat rolled down his face.

"Young mistress, your father ... your father passed away. We waited and waited for you. This is the seventh day of his passing. Thank goodness you are back. Tonight, his spirit would return to visit us. At least you are here now. Big mistress needs you. Come, come with me," he said hurrying them into the front courtyard and towards the main door.

"How, how did he die?" Her voice broke. She could hardly take in the news. Up until then, she had held on to the hope that it was all a mistake and that the mutterings of the crowd were not true.

"Mistress will tell you." Ah Sook guided them past a marquee set up in the courtyard. Shao Peng turned in shock to stare. Within its confines, several gaming tables were laid out for mahjong. People were playing the coloured tiles as though it was any ordinary day. *Snap, clack*; tiles were thrown into the centre of the table and fresh ones drawn and reassembled.

"What's this?" she asked. Her amazement was followed quickly by anger. She would have shouted and yelled at them but for Ah Sook.

Without breaking his stride, Sook hustled them into the house. "They are playing a game to while away the time. It helps keep them awake so that they can guard your father and protect him from evil spirits. It is not easy for them to stay awake for so many days. Come, come!"

He did not give her any opportunity to protest. He beckoned her to follow him. There, in the centre of the big hallway, was the coffin, rested on four stools. It was uncovered. A feast was laid out on the altar: dishes of chicken, roast pork, boiled rice and oranges accompanied by rice wine in little porcelain cups covered the altar table. Incense and smoke from joss sticks filled the room.

It was surreal. But all Shao Peng could think of was her father lying within the coffin. She dropped Li Ling' hand and rushed to the coffin. She fell on her knees. Immediately, she felt guilty. She asked herself if this was against her new religious instruction. Yet she felt that it was the most natural thing to do. She told herself she was not doing anything un-Christian; she was not praying to her father. She had no inclination to light joss sticks. She did not believe in the importance of food offerings to those in the other world. She felt only the need to kneel and ask for forgiveness. Surely that could not be wrong? All through the journey she had planned to confront her father and make him change his mind about her marrying Jack. She had thought only of herself and her selfish needs. She sobbed. Now there was no opportunity to seek forgiveness and reconciliation with a father whom she had loved with all her heart, yet with whom she had so many differences. She sobbed until her eyes burned. How could it happen? Why?

She felt a hand on her shoulder and then someone was drawing her up. She turned to see her stepmother.

"Wear this," Rohani said, handing her a black robe and a shroud made of sackcloth. "Your brother will be out soon. He is conferring with one of the managers."

Rohani watched on while Shao Peng struggled into her sackcloth. "For now," she added, "it is best that you light up joss sticks in offering to your father."

Shao Peng shook her head to protest.

"People are waiting and watching. I know you hold a different faith. So do I. Do it even if it is just to appease them and keep the peace. It will help stop their tongues from wagging."

Against her own inclination, Shao Peng took the joss sticks. She agreed with her stepmother. She could feel people's eyes on her. Clasping the joss sticks firmly with both hands, she knelt and raised them up high and then bowed three times, lowering her forehead to the floor. She could almost feel the imperceptible sigh from spectators in the background as if they were waiting for this moment to commend or to condemn her, the errant daughter. Then she placed the joss sticks into the urn on the altar. Tears continued to fall unchecked down her face.

"Come," said Rohani, "let's go to your room where we can talk. You are not allowed to look at your father's face. They have covered it with a piece of yellow silk. So there is little point in staying here with the crowd. Your brother will take care of the town people coming to pay their respect to your father. They have been flooding into the house every day. Meanwhile I'll ask one of the servants to take the girl up to your room. You'll have to tell me about her later. I don't even know her name or why she is here."

***

"Your father just keeled over," said Rohani in a matter of fact voice. "There were no warning signs. He seemed perfectly fine. We just had lunch and Siew Loong was coaxing him to eat some mandarin oranges, when he placed a hand over his heart, turned a deathly pale and then fell. His head landed on the bowl on the table and sent it crashing onto the ground. Then it was mayhem."

The shadows under Rohani's eyes told of sleepless nights but other than that there was little emotion on her face. Shao Peng wondered why. She had expected her stepmother to be desolate. Perhaps she had already wept for seven days and there were no tears left.

"Was he still cross with me?" asked Shao Peng looking more closely at Rohani.

"What with? Your wish to become a Catholic nun and do good deeds or your refusal to marry the man he chose for you?"

"Both. I need to know for I cannot bear that I had in any way contributed to his death. I am so, so sorry for the hurt I caused him."

'Dear girl, let it go. Yes he was angry. It was more with himself, at least when he had time to think it over. He said that your crazy ideas took root when he left you under the care of an Englishman when you were young. He felt it was a natural progression for you to fall in love with an Englishman. He also blamed himself for your conversion to Christianity. He said he was the one that put you in contact with the nuns. After all, it was he who supported the nuns in their quest to start their school. If he had not done that, you would not have met them."

Shao Peng hid her face in her hands. She gave vent to her sorrow and allowed her grief to brim over.

Rohani looked away. She gazed out of the window. Outside the sky was bleached white with rolling clouds skittering across the blue. "Your father said harsh things to you on the spur of the moment. When you were absent, he spoke of you every day. It is a testament to his love for you. Unlike his love for me. He left me little that shows it."

Shao Peng raised her head. Her stepmother's voice and words shook her out of her own misery. She sounded bitter. Shao Peng sensed that something was wrong. Taking her stepmother's hands in hers, she asked, "Are you cross with father? What had he done?"

"I'll tell you another day. Tell me about your aunt. And who is the girl that you came home with?" she asked.

***

That night Shao Peng kept to her room. Numb with grief and stricken with guilt, she blamed herself over and over again. She went through in her mind every minute detail of her quarrel with her father. Her head throbbed. Outside, the chanting of Buddhist scriptures went on the whole evening, accompanied by loud clashing of gongs and bells to help the deceased cross over the river of death to the other world. Near the marquee where an all night vigil was led, prayer money was burned to ensure that the deceased would be amply provided for in the after life. The smell of joss sticks seeped into the room. Curls of grey smoke permeated the air.

Li Ling huddled closer to Shao Peng.

"Sleep! I am with you so don't be frightened," said Shao Peng.

"Is it true what they say? That your father's spirit will be back tonight?"

"No," replied Shao Peng tucking the thin cotton bedcover over her charge.

"Do you not believe what they say?" The girl crept closer, turning on her side to face Shao Peng and drawing her knees up to her chest in a tight ball. She had heard her mother say the same when the farmer in the next field lost his mother.

Shao Peng brushed the hair out of Li Ling's eyes. "Not really." she said softly. "I went through the rites because I was expected to. If I did not, the people gathered today would think that I am disrespectful, and worse, that I did not love my father. It has nothing to do with my belief."

Sliding down the bed, Shao Peng took a pillow, plumped it up and tucked it under her head. "I don't think my Church would really object," she said more to herself than to her charge. She was filled with guilt because she had given in to the lighting of joss sticks. "I am neither a Buddhist nor a Taoist. I am not even sure if my father was one or the other. He was very relaxed as far as religion was concerned. My stepmother, for example, keeps another faith and she holds it close to her heart. My father never objected. He wouldn't have minded if I had not lit joss sticks for him. I did it because of the other people."

She rolled over and took Li Ling's hand. "Do you understand what I am saying? It is important for the family and community, and in a way for myself, that I show esteem for my father. I loved my father. I regret, with all my heart, the harsh words I said to him. I have not been a dutiful daughter and, in our custom, that is a major sin. I did what I did to say I was sorry."

Outside the loud chanting had diminished to a monotonous murmur. Li Ling had fallen asleep. Shao Peng pulled the sheets to her chin and closed her eyes. She was now once more Shao Peng. In this house, no one would call her by any other name. Mary did not exist as far as her family was concerned. Her mind drifted over the events of the past month. The journey had opened her eyes. She was no longer sure of her feelings, even of her desire to be a nun. Was it a form of escape? She recalled the words of the people she met in Guangdong, their antagonism to all things foreign and to Christianity. The villagers had protested when she visited them with Dr Elizabeth. They had called the Mission a seat of hypocrisy. "First," they hissed, "they ensnared us with opium then they called us immoral degenerates to be converted and saved." She recalled the scene at the dockyard. The dockworker had pointed blatantly at the cargo—crates filled with bibles unloaded alongside crates of the opiate. Her mind reeled; nothing was clear anymore. She had set out to China with such clarity of mind and returned with such confusion.

She turned on her side and tucked both hands under her cheek. It was wet. Was Jack still in Malaya? She wondered. Did he know of her father's death? Was he waiting for her as he had promised when she last saw him? With a sigh filled with self-loathing, she turned over pulling the sheets with her. How could she be thinking of Jack when she was mourning her father? What kind of daughter was she?

Next to her Li Ling slept on; her breath interspersed with little cries of distress.

Poor girl, thought Shao Peng. She was torn between worries for herself, regret and sorrow over her father's death and compassion for her charge.

Chapter 7

THE SUN STREAMED through the open shutters and a light breeze lifted the curtains. It brought into the breakfast room a lingering scent of joss sticks from last night's vigil. There was no escape from it. Shao Peng and Li Ling took their seat at the table, next to Rohani.

"Good morning," they said.

Rohani nodded in response and gave them a grim tiny quirk of a smile. It did not reach her eyes. Her hands lay listless on her lap. The room fell silent, a heavy silence that hung like a hot damp curtain that smothered the air. No one, it appeared, wished to talk. It was strange, Shao Peng thought, that they were seated down to breakfast; that the mundane act of living continued in the midst of death. She turned to take a closer look at her stepmother. She saw her swollen eyes and her pallor.

She understood them; they were marks of grief. She wondered, however, why her stepmother should look so bitter? The corners of her mouth were turned down. What could have caused it? Her stepmother's reticence and comments last night about her father troubled her.

If Rohani sensed being observed she did not show it. She made no attempt to look up or respond to Shao Peng's overtures.

The silence dragged on while they sat waiting for Siew Loong. The servants loitered by the sideboard moving bowls of congee around, as though moving them would stop it from congealing. Breakfast would not be served until he arrived. He was the new master of the house and despite being years younger than Shao Peng, she knew that she had to give him the respect that their father had previously commanded. She remembered her father saying to her when she first set eyes on her brother. "He will be called Siew Loong, little dragon," her father had explained, "and when I die, he will assume the role of *tai loong*, the big dragon." So now even Rohani, his mother, had to give him precedence.

Shao Peng fiddled with her hands for want of something to do. It was awkward to sit in silence. There were so many questions she wanted to ask. Deep in thought she did not notice Siew Loong's arrival until she heard the sharp sound of a chair drawn back. She reached over and took hold of her charge's hand under the table. She wanted to reassure Li Ling as much as to be comforted herself. When she last saw her brother harsh words had been exchanged. He had chastised her. He had accused her of foolhardiness. He scolded her for what he thought was her disregard for their father, for wanting to go to China against her father's wishes, for not obeying. She had bridled with indignation, for wasn't she the elder and by many years? She looked up and saw her brother's unwavering gaze. She immediately expected the worst. Would he rage at her again? Could she stop herself from answering back? Of course, he had been right. She should not have gone against her father's wishes. Now she couldn't even say sorry to her father. Yet, was she wrong in going to China? For not going would mean that she would not have seen her beloved aunt. She could not stand the suspense of waiting to see Siew Loong's reaction. She stood up; her chair toppled over and hit the floor with a resounding bang. She was horrified that it would be misinterpreted. She looked up from the fallen chair to her brother. With a rush of relief and joy she saw that he was already coming towards her and he did not seem angry. He reached her. They stood looking at each other and then he placed both hands on her shoulder. "Welcome home," he whispered.

"Am I forgiven?" she asked.

"There is nothing to forgive." He seemed reluctant to say more. Instead he turned his attention to Li Ling. The girl's anxious face was turned up towards them, looking from one to the other. He was struck by her soft brown eyes with their fringe of dark lashes. "And who is this?" he asked.

"My charge. Her parents begged me to take her with me. Their warlord had wanted her to be his concubine."

"*Ahhh!* My sister! Always the champion of the needy! You get it from father."

He placed a hand on Shao Peng's elbow and led her away from the table. He had more urgent worries on his mind than his sister's concern. He lowered his voice and, casting an anxious eye in the direction of his mother, said, "Father has set aside money in his will for the upkeep of four women. Apparently, he has built a house for them. He left no explanation as to why, probably because he did not expect to die so suddenly. Of course, his actions have sparked off all sorts of rumours and gossip. I give very little credit to them. Mother, however, is devastated."

"*Bodoh!* Stupid!" interjected Rohani. She suddenly came alive. She rose to her feet and jabbed her finger at her son. "I am not deaf. Neither am I as easily taken in as you." She was livid. Her eyes were like fire. "There can be only one reason why he provided for them. They are his mistresses. To think that I trusted him." Her voice broke and she sobbed. "To think of the years of hardship I went through with him only to find at his death that he had other women! That he had betrayed me! I blame myself for my naivety." She fell back in her chair, exhausted by her emotions and anger.

"No mother, it might not be true. They might not be his mistresses. There will always be people who would think the worst. You should not give credence to such idle and vicious gossip. Father was a good man. You should not wipe out your good memories by believing in such nonsense. I hear that some of the young women are poor orphans whom he had rescued from a life of prostitution. Perhaps, he felt you would not believe him. Hence he made no mention of them to you. It would seem he is justified in his belief."

"Of course, you will defend your father." Rohani's face was red with anger and exasperation. "His will provides for these women. What about me? He made no separate provisions for me, his wife!"

"You are his wife, my mother. He thinks you will be automatically entitled and cared for by me," said Siew Loong.

"Brother is right. You will be taken care of. You are still the mistress in this house."

Shao Peng took her stepmother's hands in hers. She stroked them gently to stop their trembling. She had never seen her like this.

The sharp words were totally out of character. "Remember how father gave a building to the nuns to help them. He did not share their religious belief. He still did it. So in the same way, he could well be looking after the women while not having any untoward interest in them. Why don't we go and see for ourselves?"

"No," wailed Rohani. "You go. I cannot bear it if it is true."

***

After breakfast, much of which was left uneaten, Rohani returned to her room. Her outburst had left her exhausted. Li Ling was asked to go with her and to keep her company.

The siblings found themselves on their own, sitting across the table still littered with the morning's meal.

"So how did your trip go?" Siew Loong asked his sister.

Not wishing to speak across the wide expanse of the table, Shao Peng stood up to go to Siew Loong. The room swam before her. The weariness of weeks of travel caught up with her. She had hardly slept the previous night. She was fine earlier in the morning helped by the rush of adrenalin that was fuelled by her anxiety. She had been so worried about her brother's reaction to her return. Later, her concern over Rohani had pushed aside her own fatigue. Now the tiredness came upon her suddenly. Her head spun. She sat down.

"Stay there! Don't get up!" Siew Loong ran to her side. He crouched down, dropping one knee to the floor.

"Aunt Heong Yook died," she said, her voice was so low that it was hardly a whisper. Her lips trembled and a tear rolled down her cheek. Everything had become too much for her. She needed to talk and unburden herself. She wanted her brother to understand why her aunt was so important to her, why she had gone to China. She didn't want him to view her badly. "You have not met her. She took care of me when I was little and, as you know, she brought up father."

However, the mere act of unburdening brought out another torrent of tears. She had lost two people she loved in quick succession. She did not know which of the two losses hurt most. Her aunt who had loved her so unreservedly or her father from whom she craved love and who she was never sure returned it, until now when it was too late.

"I brought aunt's ashes home with me. May I place them in the ancestral hall alongside father?" Shao Peng was worried that she had been presumptuous in bringing the ashes home. Her brother did not know the aunt, having never met her. There was a period when her father forbade any mention of Heong Yook because of a misunderstanding between them.

"Of course. Father did talk about her after you left for China. I shall speak to the temple priest about it." He felt a flash of relief. He had expected there to be more serious matters that his sister wished to bring up. He had so many worries; he could not bear to have another added to them.

"There is something else I have to tell you," she said.

Siew Loong saw the trepidation in her face. "What is it?" he asked with concern.

"Nothing..." She hesitated.

He raised an eyebrow. "Nothing?" he echoed.

With a start Shao Peng saw, for the first time that morning how the weight of responsibility had aged her little brother. He spoke like one with cares that extended far beyond his eighteen years.

"Aunty Heong Yook left me the pottery and the house in Beiliu. They sound grander than they are," she hastened to add. "The buildings are run down and business is almost non-existent.

There are no workers, no production and no buyers. I just thought that you should know." Siew Loong had been bequeathed the entire Ong estate. As a girl, she had received nothing. She was expected to marry and leave home. Yet she wondered if her brother would mind her small inheritance from an aunt. Would he mind being bypassed? She wanted his approval, his blessing. She couldn't bear to be estranged from him again. She wanted him to hear of it from her and not from someone else.

"Let us talk about it later. I have to rush." He got up, again relieved that it was not an important matter; his hand brushed her shoulder as he readied himself to leave.

"I also want to talk to you about..."

"Later, I promise," he said already striding off.

"Jack. I want to talk to you about Jack," she whispered lamely to his departing figure. Shao Peng sighed with exasperation. "Is there no one in the house who has time to listen? Is my future now in the hands of my little brother?" she asked aloud.

"I think so."

Shao Peng whirled round. She saw Li Ling. The girl had emerged out of nowhere and stood now at the doorway.

"What did you say?" Shao Peng's voice was sharp. She had not expected the girl to be there and certainly not to express a view on such matters.

"A girl is like a flash of water, insignificant, born to serve and obey the men in the house."

Shao Peng went to the girl. She regretted her brusqueness. Li Ling was trembling, her body poised to dash away. Someone must have told her and she was repeating by rote. "No, that cannot be my fate," Shao Peng said more gently this time. "And it will not be yours. Go! Go to your room. I'll come for you after the funeral procession."

Li Ling turned and ran. Horrified that she had offended Shao Peng, she skidded through the polished hallway in her hurry. She ran up the stairs taking two steps at a time. Once in her room, she sat on the bed. Taking the corner of her tunic top, she stuffed it in her mouth and chewed. She regretted speaking out loud. She wished her mother was with her. No one wanted her around. First they asked her to stay with the plump dark lady who spoke Chinese in a strange accent. She sent her back to Shao Peng. She didn't understand why the dark lady they called Rohani spoke so sharply to her. And now Shao Peng sent her back upstairs. Tears rolled down her cheeks. They splashed on to her blouse top leaving dark patches. She sank into the bed and drew her knees up and sobbed. What did they intend to do with her? Would they send her away? Her mother had explained her fate. If that were not to be, then what would be? She thought of home. She longed for the wide-open paddy fields and the seamless sky overhead, the freedom to play and run. Most of all she missed her brother and her parents. She wished she could go home. She was frightened. She did not want to be alone in the house. She thought of the coffin in the parlour. The man, Ah Sook, had talked of returning ghosts. She could not stay in the room. She scrambled out of the bed and ran down the stairs.

***

Downstairs, in the front parlour everything was quiet. Plumes of smoke spiralled from the stubs of the remaining white candles and the scent of joss sticks was everywhere. Servants glided soft footed on the marble floor, refreshing the wreaths and flowers strewn all round the coffin. It was a moment of quiet before the funeral procession.

Shao Peng stood at the threshold of the parlour. She looked across to where the coffin stood; her legs were like lead. She felt as if she was in a dream. Even now she could not believe that her father was no longer. All her life, he had been the epicentre of her being, even when she was not with him and under the care of Janidah and Uncle Grime in Singapore. His words had been the unwritten code for her to abide by, even though she rebelled against it. Now she was lost. Her chest tightened with remorse and sadness. She felt crushed by the weight of it all. If only ... if only ... she hadn't said those harsh words. She clenched her fist and bit her lips to stop herself from howling aloud and rushing to the coffin. Forgive me, she wanted to cry. Yet no sound came, just a shudder that shook her body until her teeth chattered.

She felt the gentle touch of a hand on her shoulder. She turned. "Uncle Grime, Janidah!" she exclaimed. They took her in their arms, cradling her with the warmth of their bodies, three bodies folded together. She allowed herself to be petted, hungry for the comfort they gave her, reminded once more of the time she spent with them in Singapore. Her formative years, her father had said with a heavy sigh. "No wonder you are so argumentative. Remember, you are Chinese, not English. Have you not heard of the word *guai*? You listen and you obey."

"I...," she began, disengaging herself from their embrace.

"We know," Janidah said. "There is nothing that cannot wait until the funeral is over. We'll talk then."

Chapter 8

Jing-jing was disappointed. After the long journey, she had expected to be welcomed and made much of by her husband. Instead, she hardly saw him. She blushed with shame. She recalled her loud boasts on board the ship. She had told everyone how she would be feted when her husband saw her. Of course, she reasoned, she had only just arrived. He could not just leave off work and be with her. Still, to go off for one month just one day after her arrival was too much to bear. How could she occupy herself? The house she was left in was just a tiny room, with walls made of woven bamboo strips. The kitchen, bedroom and sitting area were rolled in one. All it had was a wooden bed, with a chamber pot tucked underneath, two wooden chairs and a wood burning stove that served as her kitchen. She looked up at the ceiling. Sunlight streamed through the hastily put together dried thatch that he called *attap*. A lizard scrambled across a rattan beam as though aware of her scrutiny. Before Cheung left, he had promised that he would mend the roof when he returned. He said he would give it his first priority, smiling sheepishly at the large drops of rain that splattered into the bucket placed strategically below the roof aperture. He explained that he had to work and that her ticket had cost his entire savings. He was not allowed leave; the one day he took was already a compassionate gesture from his boss. He could not ask for more. He must earn if they were to live.

Jing-jing sighed. She could hardly recognise her husband after three years. He had grown so old and troubled as though the whole world's worries were on his shoulders. She took a broom and stepped out of the hut. Perhaps she could sweep away the debris and dried leaves in their small compound to while away the time. She mustered a smile and hummed a tune to cheer herself up.

She swept, quick deft strokes. Clouds of dust rose. Soon she was covered with it. Her hair, clothes, arms and face were grey with dirt. The jubilance that she tried to muster seeped away. She stopped and wiped her forehead with the back of her hand.

Someone called. "*Heh!* Are you new here?"

Startled, Jing-jing jumped. Standing opposite was a woman with a basket of clothes tucked under one arm. Jing-jing had not noticed her presence until she spoke. How had she come into the compound?

"I have not seen you before," the lady continued, her eyes crunched up tight against the hot sun and a smile on her face. "I am your neighbour. People call me Ah Kum as in the word gold. *Huh!* I wish. If I was truly *kum*, I would not be living over there." She pointed to a group of wooden plank houses beyond a grove of trees some distance away. "I am on my way to the river. A boat is expected any time from Port Klang. It will bring fresh supplies from the coast. Would you like to come? We can draw water for washing from the river. You certainly look as if you need a wash," she teased.

Jing-jing found herself smiling in response. Cheung, her husband, had warned that she should be careful whom she befriended. "The community here," he explained, "is a mishmash of people thrown together from all walks of life, some of which are less desirable than others. Just be careful with whom you keep company. If you have a problem, the best thing would be to contact the old retainer in my boss's household. We all call him uncle, *Ah Sook*, as a mark of respect. Ask any one. They will know him. He would help you." Then he had taken her in his arms, giving her little time to air her misgivings.

Jing-jing tossed her head, recalling the way he had held her, reassuring her that she would be fine. It was all well and good except that she could not be expected to keep to herself without anyone to talk to. Shao Peng had promised that she would visit yet had made no contact. It was for the best. She wouldn't want Shao Peng and the others to know of her present circumstances. She should have kept her mouth shut and not boast during the journey on the ship.

Jing-jing returned her attention to the woman. After a moment's hesitation, Jing-jing decided that she would make up her own mind as to what was best for herself. She didn't need Ah Sook to tell her that the woman, Ah Kum, was harmless. "I have some clothes that need washing. I'll come with you. Wait here! I'll fetch them," she said.

To Jing-jing's chagrin, Ah Kum followed her into the house. She plunked down her basket of clothes on a wooden chair. "You should do something about this place," she said, pointing to the hole in the roof. "You can have all these fixed easily. It won't cost much. Come, let's go and I'll tell you."

Jing-jing eyes lit up. Her earlier annoyance at the woman's audacity disappeared. It would be good if she could make improvements to the place. Cheung would be proud of her. She grinned. At last, she had a chance to prove her worth. She dreamt of the letters she could get Cheung to write home to his mother. She'll show her mother-in-law; make her eat her words for saying such nasty things about her laziness.

**

Two miles away, across the river Klang, the sparsely scattered ramshackle wooden huts gave way to two-storey terrace brick buildings with tiled roofs. They lined the network of narrow streets that wove and meandered through the town centre. Shao Peng's house stood apart from these terrace buildings. Fenced off by its own high brick walls, it overlooked a road that linked it to a nearby rice and tapioca mill. The mill was one of the many ventures her father had built during his lifetime. From there, the road joined the main streets of the town centre. As the funeral possession moved slowly out of the gate of the house into the mill compound and then into the main street, it gathered in size. More and more people joined it until it resembled a human throng moving ponderously across the town.

Li Ling watched the procession from the porch. She heard the clashing of the cymbals and the loud wailing that followed it. She stayed on her feet until she could not see any trace of the procession nor hear any of the loud music. The last of the stragglers had gone. All that remained were the white banners and lanterns hung at the top of the gateposts. They swung lazily in the warm breeze saying their own farewell.

She was reluctant to return to the house, reminded still of the servants' tales of ghosts and spirits that might be lingering within. She sat down on the steps and drew her knees up, resting her chin on them. I'll wait here, she thought, until Shao Peng returns.

Time passed. The sun moved steadily across the sky. By midday, it shone with such fierce intensity that every corner of the ground was filled with its penetrating heat. The road shimmered, throwing up a haze of warmth that played tricks with her eyes. Hunger gnawed. She stood up and made her way to the back of the house where the kitchen lay. There would be someone in the kitchen, she thought. She shivered despite the warmth. She didn't want to be in the house alone.

The kitchen was cool and dark. The servants had drawn down the wooden slats in the window. Large vats of water stood by the doorway. Next to them was a row of wooden clogs. She recalled the servants wearing them the previous night when they swept the ground of its litter of ashes left over from burnt effigies and paper money. Now they stood like miniature sleeping sentries on the grey concrete flooring of the kitchen. This was not a part of the house visited by the master and mistress. A servant had explained that to her when she tried to flee to the kitchen earlier in the morning in search of company. "You shouldn't be here," she had smirked. Then slyly, she added, "that is, if you are not brought here to work."

Li Ling took a step over the wooden threshold. She hesitated and then brought her other foot in. She had nowhere to go. She didn't know if she was brought here to work. In fact, she did not know what her position would be, especially after this morning when she put her foot in it by venturing her personal opinion. She wandered to the table in the middle of the room. A conical woven cover of red, yellow and blue matting was placed in the centre. She lifted it revealing a dish of stewed beef brisket. She gulped. Her stomach grumbled. She had eaten nothing at breakfast. The beef glistened invitingly in its dark sauce.

"*Aiyah! Sooi nooi pow!* Cursed bun of misfortune! Are you trying to steal food?"

Li Ling turned. Ah Tai, the maid that had shooed her away that morning stood with both hands on her hips. Her lips were drawn tight with disgust.

"If you want to eat, you need only ask. Why steal? Mistress Shao Peng has already left instruction that you were to be fed. Where were you? I went in search of you." She roughly shoved Li Ling into a chair manhandling her arm. "Sit," she commanded.

Li Ling could feel a flush of heat that rose from her neck to her cheek. She was ashamed to be so accused, guiltily acknowledging that perhaps she would have taken a piece of meat from the dish if the maid had not come in. The thought made her flush with contrition. Yes, perhaps she would have 'stolen' though she had not lifted the cover with that intent. What would her mother say?"

There! Eat!" The maid slammed down a bowl filled with rice and stewed brisket in front of her.

Li Ling hesitated, still smarting from shame, made even more so because she realised that Ah Tai had deliberately slammed down the bowl and manhandled her to show that she was not an important guest.

"What? Not enough? Not good enough for you? *Huh!*" Ah Tai sneered. "I have a lot of work. I don't need you around my feet. Eat! There is nothing else. Until Mistress clarifies your position, don't expect to be served hand and foot." She ran her eyes insolently over Li Ling, from head to toe and back again. She grumbled, not caring that her grumbling could be heard. "Can't see why Miss Shao Peng says we are to treat her well. She cannot be of any importance. Look at her clothes! Rags! If she was important, they would have included her in the funeral procession, just like they had included Master Siew Loong's intended. Why, that girl is as pretty as one would wish any bride to be. And so beautifully turned out as well. Did you see the lace she wore! Those beaded slippers must have cost a fortune."

"You mean Miss Suet Ping?" asked another woman that had just stepped into the kitchen. Li Ling saw that it was Ah Kew, the other maid in the house. "The engagement is not official, just a wish expressed by big Mistress. She likes her because Miss Suet Ping speaks beautiful Malay and that suits Mistress. No wonder! Her grandmother is a Malay, just like Mistress." She hurried over and spoke in Ah Tai's ear, a conspiratorial whisper that was nevertheless loud enough for Li Ling to hear. "It seems that Master Siew Loong does not like being coerced. He wants to choose his own bride. I overheard their heated exchange the other evening. So nothing is fixed."

Li Ling picked up her bowl and began to eat. All the while though her ears strained to hear. She was shocked to learn that the handsome young Master was betrothed. For some unknown reason, it made her sad.

Ah Kew's eyes sparkled with mischief. She cast a malicious glance at Li Ling. "*Aiyah!* That girl over there, the one Miss Shao Peng brought back. I thought for a moment she was someone of importance, especially when she breakfasted with her. But, it cannot be. Look! They left her out of the family procession."

Li Ling's cheeks turned bright red. She shuffled the rice into her mouth and pretended not to hear. The maids giggled. "*Cho loh!* No manners! Who would want her as bride?" They nudged each other.

***

Back across the other side of town, the riverbank was busy. Jing-jing stood enthralled drinking in the sounds, the smell and the colours of her surroundings. Stalls with fruits and vegetables stood next to those selling cloth. Cooking utensils were laid out cheek by jowl with chamber pots and wooden stools. Wired cages with live chickens stood next to baskets filled with fish, their eyes glazed with death. The previous night's heavy rainfall had transformed the rough tracks along the bank into a field of mud. Jing-jing's feet sunk deep with each step. She was oblivious. The people and the noise exhilarated her.

Ah Kum tapped her on the shoulder. "Here, look over there where the two rivers meet. One river is called *Gombak* and the other *Klang*." She hustled Li Ling forward and pointed to a group of rough attap houses. "Huts for the *Kapitan's* coolies," she explained. "He is our headman. See there," she gesticulated to a large wooden shed adjacent to the medley of huts, "a gambling and opium den." A group of men wandered out of the shed to leer at them. "Watch out!" She giggled, her eyes coy with delight. "Many of them come to our house, preferring it to the shacks around this part of the town." Ah Kum stole a surreptitious glance at her young companion.

Jing-jing didn't quite grasp the meaning. Thrilled with the buzz of activity, she was too busy taking it all in. She had dreaded being confined to her hut with no friends. Surely she could find a friend here. She looked around. Her heart fell. There were not many women around, just a few with long braided hair buying food. She knew of them, having met some on the ship; *mah-cheh* women who had braved the journey from China to flee from bullying mothers-in-law or husbands; women who had sworn a life of celibacy and loyalty to their domestic work for pay. "I could have been one of those if I was not careful," she said to Ah Kum. "It would be awful."

"Yes, you mustn't even think of it. You are so pretty, too pretty to be tucked away in the kitchen. Come, come away!" She pointed to a pile of cloths stacked high on a rough wooden platform. "This, when made into a tunic, would suit you and make you even more beautiful."

"No! I can't afford it," said Jing-jing looking at the material wistfully.

"What about this?" Ah Kum flashed a little mirror she found amongst a heap of assorted goods in another stall. "You need a mirror to comb your hair at least."

"No, nothing. I don't have any money at all."

"*Aiyah!* How can he leave you on your own without any money? I am sorry to ask. What kind of husband is he?" Kum looked pityingly at Jing-jing.

"I have some money; it is enough just for food."

"*Huh!* In that case, we might as well just go. No point staying here if you have no money." Ah Kum whirled abruptly from Jing-jing and walked away. At intervals she turned to throw sharp accusing glances at her young friend, her face a picture of indignation. Jing-jing followed crestfallen, her earlier jubilation completely vanished.

Chapter 9

THE CEMETERY WAS located on the side of the hill that overlooked the valley and the river. Slowly the mass of people that had formed the funeral procession began to leave. One by one they wove their way down the hillside. There were no paths that provided for an orderly departure. People trampled through patches of tall grass and negotiated their way around clumps of frangipani trees and tombstones. They left deep footprints on the red metallic soil. A warm breeze blew, sending the plumes of grass seed heads nodding.

"Good *feng shui*," Ah Sook, her father's retainer explained. "Your father will be at peace here. His plot is the best," he said soothingly to comfort her. Shao Peng had wept then, tears that she had kept in check throughout the funeral procession and even when the coffin was lowered into the ground, flowed unconstrained. The finality of it all hit her.

When the last of the crowd had left, she took a step back and turned to Janidah. "Did Jack say anything to you?" she asked. "Where is he?" She saw the hesitation on Janidah's face. Alarmed she turned to Grime. "Uncle Grime, where is Jack?" she asked again, her heart pounding.

She had no chance to pursue the matter. Her brother grabbed her elbow and ushered her forcefully forward. He had overheard.

"Give father some respect. Can't you wait until we are back home before uttering the very name that was a bone of contention between you and father? What's wrong with you? You want father to turn in his grave?" Siew Loong's eyes were filled with rage. She could feel the heat of his hand encircling her arm. He pulled her to him, and brought his face close to hers. His breath blew hot on her face.

"I tell you where he is. He has left. He will be back soon, no doubt, with his wife. So just leave it." He flung her arm away and strode furiously away to join his mother.

Shao Peng stood rooted, the last vestige of colour drained from her face. She turned to Janidah. She wanted to ask if it was true. Her lips parted; no words came. Her throat was dry; it was as though all the moisture had been sucked out of it. Questions, however, were unnecessary. She could see from the discomfiture in Janidah's face that it was true. Siew Loong was not quite finished with her. Within seconds, he was back. He took her arm again, wrenching it.

"I didn't want to say anything this morning. I didn't want you to be hurt. You leave me with no choice. I realised just then that you would never be weaned off him if you did not know the truth. When you were away, he had a Malay mistress. Ask Janidah. She knows. Everyone knows except my sister. She is so infatuated that she hears nothing and sees nothing. She sees only that which she wants to see. Well!" He expelled a long drawn out breath. "You have to face the truth." With that he turned and left, striding off at such speed that clouds of dust and sand billowed after him.

"Uncle Grime, is it true?"

Edward Grime nodded, his eyes cast down and unable to meet hers. The moment passed. He looked up. "I am sorry. I failed you. I should have been more careful with the people you met when you were under my care. I had no idea that you would fall in love with Jack. I thought no more of it after you left us and returned to your father's household. I did not know that you maintained contact with him until you wrote before you left for China. Your father came to me afterwards and together we tried to find out more about Jack and his background."

Janidah placed an arm around Shao Peng. "We understand your attraction to him. There is no doubt about it. He is a very clever and charming man. Look at the way he has risen in the ranks. We were all duped. We confronted him when we learnt that he would be bringing his English bride to Malaya. He admitted it. He said that it was a marriage of convenience, that his true love was you. That, however, does not excuse him for being the cad that he has shown himself to be."

"And that he had a Malay mistress? Is that also true?"

"There are rumours," Janidah said after a moment's hesitation, "that he was having a secret liaison with a young Malay girl even while he was preparing to return to England to marry. I do not know if it is true despite what your brother said. It is just that everyone is talking about it. It has become common gossip even if it is not true. He has made many enemies from rising so rapidly in the administration. Such a relationship is, of course, still taboo for a rising star engaged in important government matters." She cast a quick glance at her husband and whispered. "The Brits are quite unforgiving in this respect. We are only too aware of it; Edward's career in the civil service, I am sure, is held back because of me."

Shao Peng did not hear this last piece of information volunteered by Janidah. Her mind was in turmoil. Once again she had shown herself to be a fool. How could she have gone against her father for Jack? His face flashed across her mind. She recalled the way he had looked at her. She had been so sure of his love that she even persuaded her aunt to give her blessing before she died. It had taken her aunt a lot to give her blessing. Her aunt had hated the way China was parcelled out between foreign powers. Her aunt was not fond, to say the least, of the English.

Shao Peng was torn between shame, anger and contrition. How could she go home to face Siew Loong, her younger brother? Yet, despite it all, Jack's face haunted her. She still wanted to be with him. Even now she could not believe that he could deceive her. Yet, how could she not believe when presented with such evidence by family members who loved her? With a shudder of self-disgust, she walked quickly after her brother.

Janidah and Grime watched Shao Peng hurry away. "I will have a word with Siew Loong. He shouldn't have told Shao Peng in the savage way he did. It was cruel," Grime said to Janidah. "I wish that the whole sorry saga would just go away."

Janidah did not reply. She too was filled with regrets. She wished she had not aired her liberal views so freely to Shao Peng when she was in her care. Perhaps she had unwittingly encouraged her ward to have modern ways that would be difficult to practise when she was back in the conservative household of her father.

***

Shao Peng sat on the bed with both arms hugging her knees and her head resting on one arm. Across the narrow aisle separating the two beds, Li Ling lay quiet. The night was balmy, filled with the constant hum of insects. Outside in the garden all the debris left from the funeral had been swept clean away. The house had been similarly cleared. Only the sweet scent of joss sticks remained; their smoke wafted from room to room, infusing the warm night air with its pungent breath and reminding the occupants of the death that had just occurred.

She slid further down on the bed and pulled the covers firmly over her. Her mind went over the day's events. After they returned home, she had gone to her brother to make amends. Siew Loong had taken her hand in his. "Look," he had said, "I am sorry for the brutal way I broke the news to you. I had meant to be gentle. It is just that when I heard you asking about the scoundrel so soon after we buried father, my blood boiled over. It was unseemly. Even now I am angry."

She could see that he was indeed getting upset all over again, just as she could tell that it would rain when the clouds darken and lightning strikes. Her brother had always been volatile; sweet, docile and gentle one moment and then without warning a burst of temper. Yet, he never bore a grudge. She squeezed his hand to reassure him. She knew she had been in the wrong. When she was told that her father was not angry with her, she led herself to believe that he had also accepted her love for Jack. So she allowed her impatience for news of Jack to overcome her sensibility. Her little brother was right. It was unseemly and uncaring. She was ashamed and she shifted from self-loathing to sadness and then to longing for Jack, a longing that was not to be.

"What now?" she whispered to herself, pulling the covers even more firmly to her chin.

The sound of shuffling sheets and a muffled sob brought her back to the present. She turned to see Li Ling looking at her and was immediately reminded that she, wrapped up with her own selfish concerns, had neglected her charge. She pushed the bed covers away and swung her legs over her bed. Dropping to her knees, she leaned over Li Ling. "Are you all right?" she asked. The girl turned away.

Hesitantly, she reached out and touched the girl's cheeks. They were damp. "Why are you crying? Was anyone cruel to you?"

Li Ling shook her head, yet tears seeped out from the corner of her eyes, big drops that glimmered bright in the darkened room. She was homesick. She was bewildered and frightened. She wanted to go home.

"Ah Tai said that you will be returning to China and I will be left here. She wanted to know whether I would be the new bondmaid for her to supervise. She called me the new *mui chai*. If that is so, she says my duty will be to clean all the chamber pots. I will have to draw water from the well and clean all the bathrooms and toilets. I am frightened of her." She recalled the rough manner of the maid and the pinch she had given her.

"I will have a word with Ah Tai now!" Shao Peng stood up. Li Ling grasped her hand and stopped her.

"No! Please! It will only make her more angry with me."

Shao Peng lowered herself until her face was level with the frightened girl. "I won't if you don't want me to. Rest assured you will not be cleaning chamber pots. I promise you. I have not had time to think things through. My father's unexpected death..." her voice trailed off. "Sleep," she said, brushing a tear from Li Ling's drenched face, "we'll talk tomorrow."

Shao Peng tucked the thin cotton cover round her charge. She got up and went to snuff out the lamp, throwing the room into immediate deep darkness. Outside a storm was brewing. She drew open the curtains slightly and looked out into the pitch black garden. Gradually her eyes became accustomed to the dimness. Clouds scurried across the sky and a strong wind howled whipping trees into a frenzy. At a distance, coconut trees were almost bending double with the wind's force. Then the sky broke open. "How appropriate," she whispered, dropping the curtains, "perhaps we will have a new start after the storm." A tear rolled down her cheek; she could taste its tangy saltiness and was surprised at the seeming unlimited supply of tears she could shed. She brushed it away impatiently. She must show more strength. She must set a better example for Li Ling.

***

It was mid morning before Shao Peng managed to locate her stepmother. She found Rohani sitting on a wooden bench beneath a bower of bougainvillea, surrounded by a small orchard of papaya and mango trees. To the rear of the mango trees, a grove of banana palms stood sentry; their ragged leaves trailing the ground. Combs of sun ripened bananas hung heavy, their golden hues contrasting with the backdrop of the wind-torn palm leaves. Next to it a solitary rambutan tree stood resplendent, its branches laden heavy with the small hairy fruit.

Rohani looked oblivious to the heady scent of ripening fruits and colour around her. Her sarong was hitched up above her ankles, and she was listlessly rolling a betel nut joint. A silver casket lay on the bench, its lid carelessly cast aside to reveal *sirih*, betel leaves plucked from the vines growing in the backyard, areca nut, and a paste of lime and spices. Shao Peng glanced away, uncomfortable to have found her stepmother so occupied. She had never seen Rohani chewing betel. Ngao, her father, disliked the practice of betel nut chewing and had forbidden its use. Whenever he passed a *kampong* he would rave at those who chewed the betel leaves pointing to their stained lips and blackened teeth and to the ground stained with their spit. "It is a widely practised social custom among the Malay people and is said to give those using it euphoria and comfort from all sorts of pain. Don't, however, let anyone in my household even try it." But he was no longer here.

"Mother," she said, the word tripping uncomfortably from her tongue. After all these years, she still found it difficult to address Rohani as *mother*. She had only done so recently because of her father's insistence. "Would you help me with Li Ling? I had promised her parents to keep her safe. I would like her to make something of herself. At the moment, however, what she needs most is love and care. She is frightened and homesick. Remember how I was when I first arrived in Singapore and you were sent to take care of me? I cried buckets." Recalling her stepmother's kindness when she first came from China, Shao Peng lowered herself and placed both arms around her stepmother's waist and gave her a hug. She hated seeing Rohani sad.

"She is thirteen, too old to be mollycoddled. You were only eight."

"Even so she is still a child," Shao Peng protested. She drew back to look at her stepmother, surprised by the curt answer.

Rohani was normally the more lenient of her two parents, softening her father's reprimands and commands.

"When your father brought women to this house, he said the same to me. Look after them. They are young and need your love and guidance. Little did I expect, when I heard your father's will provided for four women, that three at least were the same ones that he brought to me to look after."

Shao Peng's hand flew to her mouth. She was speechless.

Rohani's eyes were grave when she finally lifted her face. Shadows like bruised grapes ringed her eyelids. There was no hint of her usual sunny disposition, a disposition that Shao Peng had cherished. Her dusky skin was dull and her lips were stretched tight with bitterness. Small lines radiated from the corners of her mouth, lines grown overnight by the sprouting of sorrow. Sorrow for the loss of a husband; sorrow to discover his infidelity after lifelong trust.

Shao Peng folded her stepmother once more in her arms. Rohani seemed to have shrunk suddenly; her shoulders slouched in defeat. "*Shhh!* Do not believe in all that people tell you. It might not be true," Shao Peng said.

Rohani extricated herself from the embrace. "For that reason, I cannot help you with Li Ling. I do not trust the girl. I trust no one. I saw how your brother looked at her the other morning. I do not want her here to spoil things. I have plans that he marries Suet Ping. She is a lovely girl and half-Chinese with Malay blood. She would be a daughter-in-law I can relate to. It is time that I looked after myself. I am done with putting others first."

"Please, please don't say that. You can't mean it. Li Ling is only a child."

"Yes, that is what your father said of each and every one that he brought to this house." She got up. "I have nothing more to say. I am sorry. You will have to find some other arrangements for the girl. With those parting words, Rohani walked away leaving the silver casket and the carefully rolled joint untouched.

Shao Peng retrieved the box and packed away the betel leaves. She held the box to her nose and inhaled the pungent spiciness of its contents. With a flash, she realised why Rohani was contemplating chewing betel. It was her stepmother's symbolic attempt to exert herself in defiance of her father's wish. There were no signs of any red stains on the ground. Her stepmother lips were unstained. If she had chewed betel nut they would be bright red. She took a deep breath; she felt for her stepmother. She was vulnerable to gossip following her father's death. Shao Peng did not believe that the four women were her father's mistresses. There must be an explanation. Perhaps finding out could be the project that would help her put aside her thoughts of Jack. Jack, the mere thought of him, overwhelmed her with sadness. How could he, she lamented for the umpteenth time. Yet could she believe all that had been said of him? After all, she could not believe the things said of her father.

Chapter 10

IGNORING THE CURIOUS looks cast her way, Shao Peng went into the mill in search of her brother. She forced herself to look straight ahead. Heads turned and a murmur could be heard from the workers assembled in the plant. She maintained a firm set to her chin and clamped her lips tight. Ah Sook had told her of her brother's whereabouts and had suggested that he accompany her to the mill. He was mortified when she declined his offer.

"Miss ... you cannot go on your own. You are the boss's eldest daughter, a *tai siew cheh*. You can't go amongst your father's workers. They are all men. It is not done. Let me go with you."

"I have been to China on my own and I have returned unescorted. I am sure I shall be fine. Don't worry."

He had shaken his head, a deep furrow of concern etched between his brows. "*Siew cheh, y*ou are not a servant to go hither and thither on your own. Your father, if he was here today, would be most displeased."

Shao Peng smiled nervously at the recollection. Ah Sook was right. She could hear the men sniggering. When she was with the Mission, it had somehow seemed fine to go out unaccompanied. Men stared not because she was a woman. They were just astonished to see a Chinese lady in a Christian habit. Now she was keenly aware that it might not be appropriate for her to venture into a man's domain. She had not felt so ogled even when she was in China. What a difference her nun's habit had made. She felt and thought differently then. Shedding the habit and adorning her Chinese clothes once more seemed to have made her a different person, more vulnerable; the customs of old closing in on her. She pulled her sleeves down to hide her hands and bowed her head low to hide her face. She should, of course, had known this before striding off without a chaperone. Here in Kuala Lumpur's Chinatown, men still outnumbered women. She cast her mind back to her journey from China. She had been pleased at the sizeable number of women travelling on the ship. However, their numbers remained small in this corner of the world despite the easing of restrictions on Chinese women's travel to foreign lands.

A loud exclamation of surprise jolted her out of her reverie.

"Sister, what are you doing here? You should not come on your own. Come, come into my office." Siew Loong threw open a door and waved her in. "I heard a commotion and came out to see. Why didn't you get someone to come with you? What can be so urgent that you couldn't wait until I came back this evening?"

She forced herself into the present. She became immediately defensive when she saw the scowl on her brother's face. All her careful planning of what to say fell by the wayside.

"No I can't wait till this evening," she retorted. "I need your help now. Mother doesn't want Li Ling in the house. She thinks that she might be a distraction for you. She compares her to the young women that father brought to the house. Can you persuade her to change her mind? Li Ling has nowhere to go. I promised her parents to take care of her."

"How can she think that? She is only a young girl." Vexed, Siew Loong slammed the door shut.

"Well she is thirteen and you are only some three, four years older? And of course, Suet Ping, your intended and mother's choice, is about the same age as Li Ling. I suppose if you look at it like that, you can't blame her."

"Poor mother," he said. His face softened. "She is angry and hurt and lashes out at everything and everyone. I shall try to persuade her." A look of resignation settled on his face making him look much older than his years. "I can't promise she'll agree. For the moment, keep Li Ling out of her way."

"I was thinking of taking her with me to visit the nuns. Perhaps this is a good time."

Siew Loong frowned. "Are you considering joining the Mission again? Or are you using this as an excuse to go to the European settlement across the river?"

She reddened under his scrutiny. "No. I am going just to tell them news I brought from China and to thank them. Li Ling and I will then be out of mother's way." She could feel her heart beat quicken; she was sure he could read the guilt in her face.

He gave her one final searching look. "Take the rickshaw," he said. "Ah Sook will go with you. Be back early. You are not thinking of seeing him? He ... Jack ... is not in town you know. I told you."

She went even redder. "I might try to see Uncle Grime before he returns to Singapore."

"You might, but must you?" He glared at her. He was plainly annoyed and irritated.

"Perhaps not today," she added in haste.

"Go if you need to check on what I told you. This will be the last time you go to the European sector. You hear me? Father would wish that. He told me as much. You just have to forget your *gwei loh* upbringing and be Chinese. The British administration would not have segmented this town on ethnic lines if they wished us to integrate."

"What about you? You are half-Malay!" she blurted out even before she could think it through. Horrified, she clapped her hands to her mouth as though she could stifle the words that had already rolled out.

"Yes, and I am proud of it. Know this, however," he leaned towards her, his eyes unflinching, "I am also my father's son. Mother accepted that when she moved out of our old house to this part of town."

Her acceptance might now be slowly eroding, thought Shao Peng. She held her tongue. It was not her place. She reminded herself that her little brother was the head of the household. She reined in the resentment that even now surged when dictated to by him. She swallowed hard and looked away.

Siew Loong gave little indication that he had noticed the resentment that crossed her face. He merely rose and escorted her out of the room and into the main thoroughfare of the mill. They were immediately engulfed. Piles of cassava lined one side of the wall. On the opposite side, sacks of rice lay on their sides in neat rows. Between the stacks of rice and cassava, coolies unloaded more bags of grain from bullock carts that had been brought into the mill. They hurried past to pile them against the wall; their backs bent double by the weight of the bags. Others wheeled in barrows of the brown tubers for stacking. The air was filled with dust and a fine sheet of white covered every nook and cranny.

Despite its proximity to the house, Shao Peng had never been in the mill before. Snatches of conversation between her father and brother kept her informed of the business. She looked on with round-eyed amazement at the activity. No one stared at her; she was with her brother.

***

The rickshaw carrying Shao Peng and Li Ling bumped gently along the dirt road towards the hilly rainforest nicknamed Pineapple Hill, *Bukit Nanas*. Shao Peng turned and saw that they had left Chinatown and the River Klang behind. They were on a by-way flanked by forests.

"Tell him to stop. He needs a rest. The poor man has been pulling this carriage, walking at a trot and barefoot for nearly an hour," she said to Ah Sook who was striding alongside the rickshaw. "The remaining travel will be uphill. Luckily Sister's Magdalene's place is just a short distance up from the foot of the hill. Even then, we should take a break. You too must be tired." She peered from under the canopy of the rickshaw. Perspiration soaked through Ah Sook's tunic. She regretted her brother's instruction to bring Ah Sook along. He must be tired for he was not a young man.

"I am fine. A short rest, however, is welcome. We shouldn't

stay too long. You have to remain in the rickshaw. Your brother has given me strict instructions. Last month, not far from here, a woman was kidnapped. The perpetuators were caught and they had their hands chopped off. This seems to have helped check the lawlessness around this area. No incidences of crime have been reported since then." He smiled when he saw the alarm in her face. "Don't worry. Your brother wouldn't have allowed you to venture out so far with just the rickshaw man and myself as companions. Look behind you. See the two men following our carriage. They are ours. He didn't tell you; he didn't want to alarm you."

"I didn't realise. What about the previous times I visited the nuns? Was I accompanied?"

"Of course," Ah Sook said with a smile.

So my independence was not independence after all, Shao Peng mused. She turned to Li Ling, seated beside her. "I am a fool," she said in English to her charge, knowing full well that Li Ling would not understand, "don't be like me."

"Your father took great care to ensure your safety to China as well. Didn't you wonder why the whole trip was so smooth? I know he made contacts in China for your safety and of course the Mission also promised him that they would take care of you. He had done much for them, as you know."

Her eyes misted. The revelation took her by surprise. She remembered the heated words she exchanged with her father when she insisted on leaving for China. Once again, she found herself in the wrong. How could she have thought that her father did not love her? She fell silent. She wondered if there was anything that she had done that was right.

Two women passed the carriage. They carried a tub of laundry between them and seemed in a hurry.

"Jing-jing," Li Ling called out waving wildly at the fast receding figures.

Immediately, Shao Peng stepped out of the carriage, hoping to run after the two women. Ah Sook stopped her.

"No miss. You mustn't. We have to leave now. They are heading towards that muddy track. It leads to a small settlement of shanty huts. Not a good area. In any case, we would be late and we have to return home early. We promised Master."

**

The rickshaw crunched to a stop on the gravel path a short distance from a small wooden building, painted green. Children's voices rang from within. Before Shao Peng and Li Ling could alight from the carriage, a handful of children ran out from it. They whooped with joy and immediately ran to play in a little sand pit by the side of the building. Two nuns followed them. They emerged from the cool darkness of the interior and stood by the doorway to accustom their eyes to the glare of the sun. One brought a hand up to shade her eyes. A bright smile broke out from her face and her eyes crinkled with delight when she saw them. "Shao Peng, she said. "Come in! It is a long time since your last visit. When did you come back?"

"Sister Magdalene, Sister Teresa," Shao Peng cried holding out both hands to them. "I came back less than a week ago. How are you? Where is Reverend Mother?"

"She is in the classroom, clearing the mess and tidying away the books." A smile as bright as sunshine lit up Sister Magdalene's face. "We have about seven pupils now," she said with pride, "and we are expecting the numbers to increase. Come, this way. She would be very happy to see you. We have such good news. A benefactor has offered to help us get a larger accommodation with potential to house sixty students. Praise the Lord. Just in time before the Monsoon arrives and the dirt floor here becomes a sea of mud." She turned to look at Li Ling. "Bring her along. Perhaps she would like to join us. She would enjoy the new school. It will be housed in the Victoria Hotel if the fund-raising succeeds."

"What a wonderful idea." Holding Li Ling's hand in hers, Shao Peng followed the nuns into the building. She looked around. Nothing much has changed since she last saw it. A cupboard, a small table and a scattering of stools were all there was in terms of furniture. Light streamed in from the doorway. There were no windows and the door was kept perpetually open to allow light into the room. Once a large garden shed, the three resourceful nuns had turned it into a classroom.

Reverend Mother was on her knees by a cupboard, reaching into its bottom shelf when they entered the room. She stood up immediately. Brushing the dust from her habit, she walked to Shao Peng. "Welcome back," she said. She smiled, a broad beam that stretched from ear to ear, transforming her face. Then the smile disappeared as fast as it came. She dropped her voice. "I am sorry to hear your loss. Your father was a good man." She broke off momentarily to allow Shao Peng to recover and then ushered her to a seat. "It is good to see you. Tell me all about your trip to China. What are your plans now?"

Shao Peng hesitated, her eyes clouding over. "First I need to talk to you about Jack." She looked at her charge. Sister Magdalene saw the hesitation. She bustled forward and led Li Ling away. "I'll introduce you to the other children," she said.

***

Throughout the ride home, Shao Peng wrestled with her thoughts. What she learnt from Reverend Mother threw a different light on the stories of Jack recounted by her brother. It was true that Jack was in England with his bride to be. But before he left he went every day to see the Reverend Mother to ask for news of Shao Peng. Reverend Mother had described him as desperate to see Shao Peng. Her heart leapt at the news. "He missed me," she murmured to herself. She was willing to clutch at any straw that could tell her that he was not the cad her family had made him out to be. "Why did he not wait for me? Why was he marrying someone else?" she had asked.

"His parents had summoned him back. His father was poorly and wanted to see him settled. You were not here. You had indicated that you would not be able to marry him and were contemplating taking the vows. He had waited almost six years. He was torn between his father's request and you. The girl was a childhood friend."

Shao Peng's heart softened at the news. How could she deny him his duty to his parents and expect him to accept her duty to hers? Somehow, Reverend Mother's words eased the pain in her heart. She had felt such shame when she thought that she had been fooled. Her pride had been injured. It had eaten into her very core and self-belief. A tiny whisper of a smile escaped her lip. He did love her.

She grabbed Li Ling's hand. "I am a fool you know," she said in English to her uncomprehending charge. "I am so mixed up that I do not know what I am or what I want to be. Life is so complicated. It is never black or white."

Li Ling squeezed her hand in return. She did not understand the words; she realised though that Shao Peng was troubled.

"Yet," Shao Peng continued aloud, "it changed nothing. It remains that Jack and I cannot be together." Her lips trembled. She despaired. It was as though her whole being had been hollowed out and nothing was left except a sense of hopelessness. "Perhaps it is meant to be. If he had just waited..."

She stared unseeingly at the scenery that unfolded. The carriage wheels rumbled across the rough track accompanied by the soft pattering of the rickshaw puller's feet pulling ahead of them. The sun was dipping to the west and the river glinted bright under its setting rays. Beside her Li Ling's head was soon bobbing and rolling with the motion of the carriage. Shao Peng reached over and gently placed an arm around the girl. She drew her close until Li Ling's head rested in the crook of her neck. She brushed the tendril of damp hair from the girl's forehead. The warmth of their contact was comforting. Poor girl, Shao Peng thought, not much of a day for her. I know what I must do; I shall help with the school. I shall teach. That much I can do with the education I have been given. With time and with work, I will heal.

Chapter 11

"You help me find out more about the women and I might let Li Ling stay."

They were in the courtyard. Rohani was resolute when she uttered those words to her stepdaughter. She looked more like herself, more in command and less of the broken distressed woman she was the previous day. She was dressed and combed. There were tiny white jasmine flowers threaded around the coil of hair worn at the nape of her neck. They blended and matched beautifully her white lace *kebaya* top. She adjusted her sarong and sat down on the wooden bench. She did not invite Shao Peng to sit.

"What if my findings are not happy ones for you? Would you take it out on Li Ling?"

Rohani did not seem to hear. "Ah Sook and the servants might tell you things they would not confide in me," she continued. "I am an outsider in my own house. Yes, you are better placed to get the truth than me."

Rohani stared wistfully into the distance. "I feel so lonely here. This part of the town has grown and grown with more and more Chinese people. I am increasingly isolated. Yet not far from here, the British Resident has set up a village called *Kampong Baru,* and designated it a Malay Agricultural Settlement. It will be exclusively for Malays. Perhaps I should move there. I long to hear my own language spoken, to be with my own people..." Her voice trailed off.

Shao Peng lowered herself next to Rohani and took both her hands in hers. "Please don't. You have been so happy here until you found out about these other women. Even if they were father's mistresses, I am sure that it did not lessen the love he had for you nor the happiness you both shared. Did he at any point make you unhappy when he was alive? I have never seen a cross word between you. When I was a child, I was jealous of the close bond between you two. I felt left out then."

Rohani nodded. "Yes I have been very happy. When I lost Siew Wong, your little brother, your father was wonderful to me. He comforted me throughout. He did not blame me when I failed to give him another son. We have Siew Loong, that is enough, he would say when I was desperate with my failure to conceive another."

"There you are. What matters are the good memories you have of him. Perhaps finding out more is not a good way forward. What would it achieve? You can't change his will."

"Is that what you are doing for yourself? Not looking back?"

"I am trying. I know it is not easy. I love Jack. No one understands. Now it is too late. He is marrying someone else."

"I can't leave it alone," confessed Rohani. "I dread knowing. Yet I have to know. It is torturous. Help me and I will help you with Li Ling." She lowered her voice to a conspiratorial whisper. Her eyes gleamed. "I can also help you with Jack. I know the whereabouts of the girl people say he had a dalliance with. You can see her and ask her yourself."

After Rohani left, Shao Peng stayed in the courtyard. Once again the mention of Jack stirred up in her a confusion of emotions. Did she want to know about Jack's alleged dalliance? She would be doing exactly what her stepmother was doing. Yet not knowing was killing her, just as not knowing was torturing her stepmother. She sat down and stood up again. She must push away these unwanted thoughts. She had to start anew. To do that, she had to immerse herself in work. She looked up. A mass of dark grey clouds moved across the sky, obliterating the sunlight with their ominous gloom. Any moment and the monsoon rains would be here. She could feel the dampness of the hot air building around her, a whirlpool of heat and humidity that was as oppressive as it was suffocating. She felt gripped by inertia. Yet the only way to break out of her grief was to act.

***

Some distance away in the shanty settlement, the monsoon had already arrived. Rain pelted down, fast and furious. *Ping! Ping! Ping!* It fell with relentless energy. The pail, so strategically placed under the leaking roof, filled over and water spilled onto the dirt floor; the damp spot spread like an ever-widening circle of leaching blood. Jing-jing ran to place another basin on the spot. She removed the overflowing pail and ran with it to the doorway to empty it. Over and over she did this, running into the house and out. She was drenched to the core. Outside the wind howled. She jumped each time lightning struck or the thunder roared.

It was morning before the rain eased. The air was still damp and the sky remained overcast. Huge cauliflowers of clouds dominated the skyline, their greyness outlined by a sun struggling to break through. Jing-jing stepped out of the hut dragging one foot in front of the other. Her legs were heavy with fatigue. She looked up and saw that parts of the thatched roof had lifted leaving an even bigger opening in the roof. The dislodged fronds rose and fell with each gust of wind. When it rains this time, she thought, no basin or pail would be able to cope. She looked around her. People were coming out to examine the damage to their property. There was not one familiar face amongst them. How could her husband leave her to this? Why didn't he repair the roof before she came? She had accepted his explanation that his boss had refused him leave and he needed to earn every penny he could, having spent all his savings on her ticket. Not now! She was angry. It would be three more weeks before she saw him. How could she stay here? Tears of self-pity rolled down her cheeks. They mingled with the drizzle of rain that had resumed. She looked at her feet. Her ankles were smeared with mud and her shoes were in tatters. They squelched in protest with each step she took. She fell to her knees and, clasping herself with both arms around her waist, sobbed.

After a while, spent and yet oddly relieved, she sat on her heels unmindful of the green and grey slime that caked her trouser bottoms and stained her arms and face. She looked across to the grove of plank houses Ah Kum had pointed out. They looked in good order. She rose to her feet and made her way there. She ignored the fallen branches, the rivulets of brown muddy water that ran down the track, the potholes and the debris that cluttered the ground. She paid little attention to the pelting rain that had once again resumed its unremitting force. She was oblivious to the wind that whipped around her; she did not see the wildly swaying coconut palm trees. Her one thought was to get to Ah Kum for help.

**

In the Ong household, Ah Sook was having a heated discourse with Shao Peng.

"Could you not wait Miss until the rains settle before setting out again? We would have to take the bullock cart this morning. It is too muddy for the rickshaw. Even then it would not be an easy journey." Ah Sook clutched the end of his tunic and tugged repeatedly at the seams, worrying it until his usually neat uniform was crushed. Ever since the young mistress's return from China, he had been made to go from place to place to accompany her. He did not approve of her unladylike behaviour. If he could voice his true feelings he would consider her actions not just unbecoming but downright unacceptable. He was adamant that she should be persuaded against it this time.

Shao Peng was equally determined. "I know it sounds unreasonable," she said. "Believe me, if I could postpone our trip I would do so. The trouble is who knows when the rain will stop? The roads might become even worse in the next few days. It might even flood. In any case the Klang River has not overflowed today. We do not have to travel far. We just need to go to the edge of Chinatown and cross the river."

"You mean to the new estate bought by the *Kapitan* for making bricks? It is still an undeveloped area. Why do you wish to go Miss? If you must, do it another time."

"It will be fine. With the bullock cart you would not need to walk. We don't need to take Li Ling with us. She will stay behind."

He stared at her, his mouth twitching with suppressed anger. She returned his stare, her face equally dogged. Finally, he bowed and without a word strode off. Shao Peng stayed still to watch his departing figure; his back was like a ramrod, stiff with resentment. She knew he was not pleased. She would have to think of a way to mollify him. Her mind cast back to the conversation she had with her brother the previous evening.

***

Dinner had been a miserable affair the previous evening. Rohani was wrapped in her own thoughts. Siew Loong said little. The servants brought dish after dish to tempt their palates. Most were sent away uneaten. Shao Peng could see that her brother was worried. A wreath of worry lines appeared to have sprouted overnight on his forehead. She could not imagine how she would have coped if she was in his position. To be thrown into father's shoes overnight, to be responsible for the lives of many people, to take over the large and varied business and, not least, to care for his mother and his father's other women! What would she have done?

As the rain fell fast and furious outside, the silence in the room became unbearable and uncomfortable.

"Can I help?" she asked her brother after her stepmother left the room.

He looked up, met her gaze and then said: "Would you?"

"Of course, if I can."

"Just before father died, he had put in place a contract to buy more land. He was very much taken up with the idea of growing rubber."

"Rubber?" she asked in surprise. It was not quite what she expected to hear. She heard of the plant from Jack. He had been very excited when Hugh Low, the British Resident in the northwest state of Perak, brought the plant into the country.

"Yes, rubber. Everything is still in an experimental stage. The few seedlings brought in some years ago have matured. The possibility of growing them in plantations is now being discussed. Before father died, he said that he wanted to be in a position to move ahead if the experimental planting succeeded. I would like to carry out his wish. However, I do not know anything about rubber. I need time to learn this. I hear that someone called Ridley is travelling around the country encouraging people to grow it. I am going to see him. The tree takes seven years to mature before we can tap it. There will be risks. A lot of capital has to be invested and seven years is a long time to wait for a return. Even the European planters are hesitating. They prefer coffee. So I really need to spend more time to study the crop and work out the feasibility of investing in it. My plate is full. Rubber is not the only thing I need to tend to. There are the other existing businesses to be taken care of as well."

He paused; a wary look crossed his face. "So sister, I don't have time to carry out my promise to mother regarding the four women. Could you help me out with it?"

Shao Peng leaned back into her chair. So, she thought, this was why he was telling her about rubber. He was setting his case for her help. "Tell me what you want me to do."

A sheepish grin appeared on his face, transforming it. She could see his relief that she had not taken umbrage. "I don't know really. I am sorry to land you this unpleasant task. What mother wants to know is whether these women were father's mistresses. That is the main thing troubling her. Then, we will have to decide what to do with them."

***

By the time Shao Peng reached the house where the four women lived, she had got out of Ah Sook some information about her father's relationship with them. He had see-sawed in his revelation, hinting and not confirming and then withdrawing his statements altogether. It left her completely confused. With a thumping heart, she got out of the cart and went to the front door of the house. Although a canopy had been put up over the cart, she was drenched. The strong wind had lifted the canopy most of the way and allowed the rain to lash in. Her clothes stuck wet on her body and her hair hung soaking and dishevelled. Rivulets of water trickled down her face. They ran down her neck and body and fell in a pool on the ground. In vain she tried to dry herself and wring the water from her hair. She gave up. They would just have to accept her as she was. She walked up to the door and banged on it. She looked around. The house was substantial and made of bricks, not like the wooden plank houses so common in this area. From within, voices rang out. Women's voices mingled with those of a child! She glanced quickly at Ah Sook standing next to her. A child! She looked questioningly at him. He avoided her eyes and looked away. There was no turning back; she straightened up and adjusted her wet clothes. She knocked smartly on the door. *Rap! Rap! Rap!*

"Coming! I am coming!" came a voice from within. "Who could be visiting on such a day?"

The door opened. A woman peeked out. She stared at Shao Peng's bedraggled figure. Her eyes, wide with surprise, shifted to the man standing next to her. She recognised him immediately and broke into a smile. "You," she exclaimed to Ah Sook. She opened the door further and moved aside to let them in.

Shao Peng stepped in, disconcerted that the woman seemed to know Ah Sook well. Behind her was a boy, three or four years old at the most. He was dressed in black, the colour of mourning. More women drifted into the room. She made a mental note. Four! They too wore the colour of mourning. All of them were young, much younger than she was, except for one.

Ah Sook stepped forward to introduce them. "Miss Shao Peng, Mister Ong Ah Ngao's eldest daughter."

Without prompting the women moved closer together. They looked afraid. The eldest of them pointed to the group of chairs arranged around an ebony table. She indicated that Shao Peng should take a seat. Shao Peng declined pointing to her own clothes wet with rain.

So, thought Shao Peng, taking note of the well-appointed room with its furniture inlaid with mother of pearls, father had provided this household well. She kept her face neutral and smiled. "I come on behalf of my brother," she said breaking the silence.

"I am Ah Chu their mother," the eldest of them explained pointing to the three young women. The little one is my grandchild, Mr Ong's son. Swee Yoke is his mother. Swee Yoke is my youngest."

It was with great difficulty that Shao Peng held back the gasp she would have emitted. Ah Sook had made no mention of children. When she heard a child's voice, her suspicion was aroused but to hear it confirmed aloud that her father had an affair and a love child, like it was the most normal of things to have occurred, was a shock. She thought of her stepmother Rohani and her heart went out to her.

She glanced at Swee Yoke who had not uttered a word. Swee Yoke, beautiful jade, a name that suited her because she was exquisite. Why! She could not have been more than eighteen, much younger than me, thought Shao Peng. How could her father...? She grew hot with anger. She felt betrayed; she felt her stepmother's betrayal. She braced herself, her fingers curled tight into her palms, her nails biting into them. She had learnt all that she wanted to know. She wanted to leave immediately.

"I am sorry to drop in so unexpectedly." She racked her head for something appropriate to say. "We did not know ... we did not know of your exis... until last week. Father never mentioned." Desperately, she turned around to seek Ah Sook's help. He looked away. "...I shall come again at a more convenient time." She looked at the little boy. The reality of it all hit her again; he was her half sibling, just like Siew Loong. He was so young, so tiny he could be her child if she had married. She remembered her stepmother's words when they last spoke. Rohani had said that her father had not blamed her for not having more children. Shao Peng's anger grew tenfold. She knew the reason why he didn't. She hurried out of the house.

***

Shao Peng rounded on Ah Sook the minute she got into the bullock cart. "Why didn't you tell me? Why didn't you say there was a child involved? You said that my father was very fond of the women. That could mean anything. You led me to believe that he was fond of them as young defenceless women."

"Miss, Big Master swore me to secrecy. He said that he loved Big Mistress and didn't want her to know. It was not my place to tell you."

"What else haven't you told me? Can't you see how it is going to tear Big Mistress to pieces?" Shao Peng's chest heaved with emotion. She loved her father, had yearned for his love when she was little and had thought it was not reciprocated. Events in the last few days convinced her that he did love her. And now this! Just when she thought she found some semblance of security! Could she ever trust any one again?

"But Miss, Mistress need not know, must she? Big Master loves her. He is a man. Please understand that a man can love several women. Look at all your father's contemporaries. When you compare him with the others, what he did is nothing. Can't you comfort her and think of something to tell her?"

Shao Peng turned away from the old retainer. She didn't want to hear any more. She would talk to Siew Loong. Together they would think of something. The cart rolled forward pulled by the bullock. The animal plodded on while the wind blew with increasing frenzy. They crossed over the river swollen beyond recognition. Water, dense with grey silt, spilled over its banks pouring its torrent over roads and fields. The water reached the ankle of the bullock. By tomorrow, much of the town would be flooded. A sigh escaped her. Thoughts of her family and her own situation chased through her mind, one after the other until she could not fathom which was which and which was worst. She closed her eyes and lifted her face to the rain, letting it cleanse her; hoping that it would also cleanse her thoughts.

***

"Of course you must stay while the storm lasts. My madam insists." Ah Kum handed a set of towels and dry clothes to Jing-jing. "There, change into this. You can't wear those wet clothes. You will catch a cold."

"I am trying to find someone called Ah Sook. He works for Mr. Ong Ah Ngao. My husband told me the address but I have forgotten it. He assured me that everyone knows him and I should look for him if I am in trouble."

"Yes, yes. No problem for me to give you the address. I guarantee you though he would not be able to see you at this moment. His boss, Mr Ong, the one you spoke about, has just passed away. And look," she pointed to the raging storm outside, "who is going to go out in this weather?"

Ah Kum bustled around Jing-jing to make her comfortable. She gave her a cup of hot tea. She offered her a plate of peanut brittle. She sat the girl down; she made soothing noises while she dried Jing-jing's hair; she was the epitome of kindness itself.

Jing-jing was grateful. When she set out to find Ah Kum that morning, she had been worried about the reception she would get after their parting the previous day. Ah Kum had been so curt. Now she was all kindness. And the lady of the house too had been so kind.

Jing-jing sipped the hot tea and looked around her. Unlike Jing-jing's abode, the house was sturdily made. A central corridor ran through the entire building with rooms branching off from it. The house had a narrow frontage but was very deep. In the front room, a small altar with offerings of mandarin oranges, red candles and joss sticks adorned a corner. Chairs lined the room. From a distance, the *click clack* of mahjong tiles could be heard. She turned towards the source of the sound. She saw a figure walk past. Ah Kum quickly closed the door.

"Come, rest. Stay in this room. Don't worry about your house. It can be fixed. Look, my boss has given me some money for you. Take it. You can repay us later. For now, just rest. I'll leave you to do that," Ah Kum said with a smile.

Outside in the corridor, Madam Lily was waiting. "She is pretty. She would do. " She rewarded Ah Kum with a pat on her shoulder. "Well done!" she said.

Chapter 12

AFTER SHAO PENG LEFT, Ah Chu gathered the young women together. In the candlelit room, they sat in a circle, clustered close together, knees touching knees, their heads bent. They spoke in whispers. There were no others in the room, save the little boy fast asleep on a mat. The maid was in the kitchen, yet they felt that they had to speak in hushed voices. The flames flickered, sending long shadows onto the wall. Outside the wind howled and the rain continued its incessant downpour.

"Listen to me. You heard what I said. Mr Ong fathered Swee Yoke's child. That will be our secret. On no account should you say anything different," Ah Chu looked in turn at each of the young women. Her eyes held theirs, seeking their connivance.

"I feel bad about it. He has been so kind to us. I can't bear the shock and sadness on his daughter's face," cried Swee Yoke.

"It will be even more unbearable if they were to know the truth. We could be kicked out. The young Mr Ong could stop our allowance. How are we to live? How are you going to bring up your son? Do you want everyone to know your shame? Do you wish to go back to your previous existence?" Ah Chu's voice was sharp. She glared at her youngest daughter. "Don't you agree that what I did was for the best?" she asked the other two women.

Hui and Huan nodded solemnly. The two sisters dropped their eyes, unable to meet Ah Chu's gaze. How could they say otherwise? They owed her so much.

Ah Chu grabbed Swee Yoke's hand, enclosing it tight in hers until the girl winced. She wanted to shake her beautiful young daughter. "You heard Hui and Huan? Don't jeopardise their lives by being virtuous; you say what I tell you to say." She turned to the two sisters. "Remember you are my daughters. Ah Sook won't tell on us. He is my kinsman. His father was my mother's brother. I doubt Mr Ong's son would pay for your upkeep unless you were closely related to Swee Yoke and me. Just being clansmen from the same village in China would not be sufficient reason. You don't want to be out on the streets do you? And he won't pay for us if we don't establish a strong enough stake."

"Mother," cried Swee Yoke, "is there no other way?"

"No," Ah Chu insisted. She was determined and shook her head vigorously to emphasise her point. "I have thought it through. You might have to give your boy to Mistress Ong. Ah Sook says she longs to have another son. She lost one of hers to the shivering sickness. That will sweeten her up. Then we can all stay together. Our future would not be bleak as it surely would be if you do not do as I say. Remember how it was when we first arrived in this country."

"No! Please don't take my little boy," sobbed Swee Yoke.

"You are young. You can have another." She reached over and brushed aside a lock of hair that had fallen over Swee Yoke's eyes. "You might still find a suitor despite your shame, a shame you brought on yourself. At least Hui and Huan had justifiable reasons for being what they were. They were sold to a brothel and Mr Ong rescued them when he heard of their plight from Ah Sook. You!" Ah Chu wagged her finger at her daughter; her voice became stern. "You have a child because you allowed your master into your bed!"

"No mother. You know that it is not true. He forced himself on me and for that his wife had me beaten and thrown out. Mr Ong saved me. You didn't even come to my aid."

Ah Chu's eyes misted for a moment. She knew she was being unfair. Her young innocent daughter was just a pawn, dispensable like all women were. Like she herself was. When she first came to this country to find work, no one took her in until that rogue of a master saw Swee Yoke. "We'll employ both you and your daughter," he had said immediately. She was so happy for the work. Unwittingly she had tried to win her master's favours by encouraging Swee Yoke to serve the master, bringing him tea and his shoes, massaging his shoulders when he requested. Swee Yoke did as she was asked. She was the obedient child Ah Chu brought her up to be. When Ah Chu learnt that the master had forced himself on Swee Yoke she had allowed herself to be beguiled by the possibility that he would take her for his concubine. So she did nothing. Yet, she reflected, what could she do? She had not reckoned on the master's wife. Yes, she was at fault. She knew it deep down and she wanted that guilt buried. The memories brought back the image of Swee Yoke, her clothes torn and bloodied, her body bruised and her lips swollen. She pushed it away.

"*Suan le! Suan le!*" she cried. "Let us not dwell on the past. We have to think of the future. And being out on the streets is not a future we want. Your son will always be yours. We will find a way to make sure he knows," she comforted.

***

The monsoon rains did not falter for two weeks. They went on and on. Both the River Klang and Gombak burst their banks. Torrents of brown muddy water coursed through the town, destroying everything in its path. Many small thatched huts were washed away. Even the newly built police barrack was brought down. Pieces of wood, bits of thatch, pots, beddings and furniture floated merrily down the river. Some lodged themselves on riverbanks where the exposed roots of trees stood; others were thrown helter-skelter by the rush of water down the valley. Jing-jing made several desperate attempts to go home. When she succeeded, she found half the roof gone. Standing knee deep in swirling water, she could only gape with disbelief at the carnage before slowly trudging her way back to Ah Kum's. This time her reception was cooler.

"You have been here for two weeks now and my madam has fed and clothed you. If you wish to stay longer you will have to think of a way to repay her. I think she is thinking of putting a small charge on your accommodation." Ah Kum handed Jing-jing a towel. Looking archly from under her brow, she brought her hand up on Jing-jing's arm. She stroked it gently, feeling the firmness of the arm, the smoothness of the skin, her eyes all the while on the young woman. With a voice as smooth as silk, she said, "There is nothing to stop you from using your assets to improve your life. No one needs to know, certainly not your husband."

"What do you mean?" Jing-jing took a step back. Goose bumps appeared on her arm and she shivered. She was not sure if it was from the cold or Ah Kum's touch.

"I don't mean right now, right this minute. *Huh!* Who is coming here with the raging storm outside? And look at this house. Water has seeped in despite our efforts to keep it out. Afterwards, when the storm has blown over, Madam expects business to return to normal. Then you can help." She busied herself with the tea bowls on the stand. "It is only right and honourable that you return her favours."

"What do you mean? How?"

Ah Kum laughed, a cackle that rose from her belly to burst forth in a sharp series of barks. "You cannot be as innocent as that! You are teasing me. You must know what this place is?"

"I ... I don't know. Your Madam's place of residence...? That is what you said and the girls ... clans women from your village?"

"And why are we all here?" Ah Kum grinned and wagged her finger at Jing-jing. "Come, come! You don't expect me to believe that you had no clue."

"Please don't tease me. I am a village girl. Until I came to Malaya I had never been out of my village. I can count on one hand the number of times I had been allowed to go out on my own. All I know is what you told me."

Ah Kum winked. "This is a gambling den besides other things."

"But ... but I have not heard ... seen any gambling..." said Jing-jing lamely. She suddenly remembered the sound of mahjong tiles on her first day here. Since then, she had heard nothing. She had been more or less confined in the room and she saw and spoke only to Ah Kum.

"Well then you are blind," said Ah Kum, "although I have to say, with the weather being what it is now, business has been slow. Look! All Madam wants you to do is to help out with the drinks to customers. With the money you earn, you could repair your roof."

Ah Kum walked to the door before turning to face Jing-jing. "Think about it," she said and closed the door sharply behind her.

Jing-jing heard a click. She ran to the door, it would not open; she banged on it, calling out to Ah Kum all the while.

"Don't make such a commotion. I'll open it when you become more reasonable," said Ah Kum.

***

"Here, take this broom and help. Don't just sit there like a Buddha," cried Ah Tai.

The maid was furious. While the house had not flooded like the rest of the town, the rain had poured into the central open courtyard splattering on to the surrounding tiled floor. Ah Kew, the second maid had slipped and twisted her ankle leaving Ah Tai with all the work. She grumbled as she flicked the long bristled broom along the surrounding corridor. *Swish! Swish!* She wielded the broom like a weapon. "I can't do everything on my own, " she muttered.

Li Ling took a broom and swept after her; then she followed up with a dry mop. Soon the tiled floor glistened. When they finished, Ah Tai stood with one hand on her hip. "You are not a bad worker, after all," she said. "Maybe we can make some use of you." She grinned showing a row of yellowed teeth. "I'll let you have some of Ah Kew's famous sesame buns for being so helpful. Come with me," she bid the girl.

They went into the adjoining kitchen. From the recess of a store cupboard, Ah Tai brought out a bun filled with sweet red bean paste and topped with a generous sprinkling of toasted sesame seeds. "Here, eat." She placed it on the table and sat down and watched while Li Ling ate.

"You are a funny girl. Lost your tongue? Can't you say anything? I know that when Miss Shao Peng came back the other night there was a meeting between her, big Mistress and the young Master. Can you not tell me what happened?"

Li Ling shook her head. She recalled the meeting. She had gone to the dining room with Miss Shao Peng who promptly forgot her. A heated discussion followed between the three adults. They spoke in a mixture of Malay and Chinese. Li Ling didn't understand most of it. The big Mistress had cried and wailed. The food was left uneaten on the table. She remembered her hunger; she hadn't dared eat.

The following morning, big Mistress was in such a mood. She glared at Li Ling and told her to disappear. She said she could not stand the sight of her. She said that Li Ling reminded her of the other women, the ones they were discussing the previous night. So Li Ling had made herself scarce. She made herself useful to the maids.

Li Ling swallowed quickly the remaining crumbs and got up. She didn't feel it was right to say anything at all about the meeting, much to the annoyance of Ah Tai. She hastened to thank the maid and excused herself. She went up to the bedroom she shared with Miss Shao Peng. She knew that her position in the house was awkward. She was not quite a servant - the fact that she shared Miss Shao Peng's room and was petted by her differentiated her from the maids. However, the big Mistress disliked her and the servants treated her like one of them. She sat on the bed and drew her legs up to rest her chin on her knees. Then there was the young Master. Unlike his mother, he was very kind to her. He was so good-looking and gentle, Li Ling thought, quite unlike the young farmers in her village. She was drawn to him. Her heart quickened each time he was in the room. She prayed that they would not send her away; she wanted so much to stay in this house. She recalled the conversation between Ah Tai and Ah Kew in the kitchen. She wondered about Suet Ping, the girl big Mistress intended for Master Siew Loong. She wondered if she was pretty.

Lost in her reverie, she did not notice Shao Peng coming into the room.

Shao Peng walked quietly to the bed and sat down on its edge, next to Li Ling. "What are you thinking about?" she asked. She placed her arm around the girl's shoulders. Perhaps Rohani was right. Li Ling was not a child. She was a young girl fast becoming a woman. Of late, she had noticed her brother's solicitous behaviour towards Li Ling. Was it her imagination borne out of what her stepmother had said?

"Nothing," the girl replied raising her eyes.

"Nothing?"

"What is going to become of me?" Li Ling asked.

"I am so sorry. With my father's death, the floods and all ... the other things happening in the family, I have not thought in detail about the matter. Would you like to learn to read and write? When I was a child, the greatest thing that happened to me was the education my aunt gave me. Later, Uncle Grime taught me to read and write in English. Would you like that for yourself?"

"Am I not to be a servant?"

Shao Peng smiled and shook her head.

"Will I stay in this house with you and Master Siew Loong?"

Shao Peng was surprised by the reference to her brother. She observed the blush that coloured Li Ling's cheeks when she mentioned Siew Loong's name. She thought of her stepmother's earlier insistence that Li Ling should be removed from the house. Rohani had said that she might let Li Ling stay if she could find out more about her father's women. That promise might not hold, not when she, Shao Peng, was a bringer of such bad news.

"I am not sure," she replied, her eyes steadfast on the girl.

"I would rather stay here. If learning meant that I have to leave, I'd rather not learn."

"Don't you think reading and writing would be more important?"

"My mother does not read and write. She says that girls don't need to be clever; they have just to be obedient because we are like a flash of..."

"You told me," interrupted Shao Peng. "I don't agree with her. With education, you could do much more for yourself."

"Like you? I am not clever that way."

Shao Peng hesitated for a moment, then lifting her chin determinedly she said, "Yes, perhaps a bit like me, though more like the women I am going to tell you about." She drew her legs up on the bed and sat cross-legged facing her charge. She told her of the work of women like Miss Betty Langland, a missionary, who gathered together a few women and taught them to read, starting the first girls' school in the town. She spoke of another called Nurse Maclay who brought up and taught children abandoned by their mothers, and finally of the three Sisters whom Li Ling had met. "We too can do these great things if we learn."

***

That night long after Li Ling had fallen asleep, Shao Peng was still up. She got out of bed, threw a shawl over her shoulders and went out of the room. The house was quiet and shrouded with darkness; the stillness broken only by the night sounds of geckos and bats chirping as they dived through the skies. She opened the door and stepped barefoot onto the verandah. A blast of cold damp air hit her and she wrapped her shawl tighter around her shoulders. She looked up and saw the sky ablaze with stars. The rains had stopped, leaving only dampness in the air and the scent of rain-soaked flowers. She made her way round the verandah holding on to the rail and edging slowly on the wooden floor towards her favourite seat. Her foot connected with another stretched out across her path.

"You can't sleep?" Siew Loong drew his feet up to make way for her.

She sat down next to him. Her eyes adjusted to the darkness. She could see his profile. "No," she replied.

"Me neither." He shuffled further up the reclining chair. "At least the rains have eased and things can get back to normal again. Well as normal as it can get. I can at least start work." He leaned back, his own face half hidden in the darkness. "I don't know what to do about father's other family. Mother wants us to cut off all ties with them. She wants me to pay them off. Today I got a message from Ah Chu, the mother of those women. She offered the little boy to us. She said that he belonged to the main house because he is our father's son. I haven't told mother of it yet. Should I?" he asked turning to face his sister. "He is our half brother."

She looked at his young face. His hair had been cut short unlike many of the other Chinese men who still maintained their hair long and braided into a pigtail. He must have been tousling it, for it stood ruffled and uncompromising, softened only by the slight breeze that had picked up.

"I am not sure." She hesitated. "Perhaps you should tell her. She would come to know sooner or later. It is difficult to keep things to ourselves because I can see that the servants have started talking amongst themselves. Why did Ah Chu want to do that?

"She said that according to Chinese custom, the son of a concubine belongs to the first wife and that she is only doing it out of respect."

"*Hmmm*. I don't know if mother would think the same way." She took his hand and squeezed it. "What a mess! Father's sudden death had opened up, what Uncle Grime would call a can of worms. I don't want this family to split apart because of this."

"No, it won't." He gave her a reassuring smile. "And you? Are you coping?"

She shrugged noncommittally and turned towards the garden. Somewhere, an owl hooted. She could see a flock of birds flying from a tree, their wings flapping in the starlit sky. She turned back to face him. "You are right about keeping busy and having projects. I am going to help the nuns run their school. Would you agree to it?"

Chapter 13

AT THE BREAK of dawn, a dim ray of sunlight seeped through the window curtains into the bedroom. Li Ling rolled over and saw Shao Peng still deep in sleep in the bed next to hers. She sat up. Quietly she swung her legs out of the bed and tiptoed to the window. She lifted a corner of the curtain and peeped down to the garden. Two gardeners were busy sweeping the path. She looked down directly beneath her. Rohani was standing at the top of the short flight of steps leading from the verandah. Only the top of her head and her shoulders were visible from above. Li Ling was uncertain as to whether she should go down immediately to help. She knew that there was a lot of work to be done. The previous night Ah Kew and Ah Tai had grumbled that the floods had brought large quantities of debris and waste into the garden. Inevitably this meant a lot of cleaning once the floods receded. Her heart missed a beat. She saw the young master join the Mistress. His head bent close to his mother's for a minute. He appeared to be saying something. Suddenly he looked up, his gaze seemingly directed at her. Li Ling dropped the curtain. She felt a flush rise in her cheeks and a hammering in her heart. Quickly she changed into her day clothes, combed her hair and went down.

She went out through the main door and stepped on to the verandah. He was not there any more, only the Mistress remained. She turned to make a quick retreat before she could be spotted. She would go to the kitchen, she thought. Mistress would not like to see her so early in the morning. She had made herself plain. Li Ling walked quickly and quietly towards the kitchen, skirting the courtyard. The kitchen was unusually quiet for the time of the day. Ah Kew and Ah Tai would normally be busy preparing the breakfast, directing the under maids to light the fire and boil the water for the morning tea. The kitchen would be a hubbub of noise, cooking smells and activity. That morning, however, only Ah Tai was in the kitchen.

"Just in time. Help me with this," she said thrusting into Li Ling's hands a tray heavily laden with a pot of tea, a tea bowl and a bowl of rice congee with an assortment of small dishes. "Take this to the young Master. He is having breakfast on his own in his study. Mistress had hers early and Miss Shao Peng is having a lie-in. Ah Kew has taken the other maids to help clean up the mess left by the floods in the outhouse. I have had no help at all," she grumbled. Without waiting for a reply she went back to the stove.

Li Ling took the tray and carefully negotiated the kitchen's narrow doorway and back into the main house. Her heart was beating so fast she thought she would drop the tray in her nervousness. Today was her birthday. She was fourteen, a grown woman. Her heart sang with happiness. Suddenly everything seemed fine. By the time she skirted the courtyard, the sun was fully up and its bright light lit up the whole courtyard. Everything looked so pretty she thought. She smiled; two dimples appeared and her eyes lit up with expectation. She did not know why or what she was expecting. She was just happy.

Her arms strained under the weight of the heavy tray. She stopped in front of the study. With no hands free to knock on the door, she edged her body around and pushed open the door with her shoulder, almost stumbling in the process. She became flustered, not quite what she wanted to be.

Siew Loong was seated behind a dark wooden desk with piles of paper in front of him. Disturbed by the noise he looked up and saw her. "Ah my breakfast. Good. Set it there please," he indicated to one side of the desk's surface. "I'll help," he said at once getting up to clear a space. "Let me take this from you."

"No Master, it is my job," Li Ling protested, clutching the tray firmly. She felt his fingers a hair's breath away from hers. It was like a current of heat had passed through her. She glanced quickly towards the door, half expecting to be reprimanded by someone for her clumsy entrance and inability to even carry out instructions to serve a meal properly.

"Where is Ah Tai or Ah Kew? They normally bring me breakfast on days I choose to have it here."

"Everyone is busy with cleaning after the floods." She set the tray down and began laying out the bowls and dishes. She could feel his eyes on her. When she finished, she made to turn away. She changed her mind and turned to face him. "Is there anything you wish me to bring you?" she asked, her cheeks a bright pink.

Siew Loong glanced at the tray and then at Li Ling, a bemused look on his face. "Perhaps you could come back and take the tray away. I need the desk to work. Say in half-an-hour's time."

Li Ling turned to go. He reached out and stopped her. "Do you like it here?" he asked, his hand still lingering on her arm.

"Yes! Very much," she replied with a smile. Her heart sang with joy.

***

"That's the situation mother," Siew Loong said. "I am sorry that father hurt you; I know that nothing I say will make it better." He glanced at his sister. Shao Peng saw the look he gave her and threw in her support.

"From what we hear, it could only be a moment of weakness that led him to form a relationship with the girl, Swee Yoke. Initially his intention was just to save them from their fate." Shao Peng took hold of her stepmother's hands and held them fast. "Please, please don't be upset," she said.

"The thing is, mother, do you want to have the little boy?" Siew Loong asked.

"What! To be reminded of your father's folly! No! No! I will not have him in this house. Just send those women packing. Pay them and tell them to go."

"Not quite that easy, mother. The house has been made over to them."

"Well then, send Li Ling to that household. Tell them that they have to have her if they wish to receive any money from us. I don't want her in this house. I expect her to report the going-on in that household to me."

Shao Peng released Rohani's hands. She looked in horror at her stepmother. "Why do you dislike Li Ling so much? She has not done any harm."

"She reminds me too much of those women. They were her age when your father first brought them here. I too thought that they were young and innocent. I thought that your father's intentions could not be anything but that of a kind man. When later I heard no more about them, I thought nothing more. And look! I am a fool and he was an old fool! I want her sent away immediately!"

***

With a heavy heart, Shao Peng went in search of her charge. She found Li Ling in the backyard. She wondered how to break the news. She straightened her shoulders. It had to be done; there was no way out of it. Li Ling spotted her and came running with a basket of newly laid eggs in hand.

"Look, I've found sixteen eggs! Ah Tai will be pleased. She was going to make her special sponge cake and..." She stopped. "What's wrong?" she asked seeing Shao Peng's face.

"Shall we sit over there on the bench by the mangosteen tree? I have something to say to you."

Li Ling knew something was wrong. "Is it news from my mother?"

"No, nothing like that." Shao Peng did not know how to broach the subject.

"Tell me then," said Li Ling, her body tense, her eyes wide and searching.

"I am sorry Li Ling, you can't stay here, at least for the moment, until I can get my stepmother to change her mind." She could hardly bear to see the hurt in Li Ling's eyes. She pulled the girl to her. She could feel Li Ling's tears soaking into her blouse, hot tears that seared her skin. She stroked Li Ling's head and whispered comforting words. Nothing, however, could console her. She sobbed and her body heaved as she gave vent to her distress. Shao Peng's eyes misted; she felt helpless. Surely there must be a way out of this, she thought. Her mind raced, darting from one possibility to the other.

"I don't want to go there. The servants told me of those women. They said nasty things about them. Big Mistress hates them and she hates me. That is why I am sent there. Please, please don't let them do this to me!"

Shao Peng gently eased the girl away from her and, looking straight into her eyes asked, "Would it be better if I make arrangements for you to stay elsewhere? Would it be better if I promise that I will still see you every day, that you will receive learning, that I shall teach you myself?"

Slowly, Li Ling raised her head. "Will I see young Master?" she whispered.

Taken back, Shao Peng looked deep into the eyes of her charge. She saw what she did not wish to see. She took a deep breath. "Li Ling," her voice was gentle, "why is seeing young Master so important?"

Li Ling made no answer. A blush as deep as a red rose coloured her face. There was no need for words to explain Li Ling's anguish. Shao Peng recognised them because she had been through it herself.

"His mother," Shao Peng said, "is making arrangements to marry him to a girl of her choice. It is better this way that you are not around him. It would be better for him and for you."

A pang of guilt twisted within her. She was behaving like her father. Was she interfering with other people's emotions and love? No, she told herself. She just wanted to protect her charge from falling in love like she did when there was no possibility that it would be requited.

Li Ling's eyes welled up once more. Shao Peng took her in her arms. "I'm sorry," she whispered. There was little more she could say.

***

Li Ling's meagre belongings were scattered on the bed. She was alone in the bedroom. She dragged the little bag that Shao Peng had given her on to the mattress. She began to pack, wiping her nose and her eyes as she did so. Her hands moved mechanically folding the garments and placing them in the bag. Why was it better for her that she did not see the young Master any more? A slow resentment simmered in her. She was disappointed, disappointed at being so curtly brushed aside when she had been promised so much by Shao Peng.

Chapter 14

JING-JING SAT ON the bed. Kum's taunts and laughter rang in her ears. There was no way out of the bedroom. The door was securely locked from the outside. Days passed. Jing-jing grew listless. The restlessness turned to despair. Each time they brought food, she would try to push her way out of the room only to be pushed back into it. Kum visited every day. She cajoled, she threatened and she offered to console Jing-jing with a pipe that would guarantee to make her forget her woes. Jing-jing lost track of time as each day passed. She sat most days biting her fingernails until they were raw, wondering all the while whether her husband would be able to find and rescue her. How many days before he comes back from the tin mine, she asked herself. How many days before he would realise that she had been taken? No one else knew her. She lost hope that Shao Peng would come.

How would she know of her plight? Kum had said that she had just lost her father and she lived on the other side of the river well away from these shanty settlements. She must conclude that all was well if Jing-jing did not contact her. Jing-jing regretted once again her boastfulness at their parting. She had blithely claimed that she needed no help because her husband would see to it all. She recalled Lai Ma asking her to keep in touch and how she had gaily replied that it would not be necessary. She remembered the hurt in the older woman's eyes.

Rap, rap, rap! She whirled and went hurriedly to the window. It was boarded from the outside. Only a tiny sliver of light peeped through between the two wooden shutters. She saw a shadow move, blocking the light and then an eye stared back at her. It looked familiar. She saw a finger placed on pursed lips. "*Shhh!* It's me," it whispered.

"Lai Ma?"

"*Shhh!* Yes, it's me. I've come to get you out. I'll wait till it's dark and after the evening meal. We have to be quick. They have barred the shutters. I will have to find a way to break through without too much commotion."

"How did you find me? How did you know I was here?"

"I'll tell you later. No time..."

"*Heh there!* Are you talking to yourself?"

Jing-jing jumped. She turned to stare at the bedroom door. She could hear the clunking sound of keys and Kum muttering from outside. She glanced quickly over her shoulder. Lai Ma was gone. She ran and sat down on the bed. She began whispering to herself, talking nonsense. She feigned madness.

Ah Kum pushed opened the door; her eyes darted, searching from one corner of the room to the other. Seeing nothing amiss she rushed to the window. She pressed her face close and peered through the slat. Finally, satisfied that there was no one outside, she walked back to the bed.

"Tonight, you will get ready. Madam is tired of waiting for your answer. Your first client will be here after dinner. Don't make him wait. I will have a tray sent to you early and a change of clothes. Someone will be here to help you change. She will also bring you a drink. I advise you to drink it to make it easier for yourself. Hear me?"

Kum dropped her voice. Her tone became more conciliatory. "I only want what's good for you. Trust me."

After she left, Jing-jing slumped back on the bed. Tonight! Would Lai Ma be here in time? Would she be saved in time? She tiptoed to the window and peered out again. No one! No one passed here because this side of the building backed on to a dense thicket of bushes. She could feel her heart beat; it thumped so hard, she feared it could be heard. She chastised herself for being silly. Yet her anxiety would not go.

***

"I have made contact with her." Lai Ma was breathless. She had run all the way back to her own house. "I told her that I would come for her this evening. We were interrupted. Thank God I hid behind the thicket to listen because they were planning to make her accept a client this very evening. I fear we have to move more quickly."

"Then, we must not wait till evening to act even if we were to risk a gang war should they catch us," replied Ah Sook. "I have to warn my young Master, and warn him of that possibility. He does not know I am here. He is away on business. Miss Shao Peng sent me."

He sat down heavily on the chair and sighed. "Well at least we found Jing-jing. I only came to know of her plight when I went to her house to break the sad news about her husband and found instead a deserted hut half blown away by strong winds and rain. Poor girl. We owe her this. She came all the way from China and now ... her husband is dead. It is lucky that neighbours spotted her with that woman Kum. Kum's notoriety made it easier for us to track her down. I told Miss Shao Peng and she sent me to you. She said that Jing-jing would be frightened if we were to send a strange man to make contact."

"How do you know her husband? How ... what did he die of ?"

"He worked in a mine owned by my boss as your husband does. He was trapped in the mine when the floods came. One of the other coolies said that Cheung was not feeling well that day. He had slipped and twisted his ankle. When the water poured in, he tried to struggle. The more he struggled the faster he was held by the mud. The others tried to help him. They couldn't do much. The torrents of water were so strong. The mine was caving in. They were forced to abandon him. Poor man! Poor woman! We must try to help her. I am sure both my young Master and Miss Shao Peng would provide for her. But enough talk of this! We have to get to Jing-jing. I shall organise some people to go with you."

Ah Sook hurried out of the house and came back almost immediately with three burly men. Lai Ma gulped, for the men wore loose tunics that were unbuttoned leaving gleaming bare torsos. Two of them had scars, which they seemed to wear with pride. They looked ruthless. She dropped her eyes in embarrassment and fear.

"They will help stand guard and take down the bars barricading the window shutters. Then Jing-jing will have to climb out of the window. Everything has to be done very quietly. We don't want a gang war if we can avoid it. It is fortunate that there are no windowpanes. You should go now. Then bring her to Miss Shao Peng. The men know the way. That house is well known to them. I will go back to Miss Shao Peng now to report on this."

***

Of the three men assigned to help Lai Ma, only one accompanied her to the back of the house where Jing-jing was. The other two pushed a cart laden with pots and pans in the opposite direction. The pots rattled and clanged with each movement of the cart. They parked the cart a short distance from the front entrance of the wooden building that housed Li Ling and immediately set forth to sell their wares. A gong was sounded at regular intervals while one of the men began to shout at the top of his voice extolling the wares.

"Pots, pans, woks, all going at reduced prices. *Tai kam kah, tai kam kah!* Big discounts!" His voice boomed across the street, followed by the loud resonations of a gong. People began to crowd round him and a steady stream of haggling began.

Other vendors began to join them. They were on their way home. When they saw the crowd the two men had drawn, they changed their minds. They too parked their carts and soon started calling out at the top of their voices.

The noise brought Madam Lily out on to the street with Ah Kum following behind her. They glared at the unruly scene before them.

"Tell them to move to another spot and to keep their voices down. They are creating such a havoc it is upsetting my business," Madam Lily ordered.

Ah Kum rushed across the street. "Are you all mad? Stop this noise at once. Go! Set up your stalls elsewhere. You are disturbing the peace here."

"Who are you to tell us what to do?" yelled back one of the men. "*Chao hai! Diu nei ge loh moh!*" Stinking c...! F... your mother!"

Kum marched up to him. She dealt him a sharp slap on the face and then she spat. A huge glob of sputum landed on his eye. Commotion broke out. He grabbed her hair just as she was turning away and pulled. Her head snapped back. She retaliated. She jabbed her elbow into his middle and then she clawed his face. Her sharp nails caught his eyes. Pans, pots, sticks flew. Everyone joined in the fight. Madam Lily and her women rushed out to help Kum.

At the back of the house, Lai Ma and the man called Chee were busy levering out the rough pieces of wood nailed on to the window shutters. The noise they made was drowned by the riot. Chee made short work of the boards and within minutes the window was opened. Jing-jing meantime had moved a chair against the window. She clambered up and then out of the window into the waiting arms of Chee and Lai Ma. They ran.

Chapter 15

"WELL DONE EVERYBODY!" said Shao Peng. Lai Ma, Jing-jing and Ah Sook were gathered in the parlour. Jing-jing was still in a state of shock and Lai Ma was out of breath from hurrying all the way to Shao Peng's house. Unable to speak, she sat with one hand on her heaving chest. Perspiration rolled down her face and her hair clung damp to her neck. Shao Peng caught Ah Sook's eyes. He shook his head imperceptibly; he had yet to tell Jing-jing about Cheung, her husband. "Later," she mouthed silently to him before turning to Jing-jing. She reached out to take her hands. They were cold.

"It is wonderful to see you safe."

Jing-jing sat with her body slumped forward from her chair and her face in both her hands. She looked up when she heard Shao Peng speak to her. She was pale and her eyes stared vacantly at Shao Peng. Gone was the high-spirited boastful girl of the past. Shao Peng dropped to her knees and took her in her arms. A tremor ran through the girl's body. Jing-jing's teeth started to chatter. She pushed Shao Peng away.

"If ... if Lai Ma hadn't come for me, I would have been forced to go with a man. I do not know how I could ever face my husband again. It is all my fault; I shouldn't have gone to Kum. Cheung warned me against people like her when he left. Please don't tell him. I don't know what he would do. Even though nothing happened, I am tainted." She crossed her arms and held herself tight to stop her shivering. "I doubt Cheung would want me back. What if he tells his mother?"

"We won't tell," Shao Peng exchanged a look with Lai Ma. "What we must plan now is how to keep you all safe. I think that staying in this part of Chinatown would be dangerous. Word would get around that you are here. Ah Sook says that Madam Lily has the support and protection of gangsters. All brothels are affiliated in some way to the triads. We don't want them to come after us."

"You can definitely expect skirmishes of some sort," chipped in Ah Sook. "But don't worry, we too have men that will protect us. "

Shao Peng looked at him in horror. "You mean we too are protected by members of secret societies? Why did we involve such people?"

"Miss, how can we not? Every one of us is involved in one society or the other. Even you, although you might not know it. We are associated through our clans; the Hakka people are in one society, the Hokkiens in another and so on. Who else would come to your help?" He looked pityingly at Shao Peng. He wondered at her naivety. Hadn't she heard of the Ghee Hins and Hai Sans?

Shao Peng fell silent. There was so much she did not know. Embarrassed, she thanked Ah Sook and sent him away.

"I think the best thing for us to do is to find a secure place for all of you."

"You mean me as well?" asked Lai Ma. "I can't go. My husband will be returning soon. He would be worried if he didn't find me at home."

"My husband will also be looking for me," Jing-jing said.

"Yes, all of you will have to leave here, including Li Ling. I have a plan. Do not worry about your husband Lai Ma. I shall take care of it. I'll get word to him. Why don't you go up to your bedroom? We have prepared one for you for tonight. Ah Kew will take you up. I would like to speak to Jing-jing alone."

Lai Ma stood up. Her eyes lingered on Jing-jing who sat with her shoulders hunched. Lai Ma turned to walk away. She placed one foot hesitatingly in front of the other. She stopped. She walked quickly back and placed a hand on Jing-jing's shoulder. She squeezed it gently. She wanted to say some comforting words. She could not. Jing-jing caught her hand and thanked her. Slowly Lai Ma walked out of the room towards the stairway. Even before she reached it she heard Jing-jing's cry, a howl that came from the very pit of her stomach. "No! No!" she cried.

***

The house was quiet. Increasingly, Shao Peng found solace in the quiet when everyone was in bed. The darkness and the night sounds of insects and birds suited her. She sat on the verandah, her legs stretched out in front, her head resting on the back of her favourite long rattan chair. She closed her eyes and allowed the silence to wash over her. She breathed deeply of the jasmine scented night air. It had been a traumatic day. Since her return from China, they had been inundated with one crisis after another. At times she could not breathe. Nothing seemed straightforward.

Only in the quiet of the night when she was alone, could she try to put some semblance of order to the different events. It would be wonderful, she thought, if they could have one problem at a time but life was not like that. When troubles come, they do not come singly. She gave a wry smile. They certainly had the effect of pushing her preoccupation with her own personal problems aside. Yes, her own personal conundrum must take second place because nothing could change its outcome. Jack was married and whatever he might or might not have done, whatever was said of him that was true or not true, the fact was she could not be part of his life. The sudden realisation of this freed her. There was utterly no need to pursue the 'truth'. All that mattered were the memories of their love in the past, not what was unattainable in the future.

Tears rolled down her cheeks; she tasted their salty tang. She let them flow; she did nothing to wipe them away. And as they flowed her acceptance of what she considered the inevitable grew. Her eyes grew heavy. She drifted off to a deep slumber. She did not hear her brother coming to sit by her nor the blanket he placed over her. She did not know that he had returned home.

Chapter 16

AT THE CRACK of dawn, when the sky was still overcast with the darkness of the previous night and when light was just a gleam of pale silver between grey clouds, Ah Sook brought the pony cart to the back of the house. Siew Loong had gathered together his clansmen from the Hai San Society. They now stood ready, waiting for the women.

Shao Peng came out first with Li Ling in tow. She grasped the girl's hand firmly in hers; she had earlier tried to reassure her charge. She spent time trying to explain to her. Li Ling hardly responded to her touch or returned her gaze. She showed her reluctance by keeping her face devoid of expression and her eyes cold and bitter. How could a young girl show so much by doing so little, wondered Shao Peng? Now she dragged her feet, and Shao Peng had to slow down. Holding her hand became a strain.

Lai Ma and Jing-jing followed them out. Both looked tired and worried. They had slept little the previous night. Jing-jing was overcome with grief and shame. Lai Ma fretted about how her husband would react when he found out that she had abandoned their home. Both women had dark shadows under their eyes. One by one they clambered onto the cart. The ponies fretted over the long wait. They raised their hoofs and neighed; the cart rolled and shifted. Finally when they were all in the cart, Siew Loong came to wish them farewell. He spoke softly to each one of them. When he finally came to Li Ling, he took both her hands. "Take care," he said, "I ... we shall miss you." He held her hands in his for a moment and then released it, the tips of his fingers brushing hers as he did so. Shao Peng glanced sharply at her charge and saw a small flicker in her eyes. Then it was gone.

The cart rolled forward with the clansmen on horseback following them.

***

By the time the sun had risen fully and the morning dew on the long blades of wild grass by the wayside had been replaced by a coating of dust, they were in the driveway of the Sisters' school. The women clambered down from the cart on to the dirt path and stared at the small green wooden building in front of them. A woman dressed in a black robe and with a white wimple emerged.

"Come in, come in." Reverend Mother Andrea opened wide her arms in welcome. She took one long look at the women, saw their downcast faces and said immediately, "tea, hot tea is what you need after the morning's journey." She smiled and ushered them into the one-room building. The children in the classroom stared with round-eyed astonishment at the women. They dropped what they were doing and gaped until Sister Magdalene drew their attention back to the book they were reading.

The women were showed to the back of the classroom where a small charcoal stove and a kettle were kept. The Reverend Mother busied herself with tea. She measured each spoonful of the leaves with care. "We have very little privacy here, I am afraid," she said pouring the hot water into a tin teapot patterned with pink flowers. She nodded in the direction of the front of the classroom. "As you can see, there is not much space. We use this as a classroom. In the late afternoon we go to a temporary sleeping accommodation provided by our wonderful patron. It is some distance away. It is not very convenient, although, mind you, we are very grateful for it." She poured out the tea into little cups. She held the cups close to her nose to breath in the aroma of the tea before setting them down. Her face brightened. "All this will change soon. We have been given a new residence. A hotel has been converted for our use thanks to our patron, and the patronage of your father and his associates. It is in Brickfields. It will be sufficient to house all of us. We had expected to be there earlier but the monsoon arrived sooner than expected and everything went on hold. In the next week of so, we should be able to move in."

Lai Ma, Jing-jing and Li Ling looked uncomprehendingly at the Reverend Mother. Slowly Shao Peng translated. "You will be safe in Brickfields, " she added. "Kapitan Yap owns the land. He bought it to set up a factory for making bricks. With the frequent floods, there is a decree by the British Resident, Frank Swettenham, that future buildings should be made from bricks and roofs should be tiled. Kapitan Yap has given my brother the assurance that you would be safe on his land."

"But what do we do? Have we to convert to Christianity? Do we have to be nuns?" asked Lai Ma, her face pale with dismay. This was not the first time she had asked that question. She stared suspiciously at Reverend Mother. She had this constant niggling fear that there was a plot to convert them to a new religion. "I can't do that," she said. "I am a married woman with four children!"

"No you do not have to convert. You do not have to be nuns." Shao Peng sighed for she had explained this many times to Lai Ma. "You have to help out with the school. You always said you wished to be employed. The number of pupils is expected to increase. The Sisters need help in the kitchen and carers for the children."

"*Aiyah*, why didn't you say so right from the start?" Lai Ma heaved a sigh of relief. "You made me so worried. Of course, I can help clean and care for the children. If you wish, I can even cook. Though I say it myself, my cooking is not bad at all."

"And you?" Shao Peng asked Jing-jing. "Will you be able to help as well?" Poor Jing-jing, she thought. She had an overwhelming desire to hold her in her arms to comfort her. She did not; she feared that Jing-jing would not welcome it.

Jing-jing nodded glumly, hardly conscious of what was asked of her. She showed no interest in what was happening around her. She had not spoken since her outpour of remorse when told of her husband's death. She blamed herself. Her mother-in-law had always claimed that she brought misfortune to the family. Her mother-in-law was right. She stared unseeingly out of the window. She winced. Her grief was like a physical pain. She was to blame. She was born in the year of the tiger, a *foo*, a bringer of woes. She did not care what she had to do.

"And you Li Ling, you will join the other children to study," Shao Peng said.

Li Ling averted her face. She refused to meet Shao Peng's eye. She made no response. Shao Peng looked to Reverend Mother for help.

Reverend Mother threw her a look that suggested she left Li Ling alone. She whispered in English. "She is merely sulking. The less you try to convince a sulking child the better." She paused, her eyes raking Li Ling's profile, noting the determination of the girl to show that she did not care. "I suppose she is more than a child, not quite a woman and not quite a child—a difficult age. Still, you don't want to give her the impression that sulking will get her what she wants."

Li Ling's averted face turned a bright pink. She did not understand what was said. She knew instinctively, however, that she was being discussed unfavourably. She did not like it and her resentment grew.

Blissfully unaware, Reverend Mother ignored Li Ling and continued addressing herself to Shao Peng. "Your help would be invaluable. We need teachers. A large number of people from Ceylon and India have been brought in recently for the rail works. Unlike the Chinese miners, these new immigrants come with their families. Their children will need support."

She looked brightly at the women. She could see that they were worried, although the young girl was seemingly nonchalant and unheeding of the conversation in the room.

"They have to sleep here tonight," she said apologetically. "There is no room for them in the temporary accommodation set aside for the children. We will get some bedding into this classroom. It is not ideal but at least, they will be safe."

"We are not very far from the British Resident's house. Security guards will be at hand," she explained to Shao Peng. "It is best you leave now before the women start to fret again. Come back in the next day or so. We can work on the curriculum then. For now, I am sure that between Sister Magdalene, Sister Teresa and myself, we can conjure up sufficient Chinese to communicate with your charges. This way we'll get to know them and they us."

She dropped her voice further and leaned closer to Shao Peng. "Mr Webster is back. I thought you should know. He is not..."

Shao Peng stopped Reverend Mother mid-sentence. "I don't want to know," she said. Her face was like chalk. She turned to the women. "I'll see you tomorrow. I ... I have to go."

Chapter 17

SHAO PENG HARDLY NOTICED anything during the journey home. Once ensconced in her own bedroom, she went straight to her desk. She opened the drawer and took out a sheet of paper. She sat, neck tensed, body rigid, pen poised in her hand, to write. She dipped the pen into the ink and began; she couldn't. She didn't know where and how to start.

Her thoughts were muddled. They came all in a rush, none of which were coherent. All of them were thoughts that had run through her mind a hundred times over. She wanted to say she missed him; she wanted to berate him. She wanted to ask, "Why, why didn't you wait? Why didn't you warn me when I told you I was going to China? How could you do this? Do you love her more than me? Do you love me?" They went through her head in no particular order, tearing her apart.

She pictured him with his wife. She could not bear that he was with another. She hated him. She loved him. She hated that she had quarrelled with her father over Jack. Drops of ink dripped on to the white paper. Soon it was covered with blotches of dark ink. Tears fell alongside it, turning the black to rivers of grey smudges. Her resolution to start afresh without him wavered. Yet two nights ago, she had felt so strong, so convinced that it was the right thing to do. She dropped the pen brush; not caring that the ink had splattered on to her blouse, not caring that the pen brush had rolled and fallen on to the floor. She cupped her palms over her eyes and wept.

After what seemed like a lifetime, she sat up and wiped her face with the ends of her blouse. She got up and went to the washbasin. She poured water into it and washed her face. "These will be the last time I cry for him," she said to herself, "I will abide by what I promised myself. I swear."

***

That night, when the meal was over, she went out to the verandah and waited for her brother to join her. It had become customary for the two siblings to meet and talk in the quiet of the evening. She had not spoken to him since his return from Malacca. She leaned over the wooden railing and felt the wood hard against her elbow. Turning her face upwards to the sky, she closed her eyes and moved her lips silently in prayer. She heard him even before she felt his presence next to her. She smiled. She had never felt closer to her brother than she did that moment. How things have changed, she mused. That she should be dependent on her younger brother and look to him for advice and he to her. When her father was alive, there was always rivalry between them for their father's affection. Now they looked to each other for support and strength.

"So, are they all settled?" said Siew Loong. "The house seems so quiet after they left."

Shao Peng gave an affirmative nod and turned to look out to the garden once more. She was glad of the darkening sky.

"Have you been crying?" While at the dining table, her swollen eyes had not escaped his notice. He had not asked because his mother and the servants were around. "Do you want to tell me?"

She shook her head. "It is best left unsaid. Speaking would cause me to cry and I don't want to cry. I am just being selfish, wrapped up with self-pity. I don't have new problems, just the same ones that I can't seem to shrug off." She smiled wryly. While the corner of her lips quirked her eyes were filled with pain.

"Is it about Jack?"

She could not bring herself to admit it. She looked down over the railing.

"I know he is back. His name came up when I was in Malacca for Ridley's introduction of rubber to Chinese cassava plantations."

She waited for him to say more. She had a hundred questions. She dreaded asking them. A long silence followed. So they stood side by side looking over the railings into the dark while the night sounds surrounded them like a thick velvet cocoon. After what seemed like eternity to Shao Peng, she heard him say, "He is not married. I thought I should at least clarify this after all that I said of him."

Her heart leapt. She held on to the railings, every limb tense with excitement. She stared ahead. She was afraid that she would give herself away. She was not sure how her brother would react if she were to jump with joy.

"His father died and he was freed from the marriage. The girl apparently had no wish to marry him because she didn't want to come to Malaya." He turned to her. "Do you still wish to marry him?"

Her mouth went dry.

"What about the Malay girl, his mistress? We should at least find out before making a decision. I am not going to allow my sister marry a philanderer."

"You mean you would not object to our marriage if he is wrongly accused?" Shao Peng's eyes were wide with disbelief. Her heart sang.

"You know I was always on father's side and backed his view. However, now that I am myself subjected to a marriage that I am not keen on, I am slowly coming round to the idea that ... that perhaps, being as old as you are, I should let you make up your own mind." He grinned; his eyes twinkled with mischief.

Shao Peng's hand flew to her face.

Siew Loong's face was serious when he continued. "I had a long talk with Uncle Grime and Aunt Janidah after father's funeral. Since then, I have had time to reflect on it. If they can be so happy together, then perhaps a mixed marriage might not always be bad. You should know, however, that it wouldn't be easy."

She was lost for words. She could only smile. It was like a beam of sunshine that lit up the night. She refrained from throwing her arms around her brother; it was not done. She didn't want to be told off for her 'foreign ways'.

"Anyway I can't stand that glum face of yours day after day," said Siew Loong with feigned anger that did not quite conceal his delight that his sister was happy.

***

At the first break of dawn, when daylight was no more than a pale wash of grey, Shao Peng was up. Sleep eluded her. She dressed quickly and went in search of her stepmother. She walked barefoot out of her room towards the wide central stairway and turned into the corridor that led to the eastern part of the house. It was a part of the house that she rarely entered. Her father had declared it his sanctuary. After a day's hard work, he wanted to be with her stepmother and the quiet that it afforded. Shao Peng had envied Siew Loong when they were children; he was younger and somehow managed always to charm his way into these quarters. She moved quickly toward the closed door; she knocked. There was no answer. She waited for just a second or two; then she pushed open the door and entered the room.

Rohani was kneeling on a mat, her buttocks resting on the pale upturned soles of her feet. She did not turn around. She continued with her prayers, prostrating herself low until her forehead touched the ground.

Caught by surprise, Shao Peng stood at the doorway. She held her breath. She felt like an intruder. She had never seen Rohani in prayer. Religion was never discussed. It never cropped up. She knew that her father respected Rohani's prayer times and abstinence from pork. It never seemed to interfere with the household activities nor the management of meals they ate together, even though her father was not a Muslim. Somehow, they accommodated each other's practice. How did they do it? Until now she never gave it any thought. She just took it for granted. Now it hit her because she herself might be at the brink of a marriage with someone with a completely different background.

She stood in silent admiration of her stepmother, wondering at how her stepmother had managed to balance the two cultures.

At least with Jack and herself, religion would not be a bone of contention. She smiled at the thought, excited by the prospect that they could marry. There was just one more hurdle to go, she thought. She waited quietly at the doorway, trying hard to instil patience in herself.

"Why this early?" her stepmother asked when she completed her prayers. She got up and invited Shao Peng into the room.

"Remember you said you could take me to Kampong Baru, the village set up for Malay people? You were going to show me the girl ... Aishah ... the one rumoured to be Jack's ... Well, can you do it? "

"Are you sure you want to know?"

"Siew Loong said that if I know for certain that Jack did not have a ... a relationship with her, he'll let us marry." She blushed. "Of course that is if Jack still wants to. I have not spoken to him." Her cheeks turned a deeper pink. She wondered if she was being presumptuous. What if Jack no longer felt the same?

"When?"

"Today? I am going to the Convent this afternoon. We can do it this morning."

A loud knock interrupted them. "Mistress, is Miss Shao Peng with you? She is not in her bedroom. Someone is here to see her."

"At this hour! Who could that be?" said Rohani.

***

Shao Peng took her time going to the main hallway. Ah Fatt was vague as to who the caller was. Ah Fatt was new to the household, having arrived from Hainan a couple of months ago. He spoke mainly Hainanese and normally would not be called upon to greet guests because not many spoke that dialect. He was only standing in for Ah Kew whose ankle was playing up once more.

Shao Peng ran her fingers through her hastily combed hair wishing all the while that she had paid more attention to her dressing this morning. She paused for a second in front of a mirror and looked at herself. She grimaced and then stepped over the half moon doorway into the front room. She stopped. It could not be!

Standing with his back facing her was Jack.

He turned when he heard her, his hat in his hand. With four big strides he was beside her. He held her arms and his eyes searched into hers. Then he pulled her to him, brushing his lips against her temple.

For a split second she resisted but her body refused to do as she willed. She gave up and buried her face in his chest. She breathed in his scent.

"I missed you," he said.

"I ... I..." She pulled away; she was suddenly overwhelmed with anger. "Why did you leave without a word? You were going to marry someone else..." Her voice broke.

He pulled her back into his arms, and his jacket once more muffled her voice. "Please, let that be for the moment. I'll explain. Please let us have this moment and think of nothing else." His lips were on hers, stopping any further protestation. She tried pushing him away. She couldn't keep up with the struggle. The comfort of being in his arms muted her anger. All she wanted at that moment was to be loved and to cast aside the shadows of the past months. She longed for peace and love. In his arms, she felt she had that for the first time since her return from China. They stood there oblivious to everything, he with his arms round her and his lips tracing the tendrils of hair that had escaped on her temple, and she nestling into his jacket. She could feel his heartbeat and he hers.

"*Ummph!*"

Shao Peng broke away. Siew Loong was standing with arms folded across his chest, looking at them. His expression was fathomless. He looked from one to the other. Then he turned and strode back into the house. "Remember what we agreed last night! Until then, he should leave!"

Shao Peng broke free. "You have to go now. My brother promised he would not stand between us if the rumours about you and Aishah are proved unfounded."

"Aishah?" A look of bewilderment crossed Jack's face. Impatiently he brushed aside the lock of hair that had fallen across his forehead. "Aishah? The girl that was sent to clean my quarters?"

He let his arms fall to his sides. The look of incredulity on his face was replaced with hurt and then anger. "Do you believe in the stories, whatever they may be?"

He stepped back. Then he turned and left.

***

The bullock cart trundled into *Kampong Baru* and Shao Peng found herself in a different time warp. The contrast between the street she lived in and the village they arrived at could not be greater. It was like leaping from the hustle and bustle of activity to a space where everything moved slowly, where the act of breathing was in itself sufficient to count as motion. Even the air, hot with a hint of the turmeric spice, smelt different. From the corner of her eye, Shao Peng could see the glimmer of excitement in Rohani's eyes.

"At last!" Rohani clambered out of the cart. "I wanted to visit the moment I heard about this place. No one was interested in accompanying me here. Both your father and brother were always busy. It reminds me so much of the village I came from, where your father first met me."

Shao Peng looked at the little wooden houses on stilts, the banana groves with their bedraggled palms, the colourful sarongs strung out to dry and flapping in the wind and the children with brown torsos bared to the hot sun, playing in the dirt. She realised why Rohani had carved out a garden that mirrored such a place. The depth of her stepmother's homesickness touched her deeply. She understood why her stepmother had chosen Suet Ping for Siew Loong. She longed for someone she could relate to and Suet Ping being half Malay provided her that.

Mindful of her own quest, however, she placed a gentle hand on the arm of the excited Rohani. "Where is Aishah?" she asked.

Rohani pointed to a group of men squatting idly by the path. The men were brazenly staring at them. "Ask them. I know only that she lives in this village."

When asked, the men pointed them in the direction of the river. They gawked at the two women. Every now and then they would drop their eyes, shift on their haunches, and mumble to each other before continuing with their staring. They did not often see Malay and Chinese women together, at least not in this village where all the residents were Malay.

Shao Peng was too preoccupied to notice. She boarded the cart and they moved in the direction of the river. She could not keep calm. She could feel her heart beat go faster and faster. She had started the journey feeling confident that she would be able to clear up any misunderstanding so that she would be free to marry Jack. Now that she was here, she found her confidence ebb away.

A number of women were washing clothes on the riverbank. They were singing and chatting. Their voices rose and fell in rapid cadence. They stopped when they saw Shao Peng and Rohani.

"Aishah?" Shao Peng heard her own voice squeak. "Is anyone here called Aishah?

A young woman detached herself from the congregation of women and came forward. "*Saya* Aishah." She was the colour of dark honey. Shao Peng's heart fell. She absorbed the symmetry of the woman's face and her large eyes framed with long dark lashes. She was the most beautiful woman she had ever seen. How could any man resist her?

Rohani saw how Shao Peng had turned deathly pale. "Leave it to me. My Malay is better. I'll speak to her," said the older woman. She beckoned the girl to follow her. Shao Peng stood aside. Aishah brushed passed, her buttocks undulating under the tight sarong. She glanced back at Shao Peng, and smiled.

Shao Peng stood rooted. Her legs refused to budge even though she wanted to move nearer to listen. She watched Rohani speak; the girl's eyes slid in Shao Peng's direction. She nodded emphatically. The thudding in Shao Peng's heart did not stop.

***

After Jack left Shao Peng, he went straight home. He ran up the short flight of steps that led from the front porch of his house to the verandah that skirted it. He entered the house. It was quiet. No one was around. He hurried to the back. He found his valet, a young Chinese called Wang, polishing shoes. Startled, Wang dropped what he was doing and got up. He was not expecting his boss.

"Master, you are back. I didn't hear you ring for me."

"I didn't. Come with me." Jack led the way into the drawing room. "Are you aware that there were rumours about Aishah..." Jack could not finish his sentence. He felt it was unseemly to ask his own valet about rumours concerning himself. "What do you know about Aishah?" he asked instead.

A smirk crossed the man's face briefly. "Aishah? She used to clean here. You know her, Master. She says you often gave her gifts, a roll of sarong, once even your shirt. She is not here now. She left once you went to England. She is back in her *kampong*." From under his eyebrows, Wang observed his Master's reaction. He had been extremely irritated when Aishah showed off the things she received. He had been jealous, afraid that his own importance to his Master would be diminished by a mere slip of a girl.

"Yes, yes! I remember her. Did she say why she left? Were there any rumours surrounding her departure?"

Wang did not answer at once. A sly look crossed his face. He remembered how he had teased the girl and accused her of bedding his master, how the others joined in until she could not stand it any more and had fled. Good riddance to bad rubbish. He now looked up and returned Jack's searching gaze. "No Master. Just that she was lazy and did not wish to work. May I bring you a drink? It is a very hot day."

Jack picked up his *topi* and placed it on his head. "No. Thank you. I am going out."

He strode out of the house into the scorching hot sun and walked briskly to the British Resident's house. He needed to clear his mind. He thought of George, his best friend. George was the district officer from the neighbouring state of Negeri Sembilan. He was visiting Kuala Lumpur. He would ask him if he heard of rumours concerning him and Aishah.

As he walked, his mind went back to recent events since his return from England. He remembered, in particular, the silence that greeted him when he entered a room. He had thought little of it then. He had attributed it to news of his broken engagement. Everyone had expected him to be married and they were embarrassed to speak to him. He now realised that he was snubbed for a different reason. He recalled the first day of his return when he was asked to join the Resident for dinner. The women averted their gaze when he looked or greeted them. Gone were the smiles and friendly greetings of the past. The lady seated next to him had barely a word to say in response to his polite conversation. Surely, he thought, his gifts carelessly given to the poor girl who had so little could not be misconstrued.

***

"Well old chap," said George, "you have yourself partly to blame for the plight you are in. I did warn you that the natives here are childlike. You should not encourage over-familiarity. There should be a strict division between employer and staff. It is for good reason that we have this policy of segregation. It is no good you saying that you gave her gifts because you pitied her. That act in itself would lead to all sorts of misconstruction. My servant is a friend of your valet, Wang. He apparently told everyone that you favoured Aishah. He hinted that she bedded you. As a man, I can't say I blame you on that score. She is beautiful. You should, however, try to keep such things from the public's view. These things do happen." George looked pityingly at his friend. "It should just appear not to."

"I didn't bed her. I love Shao Peng. You know that."

George took a big gulp of brandy and looked appraisingly at his friend. Sometimes he wondered how Jack could be so brilliant and then so naive when it came to matters of the heart.

George decided that he should try to steer his friend away from such ill-conceived thoughts of involving himself with a local. "I thought Shao Peng turned you down. Again, even with her, you are not conforming to what is expected of us as representatives of the British Crown. The people above us don't like it, you know, consorting with the natives. As far as the Administration is concerned, she is not English and that is that."

"I don't care a damn about what the Administration thinks. Funnily enough, Shao Peng's father thought exactly the same way. I am not good enough for his daughter because I am not Chinese!" Jack ran his hand through his hair, almost tugging it in his frustration.

"I wish you good luck." George finished his drink and placed the glass down with a sharp bang. He knew that Jack would not change his mind when it came to Shao Peng. Well, he gave it a try. "Duty calls. I have to go to the Resident now. I shall put in a good word for you if I am asked. There is little else I can do. "

***

"What did she say?" Shao Peng asked Rohani, the minute she had a chance.

Rohani waited until Aishah could not be seen and the last of the women by the river had left. She knew Shao Peng was anxious and thought for a while to choose her words carefully. It had not been easy to fathom all that Aishah told her. She had to separate the facts from the fiction.

"She clearly is quite besotted with her master," she replied. 'She tells me that Mr Webster *sayang* her. He gives her things. However, the word *sayang* means a range of things. It does not necessarily mean sexual love or love between a man and a woman. You *sayang* a baby, you *sayang* a child, you *sayang* your cat. If she had said *cinta*, I would be more concerned. From what she told me, I think it merely means 'fondness' as he would a pet or a child. In any case, what is most important is that she has not slept with Jack, the way it was rumoured. I specifically asked her, both indirectly and directly. From what I gathered he had been mainly kind to her."

Relieved, Shao Peng clasped both hands to her face. She wanted to jump for joy. "Would you tell Siew Loong? If I told him, he might not believe me."

Again Rohani did not reply immediately. She lowered herself to a wooden bench and patted the seat next to her. She beckoned Shao Peng to sit. "I have one condition. I would like you to be friends with Suet Ping," she said. "I would like to have her with us more frequently, and when she is in our house, she needs a friend. Your brother shows no interest. I don't want her discouraged. Having you as a friend would help the situation; it will help tide over awkward moments. Your brother could be quite trying. Moreover, as her friend, it gives me a reason to invite her over. It gives her a reason to stay. Would you help?"

"I don't want to be involved with any scheme to make my brother marry Suet Ping."

"You are not asked to do so. There is no scheme. I just want you to make her feel comfortable when she comes to us. You were so good to that girl Li Ling; can't you be equally kind to someone I like? How is being kind to a young girl make you a culprit to my scheming, as you so uncharitably put it?"

Shao Peng felt trapped. She stifled her misgivings. "All right, I will try to be kind and friendly; nothing more. Will you tell Siew Loong then?"

Rohani reached over and took Shao Peng's hands in hers. "Thank you," she said.

Chapter 18

THEY STOOD HIP TO HIP, arms entwined around each other's waist. The river gleamed darkly before them. Across the opposite bank, the jungle loomed large, its shadowy movements caught by the moon above. Every now and then, the silence was broken by the sounds of birds and animals. Shao Peng nestled closer into Jack's arms and sighed.

"Bliss," she murmured into his chest. "How did you find this place?"

"George. It is his secret hideaway. It was generous of him to lend it to us."

"It is perfect."

Jack could feel her smile without actually seeing it. "I am sorry. It has not been quite the wedding I wished you to have."

"Everything is perfect. I don't need a grand ceremony or beautiful clothes or lots of people to make it perfect for me. You make it perfect."

She raised her face. He leaned down and kissed her. Her lips felt velvety soft. "I wish it had been a bigger event for you. I hope you will not regret it."

She nestled into his arms. "No I won't. I like it the way it was, with my stepmother, brother, Uncle Grime and Janidah attending. It is only right. My father had only just passed away. Any lavish celebration would be unseemly."

"I suppose."

"And we do not want to ruffle too many feathers in the British Administration either. I know that they do not approve your marrying me."

"I am not worried about what people think."

"I am for your sake. In fact, I have taken matters into my own hand. I have asked Aishah to work for us. Do you mind?"

Astonished, Jack pushed Shao Peng away until she stood at arms length facing him. "Why?" he asked.

"I hope this will stop any further rumours. If I, as your wife, wish to have her around, it should be proof enough that there was nothing between you and her. They will have to find other things to gossip about."

He gathered her into his arms, "Mind? Why should I mind? With you beside me, I am ready to face any obstacles." Jack buried his face in her neck. Then, clasping her face with both his hands, he kissed her again. Shao Peng sighed with contentment. All the doubts, worries, troubles and cares of the past years slipped away.

***

They moved to Ampang, an area that had developed beyond recognition from the days when her father, then still a coolie, bought his first house. Rohani professed that her happiest days were spent there.

Shao Peng ran a hand over the teak console, the wood smooth and warm beneath her fingers. She sighed with happiness at all that she saw around her. She loved her little house. Perhaps happiness was infectious, she thought. She was happy, so happy that she could not believe such joy was possible. Everything was perfect except ... Shao Peng sighed and turned to Aishah who was trailing behind her. "From tomorrow, I have to return to work. I shall try to come home before Master. There will be some days, however, when I will not be able to do so. So on those days I'll have to leave you to look after him. Shall we go through the things you have to do?"

From under her eyelids, Aishah stole a quick glance at her Mistress. She averted her gaze before Shao Peng could notice and looked down again.

"Ask me if you don't understand," said Shao Peng kindly, thinking that the girl was not saying much because she was either shy or didn't comprehend. They moved from room to room with Shao Peng detailing what needed to be done, finally ending in the little anteroom next to the master bedroom. It had been converted into a shower room. A bucket tied to a rope was hung high up. The rope was released to allow the bucket to descend and dip into a large tub of water that stood on the floor and was then pulled up towards the ceiling until it caught. A tiny jerk would allow the bucket to tip over and water to cascade down. The water would run off between the floorboards to the ground below.

"Make sure that the tub is full so that Master can bathe when he comes home from work. Also make sure that you mix two buckets of hot water into the tub. Otherwise the water will be too cold. This is an experiment. Master is not used to ladling water and sluicing it over himself." Shao Peng smiled to herself. She had thought the bucket shower a strange idea when it was so much easier to just ladle water over one's body to wash.

Aishah said little as she followed her mistress around. It bothered Shao Peng that the girl was so quiet so she took both the girl's hands in hers. "If you need anything, if you have any problems at all, please tell me."

"*Semuanya baik*, everything is fine." Aishah replied softly. She moved her hand away. "I know what to do. I have looked after Master before."

"Well then, I shall leave you to it." Shao Peng was pleased to have elicited a response at last from Aishah. "I am going to read up for tomorrow," she said and, turning to give Aishah an encouraging smile, walked away to the little study next to the sitting room.

Aishah stood still looking at Shao Peng's departing figure. Then she went to the rear of the house and out through the back door and then down the flight of steps to the kitchen. Her room adjoined the kitchen. She slipped into her room and sat on her bed. She stared out of her window into the backyard. A tear rolled down her cheek. She wiped it away.

Chapter 19

THE AIR RESONATED with the buzz of insects. It was as though everything contrived to drive her mad with boredom. Venting her anger, Li Ling kicked a stone and watched it fly and fall midway into the river. Not satisfied, she kicked again, digging the toes of her sandal deep into the mud to dislodge another stone to hurl across the river. Water splashed up, its muddy brown sludge spattering onto the shirt of a young man walking by.

"*Heh!* You!" he shouted. Before he could say any more, Li Ling ran. She ran as fast as she could back to the school. She was supposed to be attending the vegetables in the school's backyard. This was one of her responsibilities during weekends and she begrudged doing it. There was nothing she was happy with at the school. She was not interested in learning. She did not like the other children. She had nothing in common with them. They were much younger than her. In her eyes, they were mere infants playing childish games and talking silly things that were beneath her. She resented having to work with Lai Ma and Jing-jing. Shao Peng had promised her that she need not work. Feeling cheated, she took it out on the two women. She barely spoke to anyone. By confining herself to herself, she grew even more miserable and resentful. She had not seen Siew Loong since she left the house. Only he, she felt, was genuinely kind to her. She blamed Shao Peng for building up her hopes and dashing them as sharply as they had been raised. When she learnt of Shao Peng's marriage, she became even more resentful.

"All those promises she made me! She forgot all of them She said I was to be her sister. Such empty words! I was not even invited to her wedding. I would have been able to see young Master if I had gone," she grumbled.

She took up a can and began walking along the paths between the vegetable beds. Her attempts to water the plants were desultory. She could not stop thinking of that morning when she brought Siew Loong his breakfast. She replayed in her mind every gesture, every word he said to her. Her hands still tingled from his touch when he took them in his and bade her farewell. He had reserved his attention for her and her alone, she thought. She loved the young Master and the Mistress had deliberately separated her from him. Shao Peng had connived with her stepmother in this.

Lai Ma watched from the kitchen window. She shook her head with despair. Li Ling was wasting the chance to better herself with learning. The sisters complained that she took no notice of the lessons. She had changed from the frightened girl that boarded the ship to a surly young woman who thought she was better than others. Unable to stand the way Li Ling was treating the plants, she rushed out and grabbed the can of water from the girl.

"I'll do it. Look! You have trodden on the vegetables. You should look where you are walking. Why can't you do a simple thing like this? I just don't understand why Miss Shao Peng thinks so highly of you. She is coming this afternoon and she has asked specifically to see you. So try to be a bit more amiable."

"She is not Miss Shao Peng, she is Mrs Webster. I want nothing to do with her."

***

They did not realise they were being watched.

Da Wei had hurried after the girl who ran like a deer when he shouted. He saw her push open a gate and disappear behind it. He was livid. He did not appreciate being splattered with mud, and certainly when he yelled at her, he expected at least an apology.

He circumvented the fence and found a gap between two planks that had been hastily put together. He peered through the gap. He saw her. Up until then, he had not had a proper look at the girl. He smiled. She was beautiful, he thought. He must certainly get to know her. He was about to find a way to clamber up the fence when he saw an older woman come out. There was an exchange of words and then he saw the girl slip away.

***

"Why doesn't she want to see me? asked Shao Peng. I brought her new clothes and books. Reverend Mother told me that she is not interested in reading. So I brought her books with pictures and words hoping that they might whet her appetite for reading. I was planning to spend some time with her on these."

Shao Peng placed the pile of books and clothes on the table. She was exhausted. She sat down and looked forlornly at the doorway, hoping that Li Ling would appear. She had made a special effort to visit. Torn between Rohani's demands that she help out with Suet Ping, her promise to assist her brother and her work at the Convent, she had been going home later and later. Jack had lamented that he hardly saw her.

"I don't know what's wrong with Li Ling," replied Lai Ma. "Give her time. She might come around. I think she wants to stay with you in the big house. In any case, she can't do it because you are married and have your own home. She is a selfish and wilful girl." Lai Ma hesitated. She was not sure whether she should say it but she couldn't hold her tongue. "I think you have spoiled her too much, Miss Shao Peng."

"I might have. I remembered how hard it was for me to leave my home in China and come here to an unknown land. I felt sorry for her. I was planning that she could come to me once I am more settled."

Lai Ma nodded sympathetically. "Stay here for a moment. I'll try to persuade her to come out of her room."

Minutes passed. Lai Ma came back. She shook her head. "I knocked and knocked on her door. She wouldn't answer. Leave her be. Leave her to her tantrums."

Shao Peng got up. "Tell her these are for her, will you?" she said, handing the books and clothes to Lai Ma. "I hope she will like them. I will be coming tomorrow to help with the classes. Perhaps she will talk to me then. Now I have to go to my brother's house. Miss Suet Ping is there and I have promised to visit."

"Is ... is she the intended for young Master?"

Shao Peng did not reply. She realised her answer would be relayed from one to the other. She pretended not to hear. Li Ling, however, heard. She had had her ears plastered to the adjoining wall and had strained to listen to the conversation between the two women. Hearing the name of Suet Ping reaffirmed her belief. Her heart hardened further against Shao Peng.

Chapter 20

THE FOLLOWING DAY, Da Wei went to the riverbank to wait for Li Ling. He did not know if she would be there; he went anyway. He had spoken to people and made many enquiries. They were too happy to tell him. Not everyone was pleased about the school. For some it was another foreign idea that would lead to false aspirations. From the local grapevine, he was able to piece together a picture of Li Ling. He knew she was unhappy in the Convent. That would be his leverage. He learnt too that she often played truant, escaping from the confines of the classroom or the kitchen garden to come to the river. He was told she was often found just before dusk, sitting on a boulder by the twist of the riverbank.

He sauntered up and down the path. He was by nature impatient. Yet on this occasion, sensing success, he was patience itself. He looked around the neighbourhood, casting his eyes on the dwellings nearby. He marked out the various paths around the school building and took note of the front and back gates to the building. After a while, he hid himself amongst the long grasses by the wayside. A breeze picked up pace and the grass rustled, swaying and bending with the wind. He took no notice of them; his eyes were fixed ahead. Then a small smile appeared on his face. She had come.

Li Ling had hurried out of the house as soon as dinner was over. She could not stand a moment more of Lai Ma's nagging and advice. Throughout the washing up in the kitchen, Lai Ma told her that she was lucky and that she should be grateful. Who is Lai Ma to tell me what to do, Li Ling thought; her eyes were fierce and her mouth petulant as she recalled the exchange with Lai Ma in the kitchen. She sat down on the boulder and took off her shoes. She dipped her feet into the river. The sun was sinking low into the horizon. She had about half an hour before she had to return to the Convent. She told Jing-jing she needed to finish some weeding in the kitchen garden. She knew no one would look for her if she stayed away for just that time. Resting both elbows on her knees she leaned forward and cupped her face with the upturned palms of her hands. She tried to catch an image of herself in the water. She did not hear Da Wei until he was standing behind her. Startled she turned and let out a gasp.

"I am sorry. Did I frighten you? I worry that you might fall into the river. You were leaning far too forward."

She got up. "I have to go. Let me pass."

"Of course." He stepped aside to leave a passageway for her. "You might wish to put on your shoes first." He pointed to her feet.

She looked down and saw her bare feet, blue with cold and still dripping from water because she had withdrawn them quickly. She blushed.

He bent down and retrieved the pair of shoes she had earlier carelessly cast aside. "Here," he said, giving them to her.

She took it. Nonplussed, she stood unsure of what to do next. It seemed ungrateful to brush pass him as she had earlier intended. Yet, she was reluctant to thank him because after all he was intruding into what she considered her space.

"I often come here myself," Da Wei volunteered, hoping to draw her into a conversation. "I live about a mile away. I come here to stroll and think after a day at work at my father's store. We sell general merchandise. I manage it."

Pretending nonchalance, she swept her eyes over Da Wei. He seemed harmless enough now that she had a closer look at his face. She thought him quite pleasant looking, and certainly not someone she needed to fear. He was clean-shaven and wore a smart blue jacket and matching loose trousers. Moreover, he said he was a manager. She relaxed.

Da Wei noticed the change in demeanour. He lowered himself on another outcrop of rock. He was careful not to get too close and alarm her. Without a word, he handed her his handkerchief and pointed to her wet feet.

"You can keep it. There are plenty where it came from. We sell all sorts of things. Clothes, handkerchiefs, food, toiletries..."

Li Ling's curiosity was aroused. She took the handkerchief. She made no move to leave.

Da Wei searched into his pocket and fished out a mouth organ. He brought the instrument to his lips and he began to play. Li Ling was captivated by the way his lips moved, pursing and blowing into it. She recognised the tune. It was a love song that young women sang in China. She had heard it sung many times during harvests.

"Do you like music?" he asked pausing for a moment, his eyes flicking quickly over her.

She nodded.

"My name is Da Wei. What is yours?" He pretended he did not know.

"Li Ling," she answered.

He picked up his mouth organ and played another tune. "This is for you. A pretty tune for a pretty girl. A merry tune to wipe the sadness from your face."

When the tune finished, Li Ling got up. "I have to go. I will be missed."

"I shall be here tomorrow," he said. He took a fan and with a flick of his wrist he opened it. "Take it. Remember, I'll be here."

Hesitantly, she took it. It smelt sweet, of sandalwood. She smiled and their eyes met. No one had ever given her such a precious gift.

Li Ling hummed a tune all the way home. It was the tune played by Da Wei. She was flattered to be called pretty. She sniffed at the fan; its sweet scent gave her a sense of well-being. He was not handsome like her young master, she thought. Yet she was thrilled by the idea that he wanted to see her again.

***

Li Ling met up with Da Wei every evening. He showered her with gifts. It could be a pretty pair of hair slides, satin slippers, sugared plums or even sesame biscuits when he learnt that she liked them. She began to look forward to their rendezvous. She enjoyed the secrecy; she enjoyed the flattery; she felt special.

One evening when they were sitting together on a boulder, he slipped his arm around her waist. She froze. He felt her body become rigid and released his hold. He pretended that he had mistakenly touched her and that he was reaching for something behind them. He made no other move. Slowly she relaxed. They chatted. Gradually, almost imperceptibly, he moved closer, still talking and laughing. Suddenly without warning, he pushed her down and held her there. She opened her mouth to scream. He clamped her mouth shut with one hand, his body pinning her down on the ground. "You have teased me long enough," he whispered. He brought his face down on hers. He kissed her, bruising her lips. He tried to prise her mouth open with his tongue. She twisted away. He hit her. She felt her face burn; her head fell back with a loud crack on the rock. He ripped her trousers. Then with one knee drawn up, he pushed her legs apart.

"Please, please, " she begged. "Stop!"

He ignored her pleas. He pulled out a knife. "One cry from you and I shall kill you." With the other hand, he pulled her up and dragged her into a bush. He pushed her down on the ground and fell on her. He tore open her blouse and grabbed her breasts. She struggled; he hit her again. Blood spurted out from her nose.

"You will learn to enjoy this and you will come again and again for more." His face was flushed with excitement and his eyes were crazed like a drunk. He loosened his trouser drawstring; he let his trousers fall; then he paused, hovering above her. "Look at me," he said. "Look at me," he repeated slapping her hard.

***

Later, much later, Li Ling sat up and gathered the remnant of the clothes that lay around her to cover herself. She got up slowly. Her legs were wobbly. Every bit of her body ached. She made her way to the river bank and washed. She scrubbed between her legs. Over and over again she scrubbed until her skin tingled. Then she put on her torn and tattered clothes and made her way back to the convent.

She stood outside for a while. The house was in darkness. She pushed open the back gate. Lai Ma and Jing-jing were not in. They had been recruited by Shao Peng to help out in the big house. Mistress Rohani was throwing an engagement party for the young master and his fiancée, Suet Ping.

At this time of the evening, she knew that the sisters would be praying in the small chapel towards the front of the building. Someone had left the kitchen door slightly ajar. She slid behind it and walked into the kitchen with bare feet. She tiptoed in the dark to her room. Once inside the room, she shed off her torn clothes and quickly changed. She bundled the garments and took them out to the garden shed. She hid them. She would dispose of them the next morning. Then she crept back into her room and crawled into the bed. She pulled the bedclothes over her face. Then she sobbed. She sobbed until she was hoarse.

"You come again here tomorrow. Tell anyone, and I'll cut up your face." His words rang over and over in her mind.

***

Da Wei went home in high spirits. He had succeeded as he had planned all along. He grinned. He was sure that Li Ling would do as he asked her. He had invested a lot of his time cultivating her trust. He should reward himself more than once, at least until he tired of her. Of that he was sure. They were all the same. They play hard to get initially. Once deflowered, they cling on like leeches.

He stopped outside his house and tidied himself. He dusted his clothes and smoothed his hair. His father would be home for dinner. He must be careful not to let the old man have any inkling of his secret activities. He had nearly been caught out twice before. His mother had bailed him out. On each of those occasions, she had threatened never to rescue him again unless he changed his ways. "You will be caught one day. You cannot..." she had stopped short of using the word rape. "You cannot hurt young girls like that. I had to draw on all my savings to pay the girl's father to shut him up. I don't have any more money to do it again." He recalled pleading with her. He attributed his behaviour to a devil in him that made him lose control and behave in a bizarre way. He claimed he remembered nothing of what he did. He cried and repented. He swore that he would change. And, as he expected, she helped him out again. He made sure that he made up to her by being attentive and loving. He knew she would always relent; she would never let him suffer. He was certain of that.

He went quickly to his room to wash and check his appearance. He must cover up the scratches Li Ling had inflicted on him. He would explain that he had walked into an over hanging branch. He was glad that the scratches were on his neck. The mandarin collar would probably cover them up adequately. He pulled the collar up and buttoned it up more securely. He looked this way and that, admiring himself. "Not bad," he said to his image in the mirror. The adrenalin was still pumping strongly in him. He felt powerful and invincible.

He had really wanted to play along with Li Ling for longer. She was the youngest of his victims so far. But something in him snapped when he felt her go rigid under his touch. How dare she! He threw all caution to the wind. She was asking for it.

He made his way to the dining room, humming under his breath. His spirit was still high when he saw his mother. She, however, was agitated. He could see it from the way her eyebrows were knitted together and the jerky rapid steps she took towards him, arms outstretched and a finger wagging in the air.

"Where were you? Do you know what time it is? Ah Sun said you left the store ages ago. I hope you are not up to something stupid."

"Mother, how could you say such a thing?" He opened wide his eyes with astonishment and feigned hurt. "I was searching for a present for you and now you have spoilt my surprise."

Taken back she smiled sheepishly, gratified by his reply. "All right, all right, ignore what I had just said. Come, your father wants to speak to you."

She led the way. Da Wei followed, wondering what was in store. He was wary. While he could always talk round his mother, he was never sure of himself with his father. He was the youngest in the family and had only been given a lowly job in his father's store. His father did not trust him to do much. Instead, his father had concentrated on teaching his elder brother the business. Da Wei resented it.

"When I was your age, I worked day and night, selling noodles from house to house. I carried a pole on my shoulders, balancing pots and baskets hanging on both ends. I never shirked. Look at my hands," his father would say, pushing his calloused square hands to Da Wei's face. "Your mother has spoilt you. You do nothing but play and spend money like water. You are useless!"

Da Wei was sick and tired of hearing about his father's rise from poverty to fortune. He would have to switch off if he was subjected to it again this evening. Thank heavens that he had friends outside the family who did not think like his father. They knew how to enjoy life. He made sure that he too would enjoy life. Women, young women, the younger the better, were very much part of his enjoyment. After all he was only young himself. A smile flashed across his face. He recalled Li Ling's terror. It added such piquancy to an otherwise mundane act.

"What is making you so happy, son?" his mother asked. She had turned round to speak to him when she saw the smile.

"Nothing. I just thought how beautiful you are today. All my friends tell me how gracious you look, how you seem to blossom with age rather then wither like other women."

She rapped her fan at him. "Flatterer!" She was, nevertheless, pleased.

They went into the dining room. His father was already seated. He frowned when he saw them.

"Father," Da Wei bowed.

"*Mmmm!*" his father grunted. "Late again!"

"I am sorry. I was waylaid. I had some work to attend to and..." he saw his mother's eyebrow shot up in surprise, "...and I was searching for a present for mother. I forgot the time."

"No point telling you not to do that again, is there?" His father's question was rhetorical and his eyes cutting. "We should think of marrying you to some decent girl who could reform you. But who would want a rascal?"

"Hong," Da Wei's mother interjected. "Don't say such harsh words to your son. You said you had some thing important to say to him. Surely this is not it?"

"Yes it is. I think we should arrange to get him married. That boy of yours is a wastrel. Start making enquiries. Employ a matchmaker. I think that the woman you choose should be someone mature, five years older than Da Wei. He needs someone to guide him."

Hong glared at his son. "I am hearing things about you that I do not like. Don't think you can fool me like you do your mother."

"Father..."

"There is nothing more to be said."

Da Wei fumed but held his tongue.

***

The following morning Li Ling rose before the sun was up. She had hardly slept. She crept out of bed and went in search of a mirror. She found one in the laundry room, hidden in a basket she had piled high with towels. She had hidden it there to look at herself from time to time. She closed the door gently and locked herself in. She looked at herself. This time it was not to admire or consider what she could do to make herself prettier, it was to see how she could hide her bruises. She knew they were there even without looking. They hurt. Taking a long strand of hair, she looped it to cover part of her cheeks, allowing the remainder to fall loose around her neck.

Da Wei had held her neck in a stranglehold. However, she could not disguise the cut on her lips or the swelling around it. From one basket she found a long loose tunic. She pulled it on and buttoned it up to her neck. She tugged the sleeves down until all but her fingers were visible for her arms too were bruised and scratched. Once dressed, she unlocked the door and went into the classroom. It was still very early. The school bell had not rung. It was likely that people were only just beginning to rise. The kitchen would be busy preparing breakfast. She went quickly to a seat at the back of the classroom. She did not want to meet anyone. She kept her head bowed low over an open book. She did not look up when finally other students began to arrive with much jostling and noise. She didn't look up even when Shao Peng came into the classroom. She remained seated when the others stood to attention.

Shao Peng noticed. She made no comment. Li Ling had been difficult the past few months. Any overtures would be interpreted wrongly. She understood that it was difficult for Li Ling. They did not have enough resources to stream the children by age. The class consisted of children ranging from as young as ten. Li Ling was by far the oldest; compared to the others she was a young adult. The class was further sub-divided into groups on the basis of abilities. The children were recruited from all sorts of background and were of different ethnicity. A significant proportion of them were from Ceylon and India. Some already had a smattering of English. Li Ling could neither read nor speak English. She spoke Cantonese; she did not, however, read or write Chinese. Inevitably she fell into the bottom group, amongst the youngest.

Shao Peng walked between the rows of desks. She stopped when she reached Li Ling. Squatting down she asked Li Ling if she was all right. Li Ling did not reply.

"Can you see me afterwards? I could help you with your work. If we make progress, then we can move you up to a group nearer your age. It would make such a difference."

"Leave me alone! Haven't you done enough? I want to go home; I want to return to my family." She placed her forehead on the table and refused to look up.

Shao Peng sighed. At such times it was impossible to make any headway with Li Ling. She would gladly send Li Ling back home if it were possible. It was not. A letter had arrived from China. The letter, written on behalf of Li Ling's parents, had stressed in no uncertain terms that it would be dangerous for Li Ling to return. The warlord had seized her parent's farm and they were now homeless, joining the thousands of other homeless people living on the streets. China was in chaos. She had tried to read the letter to the girl to no avail; she had shut her ears and walked away.

***

"You should have seen the feast served up for the engagement. Suet Ping, young Master's fiancée, was dressed in a beautiful hand-embroidered chiffon top. The embroidery went from the neck down in the middle and all round the hemline." Here Lai Ma stopped and illustrated running her fingers from the neck down the centre of the bodice. "Mistress Rohani had it especially commissioned. To go with the *kebaya* top, Miss Suet Ping wore a hand painted sarong."

"What colour was it?" asked Sister Magdalene who had just entered the kitchen and had been listening in. She loved hearing about local customs.

"The top was a pale peach, set off by a sarong with hues of brown and lemon," replied Lai Ma. "The most wonderful of all was the set of *keronsang* Big Mistress gave Miss Suet Ping; three jade brooches, each in the shape of a phoenix, and linked together with a gold chain! The extravagance! She wore it to pin the top together."

They were in the school kitchen. Lai Ma was giving a running commentary of the engagement party while she washed up. Jing-

jing, charged with drying the dishes said little. She was subdued, a totally different person from the enthusiastic and confident young woman on the ship.

Li Ling too said little. Nothing escaped her though. She listened intently. Her face grew more bitter with each of Lai Ma's pronouncements. She winced each time Lai Ma described the presents or when she said how happy the young couple were. The words hurt her more than the scratches and bruises on her body. Finally, unable to stand it any more, she threw down the dishcloth and walked out of the kitchen into the backyard.

"*Heh!* You haven't finished," shouted Lai Ma.

"I'll do the rest," volunteered Jing-jing. "She is probably not well. She has looked out of sorts the whole day."

***

Li Ling closed the back gate and leaned on it. She was breathing hard as though she had run. She clenched her fist and bit down hard on her lower lip until the scab, grown out of the cut inflicted on her the previous evening, broke and she bled once more. She needed to feel the pain. It was nothing compared to the pain in her heart. Life was so unfair! Why does Suet Ping be deserving of so much while she had nothing?

"Curse them!" she yelled, stamping her feet. "I curse Miss Suet Ping. May she have only girl offspring! See then how she will be treated. I will wait. I will bide my time and take revenge. As for Miss Shao Peng, the *shuang mian*! I hate her for her double face. She said that she cared for me. Yet, she let me go. I am a kitchen maid here. I don't care for the learning they force on me. It is only an excuse. She helped cement this engagement of her brother! I hold her responsible. I curse her too!"

She looked towards the path that led to the river. She had nowhere to go. The river was the only place of solace that had provided some sort of haven for her in the past months. Now even that was spoilt. Da Wei's threats boomed in her head. Should she go? Would he cut up her face if she didn't? If she didn't, where else could she go? No one wanted her.

She sat down on the dirt ground and buried her face in the palms of her hand. Da Wei did want her, at least until last evening. Even then, she convinced herself, it might be a *wanting* of some sort. No one would have her now; she was not a virgin. Her mother had warned her over and over again of the importance of virginity. She would go to him and plead. Maybe he would be kind again, like he had been in the past. She would let him do anything. Anything was better than being discarded again.

She rose slowly and walked towards the river. She blotted dry the blood from her lips and cleaned her face. He wouldn't want to see her in this state. He had slapped her hard for crying. She could still feel the sting of his hand as he whacked her, first from the left and then the right. Perhaps I deserved it. He had cried that she was a *c... teaser*. She didn't understand what it meant or that she was one. She must have been for him to get so angry. He had been so good to her until then.

So she walked like a zombie with all these thoughts muddling through her mind. With every step, her resentment of Shao Peng and Suet Ping grew.

By the time she reached the spot of their rendezvous, she had persuaded herself that Da Wei was her only way out of her terrible situation. She sat on the rock and waited. Time passed. She waited. The sun dipped below the horizon. Darkness fell. He did not come.

Chapter 21

SHAO PENG WENT STRAIGHT home after school. She hoped she would be there before Jack. Rohani had called upon her help every day in the weeks leading up to Siew Loong's engagement. Unable to refuse, she found herself returning home, later and later and, on many occasions, not at all. Today was the first day that she was free from such demands.

She ran up the flight of steps that led up to the verandah of her house. She was excited to be back so early. A smile broke out on her face in anticipation of seeing Jack. She relished the idea of spending a whole evening with him. She took off her shoes and pushed open the front door. The house was quiet and dark. Someone had pulled the shutters down. Good, she thought. It keeps the house cool. Sounds of laughter rang from within followed by a male voice. Jack! He was home! Her heart sang.

She hastened towards the sound of laughter. It came from her bedroom. The realisation stopped her in her track. She licked her lips; her tongue was dry, parched like sand baked in the sun. She hurried towards the bedroom. Her bare feet scarcely made a noise. The door was open. Jack was seated at the edge of the bed. Aishah was standing facing him. They were oblivious to her presence. While Aishah twirled a lock of hair with one finger and swayed her body while speaking, Jack had a lopsided grin on his face. His eyes did not stray from the girl's.

Shao Peng felt a rush of anger. "What are you...?" She broke off mid sentence, choked by her own rage.

They jumped and turned to look at her guiltily. They saw the wide-eyed horror on her face. Aishah hurtled out of the room, catching Shao Peng's shoulder as she did so.

Jack got up and went to Shao Peng with two strides. "You are back! You are early!" He took her by the shoulders and made to gather her into his arms.

She resisted, turning her face deliberately to avoid his lips.

"Obviously not a convenient time. Why are you back home at this hour?"

"I might ask you the same," he replied, dropping his hands. He moved away stunned by her frosty tone.

"Do you have Aishah in our bedroom often?" She had meant to be calm. She couldn't. Her voice rose. Even to her own ears, it sounded abrasive and harsh. "Do you have so much to talk about? It was obviously something that amuses both of you very much. What else do you do in our bedroom?"

She felt herself lose control, hurling words and accusations at him as he looked on in shock.

"You can't be serious asking those questions. I resent that tone of voice. You leave me alone in this house for long stretches while you attend to your brother and stepmother and dare accuse me of enjoying a talk with Aishah! She was merely telling me a comical situation that had arisen in her village. What evil thoughts do you harbour to come up with such suggestions?"

Jack was livid with anger.

"Does she have to come into our bedroom to tell you a tale? Have you thought how it would look? Would you like me to chat with the gardener in our bedroom?

"That is a totally unacceptable comparison!" Jack gave an exasperated snort and stalked out of the room.

Shao Peng heard the front door slam shut. The force of it reverberated through the walls and flooring. She sat heavily on the bed clasping her face in her hands. She got up. She had to do something. She could not have Aishah in the house. She was wrong in having her there. The girl was clearly infatuated with Jack. It had to be nipped in the bud. She was sorry it had come to this. My fault, she thought.

She went out of the bedroom and stalked into the kitchen holding herself straight and her shoulders squared. She was determined to resolve the problem. Aishah was seated at the kitchen table, a long wooden trestle stained dark with age. She turned at the sound of Shao Peng's entry. Her eyes, long like a cat's, flicked over Shao Peng. They were filled with insolence; then she tilted her head away. She said nothing.

"I am giving you notice. I don't need your service any more. I want you to leave now!"

The girl didn't move. Nor did she answer. She sat still.

Unnerved, Shao Peng took out some money from her pocket. It was intended for groceries for the school kitchen. She counted some out and handed it to Aishah. Her hand shook. "This is more than your month's wages and should see you through for at least a month if not more."

The girl stood up and snatched away the money. Then she spat. The glob of spittle landed in front of Shao Peng's feet making her jump. Aghast, she could only look in astonishment at Aishah. The girl laughed. There was no merriment in her face; her eyes were coal black with venom.

Shao Peng shuddered. She stood and watched Aishah leave. She stayed in the kitchen until she could not hear her any more. Then she went to the back of the house and bolted the door.

***

The sun disappeared into the horizon and still Jack did not return. Shao Peng began to fret. She lit up the oil lamps in the house, moving from one to the other. As each light spluttered to life, she felt calmer. She crossed her arms and hugged herself tight. How, she asked herself, did she manage to make enemies of those that she tried to help? And Jack! Where was he? What if she had been wrong? What if all the overtures came from Aishah and he was just guileless? Would he forgive her for the harsh words she said to him?

Shao Peng sat down. Her forehead was knitted together with worry lines. Time ticked by. Where was Jack? She asked herself again. She half rose and then fell back into the chair. Should she go in search of him? For once she regretted not taking her brother's advice to have more help in the house. She had wanted Jack to herself. She did not wish to have other people in the house. She reasoned that it was only a modest dwelling and could not accommodate them. Now she felt so alone. The quiet was disconcerting.

She got up and went to the window. Outside a warm breeze was blowing. It was dark and the moonlight cast an eerie glow in the garden.

Was this the end of their marriage? It could not be. She argued with herself. Surely their love could withstand this? Doubts crept in. With each minute that passed, she grew more troubled; each worry multiplied tenfold. "I shouldn't have said all that I said. I should have had more trust." She paced up and down the room.

Time dragged slowly by. Her eyes grew heavy. She moved in and out of fitful sleep in the armchair. Then with a jolt she woke up.

The front door opened. Jack stood at the doorway. His eyes were full of pain. She ran to him and threw herself into his arms. "I am sorry for doubting you. Will you forgive me?"

He kissed her, silencing her with his lips. "Come with me," he said dragging her into the bedroom.

***

Much later, in the early hours of the morning before the first ray of sunshine poured into the bedroom, they lay together, bodies entwined, her head on his chest. Shao Peng opened one eye and looked at her husband. He sensed her looking and moved to kiss her, his lips brushing hers gently and then more urgently. "I love you," he whispered, running his tongue lightly around the pink coral rim of her earlobes.

She sighed, "I love you too."

He shifted and brought her up so that she lay on top of him. She snuggled into his chest. She inhaled the morning smell of him. "I have you all to myself," she said. "We have the whole day with no one around."

"*Ahhh*," he teased, except that Aishah is always around. Don't forget."

"I dismissed her." She felt his body stiffen. He moved slightly, tipping her to the side of him.

"I see." He turned away.

She could feel his displeasure, the sudden coldness that settled like a wedge of ice between them.

"You have wronged an innocent girl."

Chapter 22

A MONTH WENT BY. Li Ling went to the riverbank each afternoon. She sat there, she waited, and she fretted. Da Wei did not appear. The days passed very slowly for her. She became even more restless. On the fifth weekend, she was asked to go to the market to buy groceries for the school kitchen. Lai Ma, who did most of the shopping and normally would not have involved Li Ling, was taken ill. Armed with two large cane baskets, Li Ling went out through the back door, into the kitchen garden and then out onto the path that linked the school with the open market. The market, which had initially consisted of a few vendors, had grown and grown in response to the ever-increasing settlement of houses surrounding the brick factories.

She walked briskly, clutching two empty cane baskets. With each step away from the convent, her mood lightened. The sun was shining and the dew on the grass was drying rapidly. She inhaled deeply the fresh smell of green. Further on a couple of skinny brown cows grazed idly by the wayside. Their tails swished one way and then the other while they munched through the short tufts of wild grass. Flies hovered around their haunches and around the pats of dung that littered the grass. Li Ling looked on, fascinated. The cows were new to the area. They came with the arrival of people from India. She had been warned to be careful of them for the small newly growing Indian community viewed them as sacred animals. The cows were there to provide milk, not meat, for the people.

Gingerly, Li Ling stepped around the animals to avoid the pats of fly infested dung on the ground. She held her breath. The smell emitted from the fast drying dung was strong and she was not used to it. She wondered about the milk and its taste. She did not remember anyone drinking cows' milk in China. She did not expect it to taste good. If it did, her parents would surely have had cows in their farmyard. In her parents' farm in Canton, they had pigs, chickens and ducks, not cows.

An Indian man came out of a hut with a pail in hand. He stopped by a cow and squatted down to milk it; his body almost bent over as he ducked his head to look under the animal He squeezed the udders; over and over his fingers pressed and pulled, first with his left hand and then his right. Streams of milky white frothed into the pail.

The distraction afforded by being out in the open, however, soon wore off. Li Ling found herself was once more plunged into the depth of despair. Her spirit had been oscillating between extremes for weeks. Sometimes she was able to convince herself that all would be well. Da Wei was bound to return. More often than not, however, she was miserable as she tussled with what she should do. She quickened her steps. She could not afford to dawdle. Just thinking of the task she had set herself made her breathe much harder. Ahead of her, she could see smoke from the brick kilns. She headed towards the cluster of Chinese shop houses to the east of the brick kilns. Da Wei's shop must be there. Someone there might know his whereabouts.

She passed the open market with its makeshift stalls. Baskets of food lay scattered on the ground. She decided that she would buy her groceries on the way back. The more urgent task was to locate Da Wei. She had no idea of what she would say to him. Even more worrying was how he would receive her. Would he be angry? Would he feign ignorance of her? What should she say to him?

The first shop in the row of five was an eatery. She peered into its dimly lit interior. The building was long and there were no windows and was lit only by the light filtered through the wide doorway in front. It was crowded with people having their breakfast. He was not there. She walked quickly to the next shop. It was a herbal store. Jars upon jars of carefully labelled dried herbs and roots stood in neat rows. Occasional jars of what looked suspiciously like cockroaches stood in between. Behind them were clusters of wooden drawers housing more herbal remedies. A man stood with an abacus close at hand, weighing the delicate herbs. Their strong smell, acrid and compelling, assailed her. She had to get a concoction for Lai Ma. That could also wait, she decided. She headed to the next shop. It was a general store. This must be it! she thought. She remembered the gifts he presented her. She stood in front of the shop's entrance and looked in.

A few people were examining the display of goods. At the far end, bolts of cloth were placed next to racks of shoes. Opposite, sacks of rice, dried fish, beans, fungus, mushrooms and shrimps were lined up against a wall. A man was behind the till. Li Ling went up to him and asked if he knew Da Wei.

"Who wants him?"

Li Ling turned. An elderly man with a black cloth cap on his head was behind her. His eyes, hard and appraising, raked over her.

"I came to ask if he is all right. I ... I haven't seen him for a while," she stuttered.

"Who are you?"

"I ... I am Li Ling. I have to go now." Li Ling turned to leave. Lee Ah Hong's hand shot out and grasped her arm.

"I am his father. What do you want with him?"

"Nothing ... nothing."

"Nothing?" He examined her again from top to toe. He noted her clothes; they were not those of a maid. Yet, she was definitely not from a wealthy family. No woman from a good family would be carrying baskets and walking out on her own. She was young. He knew his son's penchant for young females. His wife thought he did not know but he did. That was why he proposed that Da Wei be married off to an older woman to get some sense in him. Perhaps it could stop Da Wei's wild urges if he had a woman to himself.

"I have to go ... please." Li Ling pulled away.

He released her arm. Li Ling ran out of the shop. She pushed her way through a small group of men leaving the eatery. They shouted at her. Their curses and coarse comments rang in her ears.

Hong followed her out and stood at the doorway. He looked on as she ran back the way she came. A pretty girl, he thought.

She must be one of the many that Da Wei had kept secret from
his family. She was brave to come in search of him. Ah Hong
sighed. He was not going to probe too hard unless he had to. It
could open up more problems.

***

Li Ling ran all the way back to the riverbank. Dropping the
empty baskets, she clambered up the rock. Her breathing
came hard and fast. Should she have said something, she
asked herself. Had she missed the opportunity to tell someone
about Da Wei, someone that could help her? She felt sick with
anxiety. She was no nearer to finding out where Da Wei was
and what happened to him.

"I saw you!"

Da Wei appeared out of nowhere, taking her by surprise.
He grasped a hand full of her hair and yanked, jerking her head
back. Then he looped her hair round her neck and tightened.
Li Ling screamed in pain.

"I asked you. What were you doing in my father's shop?
What did you say to him?"

"Nothing. I ... I said I was looking for you."

He looked at her for a long while trying to determine if she
was telling the truth. Then he laughed. He didn't believe that
Li Ling would have the guts to tell on him. He pushed his face
close to hers and stuck out his tongue and licked her face. Can't
get enough of me? This is what you want?"

He pushed her to the ground and dragged her into the bush.
She kicked and struggled. "Stop! Stop!" she shouted.

He silenced her with a slap, muffling her cries with his hand.
She brought one knee up and with all her strength kicked his

groin. He doubled up and groaned. Surprised by her own action, Li Ling lay for a moment watching him groan and then she sat up. She waited until he recovered. Then calmly, before he could make another move, she shrugged off her clothes and walked deeper into the undergrowth of wild grass. She lay down and parted her legs, her eyes on him all the while as he made his way to her. Da Wei narrowed his eyes and looked at her body sprawled naked beneath him. He smiled.

Chapter 23

THE DISCORD BETWEEN Jack and Shao Peng hung heavily over their relationship. Outwardly nothing changed. Yet Shao Peng felt that something was amiss. She believed that Jack's smile did not come from his heart. It did not touch his eyes. They no longer lit up when he saw her. She became cautious with what she said. She thought about each word over and over again in her mind before she spoke them. Their conversations became stilted. When Jack took her in his arms, she felt as though he did it mechanically, a duty rather than an expression of longing. The more she put such a complexion on his behaviour, the more she thought that it was true. She tried to come home early. She gave excuses to her brother and stepmother. Jack, however, came home later and later. His work in the outlying villages became increasingly frequent. She did not know if these were genuine calls of duty or a means to avoid her. She could not bring herself to ask.

On one of Jack's travels, Shao Peng went home to her brother's. "Jack is away again?" Siew Loong's pronouncement was more a statement than a question. "You should not be at home on your own. Take one of the maids with you. Take two, in fact. Mother, I am sure, would be able to spare them."

He leaned closer to Shao Peng. "This might slow mother down a bit. She is going through my wedding arrangements like there is no tomorrow," he lamented ruefully. "You know I am not looking forward to it. "

"Suet Ping is a sweet girl."

"*Ha!* She is not of my choosing." I am going through with this for the sake of mother. She is fixed on the idea and is attached to the girl. Mother said that she would return to her *kampong* to live a life of solitude if I refused the marriage. What would people think if I allowed that to happen?"

He threw a sideway glance at her. "You were brave. You fought against your arranged marriage. I am not. I can't stand the squabbling. I don't want to let mother down. She is fragile, what with father's death and the discovery of his other women."

"I understand how you feel. We are bound by custom to accept arranged marriages and we fight against it. However, love marriages do not come unencumbered."

"Are you having problems with yours?"

"Not really. It is just a little misunderstanding. It will sort itself out."

"Then why..."

"Everything is fine. Let's change the subject. What did you decide to do with the women, particularly Swee Yoke and the child she claimed is father's?"

"I made a settlement and they have signed an undertaking to relinquish all future demands."

"You think the boy is really father's?"

"Who knows? Both mother and I are unwilling to allow this to become public knowledge and they were only too happy to take the money. It will be a good clean break. I do not wish it to hang over us. I hope to go into partnership with a British firm to grow rubber. Any gossip would undermine this ambition. I certainly do not want a half-brother challenging my inheritance."

"How are you going to get workers for the plantations?"

"From India, the same way as our British masters. They recruit labour from that subcontinent for their sugar and coffee plantations here. I will have to raise money and send a broker to India to recruit the workers directly. There will be a huge outlay initially. Advances will have to be made to bring them over and accommodation built to house them. It will not be straightforward. We would have to work through three parties, the India Office, the Colonial office in London and the Government offices in the Straits Settlements. So that is why I thought a partnership with a British firm would be a good idea. It might help reduce the red tape. Does Jack have any connections in this area?"

She shook her head. "I don't know." Jack, she thought, would probably not divulge anything to her. He didn't trust her any more. She got up. "I have to leave." Impulsively, she reached out and hugged her brother.

"Take a maid with you. Anyone. You have my permission. Try to make your life slightly easier," he said ruffling her hair.

***

She went home with Ah Kew. The house was ablaze with light when the pony cart turned into the driveway. The front door was thrown wide open. Her first thought was that something was wrong. She rushed up the flight of steps and ran into the house. There was no one in the front room but voices came from the sleeping quarters. She followed their sound.

A man emerged from her bedroom. His face was grave when he saw her. He put out his hand and steered her aside. "Mrs Webster? I am Doctor Rodwell. Before you go in, " he said, "I have to prepare you. Your husband is ill. It is malaria. He is being well looked after now and is resting."

Shao Peng paled. She made to push past him. He stopped her. "Calm down. You will make him more anxious if you are anxious. Look at your heartbeat," he said with his finger on the pulse of her wrist. "He is, as I said, being attended to. Your maid is bathing his forehead now to bring his temperature down."

"Maid? What maid?" she asked trying once more to push pass him.

"Mrs Webster, the best thing you can do for him is to keep calm and cheerful." He steered her firmly to a chair. "Take several deep breaths before you go in. I am going to get my boy to fetch a prescription from my house. I left in a hurry when your maid came to me."

Shao Peng stood up. Her legs were wobbly. She walked into the room. Her heart fell. It was as she had guessed. Aishah was with Jack. She was bathing his forehead and didn't bother to look up when Shao Peng came into the room. She ignored Shao Peng and continued her administration. She acted as though she owned the room and Shao Peng was the intruder.

Shao Peng went to the bed. "Thank you. I can manage. You can leave now." She said it quietly, not wishing to create a scene.

There were so many questions that she wanted to hurl at Aishah. She couldn't without losing her own dignity, without upsetting Jack. She struggled to contain her jealousy and suspicion. She did not want to make the same mistake again. Jack was her main priority.

Aishah did not reply nor did she budge from her position next to the bed. A groan escaped Jack's lips. Shao Peng wanted to get nearer to her husband. She could not, short of pushing Aishah away. She looked up and caught Ah Kew's eyes. She had followed Shao Peng into the room and watched the interactions between the two women. She guessed. The grapevine in the servants' quarters had been teeming with gossip about the young mistress's situation. Help me, Shao Peng's eyes pleaded. Ah Kew nodded. She came forward and grabbed hold of Aishah's arms and dragged her away. "*Pergi!*" Ah Kew hissed. "Leave, or I shall tell the headman in your village."

The women tussled. Jack groaned again, his eyelids, pale and blue veined, fluttered; he tried to open his eyes. Sweat dripped from his forehead. His shirt was wet. He tried to rise from the bed. Shao Peng threw her arms around him and placed her lips on his. They burnt like hot coals. Stripping him of his wet garments, she dried and dressed him. She was shocked by his thinness. How could he have lost so much weight in such a short time? She ignored the struggle between Ah Kew and Aishah. Little shrieks of anger were interspersed with strings of curses. Ah Kew was the stronger and was not averse to using force to push Aishah out of the room. Once they were out of the room Shao Peng bolted the door from inside. She had no time to speculate on how Aishah knew Jack was ill and how she came into the house. Brushing these questions aside, she rushed back to the stand beside the bed. On it stood the basin of water

Aishah had used. She emptied it and poured fresh cool water into it. She wrung out a flannel and kept it on Jack's forehead, changing it at intervals. Throughout the night, she remained by his side murmuring reassurances. "Please, please," she prayed, her hands clasping his fevered ones, "let him come through this. Forgive me," she whispered in Jack's ears. Over and over she told him she loved him.

***

Aishah ran into the garden with Ah Kew giving chase with a broom. Once she was safely out of the compound, Aishah stopped. She stayed still until she was sure that Ah Kew had returned back to the house. Slowly, cat-like she crept towards the hibiscus hedge that surrounded the property. The hedge was uneven in height and she could see easily above the shorter shrubs while still staying hidden behind them. She knew the compound well. She had been hiding in this very spot day after day, watching and waiting for Shao Peng to leave for school. She knew that shortly after Shao Peng left, Master Webster would emerge. On a fine day, he would choose to walk to his office just a mile or so down the road. On rainy days, a pony cart would be sent for him. Unknown to him, Aishah would follow him to work and then back to the house. She would arrange for him to see her by chance, sometimes appearing in the footpath just as he turned a bend. She would ask after his health and he would enquire after hers. He would often slip her some money. Aishah knew that her master felt guilty about her dismissal. She played on it, telling him of her impoverished circumstances. She brought him little gifts of food: a sun ripe banana, an egg she found and boiled or a handful of peanuts she has gathered. She expressed concern that he had to return home to an empty house. He was touched. She never spoke badly of Shao Peng. She never referred to what Jack believed was her unfair dismissal. The more she spoke well of Shao Peng, the more Jack felt that his wife was wrong in suspecting such a charming and delightful young girl. He became increasingly aware of her, and of the almost sinuous way she moved her body beneath her sarong. He found himself remembering her eyes. They looked at him with such disarming frankness and ... He stopped himself. He could not ignore it. The word that came to mind was adoration. With a guilty start, he would break off their conversation and excused himself. Aishah sensed all his moods. She waited patiently.

She crouched down behind the hedge and began to scour the ground. With bare hands, she dug deep into the earth and took out a little bag. She shook out its contents. A rag doll with black hair fell out. She had taken the hair from Shao Peng's hairbrush. Aishah spat. A globule of spittle landed on the doll. Then she tied up the doll's limbs into knots and wrung them tight. Closing her eyes, she began to chant under her breath, rocking on her haunch. When she was a child she had seen a *bomoh* doing the same. Curious, she had followed him around. When she reached womanhood, he taught her the dark arts. Her chanting grew in fervour and she went into a trance. She prayed for Shao Peng's death. It would free her master. She did not believe that Shao Peng deserved her master. It was Aishah who looked after him. She, Aishah, deserved him.

***

When morning came, Shao Peng was slumped on the bed. She had nodded off and her head had fallen over Jack's chest. He opened his eyes slowly and with difficulty for the lids were stuck together. He brought his hand up and placed it on Shao Peng's head. She shifted and then sat up with a jolt. "You are awake! How are you feeling?"

"Rough."

She could hardly hear him. His voice was hoarse and weak. She placed a hand on his cheek, feeling the roughness of it. "Let me get you a drink of water." She got up and poured some water into a glass. Gently she lifted his head and brought the glass to his lip. "Thank God the fever has gone. How long were you like this?"

"I don't know. I was in Klang. Then they brought me home. Aishah was here. She fetched the doctor."

"I am sorry I was not home. I was here every day except for the very day you needed me. I am so, so sorry. Will you forgive me?" Shao Peng gulped. She didn't want to cry.

But Jack was already exhausted. He closed his eyes and took her hand in his to give it a little squeeze. "Nothing to forgive. How were you to know?"

"I love you," she whispered in his ear, hovering above him, watching every movement and flicker in his face.

"I know. I love you too."

She placed her lips on his forehead. They were cold and clammy. "Please, please get well."

He didn't answer. He was already asleep.

Chapter 24

Li Ling did not know what spurred her to take off her clothes, except that she was desperate. Intuitively she felt it was the right thing to do for she had nothing to lose that she had not already lost. He would have taken her even if she had resisted. She had to take the chance and do whatever it took to win Da Wei back. She felt that she had succeeded. In the past weeks, he was the one waiting by the riverbank. It gave her a feeling of power when she saw his desire. She began to experience pleasure where once there was revulsion and pain. He did things to her that she could never, in her wildest dreams, thought possible. She could not extricate herself from the opposing sensations of loathing and lust that engulfed her. She began to enjoy their trysts even when he hit her. She could not wait for the evenings, for when she could meet him. Later, back in her own bed, when every one was asleep and the only sounds in the bedroom were those of Lai Ma's gentle snoring and the occasional sighs and sobs from Jing-jing, Li Ling would go over in her mind the events of the past month. A plan began to take shape in her mind.

Lai Ma was the first to notice her change. "Something is not right," she complained to Jing-jing. "Li Ling remains sulky as always. She says little and scowls a lot. She is totally indifferent to whatever we say to her. Yet at times, when I catch her unaware, she looks smug."

"It must be your imagination," answered Jing-jing.

"*Mmmm!* I don't think so. She is hiding something. Haven't you noticed that all of a sudden, she neither looks nor behaves like a young girl? I can't put a finger on it. Something is not right."

They were in the laundry room. Jing-jing was heating up the iron pan with hot coals and ironing and Lai Ma was folding the clothes and putting them away. They continued their work in silence. Jing-jing had become more and more withdrawn and quiet. She had already approached Reverend Mother to ask if she could become a novice nun. She was not interested in Lai Ma's frequent observations of Li Ling.

"Look! She is coming back from the yard with another basket of laundry. Observe her will you? Tell me if you see any change." Lai Ma stopped and pretended to fold the clothes with renewed vigour.

Li Ling dumped the basket on the table. Her eyes swept over the other two women. Her glance was curt and insolent. She was spoiling for a fight. She swore that if Lai Ma were to say just one word, she would unleash a string of curses on her. When neither of the two women responded, she turned to walk away. Her *samfoo* blouse caught a snag on the table and the button on her blouse popped. For a split second when that happened, her waist was exposed. Lai Ma stifled a gasp.

"What?" cried Li Ling rudely. "Something troubling you?"

'You've put on weight!" Lai Ma could not contain herself.

"Weight? Look at you! *Fei chui!* Fat pig!" Li Ling left without another word. Taken by surprise she forgot the string of curses she had wanted to unleash.

Lai Ma jumped up and rushed over to where Jing-jing was. "Did you see the girl's bosom? That was what was troubling me. She's grown so big here," Lai Ma indicated, pointing to her own busts. "Did you see how tight she bound her breasts when her blouse lifted? And her waist! "

"Maybe she has just put on weight."

"No! No! I better tell Reverend Mother or Miss Shao Peng."

***

Li Ling, standing outside the laundry room, heard the exchange. She put her hand on her breasts, pressing them gently. They felt tender and engorged. Her new breasts had added piquancy to their mating; it had aroused Da Wei to greater fervour. She closed her eyes recalling the pain that shot thorough her when he kneaded and bit them. Warmth spread from her groin upwards to her breast. Her neck and face went a deep red. She took a deep breath. She must pull herself together. She would have to act. Perhaps this was the opportunity she had been waiting for.

She heard Lai Ma come out of the laundry room and went up to her immediately.

"Lai Ma! I am sorry for my rudeness. You are right. I am in trouble." She rolled up her sleeves and pulled down the collar of her blouse. Her chest and arms were covered with bruises and bite marks.

Lai Ma let out a cry. She was shocked. "Who did this to you?"

***

"You should have come to us straightaway. Why did you keep it to yourself? Why did you keep it to yourself? How long has this been going on?"

"I was ashamed." Li Ling lowered her head. She didn't want Lai Ma to look into her eyes. "He forced me and warned me against telling anyone."

"Do you want to get rid of the baby? I do not know how ... I ... we have to find someone to do it. We have to keep it from Reverend Mother and the Sisters."

"I want to keep the baby." Li Ling looked pleadingly at Lai Ma.

Lai Ma thought about her own children. Would she want an abortion if she was in Li Ling's position? Yet, how could Li Ling keep the baby?

"I want him to marry me."

"*Aiyah!* You silly girl If he wants to marry you he would not be doing such things to you."

"I know he does not want to marry me. That's where you come in. You see, if I went to his father, Da Wei would just deny everything. He would say the baby is not his. I want you to testify that you saw him with me. Can you do that? Please?"

Lai Ma hesitated. She didn't want to be involved. Yet, how could she refuse? She couldn't let an innocent girl suffer such injustice. Reluctantly, she nodded. She marvelled at Li Ling's composure. She had not even shed a tear during her tale. What could have made a young girl's heart so hard that she was not even able to cry? Lai Ma regretted taunting and teasing Li Ling in the past. She must try her best to help. Of course Li Ling had to force the scoundrel's hand in marriage. Otherwise who would want her? She was a damaged good. "You are a brave girl," Lai Ma said.

"No one must know of this. Don't tell Miss Shao Peng. I don't want her involved."

"I think we should let her know. She is very fond of you and would help." Lai Ma was troubled. Li Ling seemed so in control. Suddenly a thought struck Lai Ma. She wondered if she was being manipulated, and was immediately ashamed. She chastised herself for being paranoid. She told herself that Li Ling was just a young girl, wilful no doubt, nevertheless still a child.

Shao Peng was the last person Li Ling wanted to involve. Her eyes flashed with anger at the thought. She hated Shao Peng. She attributed all her problems to her. If she succeeded in getting Da Wei to marry her, she would not want Shao Peng to know of the circumstances that led to it. She wanted to be able to hold her head high. People should only know that the son of a wealthy man married her, not why he did it or how he was forced into it.

She pushed aside her thoughts and recovered her composure. "No Lai Ma," she said, her voice soft and pleading, "Miss Shao Peng has enough worries of her own. We can do it together. Just you and me. You are an intelligent and resourceful woman. We will manage together." Li Ling threw her arms around Lai Ma and hugged her tight.

Taken back, Lai Ma's arms hung by her aside. Then slowly she brought them up and returned Li Ling's hug. "Then I shall not say a word. I still believe that we should. However if you are opposed to it, I won't. In any case, she is at home tending to her husband who is very ill. Perhaps you are right, she won't want to be troubled, at least not right now."

Chapter 25

THE LAST FEW DAYS were sheer heaven for Shao Peng. Jack was recovering well and she was able to spend all her time with him. Ah Kew proved to be a treasure. She cooked, washed and served the meals. Shao Peng had not realised how wearing it had been when Aishah did those tasks. That sense of being watched, of being found wanting, of tension and competition, vanished with Aishah's disappearance. Shao Peng became more relaxed and her outlook on life more cheerful.

Holding the bunch of hibiscus she had gathered from the hedge, Shao Peng ran up the flight of steps to the house and made her way to the kitchen. Jack was having his afternoon nap in the bedroom. Ah Kew was preparing tea.

"Look! Aren't they beautiful? Such glorious pinks and reds! I am going to place them on the bedroom windowsill. Master will see them when he wakes up for tea." Shao Peng grabbed a glass vase. She filled it with water and began arranging the flowers. The air was infused with the scent of the blooms but was soon overpowered by something even stronger, something distinctively rich and delicious. "What do you have in the oven? It smells wonderful."

"Biscuits," said Ah Kew. Her face lit up with pride. "English ones made with that *chow gow yow* smelly cow oil. It is for Master."

"You mean butter? It is not smelly! We are very honoured to be given it. It is difficult to come by and even more difficult to keep in this heat." Shao Peng had been delighted when the butter was delivered to the house. Months had gone by since they got married and they had not had a single invitation from Sir Frank Swettenham. It worried her that the British Resident might have had to succumb to social pressures and was excluding them from what was considered select society. She knew that their marriage had been much discussed and frowned upon. She worried that Jack's career in the civil service would be compromised by their marriage. The arrival of the small pat of butter from *Carcosa,* the Resident's house, gave her some comfort. Her worries were perhaps unnecessary.

"The boy that brought it showed me how to make them. He is from Hainan and is the new boy at the Resident's house. I don't know if they will be nice."

"They smell good." Shao Peng popped one into her mouth. It melted on her tongue, rich sweet crumbs that made her sigh with pleasure. Ah Kew beamed. She was delighted. In the Ong's main house she was only the second maid, for Ah Tai presided as the cook and first maid. Ah Kew relished her new role in Shao Peng's household.

Balancing the vase carefully in one hand, Shao Peng was about to leave the kitchen when she stopped. "When I was gathering these flowers, I saw a patch of ground by the hibiscus hedge that looked as though some wild animals had been burrowing into it. When you see the gardener, tell him to check it out. He could grass it over because it looked quite unsightly."

"I'll tell him later this afternoon. He will be here in about an hour or so."

***

It was late in the afternoon. Shao Peng tucked the blanket round Jack's knee and set about pouring tea into the pretty porcelain teacups that had been Siew Loong's gift. Setting the cup and saucer down she handed a plate of biscuits to Jack. "Ah Kew bought the milk from an Indian cowherd living near the brick kilns. Until the arrival of Indians, no one reared cows for milk. Milk doesn't keep. We kept this in a pail of ice cold water from our well. So this is pure luxury."

While she chatted gaily, Jack's eyes started to droop. He tired easily. Shao Peng saw his pallor and was immediately concerned.

"Are you all right?" she asked, placing her palm on his forehead. It felt slightly clammy.

Jack nodded to indicate that he was fine.

"Should I shut this window? The breeze is quite strong. I don't want you to catch a chill." She got up and drew the window, wedging it with a piece of wood so that it stood slightly ajar for fresh air to come in.

"Don't fuss. I am fine. Sit down!"

Hurt by his tone and the irritation on his face, she was unable to move, her legs wooden, unyielding to the task demanded of her.

"About Aishah," began Jack, "can't you give her back her job? The poor girl is finding it hard to make ends meet. You know she has no one except for an uncle. She lost her parents when she was very young. Life cannot be easy for her now."

Her heart went cold. "We have Ah Kew. I don't need her and even if I needed someone, I wouldn't take her."

Jack opened his mouth to protest.

"I don't want to discuss this." Her voice went up a notch louder than normal. It sounded heartless to Jack.

"What have you against that poor child?"

"Poor child! She tried to take you away from me. She is rude. She spa..."

"Stop! Stop! I don't want to hear you bad mouthing someone. It only makes you sound vile."

"So you are taking her side against me."

Jack gave her a look of utter disgust. "I am tired. I am going back to bed."

He got up, wobbling with the effort. She went to him immediately. He brushed her hand away and refused her help. She looked helplessly at his retreating back. "What have I done?" she asked herself. "Just when everything seemed to be going so fine!" A pain shot through her, a gripping sharp pain that seemed to explode from within. She doubled up, clutching tight her middle. Her arms were numb and her legs felt like jelly.

In the garden, Ah Kew was showing the gardener the patch of ground that needed work. He swung his hoe up and brought it down with force. The blade broke through the earth. It came into contact with a soft object. Loose soil flew up. He dropped down to a squat and reached into the soil. He fished out a doll; it's limbs bound and ungainly. It stared at him with sightless eyes.

The doll was smashed into two. He dropped it. "Black magic!" he whispered, fear in his eyes.

Ah Kew stared at the doll. She was speechless with shock. From within the house, she could hear her master shouting. She rushed inside.

***

"Over there," pointed Li Ling, "the store third from the left belongs to Da Wei's father. We will wait here to see if he is in."

"What about Da Wei?" asked Lai Ma. "What if he is there?"

"He won't be."

"How do you know?

"He told me."

"What? Are you still seeing him?" Lai Ma shouted. "What's wrong with you?" Before she could say any more, Li Ling hugged her, pressing her face close. Lai Ma's anger melted away. In some ways, Li Ling reminded Lai Ma of her children. They needed her just as Li Ling needed her now. She liked being needed. It had been such a long time since she saw her children and it would be many years before any of them could come to Malaya. For now Li Ling was her surrogate daughter. Yet, fond as she had become of Li Ling, she could not dispel the niggling unease she had about the girl. She struggled with her conscience each time she went along with Li Ling's suggestions.

Unaware of Lai Ma's thoughts, Li Ling, her arms still around Lai Ma, whispered. "I have to see him, otherwise he would suspect something is wrong. He has to keep his mother company today. That is why he will not be in the shop." Li Ling recalled his haste to leave after their last assignation She touched her breasts, recalling the brutal way they had been handled. "He has no idea at all that I want marriage. If he has any inkling at all, he would put a stop to it." She drew a finger across her neck.

And, that, thought Li Ling, would be the end of their trysts and her hold on him. She knew Da Wei would not marry her of his own volition. She believed, however, he would not dare refuse his father if it was his father's wish. She had learnt enough about Da Wei to know that. She had to work on the father. She was sure that she would be able to persuade him.

Lai Ma could not find anything to say in reply. She saw the way Li Ling touched her breasts and the knowing expression in her face. It was not the face of innocence. It troubled Lai Ma. Where, she asked herself for the umpteenth time, was the naive girl who boarded the ship to Malaya?

An elderly man came out of the store followed by some young coolies. He pointed to some crates and went into the store again.

"That is Da Wei's father, Lee Ah Hong. Come, let's go." She got up and walked across the street giving Lai Ma little chance to change her mind. Lai Ma followed.

Chapter 26

"*LOW POH!* OLD WOMAN! The wedding will have to be cancelled. This girl is expecting our son's baby. Although I am a hard man, I couldn't but pity her. The things our son did to her. If she reports him, he would get years of imprisonment and hard labour. She was black and blue all over, everywhere except her beautiful face." Hong was quite taken by Li Ling. He remembered her from her first visit to the shop and had admired her pluck.

"How could you believe her? Did you ask Da Wei? It could be someone else's child."

"She brought another woman who swore that she saw them together. Both gave a detailed account of the assignations by the river. The girl was able to describe every birthmark and mole our son has. Some of these are in places that even you as a mother would not know. They made such a commotion. The poor girl was weeping. Customers crowded into the shop to see what was going on. The shop attendants stopped work to listen. I was so embarrassed. The thing is, old woman, I couldn't look them in the eye and swear that our son would never do such a thing. You and I know that this has happened before though thank God, a child was never involved."

"No! No! Lies!" she protested.

"Don't interrupt!" shouted Lee Hong. "I know that you paid off the other victims. Don't take me for a fool! Unlike the other girls who did not want their names made public, this girl is not so averse. She is not willing to take a payment. She wants nothing short of a marriage."

"*Huh!* For all we know, she was a willing partner in this."

"Then you should see her bruises. Don't deny it, he can be violent. What about the last time...."

"You don't have to talk to me about the last time. He promised that he would never do it again."

"And how many times has he promised in the past? Well I am not going to argue with you. It is useless when it comes to Da Wei. You spoiled him. It is your fault."

"My fault? If you knew what he was doing, why didn't you come right out and confront him? Instead you went out of your way to make him unhappy. You drove him to take it out on girls."

"*Aiyah!* Now it is my fault! Just keep to the crux of the problem. What can we do? The whole town knows of this by now. We cannot live it down."

"There is just a week to the wedding. We cannot cancel it without forfeiting all the bridal gifts."

"That is the least of our worries. Think, woman think! If she reports him, Da Wei will go to prison."

"I am thinking. Give me time!"

Mrs Lee would not be hurried. She paced up and down the room leaving Hong to chew his fingers in frustration.

"Bai Choo is seven years older than our Da Wei," she said finally. "She is not pretty. She is an old maid. No one has proposed to her before. She gets to marry our son only because you wish to punish him with an older woman knowing that he prefers them young and nubile. We won't be able to retract the offer of marriage easily. I suspect her parents will not agree to such a last minute withdrawal. However, if they are so keen to get their daughter married then perhaps we could get them to agree that Da Wei take this young girl as second wife. We could increase our gifts to make the proposal more palatable."

"Good! Good! That might work. We will call the wedding ceremony double happiness." Ah Hong was about to get up when he sat down heavily again. "The girl Li Ling might not agree."

A sly look crossed Mrs. Lee's face. "The girl's parents are in China. She has no one here. Do we have to tell her everything? Can we not just send for her in a wedding sedan and let her go through the wedding rites without explaining? We will have the wedding ceremony for Bai Choo and then the sedan would arrive with this girl. The girl would have to serve tea to us and other elders in the family. Let Bai Choo be served tea alongside the other elders. The girl wouldn't know she is serving tea to the first wife and in doing so accepts her position as second wife."

Ah Hong looked doubtful. He stroked his chin and played with the single black hair that sprouted from a mole in his chin.

"The girl only wants Da Wei to marry her. *Fan to sook!* The rice is cooked! You can't undo something that is already done. I am sure she would accept anything in order to be married to Da Wei," she said to her husband. "There! It is settled," she concluded without waiting for a reply. She could see from her husband's hesitance that he was bending to her will and she needed just to give a push to propel the idea along.

"Not quite. Call Da Wei in. I want to give him a piece of my mind."

"*Low yeh!* Old man! There are more important things to get on with. What would scolding Da Wei achieve at this point?"

"Fine! Fine! You win as usual. Remember the girl is called Li Ling. Don't call her *girl*. She might well be carrying our first grandson."

***

Shao Peng had a vague recollection of a sharp pain and of falling. She remembered nothing of what followed. When she woke up she was in bed and Jack was sitting by her side. He looked worried yet pleased.

"What happened?" she asked him.

"You fainted, clutching your belly in pain. We sent for Doctor Rodwell." Jack smiled and his eyes twinkled with delight bringing warmth to the pallor that had coloured his face for weeks. "He said you are with child, our child. Everything is fine."

Shao Peng squealed with joy. She was not expecting this. Her period had always been irregular. She had been late several times before and they were all false alarms. She was beginning to fear that something was wrong and that she could not conceive.

"That is wonderful! Are you happy?" she asked.

Jack took her hands in his. "Absolutely delighted. You have to take it easy though. We cannot have you falling over again. Rodwell thinks that the pain might be a stomach cramp. Did you eat something that didn't agree with you? You might be tired and rundown. Looking after me this past week couldn't have been easy."

"Why don't you get into bed and rest with me?" She patted the mattress next to her. Her eyes were full of mischief. All thoughts of their earlier quarrel were temporarily forgotten.

Jack got up from the chair and went to the other side of the bed. He lifted the sheet and slipped in. He drew her near to him and she rested her head on his chest. Her neck lay snug in the crook of his arm and she sighed happily.

After a while, Jack whispered in her ear. "I think I have to sleep. I am tired. I kept awake the entire time you were out and when Dr Rodwell was here. I confess I am dead beat."

"Close your eyes. We will both rest," Shao Peng snuggled a little closer. After a few minutes, she whispered. " I think I might be six weeks pregnant if I count from my last period." He didn't answer. She raised her head slightly to look at him. Jack was already asleep. She slid further down and rested her head once more on his chest. A sharp pain shot through her making her gasp aloud. She couldn't move. Her eyes rolled and she passed out.

When she woke up, it was as though nothing had happened. Gingerly she placed her hand on the spot where the pain had been. It felt perfectly fine. She raised her head to look at Jack. He was still fast asleep, his chest rising and settling with his breath. She disentangled herself and, lifting his arm gently, placed it on a pillow. She slid out of bed and went to the door. She tiptoed out of the bedroom, went passed the sitting room and down a flight of steps into the kitchen. Ah Kew was not there. A young girl was by the wash basin.

"Who are you?" Shao Peng asked.

"Ah Kew has asked me to help out for the moment. She is in Master Siew Loong's house."

***

Ah Kew placed a creased and soiled brown paper bag in front of Rohani. "This is what we found underneath the hibiscus hedge."

Rohani took the bag, her fingers curling around the top, her nails pressed white against the rim. She pried it open and peered in. A smell, foul and rancid, rose from its depth. She drew back. Beads of perspiration broke out on her forehead. She went deathly pale.

"I brought it here because I do not want to upset Miss Shao Peng or my master. The gardener said that this was black magic. I think so too. Miss Shao Peng had a bad attack of pain just when we fished the doll out of the soil. Someone planted it there to make mischief and to frighten her. That is why I kept the doll from her and brought it to you instead. I do not want her scared. I suspect Aishah did this. We threw her out. She hates our young mistress and she is taking her revenge."

"What can I do?"

"I don't know." Ah Kew was certain her Big Mistress could do something. Weren't such things common practice amongst her people? The gardener admitted as much.

Rohani got up and paced the room. She had a blinding headache and began rubbing her temples vigorously. "I really do not know what you think I can do. Do you think I practise such wicked arts or know people who do? I can't undo such things. In the first place, I don't believe in them."

"Master Siew Loong would be pleased if you could help out. He is very fond of his sister."

Rohani glared at Ah Kew. She was shocked by the servant's cheek. She lost her temper. "I don't need you to tell me my son's feelings nor wishes. Now get out!" She felt that Ah Kew had overstepped herself. All the servants did that with her. She suspected that it was because she was Malay. It was at times like this that she felt even more strongly the need for an ally. Suet Ping, when Siew Loong marries her, would provide her the support she so sorely needed.

"I am sorry. I am worried for young mistress." Ah Kew realised her mistake but she did not want to leave without a firm promise of help.

"Get out!"

"Miss Shao Peng is expecting. She needs your help quickly."

"Get out before I change my mind and do not help at all!"

Once Ah Kew left Rohani resumed her pacing of the room. She too was worried about Shao Peng. She didn't believe in black magic. Yet she had a niggling fear of it. The belief and practice of the occult was entrenched amongst some and there was no escaping it, whether one believed in it or not. The soft down on her arms rose. She shuddered. Did she unwittingly put her step-daughter in harm's way by introducing her to Aishah?

Chapter 27

DA WEI WAS BORED. He was angry. He hid both emotions under a mask when he was with his parents. He fawned, smiled and bowed to them like a dutiful son. Underneath it all he was fuming. He took out his anger on his two wives.

He disliked Bai Choo intensely. He did not bother to conceal it. Why should he when she had been forced on him? He did not spend the wedding night with her. On the first night, he went, instead, to Li Ling. This was a tremendous loss of face for Bai Choo, who had already been sorely humiliated from having to accept a second wife on her own wedding day.

Da Wei went to Li Ling not because he favoured her. He went to punish her for her treachery. If she had suffered from bruises before, her hurt was magnified on that wedding night. Now that she was his wife, the excitement and lust he felt for her vanished.

He looked at her growing belly with loathing. He laughed at her. He pushed and slapped her and then rejected her. Her enlarged breasts which had thrilled him before lost their hold. While she could accept the physical abuse and had even grown to enjoy it in their earlier union, she suffered the psychological rejection and torture, immensely. She had imagined that she had become indispensable to Da Wei for hadn't she done everything to comply with his sadistic demands. She had done it for marriage. She wanted respectability. She wanted to be mistress of a house. It was never going to be realised. She was second wife. When she found out that she had been tricked, she saw her hopes to be someone of importance dashed to the ground. She blamed Shao Peng once more for her ill fate.

Tired of Bai Choo's moaning, Da Wei's father had insisted that he divided his time equally between the two women. "Make sure Bai Choo conceives, just in case Li Ling's child is a girl." Those words rang in Da Wei's ears and he became even more resentful. He began to look outside again to satisfy his needs. Bai Choo took comfort in Li Ling's neglect.

***

Shao Peng was seated in Reverend Mother Andrea's office. Shelves lined all the walls except for the one that had a window. On the windowsill, a jam jar of wild flowers stood in lonely but colourful isolation, the only concession to what otherwise was a purely utilitarian room. Books, papers and files were everywhere. Despite shelves already packed full with books, books piled high on her desk while others were stacked on the floor. In the heat, the smell of paper and dust filled the room.

Please excuse the mess. I just can't find time to tidy it all up."

"And I am sorry to say I will add to your troubles," said Shao Peng. "I won't be able to come in to help with the teaching. I have been feeling rather ill."

"Don't you worry. We will take each day as it comes. You take care of yourself. I am so happy for you and Jack. God bless you both and the baby." Reverend Mother Andrea took both Shao Peng's hands in her own big capable ones. She did not like Shao Peng's pallor. "Is Dr. Rodwell able to diagnose what caused these sudden attacks of pain?"

Shao Peng shook her head. "He is puzzled as I am. One good thing, however, is that the baby is fine. He insists I rest, though."

"Well then, you rest." Reverend Mother had heard of the doll and the rumour of black magic. She shrugged it off as the unfortunate belief of some misguided souls. Shao Peng's pain was more likely to be a coincidence. She believed, however, that the culprit should be caught. Shao Peng's face was clearly showing signs of strain and stress. She had never seen her so thin and pale.

"What happened to Li Ling?" asked Shao Peng.

"I was not going to bring it up if you didn't. Well she left us. She is married into the Lee family, who own the big general store in Brickfields. She is expecting a child."

"You had no inkling of what was happening when she was here?"

"No one knew except Lai Ma. She is a good worker and a kind woman. I just didn't understand why she abetted Li Ling in this. She is keeping quiet and is not letting out much. What we know is that one day, Li Ling just disappeared. Apparently a sedan was sent to pick her up somewhere along the river. It did not come here to the convent. She didn't take any clothing or belongings with her. It was all hush-hush. When we found out we were very upset. She didn't even say goodbye." Reverend

Mother's grey eyes clouded over. "She was very unhappy here," she added gravely.

"Yes, I know," replied Shao Peng. "I am to blame."

"Nonsense. You did all you could. Now you go home and rest." She stood up and guided Shao Peng to the door. "Remember! Rest!"

***

Bai Choo bowed low before her mother-in-law. She had been hovering around her, trying to pick up courage to make her complaint.

"*Nai-nai!*" she said in a voice that could barely be heard. "What shall I do with Li Ling? She doesn't respect anyone in this house. She lies in bed till late in the morning and will not do any work. You gave us pillow cases to embroider. I tried to get her to do it with me. She flatly refused and flounced out of the room."

"*Aiyah!* You as elder wife should learn how to manage your husband's *tipsee*. If you can't even handle your husband's second wife, how do you expect me to hand over the running of this household to you?" Da Wei's mother was not sympathetic. "Be firm! Show her who is the boss. By custom, she has to ask your permission for everything, as you have to ask me for permission. Look at you! *Kuai kuai sui sui!* Like a mouse! What do you expect?"

Hurt by the cutting remark, Bai Choo hurried out of the room. Drumming up courage, she went immediately to seek out Li Ling. She found her sitting in the courtyard cracking water melon seeds, with her feet up on a stool.

"Eating again! You will be fat! No wonder Da Wei has lost interest in you."

"I am eating for two. Pity you can't eat for two. At this rate, you will never eat for two. Has Da Wei visited you yet?" Li Ling asked innocently.

Bai Choo blushed. She pretended she did not hear. "Come! We have work to do. *Nai-nai* has given us a pile of pillow cases to embroider. She wants it done by the end of the month. We have only two and a half weeks to finish them."

"I am not interested." Li Ling said showing off her fingers. "These are not made to do embroidery."

"What are they for then? Scrubbing chamber pots?" The words came out of her mouth before she could stop them. Bai Choo knew that it was cruel; Li Ling's constant taunting always brought out the worst in her.

"Your wicked words will not hurt me. It takes one chamber pot scrubber to recognise another. Perhaps that is why Da Wei never visits you. The stench must be too much for him."

Bai Choo's eyes misted. Li Ling's words hit a raw wound. Her marriage to Da Wei had yet to be consummated. Her mother-in-law had tried to pry the information from her. The white bolt of cloth that had been given to her to line the bed was yet unused. It was to be presented as evidence of their union to her mother-in-law. It stayed in Bai Choo's wardrobe. Each time she opened the cupboard, it gleamed dazzling white, reminding her that she had not done her wifely duty, the duty to conceive a child, a male child. She was not a good daughter-in-law.

"It is lucky that Li Ling is pregnant At least, we know it is your barrenness that is at fault and that it is nothing to do with our son," Da Wei's mother had said.

"How can it not be due to her son?" Bai Choo had wanted to scream at her *nai-nai*. Instead she demurred, choking her anger with a smile.

Li Ling patted her abdomen and gave a sigh of satisfaction. No longer constrained by yards of cloth binding it, her pregnancy was obvious. She did not care that the servants gossiped. She relished the torment on Bai Choo's face when she saw her growing belly. Why should Bai Choo's situation trouble her? No one had given her any love, not even her own mother. Her mother had sent her away on the flimsy excuse of rescuing her from the warlord and a life of being a second wife. What was she now but a second wife? Shao Peng promised her great things, only to let her down. If they had allowed her to stay on with the Ong family she was convinced that Siew Loong would have married her. He had already shown every signs of being in love with her. If that had happened, then she would not be in this situation. She would not be married to Da Wei. So why should she have any pity on others? They had none for her.

Li Ling got up. "I am going in to rest. Don't bother me. I'll see you at dinner." Tossing her head, she brushed past Bai Choo.

Bai Choo's hand shot out. She grabbed Li Ling's arm. Li Ling shook it away and strode out of the room.

Once ensconced in her own bedroom, Li Ling's face fell. Da Wei had not visited her for over a week. She was not going to let anyone see her hurt and her bewilderment. Once more the gods had not been kind to her. What was the point of being good? Everything that she had been taught in the past led to nothing. She would not be a flash of water that would disappear. If she disappeared she would make sure the soil was stained forever, that nothing would grow out of it.

***

Aishah waited in the field that dipped gently away from the house. She stood partially hidden by a copse of trees and surrounded by tall *lalang*. Razor like, the grass came up to her waist, bending and whipping around her with the wind, their sharp blades cutting her arms. She was oblivious. She had been coming to the same spot for days, hoping to see Jack. She wondered if he was still ill.

Impatient to know what was going on, she crept up the gentle slope towards the hedge that circled the house. She bowed low to keep her head out of view. The evening had come early. She put out her hand brushing it along the foliage to guide her way. Odd that in the dark, what was familiar became strange. The leaves rustled as she brushed past. She came to the spot where she had buried the doll. She stopped. She stooped to peer closer. Someone had patched over it with grass. She knelt down and began pulling the turfs of green; her movements were frantic and urgent.

"Looking for something?"

Aishah turned. Standing over her was Rohani and the gardener, their silhouettes dark and menacing with the moonlight above. Behind them stood her guardian, Mahmud, the man she feared above all, the man who had taken her in when she lost her parents. Her hands flew to her face; she flinched as though she had been slapped.

"Get up!" Mahmud commanded.

"Were you looking for this?" Rohani asked. The gardener handed Rohani a brown bag. She thrust it into Aishah's hand, "Look inside. Is this your doing?"

"No!"

Mahmud took a step towards her. His hand was bunched up into a fist. Aishah, still crouching, half scrambled to get away and fell back with a thud.

"Don't hit her," cried Rohani. She could understand why Aishah was cringing. Mahmud's face was alarming; his bushy eyebrows were drawn together and his moustache was literally bristling.

"*Gila!* Mad!" he shouted. "I'll teach you a lesson." He turned to Rohani. "I am sorry for all the trouble. I was not joking when I said that she is mad. She might look perfectly normal but she is not. She has obsessive behaviours. Like the time when she loved a cat. She petted it and fussed round it so much that it died under her hands. That was not the only time. There were other incidents. I whip her and she is good for a while. Then there is another relapse. I don't know what else to do. Whipping is the only thing she understands."

"Whip her? You must not do such a thing. We just want her to stop stalking Mr Webster and to stop harassing my daughter, Mr Webster's wife. That is enough. Remember, you must promise that you will not hit her."

Mahmud glared defiantly at Rohani. His lips quivered with unspoken angry words. Weakling, he thought though he did not say. He shot out his hand and caught hold of Aishah's arm; his fingers pressed into it like claws. She whimpered.

"Come with me." Without a further word, he strode off dragging the girl with him. "You won't be troubled by her again." His words echoed in the wind.

***

In the house, not a hundred yards away, all was quiet. An oil lamp was burning bright. Beneath its warm glow, Jack sat reading. Shao Peng lay with her head on his lap and her book opened on her chest. She could not settle down to read. She stared vacantly ahead, looking, though not seeing, the flying insects milling around the light. They were like ants drawn to honey.

Jack sensed her quiet and placed a hand on her forehead. "Are you all right?" he asked.

She answered by taking his hand and placing it on her lips. She kissed it. Her lips felt parched dry. The sudden pains had exhausted her. They came and went without warning. One moment she was fine and the next she was in agony.

"I am worried for the baby," she whispered. "And I am so tired."

Jack placed his hand on her belly. There was hardly a swell to be seen. "We'll get Dr Rodwell over tomorrow. Perhaps he could give you something to settle the pain."

"I don't want any opium. It would hurt the baby. Maybe the pain will vanish tomorrow."

Shao Peng closed her eyes. "I saw my stepmother this afternoon. She came to the house to see how I was. It was very kind of her because I know that she is busy with the wedding arrangements. She had someone with her. Someone called Mahmud. Rohani said that he would be working for my brother. She has been popping in with him these last few days."

"Mahmud? Does he have a scar here?" Jack drew his finger over his cheek.

"Yes. A rather nasty looking scar although it is partly camouflaged by his thick moustache and sideburns."

"I know of him. He recruits Indian workers for many of the coffee plantations here. He came to the country some fifteen years ago and worked as a labourer in a sugar plantation. Many of our planters found him able and intelligent and appointed him as their intermediary for recruiting his fellow kinsmen into this country. He commands a sizeable Indian work force, all indentured to work in these plantations. He married a Malay girl. He has no children himself except for an adopted daughter."

"It is strange that my stepmother came with him. Perhaps, they were on the way to meet Siew Loong and just dropped in to see me, though I don't quite understand why he accompanied her every day this past week. Perhaps Siew Loong is thinking of using him to recruit workers for planting rubber."

"Perhaps," said Jack closing his book.

Chapter 28

A WEEK PASSED. During that time, the pains that had racked Shao Peng's body rendering her weak and listless gradually eased. She began to sleep better. One morning she woke up to find herself totally free of pain. She must have slept through the whole night for the sun was already up. The bright sunshine that filtered through the window shutters took her by surprise. She had become used to waking up during the night. She cast off the sheets and swung both legs on to the floor. She was ravenous. She stood up, tested her legs gingerly, and went out of the bedroom in search of Ah Kew. Jack, she surmised, must have gone to work.

"*Aiyah!* Why didn't you call for me? Get back to bed!" Ah Kew was horrified by the sudden arrival of her mistress in the kitchen.

"I'm fine. I only want to get something to eat."

"Sit, sit! Ah Kew pulled out a chair. "I'll make tea and warm up some savoury buns. They are your favourite. I made them with sweet roast pork." She piled a plate full of milky white buns and placed it in a rattan casket to steam. Then she lifted the lid off a *wok* filled with bubbling hot water. Carefully she sat two pairs of chopsticks crosswise in the boiling water and placed the rattan casket on it. Soon the kitchen was filled with the warm smell of yeast and roast pork.

"Takes no time to warm them up this way."

"Ingenious," said Shao Peng, marvelling at Ah Kew's improvisation.

"You have not been eating properly for days. You must now eat more to make up for it. Thank goodness you do not suffer from morning sickness."

Ah Kew placed a bowl and a small dish of soya sauce before Shao Peng. Then she heaped the bowl with rice porridge. "Eat! There are thin slices of fish, ginger and spring onions in it. Eat!" she repeated, handing yet another dish to tempt her palate. "Pickled turnips; helps whet your appetite."

"Stop! I can't eat that much."

No amount of protest, however, could deter Ah Kew's determination that her young mistress should eat. She fussed, rushing from stove to table and back again.

"I am so glad that you are feeling better. You got us very worried. Thank the Goddess of Mercy for your recovery. Thank Big Mistress for helping out."

Ah Kew stopped and threw a guilty glance at Shao Peng to see if she heard.

"How did she help?" asked Shao Peng, picking up her chopstick.

"Nothing. Just nonsense that tripped out of my mouth." Ah Kew's eyes darted towards her young mistress and back again to the pot of porridge she was stirring.

Shao Peng caught her eye and asked, "What were you showing my stepmother and the gentleman that came with her the other week?"

"Nothing of importance. He was just interested in the layout of the house. Don't you worry about anything. Just think of yourself and the baby you are carrying." Ah Kew dropped the ladle and moved the pot of porridge over to the side of the stove. She took a basin from the cupboard, turned it over to check that it was clean, and emptied a packet of white flour in.

"I can't just sit at home and do nothing. I am worried about Li Ling. She is expecting and might need our help. I think I should visit her."

Ah Kew opened her mouth and closed it again. She immersed her hand in the basin of flour and began to knead. There was no point in trying to stop her young mistress once she had made up her mind. She failed to see why Shao Peng should be fond of a girl who rejected her advances of good will.

***

Rohani was worried. She did not trust Mahmud nor did she trust Aishah to stop her pursuit of Jack. Someone must warn Jack. Siew Loong would have to do it. Goose pimples appeared on her arms like a rash of pin pricks. She recalled the incantations and rites performed by the *bomoh* that she had unwillingly engaged.

She went down the stairs, holding on to the banister. A week to go before the wedding and everything was almost ready. It was the one bright spot in her life. She was looking forward to it. Suet Ping was such a sweet and quiet girl. She was sure Siew Loong would be won over once he got to know her. She stopped half way down the stairs and looked out over to the entrance hallway. Red banners hung on the wall, each inscribed in beautiful calligraphy with poems in praise of the main virtues expected of women: morality, obedience, modesty and diligence. Flanking them were odes to manhood, of benevolence, propriety, righteousness, wisdom and honesty. They stood like flags, billowing gently with the breeze, their shadows undulating on the marble floor. Together the teachings formed the framework of Confucius's teachings on behaviour.

Heavy red drapes hung over doors; in fact, everywhere she turned she saw a sea of red. She had allowed Ah Sook to make all the wedding arrangements. He insisted that red was a lucky colour. He explained that *hong* was the colour of prosperity, important if Master Siew Loong's business ventures were to continue to expand and flourish. She nodded and agreed. It was simpler for her that way. The intricacies of Chinese customs and traditions were beyond her. When she met Ngao, such matters did not stand in their way. They had fallen in love and that was that. Life was simple then. She shrugged. What does it matter? She had no living relatives or parents who would object and whatever was done, was done with the best intentions.

She continued her way down the steps, her mind busy. Suet Ping's family would appreciate such arrangements, she thought, and that was important. She was surprised to learn that they held on to traditional Chinese customs even more than her late husband in his later life. Although Ngao had a carefree attitude when he was young, when he acquired wealth and became associated with other wealthy Chinese families, his observance of Chinese customs grew. She had not expected her future in-laws to be so similarly inclined for Suet Ping's maternal side were Malays. One thing she was certain, they would be easy to talk to for her prospective in-laws spoke mainly Malay. She smiled, reassured that her decision to pursue this marriage for her son was right.

There was a frenzy of activity in the sitting room. A servant was mopping the floor with a wet rag, while another was on her knees buffing the tiles until they shone. Another was busy polishing the furniture with a clear thin wax. Many scurried round the room carrying chairs and setting them around tables brought in to accommodate dinner guests. Table cloths were brought out, aired and placed on the tables.

"Where is Master Siew Loong?" she asked a passing servant.

"In there," he replied, "in his office."

From where she was, Rohani could see the doorway that opened to a room to the east of the house. She walked towards it. She stopped. A man was coming out of the room. She recognised him. It was Mahmud. She slipped quickly into an adjacent room used to store linen and odd bits of furniture. She didn't want to meet him. He frightened her. He went passed her in a flurry of movements, his green tunic and brown sarong flashing by like a blur. Rohani waited until he was completely gone. Then she moved towards Siew Loong's office.

***

Ah Su poked her head through the doorway. "You have a visitor," the maid said standing at the threshold of Li Ling's room. "She is in the sitting room. Your mother-in-law is with her. Please come with me."

Ah Su could hardly see. The curtains were drawn tightly closed. The room was dank and dark. It smelt of sweat, urine and of unwashed bodies, a feral musty odour. She pinched her nose in disgust. A movement in the corner caught her eye and she moved a step towards it.

"Stop! Don't come any closer." Li Ling was huddled under a blanket. "I don't want to see any one," she said, clutching the seams of the blanket tightly to her bosom.

"It is Mistress Shao Peng from the Ong family. *Wah!* She came in a pony cart laden with gifts of fruits and baby garments for you."

"Send her away. I don't want them."

Ah Su took a step closer. "Come! *Nai nai* won't be pleased if you don't show your face. You know how your mother-in-law hates to be kept waiting. I'll help you clean up and we'll go out together." She edged further forward, her movements furtive, one foot gingerly in front of the other.

Li Ling grabbed a shoe and hurled it. It hit Ah Su, bouncing off her shoulder to crash down onto the floor. "Get out! Get out! Who needs your help? Come any closer and I'll scratch your eyes out."

Without a word, Ah Su turned and ran out. There was little that she could do. If they wanted to fetch Master Da Wei's wilful second mistress they would have to do it themselves. She was like a wild animal. Ah Su did not know what brought it on. Until a couple of days ago, the girl had been so brazen and boastful. She was under everyone's feet, volunteering her opinions on every subject and above all taunting poor mistress Bai Choo.

Li Ling bolted the door. She knew it would be a pointless exercise. The lock was not secure broken two days ago when Da Wei came to the room. He was furious with her for locking him out. Fed up with his long absence and disgruntled by whispers that he was seeing someone else, someone even younger than her and prettier to boot, she had locked her door when she heard his approaching footsteps. She wanted to teach him a lesson. She would reject him as he had rejected and neglected her.

It drove him mad. He lashed out at her. He hit her harder than he had ever done before. He tore at her clothes. "Kneel! Turn over! Grasping her hair, he pushed her head down until it banged on the floor. He mounted her. She felt the sharp stab of pains as he pushed into her over and over, grunting with each thrust, oblivious to her pregnancy, oblivious that her belly was slapping hard on the floor. He rode her like a horse. Finished, he kicked her, his foot connecting with her cheek. It drew blood.

"Try locking the door again and you will get it even worse."

He left. She sat huddled on the floor, steeling herself not to whimper, not to call for help. She would not leave the room. She did not want the other women in the house, especially Bai Choo, to see her. She would not let them have the pleasure of seeing her so humiliated. She grew hungry. The chamber pot filled till it almost overflowed. She remembered someone opening the door gently and pushing a bowl filled with rice and bits of vegetables and meat through the doorway. "Please eat for the baby," the voice said. She recognised it as Bai Choo's. Li Ling was appalled that she knew. She tried to starve herself. She would not touch the bowl. Hours passed. Night became day. Hunger gnawed. She could not help herself. She crawled on her knees to the bowl and began stuffing the rice into her mouth. Immediately, someone pushed a bowl of tea in through the gap in the door. Li Ling cried then. She was so ashamed.

Shao Peng's visit could have hardly come at a worst time. "At least I could keep my circumstances from her," Li Ling thought leaning heavily against the door, her legs outstretched before her. "I will not let her see me so reduced." Her heart hardened further against Shao Peng. Li Ling suspected that she had come to gloat.

Chapter 29

THE WEDDING DAY ARRIVED. A crowd gathered outside the Ongs' residence to wait for the bride. The people jostled for space by the roadside. Some stood on tiptoe, others on wooden crates, while children clambered onto the shoulders of adults. In the two-storey shop houses on either side of the road, people squeezed behind windows to peer out onto the street. A wedding of this scale amongst the newly established Chinese immigrant community was a rare event. Most people married simply. An exchange of vows and, if the bridegroom's parents were in the country, an offering of tea was all that there was to it. Brides, often imported from China, generally came without the accompaniment of their parents. Bridegrooms too were often unencumbered with family. Most were immigrants who had come to do manual work. In such cases, there would be no wedding ceremony at all. The Ongs were different. They were rich second generation Chinese immigrants and the bride Suet Ping was a third generation Chinese. Both families had Malay bloodlines from their maternal side. People were curious to see how the wedding would proceed.

Li Ling elbowed her way to the front, holding on to her swollen belly. People hissed at her. When they saw her they gave way. Their anger turned to sympathy. Her face was so bruised that it was just a mottle of sickly greenish grey. She flashed them a look of defiance. She could not stand the pity. "What are you staring at?" she snarled. They edged away leaving her alone and isolated in a sea of bodies.

The sound of clashing cymbals heralded the arrival of the bride. Four men carried the sedan. The bride sat within, her face demurely covered with a red veil and her hair pinned up and tucked under a traditional headgear of gold. The tassels of her headdress glittered and sparkled with each sway of the carriage. A ripple of appreciative murmurs went through the crowd.

Li Ling heard the whispers of admiration. Each one was like a stab to her heart. "How could one woman have so much and I so little?" she asked herself. "All I ever wanted was to love and marry Master Siew Loong."

She placed her hands protectively around her belly. She felt the baby's movement, a limb straining and pushing followed by another flutter. She looked towards the house. People were emerging from within. First to appear was Mistress Rohani in an embroidered top and a magnificent sarong of bold hues of red. Master Siew Loong followed. Li Ling pressed a fist to her chest to still her pain. He was in a traditional long silk Mandarin collared gown worn over silk trousers and he had a fitted red silk skullcap on his head. Li Ling searched his face for signs that could tell her that he was an unwilling participant; she wanted to believe it to be so. She saw nothing except a face that was almost devoid of expression. She could not tell if he was unhappy or happy. It troubled her. She closed her eyes and felt a tear roll down her cheek. She brushed it away quickly. It should have been her in the carriage. She recalled Master Siew Loong's face and the touch of his hand on hers when he bade her farewell those months ago. It was so unfair. How could they have forsaken her like a discarded rag?

The sedan arrived at the front porch. She saw the bride helped out of it like a delicate flower. She held a red sash with a matching silk chrysanthemum flower. Someone placed the other end of the sash in the bridegroom's hand. They bowed to each other. He smiled and led the bride into the house. Li Ling turned with a sob and fled. She ran back to where she came from, uncaring that she pushed into people. She ignored the strings of curses that followed her. She was beyond pain.

***

Siew Loong slipped into the study. He needed a moment of quiet. The noise, the barrage of good wishes, the need to smile in response and to look happy was all just too much to bear. Suet Ping was a sweet girl except that she was not one he wanted to marry. If he had been able to choose, whom would he have wanted? He remembered a face, a wistful face. He could not marry her and that was that.

Maybe in later years, when he could take a second wife, perhaps he could consider it. A second wife did not have to have the status of the first. She did not have to come from a family with an illustrious background. He shook his head to stop himself from brooding. He was building false hopes. He reminded himself that even that possibility was not to be. She was married and with child.

He sat down behind his desk. Moments later, he heard the door open and looked up. "Come in for a respite?" he asked his brother-in-law with a wry smile.

Jack smiled sheepishly back in response. "Yes, I am afraid. I am not used to ... I found it all a bit overwhelming," he said with an apologetic twist of his mouth. "I could barely understand all that was said. My fault for not totally mastering the language."

"Take a seat and join me in this," said Siew Loong. He went to a glass cabinet, a tall Victorian piece of furniture set in the alcove behind his desk, and fished out a bottle and two glasses. "Brandy. Not something that I drink; yet if I was to drink this would be the day for it." He poured a generous measure into each glass and handed one to Jack.

They sipped companionably, the liquid heat swilling in their mouth, each mulling over the events of the day.

"Happy?" ventured Jack.

"I am happy because my mother is happy. Everyone says that happiness comes from being a filial son." He took a sharp intake of breath and expelled it. He drank deeply from his glass. "When I have finished with my duty as a son, then I can pursue happiness, the sort you were referring to."

"I am sorry. I shouldn't have asked."

"You are family and hence entitled to know."

Siew Loong came from behind his desk and walked to the window. Outside in the courtyard servants were laying tables for dinner.

"Talking about my mother, she spoke to me the other day about Aishah."

Jack looked at him puzzled.

"You, I trust, do not know what transpired these last few weeks. To make it brief, she told me that Aishah tried to harm Shao Peng using black magic. They attributed the pains that Shao Peng had to her sorcery. Aishah was caught in the act. I find it hard to believe in black magic. I am, however, worried about the girl's wicked intentions."

"It can't be. She is a young girl with the mildest of manners. She is always pleasant and has a ready smile."

Siew Loong waved away Jack's protest. "You of all people should know better. A person who smiles is not necessarily good. Haven't you learnt that in the diplomatic service?" He turned around to face Jack. "Did you know that her guardian is Mahmud?"

A look of astonishment crossed Jack's face. "She never mentioned it. I knew he had an adopted daughter. I never put the two together."

"Well, he has locked her up. He says that her behaviour is obsessive and there is no way he could control her actions short of chaining her. Mother and I are appalled. We do not approve of the harsh punishment. Mother feels responsible for her present plight. We are thinking of bringing her here, to this household. This way, we could keep an eye on her. If we monitor her movements then we should be able to stop her from trying to harm Shao Peng again. At the same time, we could rescue her from Mahmud. Mother does not like the idea that she is chained."

Siew Loong kept his eyes steadfastly on Jack, watching for any signs of opposition. "It is either that or leaving her with Mahmud. However, we will help her on one condition. She is infatuated with you. You have to stop her from thinking that you reciprocate her feelings. Stop being kind to her. Tell her that you don't have the slightest interest in her. Then sever all contact. Can you do that?"

Jack was utterly speechless. He was shocked at the revelation. Could he believe all that was said of Aishah? He thought of Shao Peng's unexplained pains. He had wanted her to take Aishah back. Had he misjudged?

"Speak to mother or Mahmud if you wish to verify what I said. Ask Ah Kew too. Shao Peng doesn't know any of this and we would like to keep it this way, at least until the baby is born. For now, I have to return to my bride."

***

Jack was distracted throughout the remainder of the wedding feast. It was obvious that he could not confront his mother-in-law nor seek out Ah Kew immediately. He tried to bottle up his anxiety and questions. He glanced at his wife sitting next to him. Shao Peng was listening to one of the guests, nodding and smiling in agreement. He had not seen her so settled and serene for a long time. She was beautiful.

He remembered when they first met. She was sitting with her dance card looking lost. He had asked her to dance. They had been young then. He recalled the years of trial and tribulation that followed that first meeting, of uncertainty, of not knowing whether they could ever be together. They had fought so hard for their happiness. He would not let anyone or anything come between his wife and him. He reached over and took her hand in his. She smiled and gave his hand a reassuring return squeeze.

Jack looked around. He did not feel part of it. He felt alone and isolated in the crowd. It was noisy. The endless round of *yum seng* drove him crazy. It was of course no different to the drinking sessions and the 'bottoms-up' days of his youth in England. Perhaps he was getting old. Perhaps he should be thinking of returning to England. They would be away from all this, the intrigue, the heat, the tropical diseases, and now even sorcery. Would Shao Peng be willing? It would be tearing her away from her roots. He watched her, the ease in which she slipped from one dialect and language to the other. What would life be like for them in England? Would she suffer discrimination? Would it be worst than it is here? At least in Malaya, she had the support of her family.

"*Heh!* Give me a smile," Shao Peng said. "You look so worried!"

"Would you give this up," he indicated with his hand, "and return to England with me?

The smile went from her face. "Are you serious?"

"Maybe. Just answer me." He gave her a lopsided grin to make light of his question.

"I have never thought about it. I always assumed you would wish to stay here, that you liked it here."

"I do like it here. It is just a thought."

Her eyebrows knitted together. "Should I give it serious consideration?"

"Not now. I am just feeling a bit left out in tonight's celebration. Don't mind me."

She linked her arm through his. "I am sorry. Chinese family affairs tend to be like this. Just one big occasion to talk, eat and make merry."

A loud explosion echoed through the house. Strings of fireworks sizzled, sending sparks of fire high into the air. Soon a carpet of red littered the ground and the air was choked with smoke. Shao Peng leaned over and whispered. "I think this marks the end of our attempt to have any conversation."

Chapter 30

It was late afternoon, well after three o'clock. Ah Kew gave a final cursory glance into the basket and covered it with a white cotton towel. She had filled it with food: little buns that she had steamed in the morning, a bunch of golden bananas ripened in the sun, a handful of sweet mangosteen, the colour of ripe plums, a small bag of custard apples and a whole chicken roasted to a golden brown on the new spit the Master had built in the back garden.

"Wait! Please put this in as well," cried Shao Peng walking into the kitchen. She handed Ah Kew a bottle of rice wine. "My brother's kitchen is making a huge batch of this in preparation for the many babies that they expect to arrive in the next few years. He is giving them away in protest."

Ah Kew took the bottle reluctantly. She muttered under her breath.

"What did you say?" asked Shao Peng.

"I was just wondering why you care so much for that ungrateful wretch. She has refused to see anyone, not even Lai Ma after all she has done for her. It is best you leave her alone." Ah Kew eyed Shao Peng's burgeoning tummy. You are in no state to gallivant about town. What you need to do is to put your feet up."

"I am going to try to see her again. She can't possibly say no forever."

Ah Kew tucked the cloth around the contents of the basket. She hesitated and then uncovered it again. She lifted the bottle of rice wine and pointed to it. "Are you sure you want to give this to her? We need it too you know. Chicken cooked in rice wine and ginger is a must for pregnant women, especially after birth. If we keep this bottle, it would be nicely matured by the time your baby arrives."

Shao Peng took the bottle from her and placed it firmly back in the basket. "There are plenty where it came from." She placed an arm around Ah Kew's shoulder. "Let us be generous. I know you mean well. Come, I shall carry this out," she said reaching for the basket.

Ah Kew broke away and snatched the basket away from Shao Peng. "You must not carry anything that is heavy. I'll do it." She took the basket under the crook of her arm and headed for the door. She continued muttering. She did not approve of her young mistress's actions.

***

Life for Li Ling settled into a pattern. She got up, washed, ate and went back into her room until the next meal. She kept silent throughout the day. She spurned Bai Choo's attempt to draw her out or become friends. She was ashamed but did not want to admit to it. She listened with her head bowed when her mother-in-law chastised her for her surliness. If her eyes flashed with resentment and anger, she was careful not to let them be seen. On occasions when she met her father-in-law, she would keep a similar demeanour. His kind words were met with absolute silence. She would just stand with eyes cast down until he finished. Then she would excuse herself. She knew that it made her father-in-law sad. She could hear his sighs for he had a soft spot for her and there were instances when she was almost moved to speak. She never did. She thought it futile to reply. When her mother-in-law spotted these little exchanges, there would be a heated discussion between her in-laws. She didn't care. They were of no importance to her.

Da Wei came home less and less. Even his parents could no longer control him. He was involved with yet another young girl. In the servants' quarters, the main topic of conversation often centred on Da Wei. They would wonder how he managed to lure so many women when there were so few women compared to men. At times, the arguments and speculations became quite heated with different parties taking different views. They seemed oblivious that Li Ling might hear.

"It is because he is the son of a rich man," Li Ling heard them say. "Coolies don't get a chance. If you are rich you can have as many as you wish."

Others volunteered that all his recent women were young prostitutes. His reputation was so bad that people hid their daughters from him.

In the early days, Da Wei would make straight for Li Ling's room when he came home. The servants would wait with abated breath to see what would happen. With eyes round with excitement, they plastered their ears against the thin walls. After the fateful beating, Li Ling no longer locked her door. She made no attempt to make herself pretty. She left her hair uncombed and unwashed. Her cheeks were pinched and sallow because she stayed indoors. She grew thinner and thinner while her belly grew bigger and bigger.

Hollow-eyed, she would just gaze at her husband when he came into the bedroom. Then, without a word, she would take off her clothes and lie on her back. She kept her face empty of emotion. She would stare vacantly at the ceiling; her body was a hull without spirit, a corpse in waiting. It drove Da Wei mad. The first time she did this, he slapped her. He needed her to respond and to be frightened. Even that did not move her to speak or scream. Gradually he lost interest and his visits became fewer and fewer. Li Ling was glad. She channelled all her energy to the child within her. She ate dutifully to ensure the baby was nourished. She put all her hopes on it. She had no clear idea how the child could be her saviour; she just felt that it would be so.

***

"Let me see her ... please." Shao Peng stood at the doorstep with one foot in and a basket in her hand.

Ah Su eased open the door. "Mistress Li Ling would not like it. So don't tell her that I have let you in."

Ah Su closed the door gently and pointed to the rear of the house. "Mistress Li Ling is in her bedroom. It is the one facing the inner courtyard. I am afraid it is not very nice because that is where we do the washing. Are you sure you want to go?"

"Yes! Show me the way."

"Well, can I just leave you when we arrive near the bedroom? Mistress Li Ling can be quite fierce. If she were to see that I brought you to her, she might throw tantrums. She threw a stool at me the other day."

"I understand. Could you help me with the basket?"

"Yes, I'll carry it and leave it outside her door. As I said, she might throw a tantrum if she sees me with you." Ah Su heaved the basket up and carried it with both hands supporting its base.

Shao Peng followed Ah Su to the back of the house. She was dismayed. How could it be? They seemed to be heading towards the servants' quarters and towards the kitchen. The stale smell of cooking oil mingled with that of pickling liquid. She sniffed. Its pungency hit her; she identified it as rice wine vinegar, brine and herbs. It permeated the air. The corridor became narrower and narrower. She glanced into one of the opened doorways. The room was dank and dark. Large vats of pickles stood next to casks of soya; dribbles of the dark sauce stained the floor. Someone had forgotten to clean up.

"Where do the rest of the family live?" she asked casually.

"Oh! The big master and mistress are in the eastern side of the building and Mistress Bai Choo is on the western side. The family don't come to this part of the house often."

They stopped when they reached a small courtyard. To call it a courtyard was an exaggeration. It was a little open space with a well in the middle. All round it were tubs and brushes. A big dish of soap and a wooden scrubbing board stood in between the tubs. Above them, hung a clothes line with washing on it.

"There," whispered Ah Su apologetically. "I'll leave this with you." She hurried away, abandoning the basket on the floor.

Shao Peng looked around. She was troubled that Li Ling was relegated to such quarters. She raised a fist to the door and knocked. There was no reply. She pushed open the door.

Through the gloom, she could see a bed tucked at one end, its' bed sheet crumpled, exposing the thin mattress and bare wooden boards beneath. At the other end of the bedroom was a heavy wardrobe. A dressing table with a mirror blotched and aged with black spots, stood next to it. She stepped inside. It was airless and still. She felt a movement behind her and, almost at the same instance, the sound of a door closing. She turned. Li Ling was standing behind her. She must have been hiding behind the door.

"Why have you come?" The words were spat out, terse.

"To see you. I have brought this for you." Shao Peng tried to keep calm. She placed the basket on a chair.

"I don't want it."

Shao Peng went up to Li Ling. "Can we not just talk?"

"Go away! I don't need your help."

"Please Li Ling. Tell me what I have done wrong?" Shao Peng took a step closer. Her eyes became accustomed to the dark. Li Ling's gaunt face shocked her. When she last saw her at the convent, she was a young girl. Now she seemed to have aged a decade. She reached out. Li Ling flung her hand away.

"I hate you! Don't you know that? I hate you for building such hopes in me for a better life. You led me to believe that you loved me. I shared your bedroom. You said that you would make something out of me. Yet you allow them to send me away. I was not good enough for your brother."

Li Ling shook with anger. The words she had bottled up in her weeks of self enforced silence rushed out. She hurled accusations at Shao Peng; she shouted and screamed; she knocked over a chair; she kicked a stool and then finally she cried. She stood with both palms on her face and sobbed and sobbed. Shao Peng tried to gather her in her arms. She couldn't get close; their tummies were in the way. She tried again. The humour of the situation suddenly struck Li Ling. She began to giggle. Shao Peng took her by the hand and drew her to the bed. They sat with Shao Peng's arms around her shoulders.

"I tried to persuade my stepmother to let you stay. I failed. It was not my house, not my decision. I am so, so sorry. I had no home to offer you until I had a home myself. I wanted you to come to me when I had a house I called my own. By then you were so upset you would not accept anything from me. I wanted you to make something of yourself. I wanted you to study. You can still do that."

Shao Peng hugged Li Ling. "*Shhh, shhh!* Don't cry."

Spent, Li Ling laid down and pulled the sheets to her.

"Is he cruel to you? Does the family treat you badly?" Shao Peng swept her hand to encompass the room. "This ... this is not what I pictured for you."

With a muffled sob and halting words, Li Ling described her married life.

***

Throughout her journey home, the horror of Li Ling's tale replayed in Shao Peng's mind. She shut her eyes tight as though shutting them would stop the images of violence in her mind eyes. She could not possibly let Li Ling stay a minute longer in that household. Yet how could she remove Li Ling from the clutches of her husband? She could not involve Siew Loong. He was recently married. She knew that he was fond of Li Ling. She had often wondered at the depth of his feelings.

How would he react if he was told the full story? He might blame his mother and what use would that be, except to create turmoil within their family?

She leaned back against the seat. She was so preoccupied that she was unmindful of the jolts and bumps of the pony cart. The dirt road was filled with potholes. Floods had resulted in landslides so that the cart had to weave around mounds of earth and tree branches brought down from the hills. She recalled her first journey with Li Ling to the Convent. Life had been simpler then. How could things change so dramatically? How could a young innocent girl be so transformed? She winced each time she recalled the physical abuse Li Ling suffered. She felt nausea to think of the sexual violation. She clutched her belly protectively, cradling and stroking it. How could it be safe to bring up a child in such a world?

By the time she reached home, the sun had disappeared below the horizon. The house was covered in darkness except for the pool of light from a lantern held aloft. A tall silhouette stood beneath it. It must be Jack. She knew Jack would be worried. She had not intended to be late. It was not safe to travel in the evening with just the driver. She had been warned many times. Ah Sook would have been horrified that she had ventured out on her own with just the driver of the pony cart.

Jack was waiting at the top of the flight of steps to their bungalow. She hurried towards him. Her foot slid on a pebble, she righted herself. She heard him call out to her to slow down. She could not. She wanted to feel his arms around her, to feel safe. She ran and on reaching him, threw her arms around him. The lantern swayed precariously under the impact.

"Steady, I am here. It is all right."

"I have seen Li Ling," she said. "We must help her."

Chapter 31

AFTER THE WEEKS of frantic preparation, the days following the wedding were dull in comparison. The banners and drapes that hung and covered every wall in the Ong household had long been taken down, the floors washed and buffed to their original shine and the dozens of chairs and tables brought out to cater for guests put away. The servants breathed a sigh of relief. Ah Tai took the opportunity to put her feet up. Even idle chatter in the kitchen died down to just the occasional word and comment. The weather was once more changing in preparation for the monsoon. At times the heat was unbearable. Ah Tai fanned herself. Humidity had taken its toll in the kitchen. Everything was damp to touch. She resisted the urge to get up and wipe down the table. She was too tired. She would rest first before attending to dinner.

In Rohani's private rooms, Suet Ping was busy drawing a pattern for a pair of beaded slippers. With great concentration, she drew a chrysanthemum flower, its minute petals nestling on a sprig of green leaves. Spools of cotton and trays of coloured beads lay by her side.

"I'll have to have gold beads for the flower," she said to herself, "and I have run out."

Rohani watched from a distance. She saw how Suet Ping held her brush, her long slim fingers with their shell pink nails pressed against the pen's stem. After a while, Rohani patted the seat next to her. "Sit with me," she said.

Suet Ping stopped what she was doing and went immediately to her mother-in-law. She sank gracefully on to the cushion and turned to smile at Rohani. She waited expectantly.

"Is my son treating you well?"

"Yes, mother. He is treating me well."

Rohani dithered. Should she or should she not? she asked herself. It was almost two months since the wedding and she was disconcerted by what she had heard from the maids.

"Are you ... does he..? I mean are you feeling well? Do you have any signs of sickness, nausea, any craving for strange foods?"

"No. I don't have any illness of any sort at all. Don't worry about me. I am fine."

Rohani's eyes narrowed. It was clear that the child did not know why she was asking such questions. She tried her wheedling from another angle. "Siew Loong seems very preoccupied," she commented. "He is out of the house early in the morning and does not come home until late at night. Does he spend enough time with you?"

Suet Ping was not sure what her mother-in-law was driving at. She did not know what was expected of a husband. No one had told her what to expect or do. She knew that she had to be obedient to her mother-in-law and to her husband. Wishing to reassure her mother-in-law, she said, "Siew Loong is very good to me; he is like a brother and looks after me well."

"A brother? Surely he has ... is he sleeping with you?" The words fell out of Rohani's mouth before she could check herself.

Suet Ping blushed. She looked down on the floor. The first night, Siew Loong had offered her the bed and opted to sleep on the floor. She had felt bad and insisted that he shared the bed. Now they slept on the bed, separated by a bolster in the middle. She felt comfortable with the arrangement. She recalled the servants' whispers when they came to tidy the room the morning after the wedding night. They had looked at the sheets and then at her and then back at the sheets as though something was wanting. She recalled her mother saying that she must show red on her wedding night although she did not elaborate on how this could occur. Perhaps what was missing was this *red*. Before she could ask, her mother had switched the topic to something else saying that it was good that Rohani was not a strict follower of Chinese traditions and had done away with the custom.

"Is he sleeping with you?" Rohani asked again, looking quite alarmed this time by Suet Ping's silence.

"Yes. He sleeps on the bed with me," came the reply. Suet Ping voice had dropped to a whisper. Something told her that her mother-in-law was not happy. There was a look of desperation in her face. She was bursting to say something and Suet Ping waited patiently to hear it.

Rohani clutched the ends of her *kebaya* top, her fingers digging into her own palms. Should she explain what she meant by sleeping? She couldn't. Surely it was Suet Ping's mother's duty to do so. She should have checked before the wedding that Suet

Ping was told what was involved. She supposed her mother had expected that Siew Loong would take the lead and all Suet Ping had to do was to comply. Rohani sighed. What a mess! She was sure that the marriage had yet to be consummated. She took the girl's hand into her own and patted it.

"Have I done wrong?" asked Suet Ping.

"No, not at all. Go back to your beading."

Rohani looked on as Suet Ping once more took up her pen brush. She recalled how she was with her late husband. Love was the most natural thing for them. They were two together, alone and in love. Perhaps she was wrong to force this marriage. Siew Loong did not love Suet Ping. It showed in his daily dealings with his wife. Yet Rohani was so sure that it was just a matter of time before he would. She made up her mind. She had to give them a little push in the right direction. But how?

Rohani got up and went to the window. Outside in the garden, Aishah was stripping the yellowed fronds from the banana tree. Bunches of bananas lay in a rattan basket by her feet. She reached out to cut another bunch, her buttocks strained against the thin cotton of her sarong when she leaned forward on tiptoe. With a sharp movement of her knife, she cut through the stem and the bunch fell. She caught it expertly and laid it alongside the others. She then tidied up the fronds that she had stripped, piling them up high for the gardener to collect. Her movements were fluid, strong and uninhibited. That Aishah was aware of her sexuality was in no doubt.

Rohani looked on as Aishah worked. She had learnt a lot about Aishah. When she went to fetch Aishah from her guardian, all her anger against the girl vanished. She was shocked at how she had been treated. Even now she could see the sores and cuts on the girl's wrists and ankles. She had him unchain her. Rohani believed that Aishah's misdeed was a moment of madness, and that she could help the girl reform. Who would not be maddened by such inhuman treatment? No wonder Aishah had a fixation on Jack who had been kind. They had talked and talked. She saw in Aishah, the daughter that she never had. With Shao Peng there was always a barrier; Shao Peng hankered after her own mother and her aunt Heong Yook. Aishah had no one.

Aishah, Rohani thought, would be a good teacher for Suet Ping. She would help her out of her innocence. Aishah could talk to Suet Ping without being embarrassed. It would be good for Siew Loong's marriage.

***

In the kitchen, Ah Tai had dropped off to sleep. Her head lolled, jerking every now and then when it rolled too far back. Slowly her jaw slackened, her mouth fell open and she began to snore. The two undermaids in the kitchen looked at each other. Now was the time, they thought, to steal a little rest themselves. They dropped their paring knives in a basket and placed the turnips they were peeling aside. Between them they had peeled and shredded a dozen of these huge turnips. "Surely, that was enough," they whispered to each other. With great concentration and care, they tiptoed out of the kitchen, stifling their impulse to giggle. Ah Sum and Ah Looi were two sisters employed to help Ah Tai when Ah Kew left to join Shao Peng's household. Just thirteen and fourteen of age, they were mischievous.

"Come, let's go out that way," said Ah Sum pointing in the direction of the back garden. "Aishah is there harvesting bananas. We'll get some from her. She won't mind."

"Do you know why we are not to tell anyone that Aishah is living here?" Ah Looi asked with one foot resting on her other calf while she bent over to scratch its sole. An ant had bitten her the other day and the bite had become an angry red weal.

"I don't know. Probably in case the news reaches Miss Shao Peng. Big Mistress was particularly insistent that Miss Shao Peng should not know. Quick, come before Ah Tai wakes up."

"What must I not know?" Shao Peng stepped into their view.

Ah Sum and Ah Looi started. "Nothing, nothing. We didn't hear you," they mumbled.

"I knocked and knocked. No one answered the front door so I came to the back. Where is everyone?"

"Big Mistress is upstairs with Mistress Suet Ping. They must be resting. They won't be able to hear you. Ah Tai is also resting and we..." the sisters looked at each other guiltily, "we were going out to the back garden."

"I won't wake them up if they are resting. I'll come with you to the garden. Is the gardener here? He can get me a bunch of those lovely golden bananas. I have a craving for those. "

The two girls stared at Shao Peng and then at each other.

"Don't look so frightened, Mistress Rohani said that I am welcome to have them."

"No ... we'll get them for you." Ah Looi dashed towards the back garden and bumped immediately into Aishah, knocking the basket of bananas out of Aishah's hand. The fruits scattered onto the ground.

"*Tengok mana anda pergi!* Look where you are going!" Aishah dropped to her knees and began picking up the bananas. She did not see Shao Peng, who had rushed after Ah Looi when she heard the commotion.

Shao Peng could not believe her eyes. Instinctively she cradled her belly. She didn't want Aishah to see her. She could not bear those cat eyes glaring at her with the ferocious intensity of a tiger. She wheeled, catching Ah Sum, who was tailing her. She placed a finger to her lips and hurried away.

Chapter 32

SHAO PENG HAD GONE back to her family home to speak to Rohani. She wanted to ask her to help Li Ling. She had discussed at length with Jack the various possibilities of rescuing Li Ling. None seemed viable. The biggest problem, explained Jack, was that in matters of civil law regarding the local and immigrant population, the British administration had adopted a principle of non-interference.

"My hands, even those of the Resident, are tied. In family matters we leave it to each ethnic group to administer the customary justice they feel most appropriate. In all my years here we have never intervened. The Sultan or his chiefs resolve any dispute amongst Malays in accordance with Muslim law. Similarly, the Indian community follow Indian rules and customs as practised in India. In the case of the Chinese community in

Kuala Lumpur we leave it to their leader, the *Kapitan* China. Your brother is in a better position to talk to *Kapitan* Yap. Isn't he his personal friend?"

"I can't believe you cannot use your office to intervene."

"I am sorry. We are not in the Straits Settlements. The British Resident in Selangor has only an advisory role, even though in most situations our advice is followed and implemented. We must not be blatant about it. Our position is delicate. We reserve our intervention and advice for matters of state and economy, and never for personal matters. In personal matters, the leaders of the various ethnic groups have full power. Face is very important in this part of the world. We cannot take on family matters without causing a major outcry."

"Is there no other way? Surely if there is abuse within the family, something could be done by your administration."

"Only the local leaders can intervene in family matters. It would be unfair for us to meddle in such matters. Let me give you an example. Polygamy is widely practised here. It is not allowed under English law. Even though we are against polygamy and it is illegal under British law, we would not make families with such arrangements cast away the secondary wives. That would be cruel. It wouldn't be accepted. And as for wife battering, the issues involved are even more complex."

"So what can we do? We cannot leave Li Ling with her husband. She will not survive. She will be giving birth in a few months. How could we leave her to be kicked and abused?"

"See your brother. Ask him to get help from the *Kapitan*. See him at his office. Don't go to his house. There are too many distractions there."

But Shao Peng couldn't approach her brother on a matter relating to Li Ling without first consulting her stepmother.

Rohani would consider such a step as treacherous. So Shao Peng had gone to see Rohani only to discover that she was harbouring Aishah. Shao Peng felt betrayed.

During her journey home she mulled over her discovery. How could Rohani do that to her? Did her brother know? she wondered. He must know. He lived in the same house. Yet she could not believe that her brother would do such a thing. The arguments in her mind went back and forth and she went from anger to recrimination to disappointment and sadness. Finally, Shao Peng took a deep breath. She had to rise above her own personal grievances and to focus on ways to rescue Li Ling. She could not allow herself to be distracted. Every minute wasted was a minute more that Li Ling had to endure abuse. She could not allow time to slip away. Yet how could she trust Rohani to help her? Rohani had chosen to give a home to Aishah when she had turned Li Ling out.

**

It was evening when Jack came home. Shao Peng heard his footsteps and went out to greet him. She held a lantern up high and light spilled over the path. She watched him hurry forward to the porch taking the steps two at a time.

"What is the matter?" Jack asked when he saw her face.

"I went to see my stepmother. I couldn't bring myself to speak to her."

Jack ushered her into the house, handing the lantern to Ah Kew. It was warm in the house despite the windows thrown wide open. He took off his jacket. "Come, sit down," he said guiding her to a seat. He was troubled. He suspected that Shao Peng had seen Aishah. He had specifically suggested that she should not go to her brother's house. He wanted to tell Shao Peng about Aishah first. He could not do so without consulting with Rohani and Siew Loong. They had specifically told him not to tell Shao Peng. His first response then was that the whole idea was ridiculous and the idea of keeping Aishah's whereabouts from Shao Peng even more so. He had warned them that the servants would talk. They had disagreed with him. They were confident that it could be done. They were keen that Shao Peng should not be troubled until after the birth. For a while he believed them for Ah Kew showed no signs that she knew. Then work came in the way and days passed without him realising until the fateful day when Shao Peng came home with news of Li Ling. Events spiralled quickly then.

"Why couldn't you speak to Rohani?" he asked.

"I saw Aishah. I told my stepmother the trouble that I had with her. Yet she took her in. I see it as a betrayal. What troubled me more is that my brother must be in it as well."

"They did it for a reason."

"You knew!" She snatched her hand away. For her this was the ultimate treachery.

"Let me explain." He tried to place his arms around her.

"No!" She thrust his hands away.

He caught her in his arms and kept her there. She wouldn't look at him.

"Please let me explain. They were trying to protect you."

"Protect me?"

He told her. He explained how Aishah was chained by her guardian. While they agreed that Aishah had to be watched to prevent her from trying to harm Shao Peng again, they did not have the heart to see her so treated.

"Harm me?" Shao Peng asked in surprise. "How could she harm me?"

Jack told her. "She was practising black magic on you..."

By the end of the evening, Shao Peng was calmer. She sat with her head resting on Jack's shoulder. She was appalled by Aishah's story. She regretted sending her away so precipitously. "Poor Aishah, poor Li Ling. At least Aishah is safe now."

"Yes, and I think we will not have any trouble from her on account of me. I have spoken to Aishah. She understands that I love only you and that she had mistaken my kindness for love. Rohani is hoping to channel her need for love to a more suitable young man when the time is right and an opportunity arises."

"Which brings us back to Li Ling. What can we do?"

Chapter 33

Li Ling held on to her side. Her belly was growing by the day. She stroked it, marvelling at its tautness. How did I become like this she wondered, trailing a finger around her naval. It poked defiantly up from the round hump that was now her belly. It was like a little hillock in her engorged middle. She could hardly bend over. She shifted in her seat, hoping to ease the discomfort. She took up her bowl and chopstick and began to eat a solitary meal in her room. She suffered from constant heartburn and her mother-in-law had asked that she ate separately from the household.

"*Aiyah!*" her mother-in-law had cried. "I can't stand looking at your miserable face. Can't you stop burping? Where are your manners? It spoils my appetite. I don't want you at the table. You have to have your meals separately from us."

Li Ling took a bite. It was better this way, she thought. The kitchen had spared no effort in preparing delicious meals for her on the orders of her mother-in-law. Li Ling heard her instruct the servants, not caring that she was within hearing. "See that she eats well. It is not her that I am concerned about. I care only for the baby."

Li Ling laid down her chopstick. Her heartburn was getting worst. There was far too much to eat: chicken braised in rice wine, ginger and sliced spring onions, pork cooked with black mushrooms and wood fungus and green spinach glistening in oyster sauce. She looked up; her eyes met Ah Su. Since Shao Peng's visit a week ago, the maid had become supportive and friendly.

"*Nai-nai* says that I am to make sure you finish the food," Ah Su said. "I know it is difficult. Just try. Let me help you." She picked up a porcelain ladle and heaped a spoonful of spinach into Li Ling's bowl.

Li Ling protested and shifted in her seat once more. Of late her protests had become less vehement. She was worn down. Suddenly, there was a loud pop and a button flew and landed on the floor.

"See!" giggled Li Ling, though her eyes were bleak and bore none of the joviality that issued from her lips. "I am bursting from the seams. I can't eat."

Holding onto the table, she heaved herself up. Another button popped and spiralled onto the floor. "I can't wear my clothes any more." She had no one whom she could ask for new clothes. Da Wei no longer visited her. Asking her mother-in-law was not an option. It would just invite more contemptuous comments. She recalled her one attempt to ask for maternity clothes. The response was harsh: "You brought it on yourself. You could have had as many clothes as you could possibly wish if you had been able to keep your husband at home. After all he manages a store that sells clothes and textile. You have only yourself to blame!"

"Wait! I have an idea." Ah Su left the room with a backward glance of triumph. Within moments she returned with a small pile of clothes in her arms.

"I do not know who they belonged to. They have been in the cupboard for ages, buried under a pile of odd assortments. Someone's cast-offs, no doubt. No one will miss them. They are huge, probably for someone much bigger than you, so they should be more comfortable than your old clothes. If they are too long, I can help take them up."

Li Ling took the clothes and smiled at Ah Su. A month ago she would have screamed at Ah Su for daring to suggest that she would accept cast-offs. Her mouth twisted in a bitter grin. A month! A lifetime. She was waiting for Shao Peng to come to her rescue. She prayed that she would not forget her.

"Come, sit and eat," called Ah Su unaware of Li Ling's thoughts.

Li Ling shook her head. She held onto her belly. She couldn't eat anymore.

Ah Su placed a finger on her lip. She went to the door and closed it. She waited a while with her ears plastered to the door and then said softly. "In that case, we'll have to hide the food. I can't take the tray back into the kitchen if the food is not eaten." She hurried to the dresser and took out a silver casket used for storing thimbles and scissors. She emptied the contents out and ladled the food into the casket. "There! This looks better. The dishes are all more or less empty. I'll come back for the casket later. I'll hide it here," she said popping the casket back into a drawer.

Li Ling watched Ah Su carry the dinner tray out. She heaved a sigh of relief. Since Shao Peng's visit, things had improved. Da Wei had stopped coming to her. She had grown so big that even he would not risk harming her because his mother was keen on having a grandson. She touched her face remembering the slaps when he last came. "What if I don't have a boy?" she asked aloud. The thought was not worth contemplating. She could only pray that she could escape.

***

The mill was busy. Bags and bags of rice lay on the floor waiting to be stacked. At the other end, men were wheeling cassava into the mill to be crushed and refined into flour.

"Come with me," said Ah Sook. "We can't talk at ease here. The air is choked with tapioca dusts. It is not good for you."

He walked out of the mill and beckoned Shao Peng to follow him. It was a hot sunny day. The road simmered with the heat. Ah Sook walked quickly. By the time Shao Peng stepped out of the mill, he was on the opposite side of the road, standing patiently waiting for her. She looked up and brought a hand above her brow to shield against the glare of the burning sun. She felt queasy. Ah Kew had been disapproving when she said that she was seeing Ah Sook at the mill. "Don't go. The roads are full of potholes. The journey will be too bumpy for you in your condition. I'll get word to him. He can come to us," she said. Shao Peng didn't want the fuss. It was a good time to see him at the mill because she knew her brother was away on business.

She crossed over the road and he walked her a short distance to a teahouse. This time, Ah Sook walked slowly adjusting his speed to hers.

"I know the owner," he said as they went into its dark interior. "He has given us his own personal room. We won't be disturbed. It will be more private than my office. With business growing rapidly, I now share the small space with two other clerks. You did say that you needed to speak to me on a confidential matter."

Ah Sook looked questioningly at his young mistress. He wondered what could be so important that it could not wait. He didn't like her pallor. The greyish sheen on her face was definitely alarming. He reminded himself that it wasn't his place to comment. They were women-matters. The trouble was the young mistress had no mother and had been left to adopt all sorts of strange behaviour. Why did she rush around to deal with matters that should not concern a well brought up lady? If she had married a good Chinese man, he surely would have reined in her shortcomings. Instead, she was allowed to marry a *gweiloh* who knew no better. He shook his head and sighed. He wondered at the child she was carrying. What would it be, a Chinese or a white child? Under whose law would it come? The world had become a topsy-turvy place. If she came for his advice on that score, he would not be able to help her.

Shao Peng held on to the edge of the table and lowered herself on the stool. A woman came in with a pot of tea and tiny porcelain teacups. She said nothing and did not look at them. She poured the streaming hot tea into the cups and then left, closing the door gently behind her.

Shao Peng reached for the cup and drank deeply, ignoring its heat and the burn on her tongue. The fragrant steam and the warmth of the tea quelled her queasiness. She looked around. The room was bare except for the table and marble top stools.

"Is it safe to speak?"

"Yes Miss," he answered. Like Ah Kew, Ah Sook preferred to address her as Miss. He avoided calling her by her married name. He couldn't pronounced it in any event.

"It is about Li Ling."

Ah Sook rolled his eyes. "Not her again," he wanted to say. Shao Peng intercepted him with a wave of her hand.

"She is married and with child. She suffers terrible abuse from her husband and her mother-in-law doesn't treat her well. Can we do something?"

Ah Sook stared at her in amazement. His bushy eyebrows came together and his eyes were like slits below their hooded lids. "First of all, you must understand that under Chinese customs she has to obey her mother-in-law. Li Ling, I remember, was always wilful. You must not give credence to everything she says."

Shao Peng had not expected this. She half rose from her seat, her eyes wide with horror. "I have seen her injuries. Surely that is not allowed?"

"No. Proving her husband inflicted these injuries, however, might be difficult. Who knows? She might be inflicting the injuries on herself."

"You surely cannot believe that?"

"You can never tell with cases such as these. Even the *Kapitan* does not like to intervene in family matters. If he did, he'd find himself inundated. He has enough on his hands. He has only six policemen under him to keep law and order. Stopping fights between gangs, robberies and murders are his main priority. He would not consider squabbles between a husband and wife important work."

"Then he is wrong! Especially when the husband is inflicting bodily harm on his wife."

"Look! His aim is to make Kuala Lumpur a better town and his energy is directed towards building better houses and roads. He would not wish to deal with a domestic issue like this. You just have to accept this."

Privately Ah Sook was appalled. Hadn't Shao Peng enough on her plate? He tried not to show his disapproval. He pursed his lips to stop them quivering from indignation. A woman should know her place and probably Li Ling didn't and hence invited such censure from her in-laws and husband.

"I cannot believe we can't do anything. You did such a wonderful job when you helped rescue Jing-jing. Can't you do the same for Li Ling?"

Ah Sook had a soft spot for Shao Peng and could not refuse her when she was a little girl. He couldn't refuse her now when she looked at him with those limpid eyes.

"It was different with Jing-jing," he explained in a quieter voice. "We were dealing with gangsters then and we had the law behind us. This is meddling with someone's family. We cannot forcefully extract Li Ling from her husband. He has rights."

"What about her rights?"

"A woman has to obey her husband. If she doesn't, she opens herself to all sorts of recriminations. Please forget this whole business. You don't look well. Go home."

"Not until you promise to try to help." Shao Peng reached over and took his hand. "Please," she pleaded.

Ah Sook looked away. He was conscious of Shao Peng's pleading eyes and the pressure of her hand. He withdrew his. It was not right. She shouldn't put him in such a situation.

"Please," she begged. "Li Ling is in a terrible state. I promised her that I would help."

He did not reply immediately. The room fell quiet, so quiet that Shao Peng could hear every rustle, every breath in the room. Finally Ah Sook stood up and brushed his tunic. "Leave it with me," he replied.

Aren't you going to tell me what you plan to do?" asked Shao Peng.

"You won't want to know," he said. He went to the door, opened it and stood aside for her.

Reluctantly, Shao Peng rose and went out of the room. The conversation was over. Ever since she was a child, she knew that she could not push too far with her father. It would be the same with his old retainer, who after all was more a family member than an employee.

Chapter 34

AISHAH TOOK UP a hair brush and considered Suet Ping's reflection in the mirror. Suet Ping's hair was undone. It fell like black silk right down to her waist. Her eyes were wide with just a hint of a slant, eyes that now stared back at Aishah without any guile. Obviously, thought Aishah, she did not understand what I was saying. She, Aishah, would have to approach it another way.

Aishah began to brush the hair until it crackled. Then she parted it and braided it, revelling in its thick silky smoothness. She caught sight of herself in the mirror. She saw her brown, honey coloured hand against the pale alabaster colouring of Suet Ping's face. Strange, she thought, that the girl should have such fair skin when she was half-Malay. With a deft twist of her hand, she wove the two braids together and pinned it up with a gold hairpin. "There!" she said laying her hands on both of Suet Ping's shoulders. The girl smiled. Encouraged, Aishah lowered herself and turned the chair around so that Suet Ping was facing her. "Did you understand what I said earlier?"

Suet Ping blushed. "No!" she confessed.

"Then come with me." Aishah drew Suet Ping up from her seat and walked her to a long wooden sofa. She sat down. Mistress Rohani had specifically set her this task and told her to do it as she saw fit. Aishah didn't understand why her mistress was not able to instruct Suet Ping herself. She waited until the girl sat down. It was obvious that words were insufficient. She had spent the last half hour speaking and the girl had just blushed.

Perhaps a demonstration was better than mere words. It would at least be more entertaining. Gently, she placed a finger under Suet Ping's chin and tilted it up. With her other hand, she drew her closer. Then, she lowered her face towards Suet Ping and brushed her lips with her own. Suet Ping started and pushed her away. "When Master Siew Loong does this, you have to kiss him back. Like this," she said moving even closer. Suet Ping could feel Aishah's breast on her own and smell the muskiness of her scent. She tried to strain away. Her shoulders connected with the back of the seat and she could not move any further.

Aishah pressed her lips once more on Suet Ping's, this time parting them ever so slightly. Suet Ping froze; her whole body went rigid. She could feel Aishah's tongue as it ran over her lips and into her mouth. Suet Ping gagged. She stood up and ran out of the room.

Aishah got up and stood in the middle of the room. If Suet Ping was an unwilling student, perhaps Master Siew Loong might not be. She smiled, her cat smile. She wondered if Mistress Rohani would allow her to teach the young master instead. She wondered at all the fuss. She recalled her own childhood and the thin thatched walls with gaping holes that separated her from her mother's room. Her mother had been very generous with her favours. The uncles that came every day and night were generous in return, sometimes pressing a coin into Aishah's palm or tousling her hair to demonstrate that they extended their affection even to her. Sometimes they sat her on their knees and petted and touched her until her mother pushed her away.

When her mother died, she was bereft. Alone in the hut, some of the uncles came and comforted her and loved her like they did her mother. She did not find it strange. It was no stranger than seeing her mother with these men. That was until Mahmud came along and took over her care. He said he was her uncle. The headman in the village was glad to give her into Mahmud's care. She hated her guardian Mahmud. He wanted her only for himself and he was cruel. She had prayed and hoped that one day she would find a man who would love her like her mother was loved by all those uncles. She thought that she found him in Master Webster. The only obstacle was his wife, Shao Peng.

She went to the window and leaned out to look into the garden below. She wondered if Suet Ping would report what happened to Mistress Rohani. She shrugged her shoulders. After all, she did only what she had been told, which was to explain to Suet Ping about love and how to attract the young master. If Suet Ping couldn't understand what she was saying, it was only logical that she should demonstrate. She reached up and touched her own lips, trailing her fingers down to her breasts. She chuckled. "Such fuss over nothing," she mused.

***

Suet Ping ran out of the room and bumped into Ah Tai, sending her stumbling backwards. The pile of neatly folded clean laundry flew from Ah Tai's arms and landed in an untidy heap on the floor. Ah Tai caught hold of a chair and narrowly prevented her own fall.

"*Dew nei ...!*" Ah Tai stopped. She clammed her mouth shut to stop the profanities that escaped from her mouth. She saw Suet Ping's tear-stained face. "What happened?" she asked.

Suet Ping looked over her shoulder; her eyes were wide with shock. She shook her head and ran. Ah Tai went after her. "Stop! Stop!" she yelled. Suet Ping was too fast for her. Breathing hard, Ah Tai stopped and doubled over to hold her middle. She heard a door close. She turned and saw Aishah come out of Suet Ping's room. Ah Tai's eyes narrowed. She saw Aishah smile like a cat that had had a fish dinner. What did that woman do to make her young mistress so frightened? she wondered. She retraced her steps until she reached the pile of clothes on the floor. She picked them up, one by one and refolded them, asking herself all the while what could have happened in that room. Nothing good, she concluded. From what she had heard from Ah Kew, Aishah was just pure evil. What could one expect? she thought. A girl with such a background. Only big Mistress could fall for her stories.

With her arms full of clothes, she made her way to the linen cupboard that stood outside Rohani's room. She opened the cupboard door and began putting away the clothes. She took her time. Mistress Rohani's door was ajar and she could hear faint voices from within. She recognised the voices. She could not understand fully all that was said because it was in Malay. She edged closer to the door. Suddenly she spied Ah Sum, the undermaid. She waved her over with a finger to her lip. She pointed to the room. Ah Sum tiptoed closer. "Listen," Ah Tai whispered in Ah Sum's ear.

"Maybe I can talk to the young master instead. The young mistress didn't understand what I was trying to say to her."

A long silence followed. Ah Sum leaned closer to the door with Ah Tai behind her.

"Was Mistress Suet Ping upset when you talked to her?"

"Yes and she ran away."

"Would you not be embarrassed telling such things to young master?"

"No. Of course not. It is just a natural thing that people do. I am sure he would be more receptive. Once he knows, he could teach mistress Suet Ping himself."

"I am not sure."

"It will be all right. I promise. Leave it to me."

"I don't think it is a good idea. No! Really, it is in fact a bad idea."

"It would be fine. I would just explain things."

"Let me think about it. Don't say anything to him until I have time to think about it. I will let you know."

Ah Tai and Ah Sum moved quickly away and hurried down the stairs. Once safely ensconced in the kitchen, Ah Sum gave a brief report of what was said in the room.

"I have to go out for a moment," said Ah Tai. "Make a start with dinner. I will lay out all the vegetables and meat that have to be sliced. I will come back in an hour. Remember, not a word about this to anyone, not even to your sister. Understand? I will see that you are rewarded."

Chapter 35

IT WAS LATE AFTERNOON before Ah Sook could find time to visit Ah Chu and her family. It had been a long while since he paid them a visit. The last time was when he came with Miss Shao Peng. She had wanted to find out about the relationship between her father, Ngao, and the women in Ah Chu's household. He remembered that day clearly. The town had been inundated with water that gushed and overflowed from the River Klang and Miss Shao Peng had been distraught. He stood for a moment and then rapped on the door. It opened. Swee Yoke came out with a little boy. "Ah Sook," she cried in surprise.

"I come to see your mother," he said without the customary exchange of greetings. His face was grave.

"Come, this way." Without a further word, Swee Yoke led the way into the parlour. His solemn face told her that it was not a social call. Ah Chu was with her two adopted daughters Hui and Huan. She rose immediately and went to him with a big smile. She greeted him effusively. She was, however, apprehensive. She owed Ah Sook. Without his help, she would probably not have received such a generous settlement from Master Siew Loong. She had expected that a day would come when she would be asked to pay her dues. She often wondered when it would be.

"I have to speak to you privately," Ah Sook said.

Ah Chu knew from his voice and manner that the day had arrived. She waved the women away and sat down. Ah Sook took the adjacent chair. He bent his head close to hers and spoke softly. Every now and then, he would pause to take a big breath. Ah Chu's eyes darted towards where her two adopted daughters stood. Her first thought was that it would have to be one of them, not Swee Yoke, her own child.

From a distance, the three women, Swee Yoke, Hui and Huan, looked on with knitted brows and anxious eyes. They huddled together in search of comfort from each other. They wondered at what was being discussed and if they were to be involved.

"After this I have one other small request. It will not be a big problem for you and I will let you know the details later. Once completed, I will not come to you for any more favours." Ah Sook bowed solemnly to underline his words.

She nodded. "Tell me what to do," she replied with yet another furtive glance at the three women.

*****

When Ah Sook came back late that evening to the Ong household, Ah Tai was waiting for him. She told him what she had heard outside Rohani's room. She told him of her suspicion about Aishah and how Aishah must have done something to frighten Suet Ping.

"Where is Master Siew Loong?"

"Master Siew Loong is back. He is upstairs."

"Watch Aishah like a hawk. She might be young in age but up here," Ah Sook pointed to his temple, "is a can of worms. I do not understand big Mistress's trust in her. I cannot believe that she would entrust her with such a task as that which you described. Letting Aishah teach our young Mistress Suet Ping the art of seduction! How could it be?"

"Big Mistress is a very kind and unsuspecting person. She trusts everyone. I have spoken to Mistress Suet Ping. She won't tell me what happened. The poor child blames herself for what happened. She turns red with shame and cries whenever I broach the subject; she has now locked herself in her room. I had to make up another room for Master Siew Loong. He is there now."

"And where is Aishah?"

Ah Tai turned red. "I don't know," she said.

"You had better find her."

***

Siew Loong threw his shirt aside and strode to the window. Of late he had taken to wearing a shirt, such as that worn by his brother-in-law Jack. He found it more comfortable than his Mandarin collared tunic, especially when he had to deal with his English associates. He blended in better and was more at ease when he dressed like them.

He placed his elbows on the window sill and leaned out. Outside in the garden, all was quiet except for the soft rustling of leaves stirred up by the breeze. They whirled and dispersed and regrouped. He didn't mind having to sleep in a separate room from Suet Ping, if that was what she wished. He wondered what brought it about because he had taken care not to encroach on her private space. He was tired of his mother's attempts to coax information from him. He did not want to admit to her that he had not consummated the marriage. It was not because he didn't know how; he was just not ready for it with Suet Ping. He did not love her in that way. He closed his eyes and an image of her sweet innocent face and buttoned-up pyjamas came to mind. He knew, however, that sooner or later he would have to perform his duty.

He stretched out his arms and rolled his shoulders to release the tension in his neck and back. He knew his mother was anxious for a grandchild. She probably thought he needed a lesson in love. He grinned. He couldn't really confess that he was more than able in that quarter. When he was a young boy, he had trailed some of his father's workmen to their brothels and opium dens. He did not join them. That would not be right. His father would have found out and he would get the workmen into trouble. Nevertheless, he had lost his innocence long ago.

The door opened. He turned sharply around. Aishah stepped in and gently closed the door. She walked towards him, hips swaying, her lips slightly parted and her eyes fixed on him.

"Yes?" he asked, a brow lifted quizzically.

"Your mother sent me," she answered. She dropped her eyes and he could see her long thick eyelashes. His eyes followed down to her chest. She was wearing her sarong tied above her breasts and nothing else. His throat tightened. Through the thin cotton, he could see her breasts and her nipples. His eyes trailed further down to her hips and to her exposed legs for the sarong reached just below the knee. He caught his breath. He had never seen any Chinese women with bare legs, naked shoulders or breasts half exposed in public.

"Why? What does she want?" His voice was hoarse.

"This," answered Aishah dropping her sarong. She stood with the cotton cloth spilled around her feet. Her breasts rose and fell with each breath. He could smell her musks. She stepped over her sarong and walked to him. Siew Loong took a step back. "Let me," she said putting her arms around his neck and bringing her lips to his. He could feel her breasts on his bare chest. She pressed against him.

"This is wrong," he said pushing away even though his body said the opposite.

"Master, Master!" shouted Ah Tai bursting into the room. She stopped. Her mouth fell open and she stood gaping for a moment in shock. Then she fell on Aishah, dragging her by her hair.

"*Dew nei loh moh!, Ham kah chan!* F... your mother. May your whole family perish. What shame are you bringing to this family? You evil witch. First you upset our young mistress and now you attempt to seduce our young master!"

By then, the commotion had brought Ah Sook and Rohani into the room. Rohani, horrified, snatched the sarong from the floor and threw it at Aishah. "Put this on! What happened?" She looked at her son and then Aishah.

"I did as you told me. I only wanted to show Master the art of love."

Rohani turned bright red. Her knees felt like jelly. She went to a chair and sat down. All eyes were on her. Her ears burned with shame. She turned to her son. "I was worried about you and Suet Ping. Aishah suggested that she could speak to you so I had thought it would be in words rather than action. I hadn't even agreed to it. Never in my mind did I expect her to seduce you." Yet at the back of her mind, she had a niggling thought.

Was she to blame, she asked herself. Could she have avoided this if she had given a definitive no to Aishah's suggestion?

"She has to go," interjected Ah Sook. "I'll take care of it."

Ah Tai and Ah Sook manhandled Aishah out of the room. They ignored her screams and pushed and pulled her along.

Siew Loong waited until the noise died down. His face was cold; expressionless. "Why mother?" he asked. He picked up his shirt and left the room.

Chapter 36

DA WEI SWAGGERED INTO the room. He had only just come to know of this establishment. He was astonished to discover that there was still one that he had not visited. In the last few months he must have had visited dozens of them. With his reputation spreading fast in Chinatown, he was finding it exceedingly hard to find new prey. He had to turn to brothels instead. Even those were turning him away. They did not want to have his business.

He cursed Li Ling for that, for shaming him and exposing his deeds publicly in his father's shop. He was told that parents would lock up their daughters when he was around. Not that there were so many daughters to choose from. He sniffed indignantly with that thought. The number of women arriving from China might be on the rise, but most were much too old for his taste. New arrivals of young women were more often than not already earmarked for marriage. He couldn't risk his father's censure and rage.

He thought of Li Ling and her swollen body. He could hardly bear the sight of her. She disgusted him. Bai Choo, his first wife, so cruelly forced on him by his father, was worse; she was old and a prude. At least tonight he would be rewarded. He was told that the establishment prided itself on its young girls.

A woman emerged and beckoned him to follow her. Da Wei hesitated. She was neither young nor pretty. She smiled and murmured. "Not me. I am bringing you to the pretty one." With that she resumed her pace and he followed her. She stopped in front of a door and pushed it open. He stepped into the room. Without a word, his guide left, closing the door behind her. He grinned when he saw the girl. Not as young as he would have liked. But there was fear in her eyes and she was trembling. He felt a rush of exhilaration, of power. Without a word, he undid his belt and walked towards her. "What is your name?" he asked.

She cowered and brought both hands up protectively over her face.

"I ask you once and now twice. What is your name?" The words spat out of his lips. He swung the belt faster and faster. It swished through the air like a rattle snake.

"Huan," she replied cringing even more.

"Huan," he said, "lie down there," he pointed to the bed.

***

Outside in the street, a woman was screaming for help. Her hair was dishevelled and her clothes were torn.

"A man barged into my house. He assaulted me. He forced my daughter into a bedroom. I heard her scream. I banged on the door. He wouldn't open."

Ah Sook signalled the men that he had gathered. They had been waiting. They formed part of the vigilante force used by the Kapitan to keep law and order. The men had been tailing Da Wei for some time. Report after report had been filed against him. Each time, they were dropped. Victims from respectable families could not bear the shame of standing witness against him. Brothel owners were reluctant to charge him; they did not wish to bring too much attention to their activities. Although brothels were legitimate businesses, it was never a good idea to invite trouble when it could be avoided. They wrote off the girls who had the misfortune to be disfigured by Da Wei. They had no obligation to pay off the victims. The police had almost given up hope until Ah Sook came to them to give them a tip.

"Let's get him," they said.

***

Two days after the raid, Ah Sook was back at Ah Chu's house. Everything seemed normal and peaceful. The shutters were half shut. It was not unusual at that time of the day. The sun was shining fiercely exposing cracks in the wall and paint flaking from the wooden shutters. Patches of mould streaked grey against the white paint. Yet just a year ago, everything had been pristine. High humidity and torrential rains alternating with ferocious sunshine meant that the upkeep of the place was a constant struggle. He made up his mind. He would promise them help and they would be grateful. He would make sure that they would be well rewarded. He knocked on the door, three sharp raps, and waited.

A couple of minutes later, he was in the sitting room waiting for Ah Chu and wondering what he would see. Street noise filtered in from the windows. He tapped his fingers; anxiety brewed in his belly as he watched dust motes danced in the sunlight. Ah Chu came in with Huan. He jumped up; his eyes went immediately to the girl. He recoiled at the bloodied eyelids and the stream of gooey liquid that oozed from their corners. Her face and lips were swollen beyond recognition; the disfigurement was heartbreaking.

Huan walked with difficulty supported by Ah Chu. She declined to sit down. She couldn't sit.

His eyes slid away quickly from the sight of the girl who was wincing with pain and clearly in distress. He couldn't bring himself to face Huan. "Did you get a doctor to attend to her?" he asked Ah Chu instead.

"Yes, no bones have been broken. He had started whipping her with his belt before your men came in. She can't sit."

"I am sorry." he bowed. "Why doesn't she rest? Please, we do not need her for what we need to discuss now." His face remained steadfastly averted from Huan. He did not want to be reminded that he had contributed to her situation.

Ah Chu did not reply. She waited. Her silence filled the room like an accusation. Reluctantly, he turned to face Huan. He bowed apologetically. "Thank you," he said hoping fervently that her injuries were superficial and she would not be permanently scarred.

Ah Chu sniffed. "Wait here. I'll take her to he room." Supporting Huan by the elbow, she helped her walk away.

Ah Sook closed his eyes. He had wanted to prevent this; he had got the men to rush in straightaway. Not soon enough apparently. Da Wei must have started on Huan the instant Ah Chu left the room. Well it was done. He had to think forward and not reflect on the past. Yet images of Ngao, his boss, were forced into his mind. Ngao, to whom he owed his loyalty, would not have approved that a woman he had sought to protect from harm had been injured in such a gamble. Yet, what else could have been done? At least Li Ling would be saved and he had prevented other women from falling into harm's way in the future.

Within minutes Ah Chu was back. She glared at him.

"You came for your second request," she said. "Huan paid a heavy price. I hope it is not a request with such penalties."

"I know. Words cannot convey how sorry I am."

"*Huh!*" Her lips curled. "Let us get this over." She was abrupt. Since the event, Ah Chu's feelings towards Ah Sook had changed. She felt she had been exploited. She had not expected things to be as bad as they turned out to be. She thought that it would be a few slaps and pushes before Da Wei was intercepted. Her heart was heavy with guilt. She had sacrificed Huan for her own daughter.

"I am afraid I have two small additional requests, not one."

"No!" She jumped up, wagging her finger. "You promised just one last request."

"Listen, it is not a big request. We'll compensate you. I would like to bring a young girl here to lodge with you temporarily until we can find her a passage back to China. She is Li Ling, Da Wei's wife. She too has suffered immeasurably under him. She is pregnant. It will have to be kept secret. Her in-laws do not wish to give up the child. She is with them right now."

"So how are you going to bring her here?"

"I'll take care of that."

Ah Chu thought for a while. "I make no promises. I shall have to think about it before I agree. What is your third request?"

"I would like you to give me the address of a brothel in Singapore."

Ah Chu smiled, a contemptuous smile that made him cringe with embarrassment.

"Any preferences?" She leered, sweeping her eyes over him from head to foot. "Have you been to the city? There are over two hundred public brothels in the city, somewhat less than the three-hundred-and-fifty odd some five years ago, though still a not inconsiderable number especially if you were to include the non-registered ones. Every street has them. There are well over three hundred illegal ones; some say four hundred even. I wouldn't recommend those," she smirked. "Too dangerous, not only because of diseases but also because of *samsengs*, gangsters that have no qualms if you cross them."

He shook his head sheepishly. "Legal ones," he said lamely.

Ah Chu sniffed again, pleased by his discomfort. She knew him as a family man. A family man indeed! She became openly contemptuous.

"You have to be more specific if I am to help you. Brothels are ranked; *pau chai* for fire cracker activities, in and out and takes no more time for a firecracker to go, or do you prefer leisurely overnight stays? There are also those falling in between. So what do you want? As for the type of *Ah Ku,* they are those that are owned by the *kwai poh* and they are generally called daughters, or those called *pong nin*, young ones indentured to *kwai poh*, to pay off parents debts or *tap tang*, voluntary prostitutes, who work on their own but make use of the premise of a brothel. They might well differ in the services they provide." She winked, her lips drawn back to reveal her teeth.

He stared at her mouth. He counted taking note a missing tooth. He couldn't speak.

"You are presumably talking about Chinese brothels," she said. She took measure of him. His face was craggy and thin, his hair grey and his moustache was just a shadow of what it had been when they first met. Yet there was vigour in his movement and his eyes were sharp. The old dog might still have some life in him, she thought in amusement. Suddenly another thought struck her. She wondered if he actually intended that Li Ling be sent to one and he was vetting them for that purpose. She did not believe his story about sending her back to China.

He shook himself. "No! *Uh ...Uh...*"

"You just have to be clearer." She was enjoying his discomfort.

"It doesn't matter." Ah Sook was getting more and more embarrassed. He realised that she was playing with him. In exasperation, he said: "Just give me a list of ten non-Chinese brothels."

Ah Chu eyes widened in surprise. Non-Chinese! She'd heard rumours. She kept them to herself. "What do I get in return?" she asked.

***

"Go on then, beat me. See if I care." Head jutted forward, teeth bared and with eyes sparking fire, Aishah spun round to face her mistress.

They were in Aishah's own room, situated beyond the kitchen and adjacent to that shared by Ah Sum and Ah Looi. Aishah had been confined there since the day Ah Tai and Ah Sook manhandled her away from Master Siew Loong. Worried as to what she might do, they had watched her like hawks.

"And why would I do that?" Rohani tried to be reasonable. She softened her voice. "Haven't we, I in particular, treated you well? I rescued you from your guardian. I could have sent you back to him; I didn't because I care for your well being."

"Yes!" Aishah whirled and flung her arm out. "And subjected me to this imprisonment. I hate and despise you. Hypocrite! It is I who tried to help you. I do not know what I have done wrong. Wasn't it you who wanted me to help your son's marriage?"

Rohani took a step back, shocked at the girl's venom. "But not to seduce him! And certainly not to seduce my daughter-in-law!"

Aishah's laughter pealed across the room, like a slap on Rohani's face. "Hypocrite!" she screamed. "Why are you shocked at something that is so natural? As for your pasty-faced daughter-in-law, no wonder Master does not want her. He wants me! If you had not barged in, he would have..."

Rohani's hand shot up. She slapped Aishah. In the next moment, she was contrite, sorry for her actions. She had not wished to do that. She had liked the girl, was fond of her, mistaking her for what she was not.

Suddenly Aishah grabbed a stool and crashed it to the floor. She held its broken leg and thrust it towards Rohani. Rohani jumped back.

"Mistress, mistress! Are you all right?" shouted the servants waiting outside the door. "Shall we come in?"

"I am fine. Wait outside," replied Rohani edging towards the door.

"I am sorry," she said to Aishah. She took a deep breath. She was sorry that it came to this, sorry that she lost her temper. She thought that she could talk sense into Aishah, make her change her mind, and see her errors. She was willing to give her another chance. But the girl was unstable. It was no use.

Ah Sook had briefed her on his conversation with Aishah. She could not believe what he said. He told her that Aishah wanted to go to Singapore. She wanted to set herself up like her mother. That was the life she knew. That was the life she claimed would give her the freedom she wanted, to enjoy what she liked most, an occupation that would lead her to a man who would appreciate her and keep her like her mother had been kept. He had brought Rohani a list of brothels that catered to foreigners, Arab traders and Europeans. She fished it out of her pocket.

"Ah Sook gave me this list. It is a list of brothels."

Aishah's eyes lit up. She grabbed the piece of paper and then she returned it to Rohani. "I can't read," she said.

"I'll let Ah Sook speak to you. I came mainly to talk you out of pursuing this route. Here," she said digging deep into her pocket again. She took a small pouch. "This is for you to set up on your own." With that Rohani left the room, barely able to conceal her sadness. What had she done? she asked herself. All she had succeeded in doing was to alienate her son and made an enemy of one whom she had become fond of.

Ah Sook came into the room immediately after his Mistress left. He held the piece of paper that Rohani had returned to him. Unlike his Mistress, he had no compunction about getting rid of Aishah and sending her away as far as possible. He did not bother with any preliminaries.

"There are some sixteen brothels located in Kampong Glam, Jalan Sultan, Arab Street and Sheikh Madersah Lane in Singapore," he said. "The ten in the list have been shortlisted. They take girls of other nationalities. They do not cater to the Chinese. I don't have all their addresses. But there is one in Malay Street owned by someone called Miriam. She might be the most suitable. It is adjacent to North Bridge Road. It is registered. The other European houses in Victoria Street might not accept you, a local girl."

He eyed Aishah coldly.

She smiled.

Chapter 37

"You look rested," remarked Jack when he came through the open doorway. Behind him the sun sank low until it almost disappeared leaving just streaks of light peeking through the tree tops and spilling on to the garden. He closed the door, his hat in his hand. Smiling fondly at his wife, he made his way round to the back of her chair. He lowered his face until it was next to hers'. He could smell her scent, a warm sweet smell mingled with something unidentifiable which he associated with the baby.

Shao Peng leaned into him and sank further into the cushions propped around her. She placed her hands round her belly and gave a satisfied sigh. "I am happy. I just got news that Li Ling is now safely settled with a lovely family who will care for her until the baby arrives. Ah Sook said that it would be dangerous for me to see her. It would arouse too much attention from her in-laws who do not know her whereabouts. He won't let me have any details on how he arranged her escape. He won't even tell me where she is now. I trust him though. He will do anything for our family and will do the best he can. Da Wei apparently is in prison. On top of it all, my stepmother sent me a message saying that my brother has finally come together with his wife Suet Ping. So at last, everything seems to be falling into place."

"Good! At last you can take a little rest and give the baby and yourself some time. I have been worried about you. We don't have long to go before the baby arrives."

He had passed Ah Sook on the way home. Da Wei, he was told, had been badly beaten up. His arm was broken and his kneecap smashed. It was unlikely that he would receive treatment for his injuries. He wondered where he would be held. There were no proper facilities in the city for holding prisoners. A site for the construction of a prison had only been identified a week ago. He had gone to see it with the Kapitan. It was a former Chinese burial ground set in a dense jungle area where tigers still prowled. The building of the prison would be slow. Large tracts of the surrounding jungle had still to be cleared. Until then, prison camps would be makeshift. Prisons were not generally used. Instead, capital punishment was meted out. It was more economical and was felt to be a better deterrent to crime. He didn't think that Da Wei would be imprisoned. It was more likely that he would be given the death penalty. He was not going to say anything to Shao Peng.

He patted her shoulders and straightened up. He could feel her bones; they were delicate like a sparrow's. He ran his finger along the deep depression behind her collar bones. She was always up and about caring for one cause or another. As Ah Sook said, it was best to keep everything from her so that she could rest and look after herself.

"Come! We should eat. Ah Kew has rung her dinner bell and a wonderful aroma is coming from the kitchen. We have to do her justice and I would like you to eat properly instead of picking at your food."

Shao Peng got up, one hand instinctively around her belly. "Ah Sook mentioned that Aishah had left. That is a surprise. Do you know where she is?"

Jack did not answer immediately. He grasped her arm gently and ushered her to the table. He pulled a chair out for her. "I heard she has left to set up a business. Your stepmother has helped her with some capital."

He walked over to his own seat. "Don't worry about Aishah. Don't beat yourself up over her anymore. Let it all go. Everything has turned out for the best."

Part Two

Thirteen years later

Chapter 38

JAMES POKED HIS HEAD out of the window and shouted. "They are here!" He jumped down from the window sill where he was seated and ran straight out of the room and down the stairs. He did not wait for his mother's reply. He ran past Ah Kew and skidded to a stop at the front door. "I have it," he shouted over his shoulder to Ah Kew. He wrenched open the door and stood there with a lop-sided grin on his face and his knee length socks squashed down to his ankles.

The two girls, one ten and the other eight, looked at each other and then turned to smile at him. Their eyes, the colour of melted liquorice, twinkled in amusement at the sight of the chestnut haired boy with freckles that spanned both cheeks. "Hello," they said shyly. They held on to each other's hands.

"Invite your cousins in," reprimanded Ah Kew coming from behind. "Where are your manners?"

"Mother will be here shortly," said the elder girl. "She has just stopped outside with grandma to look at the tree in your garden. She is talking to the gardener."

"*Aiyah!* It is far too hot for them to stay out in the garden. Let me get them an umbrella." Ah Kew grabbed an umbrella, a sea-green lacquered affair with bright yellow chrysanthemums, and hurried out leaving the three children alone.

James stepped aside to let his cousins in. Suddenly he felt shy. "Would you like some lime juice?" he asked awkwardly, remembering that this was what his parents would ask him on a hot day.

"No, thank you," replied Mei Fern, the elder. "No, thank you," said Mei Kwei, the younger of the two.

His cousins were extremely polite, he thought. James was at a lost as to what to do next. He had been looking forward to their visit ever since he was told that they were coming. Now that they were here, he did not know what to do. He was a lone child and did not have many friends.

Fern and Rose, so nicknamed because Fern was part of her name and Mei Kwei, in Chinese, meant Rose, saw their cousin's discomfort. They felt sorry for him. Instinctively, they tightened their hold of each other's hand. They had each other; James, however, had no siblings at all. They could not imagine being without each other. He had told them that he had longed for a brother or a sister. Ah Kew had chastised him when he pestered his parents about it. "Don't worry your mother," she had scolded. "You would just upset her." In a kinder tone she explained that his mother would not be able to have another child. "Too dangerous, too dangerous," she said. They remembered how upset he had been that day.

"Nothing to drink at all?" he asked again still wondering what to do next.

They shook their heads solemnly. "But we would like to see your train set. Grandma said that your dad bought you one."

His face brightened immediately. "Then come with me." He beckoned Fern and Rose into a room across the hallway. They followed him. James could hear the women coming in from the garden. Ah Kew was singing his cousins' praise to their grandmother. He left the door ajar.

"Such good girls. You taught them well. They don't speak until they are spoken to and never argue," she said enthusiastically. James knew that Ah Kew was thinking of him when she said the latter.

***

It was a beautiful light and airy room. Sunlight streamed through the tall sash windows, turning the dark teak floor into a mellow gold. On either side of the windows long pearly-white muslin curtains wafted and billowed with the breeze. The sweet smell of roses drifted in filling the warm moist air with their scent.

Shao Peng stood until her stepmother had taken a seat before settling down onto a chair beside her. Suet Ping followed suit, taking an armchair at the far end. Ah Kew came in with a tray laid with tea and biscuits. No one spoke. Ah Kew's voice filled the room. The ladies nodded and smiled at her chatter. She was old and had been such a loyal servant that they felt they owed it to her to listen. Ah Kew talked and commented on all and sundry. They waited patiently until Ah Kew left.

"How bad is it?" asked Shao Peng, the first to break the silence.

"Bad," was Rohani's solitary answer. She glanced across the room at Suet Ping. She was sitting in a corner with both arms cradled around her chest as though she needed to hug herself to find solace.

"Are you okay?" Shao Peng asked her sister-in-law.

Suet Ping's eyes, swollen and red-rimmed, met Shao Peng's for a second before they look away.

The hopelessness in Suet Ping's face tugged at Shao Peng's heart. Where was the beautiful bright young girl with sparkling eyes?

Rohani bent closer to Shao Peng. Shao Peng could feel her breath hot and urgent in her ear. "Siew Loong is spending nights away from the house even when he is in town. In recent months, these occasional nights have turned to weeks."

"Do you know where he spends them? Whom he spends it with?"

"I have my suspicions. Would you speak to him?"

"Me?!"

"No one else can. Certainly not Suet Ping. I can't either. I tried and I failed. I blame myself. I shouldn't have forced this marriage on them. The marriage is such an utter failure, not only in terms of the unhappiness it has caused but also..." Rohani sighed. "It has not even resulted in a male issue. It is eight years since Rose was born and still no sign of a baby, let alone a son."

"Suet Ping cannot have a baby on her own! How could she if he neglects her!" Shao Peng's voice was sharp. Rohani recoiled as though she had been slapped. Her eyes misted. Shao Peng took her stepmother's hand and squeezed it to reassure her. "I am sorry. I understand. You only wished them well."

"It is my fault. If I was able to have another son, then perhaps all the burden would not have been on Siew Loong," said Rohani. "But not to have a male issue! What will become of the business?"

They looked across at Suet Ping. She did not look back at them. She had the heel of her palm pressed against her forehead and her eyes were closed.

Suet Ping was hurt by the whispering and exchange between her mother and sister-in-law. She could guess what they were talking about. They blame me for Siew Loong's infidelity; they blame me for not producing a son, she thought.

***

From where Siew Loong stood, the rows upon rows of rubber trees were like never-ending regular criss-crosses. Whichever way he turned, the trees were there; neat, precise and upright, seven metres between rows and three metres between trees. The trees, now in their seventh year, were starting to produce. He heaved a sigh of relief. The milky white sap that could make or break his business empire. His white gold! He had invested heavily in rubber and establishing the estate had proved to be a long difficult haul, far longer than the seven years needed for it to mature and far more difficult than he had expected.

He moved towards a tree and reached out to touch its trunk. He brushed it gently and smiled. The latex collected in the cup was full to the brim. The trees had been cut with military precision in the early hours of the morning and their bark peeled back to allow the latex to flow. By tomorrow, the process had to be repeated all over again. He would have to commend the workers when he saw them later in the day.

His eyes swept across the plantation, marvelling at the tappers moving between trees under the dappled shade. Getting the right labour for the plantation had been difficult. The locals were not interested in the work. Mahmud proved unreliable. Despite his boasts about contacts in India, he failed to get sufficient numbers to come over to Malaya. Siew Loong severed his contract and tried to recruit coolies from China. A recruiting office was established in Southern China. It failed; the Chinese workers were more expensive and many were addicted to opium. With his new foreman, Naresh, a Tamil from Tamil Nadhu, he turned once more to India and Ceylon. This time he succeeded. Accommodation, however, had to be built on the estate to house the recruits and their families. This led to further delays. Unlike Chinese immigrants, Indian workers did not generally come alone with the objective of returning to their country. He had to invest heavily in penetrating and clearing large tracts of virgin jungle and secondary forests. Many areas were swampland infested with anopheles mosquitoes. Inevitably, the mortality rate was high.

He realised that more would have to be done to reduce the danger posed by malaria. He had lost a dozen men to the disease last year, not as bad as the neighbouring estate, but sufficient to cause alarm. He had to do something to mitigate these dangers for his workers. The basic infrastructure was just not there. There were no drainage or sewage systems and torrential tropical rains created the ideal conditions for tropical diseases. He expelled a huge sigh of frustration. Once again, plantations were left to pick up the pieces for the government had done little to improve sanitary conditions.

Siew Loong headed back to his office in the base camp. From a distance, he saw a thin figure waving at him. As he drew nearer, he saw that it was Ah Sook. Something must be wrong, he thought. He hastened forward, his feet pummelling the hard ground and spitting a cloud of red dust in his tracks. Within seconds, he was drenched in sweat. His shirt clung to him and perspiration poured from his forehead.

"Why are you here?" he shouted across the stretch of land that separated him from Ah Sook. "Is it mother? The children..."

"You have an urgent message from Naresh. He said that the coolies he recruited from Kerala have arrived. The Government has quarantined them at Port Swettenham. He failed to get their release and he is not sure how long they will be detained. He is worried. He said he visited the quarantine centre and saw thousands of men literally squashed together in indescribably filthy conditions. The Port authorities say that they cannot handle the huge number of people and they are going to send them to an island called Pulau Jejerak, to be held until such time they see fit. That island too has no proper sanitary facilities; it has just a handful of latrines to cater for the thousands. Cholera and smallpox are rife. A large percentage of the detainees held last year died. We cannot afford to lose our men."

"I'll come back with you to Kuala Lumpur. I'll see what I can do." Siew Loong strode past Ah Sook and headed for the car, a black ten horsepower De Dion with a canopied roof, his pride and joy. The older man followed.

"Your mother is asking for you," said Ah Sook.

Siew Loong stopped in his track. He whirled around to face Ah Sook. "I am not going home. Don't tell her I am in Kuala Lumpur. I need space. I have done what she wished me to do. I won't do more."

Chapter 39

SU HEI FLICKED HER long braid to the back and tipped her straw hat further forward to shade her face from the hot sun. She crouched down and began to weed the vegetable patch. She would have to do it quickly before her mother woke up from her nap. Her mother did not like her doing manual work. She had other plans for Su Hei, all of which, it would seem to Su Hei, revolved around not having the life her mother had. She did not know much about her mother's mysterious past life. All she knew was that her aunt Ah Chu complained that she had extra mouths to feed, mouths that did little work in return. Su Hei hated the charity so she would work whenever she was given a chance. Yet Ah Chu had been kind to her mother and her. Without Ah Chu, they would probably be back in China. "You wouldn't want to be there," they would tell her. "China is in turmoil, overrun by foreigners, each carving a slice of the country. The people are driven to opium addiction. If you think life is hard here, wait till you see China," they would say.

Su Hei sat back on her haunch and swept the weeds into a bucket. Looking up she saw trails of long green beans hanging overhead, their pods some two feet long swaying tantalisingly in the hot sun. She would pick some for supper, she decided. Ah Chu would like that.

"How many times have I told you not to be in the sun!" Li Ling shouted. "Come in, come in. I'll do that," she said wrenching the basket from Su Hei. "Sit over there in the shade."

"Mother, why don't you let me finish what I am doing?" Su Hei tried to snatch the basket back.

"Goodness! Look at your fingernails. Look at the dirt in them. I told you to keep your hands lily-white and smooth. Why do you not listen to me? Go! Wash them and put a bit of lard on. You don't want your hands to be rough."

"I don't mind," Su Hei protested. Her mother pushed her away.

The commotion brought Ah Chu out into the dirt backyard. "*Aiyah!* You can't protect her all the time. She wouldn't want for suitors if you would only allow her to have them. She is pretty enough with her big eyes and fine features. If Hui, Huan and Swee Yoke can find husbands with their background, you won't have a problem with Su Hei. Mind you, we had to be a bit inventive about their background."

Li Ling glared at Ah Chu. Over the years, the two had grown close. With her daughters gone, Ah Chu had increasingly turned to Li Ling for comfort. They shared a secret between them, their past involvement with the Ong family. Both felt that they should be part of that family. Both nurtured a resentment over their rejection. "I have plans, big plans for Su Hei," boasted Li Ling, her lips curled in disdain. "They do not include marrying my daughter to anyone just because they have a dime or two. Don't compare my daughter to yours. Keep out of my business!"

"Well, if you do not wish for advice, then you should really strike out on your own. No one is keeping you here," retorted Ah Chu. Stung by Li Ling's reply, she glowered with one hand on her hip and the other pointing to the door.

Li Ling threw the basket onto the ground and strode off. Su Hei looked with bewilderment from one woman to the other. She ran after her mother, turning back to mime and point to the basket and the beans scattered on the ground. "I'll take care of that later," she said. She mouthed a silent sorry and hurried after Li Ling.

***

Su Hei moved listlessly around the room. Finally she settled on a chair by the bed. Li Ling's eyes did not leave her daughter. She is like me, she thought with pride. She has my eyes, my nose and my mouth; she is my spitting image.

"Aunty Chu is very hurt. Why do you say such awful things to her? Are we leaving here? Where would we go? Where could we go?" Su Hei thought of what she had seen on the rare occasions her mother had taken her to town. The dirt and the squalor shocked her except, of course, if you were to live in those big houses owned by the very rich and by the English people who ruled over them.

Su Hei was frightened. She didn't want to leave. This was the only home she knew and aside from the odd moment, Aunt

Chu was kind. She couldn't blame Ah Chu for those occasional moments because her mother could be trying and very fierce. She didn't understand what her mother said. She spoke often in riddles. Her heart did a flip when her mother mentioned the *big plans* she had for her. What were they? She had often asked without ever receiving a reply. "You just wait and see," her mother would say.

"Don't worry about Aunt Chu. Look, why don't you go and say sorry to her from me. Say that I am indisposed, that I have one of my headaches. I'll come out to apologise later when things are a bit calmer. Go! Do that and I'll come out and help with the dinner. I want to be alone for a while."

Li Ling grabbed Su Hei's hand and pressed it to her lips. "I love you. I only want that which is best for you. Remember that."

When Su Hei's footsteps faded, Li Ling got up and went to the bed. She knelt down and reached under its wooden frame. She pulled out a pile of newspapers. They were damp and had yellowed with time. Their ink stained her fingers black. Carefully, she lifted the one on the top. Setting it on the floor, she flipped through the pages until she found what she wanted. In the centre of the page was a photograph of a man. She ran her fingers over his face, lingering on his lips, and smiled. "I'll never forget you," she whispered. "We were meant for each other."

Carefully, she tore the page and folded it, placing it alongside the others she had similarly torn from various newspapers. Later, when she had made amends with Ah Chu, she would ask her to read the news to her. Shao Peng was right in one thing. She should have learnt how to read. She wondered if she should make contact. It would surprise Shao Peng because everyone had believed that she, Li Ling, had returned to China. Yet would she want to surprise Shao Peng?

She got up and went to close the door. With infinite care, she turned the key; it squeaked in protest. She waited, half expecting someone to rush in to ask why she had locked the door. A minute or two passed. She mounted a stool and retrieved a little wooden box from the top of the wardrobe. From within it, she took out a little round jade pendant. The stone felt cool in her palm; its gold trimmings in the centre gleamed brightly against the deep green of the jade. Shao Peng had given her this. This was the only item that she had kept and hidden from Ah Chu. Her mind went back to the day when Ah Sook's men first deposited her in this house.

***

Thirteen years ago

It was a day when the heavens opened up and drenched my world, washing clean my soul so that I could be reborn. I stood shivering under the inadequate shelter of the banana tree. Its ragged palms swayed and slapped against me while the rain spat sharp and vicious against my body. A streak of lightning flashed across the sky and thunder bellowed, hammering my head with the force of its sound. Instinctively, I wrapped my arms around my middle to protect the baby within. It would be any time now. I prayed that it would not be then, for I was waiting for Ah Sook's men. Through Ah Su the maid, he told me to leave the house of my parent-in-law's. I was to take nothing with me and to inform no one. Ah Su would not tell. With the help of Ah Sook, she had vanished immediately after giving me the message.

I shivered and my teeth chattered. It could be the cold; it could be fear. I was frightened and elated all at the same time. At last I would be free. A spasm of pain hit me and I doubled up, clutching my tummy even more strongly. Please, please not now, I remembered praying when yet another spasm of pain hit me. Through the pelting rains, I saw two men in black hooded cloaks. It must be Ah Sook's men. I worried that they couldn't see me. I could hardly open my eyes, so strong was the rain. I opened my mouth to shout to them, to tell them I was here. My legs gave way, just as they approached and grasped me by my arms. I felt a flush of warm sticky liquid run down my legs to mingle with the pool of water collected in the puddle that I stood in. "The baby is coming," I whispered hoarsely. They dropped my arms in haste; they jumped away as if the puddle was a cesspit of snakes. I could see the disgust on their face. "Bad luck!" They made a sign to ward off evil. Women were unclean at childbirth and remained so for at least a month. They turned as though to leave me in the puddle. I screamed after them to help; I promised them extra reward; I threatened that Ah Sook would punish them if they did not carry out their instructions. They returned and grabbed me roughly under the arm. They dragged me; my feet trailed on the ground like wheel marks puncturing wet soil. They didn't stop. The rain would wash the marks away. It would be as though I had never been. They had arranged for me to disappear. They had arranged for me return to China as soon as the baby was born.

Su Hei was born in the wayside, just a hundred yards from Ah Chu. The men left me there. There were no passersby. The rain pelted and hissed. The men brought Ah Chu to me. By the time she arrived, Su Hei had made her appearance in the world. My screams, and her cries, muffled by the loud splatter of the rains.

***

Li Ling cleared up the dishes. Su Hei had gone to bed and Ah Chu was seated at the table, nursing a bowl of tea. She clasped the cup with both hands, her knuckles tightly pressed against it. She gave a loud sniff; her mouth tightened rendering her lips into a thin line that drooped at each corner. She had barely looked at Li Ling throughout the meal and was not going to do so now.

The light from the oil lamp flickered and the shadows on the wall lengthened and waned. Li Ling refreshed the pot of tea and brought it to the table. She reached over and gently extracted the tea bowl from Ah Chu. She poured more tea into the bowl and, placing it in front of Ah Chu, sat down. "I am sorry for earlier on." Her voice was honeyed and low. She looked from under her brows to check on Ah Chu's reaction.

"I am used to it," Ah Chu replied in a huff. She refused to look at Li Ling.

"I am truly sorry you know," said Li Ling, her voice syrupy like a velvet glove upon soft skin. "I am very grateful for all that you have done for me, for keeping me here, for covering for me, for not forcing me to return to China."

"You have a funny way of showing your gratitude." Ah Chu's sniff was even more pronounced this time. She glowered at the young woman. "You might think that the passage money you gave me covered all the expenditures heaped on you, but let me assure you it had long been spent. I've kept you here at my own expense."

"I know, I know."

"Look!" continued Ah Chu, ignoring the slight hardening of Li Ling's voice, "I am still having to rely on oil lamps when other houses on the street are beginning to have electric lights. I could have afforded it if my household expenses had not included feeding you and Su Hei."

"I said I am sorry."

"Then stop throwing such tantrums! You are only a young woman, barely twenty-eight years old. You still have your looks. You can marry again. Instead, you keep yourself to yourself and have such violent outbursts of anger, most of which are directed at me or poor Su Hei."

Li Ling's face was bitter when she stood up and unbuttoned her top. "Who would want me?" She shrugged, letting the back of her dress drop, and turned around. Brown weals criss-crossed her back like meat that had been pummelled and aged. She turned back to face Ah Chu once more, and released the front flap of her tunic. Ah Chu gasped. A part of a nipple was missing and burn marks scarred the other.

Ah Chu cleared her throat. She had never seen the scars until today. No wonder Li Ling refused her help to wash or dress, even when she was ill. "Don't give up hope. Maybe..."

"Don't try to console me. Who would want someone like me with such a history and such a body? I might have had a chance when there were no Chinese women around. That is no longer the case. You know it. There is an abundance of women now." Li Ling buttoned up her dress and went out of the room to return almost instantaneously. She sat down and placed a newspaper in front of Ah Chu. "Please read this for me," she said.

Ah Chu started when she saw the photograph. She looked up questioningly at Li Ling. "Why? she asked.

"Read it for me, please," Li Ling pleaded.

Ah Chu read silently. "It is about his business and how well he is doing. The gossip is that all is not well in his home life. In his recent venture to establish a labour recruiting office in China, he met a songstress in Hong Kong. He brought her back to Kuala Lumpur and has been seen with her. The rest is about his family, his wife Suet Ping and their two daughters, Fern and Rose."

Li Ling smiled and her eyes glittered with excitement. "He has no male offspring?"

Ah Chu looked at the date of the newspaper. "No, unless his wife is expecting one since the article."

"Then, would you help me?" Li Ling drew her chair closer to Ah Chu's and whispered in her ear. "You will help me won't you?"

Ah Chu thought for a while. Her silence magnified the buzz in Li Ling's ears, for each breath she took was exaggerated by a thousand syllables. Finally Ah Chu nodded.

Chapter 40

JACK SLIPPED OUT of his bedroom slippers and edged further up the bed until his back rested on the cool dark wooden headboard. Then he swung his legs up. Shao Peng, already in bed and waiting, snuggled up to him. Tucking an arm under the crook of his she buried her face in his chest and inhaled his familiar smell, comforted by his closeness.

"Rohani is worried about Siew Loong," she said brushing away a strand of grey hair from Jack's forehead. She marvelled that he should be greying and looking more distinguished with it, while her own grey hairs were coarse and unflattering. "He has not been home for a long time. He doesn't go home even when he is in town, she says. Do you know who he is with? Is he with that songstress from Hong Kong, Annie?"

"You shouldn't ask me to tell tales on your brother."

"*Hmmm!*" She gave him a sidelong disapproving look. "Ah Sook will never say a word about Siew Loong. I have only you whom I can ask. After all, you are now working closely with him. You cannot say, as in the past, that you are a civil servant and know nothing about the going-ons in the private world of business."

"Yes I can! We work in different areas. He deals with rubber and I take care of the tin mines."

"I am not asking you about the business. I am asking if you know who he is with at the moment."

Jack disentangled himself to face his wife. He saw the worry lines etched between her brows. "Precisely, at this moment? I do not know. Siew Loong does not confide in me about his liaisons. He thinks that I would pass the information to you. He is probably right in that respect. I am putty in your hands." He grinned.

She grabbed a pillow from behind her and pummelled him with it.

"Be serious! Suet Ping is terribly upset. Something has to be done. Siew Loong's infidelities are becoming too much to ignore."

"You should not interfere. It is no worse today than it was a week ago or a month ago or even a year ago. It has been going on for some time. Suet Ping and Rohani have closed their eyes to it before. Why are they choosing to address this problem now?"

"Because ... because Rohani is not well. She wants to see my brother settled before she d... She wants him to have a son. She wants a grandson."

"Annie is just one of many. He has been careful in not tying himself to any particular woman. He just enjoys their company, I was told."

"Where does he spend his nights?"

Jack placed his hands on her shoulders and held her at arm's distance. "Dear wife, your brother works. Sometimes he spends them in the plantation campsites. There is always a camp bed in the office there. In Kuala Lumpur, he has a small bedsit next to his new office. He works sometimes till the small hours of the morning. You do not get to where he is now without hard work. Your brother must be one of the most industrious people I know. There are occasions when he spends them with a woman, I am sure. Where exactly I do not know and do not wish to know."

"I want to talk to him."

"Please don't. He wouldn't appreciate it. He is having problems with his new batch of workers from India. He is not in a good mood. I can tell."

Jack drew Shao Peng to him and kissed the top of her head. "Please direct your thoughts to what I said about James's education. We have to decide. He has fast outgrown the tutor and us."

Thank God, he thought, that we have James. He could not understand the Chinese obsession with male offspring. If we had a girl instead of a son, Shao Peng would not give up trying no matter the repercussions on her health, no matter that the doctor said that it would be dangerous at her age.

***

The following morning Shao Peng went to Chinatown. "How it has changed," she mused. She got out of the car in High Street. Under the blazing sun, a couple of motor-cars and bicycles ran alongside trishaws and bullock carts that were still in use. "Well, all except for our house," she murmured to herself, for the Ong mansion remained *in situ*, virtually the same except for the addition of another extension, turning what was previously a long mansion to one that was L-shaped. A low wall separated it from the narrow two storey shop houses in High Street. These shop houses lined the street cheek by jowl, taking over the land which had previously housed the tapioca mill. Her brother had had the mill moved to the outskirts of the town. The price of land had shot up in the town centre and building shop houses in place of the mill was too good an opportunity for Siew Loong to pass over.

Shao Peng went straight up to Rohani's rooms. She found her with Suet Ping.

"Any news?" they asked.

Shao Peng shook her head.

The light went out of Suet Ping's face leaving only dark shadows under her eyes, eyes that were puffy from lack of sleep and crying. Shao Peng's heart went out to her. She took Suet Ping's hands. "Siew Loong is working very hard and spends a lot of time in his office. He is having problems with the immigration authorities. His new recruits are stranded in the quarantine centre. His absence could be just that."

Suet Ping pulled her hand away. She made no reply. The lie hung uncomfortably between them. The papers this morning told a different story. He had been seen with someone else.

"Perhaps," Rohani said very slowly, "we should think of another tactic. I understand that in Chinese custom, it is the wife's duty to find her husband another concubine if she fails to produce an heir."

Two bright spots of red appeared on Suet Ping's face. Shao Peng turned to her stepmother in horror.

"I am only airing all the different options. At least then, we know our enemy. Hopefully, it would also be someone we could control, someone indebted to us."

"You don't have to agree to this," Shao Peng said to her sister-in-law, alarmed at the desperate sadness and hurt in her face.

Rohani hurried over to Suet Ping. She placed an arm around her. "Come, come, I am only examining all the options. You don't have to agree. I just thought that it would at least mean that he comes home and Fern and Rose could see their father. If we choose well, it would also mean that you would have an ally instead of an unknown rival. Think about it. It is just a suggestion. I am not forcing you."

With a sob, Suet Ping ran from the room.

"That was not at all kind." Shao Peng shouted at Rohani. "How would you feel if you were in her place?"

"In truth," shouted back Rohani, "I would feel terrible."

"You should retract what you said and apologise. Why don't you talk to Siew Loong? Why do you place the entire burden on her?"

"I can't talk to Siew Loong. I have tried. He avoids me. He blames me for this situation. I blame myself for this situation. I thought that with time, he would grow to love Suet Ping. She is such a nice sweet girl. How could he not love her?"

"Maybe he does not like nice sweet girls!" Exasperated, Shao Peng's thoughts went back to the day, some fourteen years ago, when she accompanied the women she had brought over from China to the Convent. She recalled the way her brother had looked at Li Ling; she had never seen him look at his wife in the same way. Li Ling was saucy, rebellious and feisty, all that Suet Ping was not. Yet he had gone on with the marriage. He thought it was his duty to be a filial son.

Rohani clutched at her chest. Her face went deadly pale. Her eyes rolled and her mouth sagged.

Shao Peng rushed to Rohani and caught her in her arms. "Ah Tai! Suet Ping! Help!" she screamed.

***

Suet Ping sat with Fern and Rose until they were asleep. The rise and fall of their sweet breath in the quiet of the bedroom was like a refuge in a storm. They had been restless. Suet Ping brushed aside the damp tendrils of hair from her children's face. The whole household had been restless following Rohani's heart attack.

Suet Ping snuggled close to her two daughters. She loved them. Yet the longing for a son, a baby boy to hold and love, was so strong, it wrenched her heart. Involuntarily, her hand went to her stomach. She believed that a boy child would help her regain her husband's affection. "For surely it was my barrenness, my inability to give him a son that lost me my husband's love," she said to herself. She blushed, recollecting the encounter with her husband outside her mother-in-law's room.

Siew Loong had returned home and stayed with his mother the whole day. Suet Ping caught him briefly before he left. He would have brushed past her if she had not placed a restraining hand on his arm to stay him. He was abrupt. She wanted to speak to him yet found it impossible to say all that she wanted to say under the circumstances. She became tongue-tied, he irritated.

The initial years of her marriage had not been bad. Siew Loong was kind and attentive. The two girls came in quick succession. Then, despite attempt after attempt, she was not able to conceive, let alone bear a boy. She sensed her husband's increasing coldness. Their love making, even to her inexperienced eyes, became totally mechanical. One day, Siew Loong stayed away from home the whole night. The occasional night became more frequent; they turned into days at a stretch, and in recent months even longer.

The room was shrouded in darkness. Suet Ping made no attempt to turn on the light. She tried to lose herself in the dark; she tried to let the dark to calm her mind. It would not stay quiet. Rohani's words that it was her duty to find her husband a concubine played over and over in her head.

Chapter 41

LI LING KEPT VERY STILL. Everyday, for the past week, she had come to this spot and waited. Rain or shine, she would be in the covered walkway fronting the double storey shop houses hoping for a chance to see Siew Loong emerge from the mansion opposite. People passed by and looked at her curiously. Shopkeepers viewed her with suspicion. She was there when they opened their store, she was there when they shut it. Often they would pointedly urge her to leave.

Siew Loong was never far away from her thoughts. She treasured every glance he had given her, every conversation they had had. They replayed in her mind through all the years of hardship and suffering. With time, these isolated incidents bloomed and acquired even greater meaning. She kept all her thoughts to herself. She would hoard newspaper pictures and articles of him. She knew little of Siew Loong's life apart from what was conveyed by the pictures. The words in the newspapers meant nothing. She could not read. She had tried to stifle her feelings and had kept away from him. She thought it would hurt too much if she were to see him. She thought that he would not want her. Yet she hankered to have some connection that would bind her to him forever and this became a dream that kept her spirit alive. When Ah Chu read her the newspaper cutting, Li Ling felt that her fate had arrived. So now, she wanted desperately to see him, to know if her feelings were still true.

A car swept past and came to a halt. Li Ling held her breath. A man alighted. She took a step forward. He turned and stared past her. Li Ling gasped. Siew Loong did not see her. He was preoccupied by his mother's illness and had hurried home from Port Swettenham. He made his way with long loping strides towards the house. Ah Sook came out to greet him. The old man bowed and when he straightened he happened to look across the road, straight at Li Ling. Li Ling stepped back quickly behind a pillar. Ah Sook remained with his eyes fixed across the road, a puzzled expression on his face. Then with a resigned shrug, he turned and followed Siew Loong.

Li Ling held her breath half expecting the old man to cross over in pursuit of her. When Ah Sook turned away, she felt a flood of warm relief. Her heart did a multiple of flips before it settled to a ragged beat. Siew Loong was all that she had remembered and much more. He was not the young lanky man in her dreams; he was filled out and hardened. She counted. He must be thirty-one!

She emerged from behind the pillar and looked across the fast departing backs of Siew Loong and Ah Sook. From the balcony another figure appeared. She recognised her. Suet Ping! A sharp stab of jealousy hit Li Ling. It was unreasonable. It was unjust, she knew. Yet, why, why should Suet Ping have him? She didn't deserve Siew Loong. She wasn't even able to give him an heir. Perhaps, the curses she had heaped on Suet Ping worked. Perhaps, it was fate and the time had come for Li Ling to lay her claim.

***

That night, Li Ling took hold of her daughter's hand and led her into the courtyard. She lit a lamp. A glow like warm melted butter cloaked them. In the open sky above, the moon peeked out from behind a cloud like a huge silver ball come out to play.

"Up there," Li Ling said, "is the moon maiden waiting for her lover. Can you see the shadow within the moon? That is Chang'e. She has waited four thousand years to see her husband. Her love, however, will be unrequited. She made a mistake. She was greedy; she swallowed the entire elixir of immortality instead of sharing it with her husband. As a result, she floated up to the heavens and into the moon where she was condemned to wait for eternity for her husband, a mortal. Each year on the fifteenth day of the eight month of the lunar calendar, women pray to the Moon Goddess. They generally pray for a good husband. Tonight, you and I will pray that she will grant us our love for she understands the pain of being separated. My love who will be your love. You and I, one heart."

Su Hei looked uncomprehendingly at her mother. Li Ling's face was serene. Her eyes were closed and a smile played on her lips. Su Hei was happy that her mother was happy. "Shall I bring out the joss sticks?" she asked scrambling to her feet.

"I have them here and more," said Ah Chu emerging from the house. She balanced a tray on a makeshift table. From the tray, she laid out a plate of mooncakes, some joss sticks and an incense holder. Next to these, she added a plate of water chestnuts resembling black buffalo horns. Then looking very solemn, she took out a needlework box. From it she took out a reel of cotton and a needle. She cut a length of the cotton.

"Here, Su Hei. Kneel down. I will light some joss sticks, which you must offer to the Moon Goddess. When they are lit and you have kowtowed three times, I shall place them in the holder. Then I want you to take this needle and thread it with this cotton, like so." Ah Chu, took the needle and held it over her head with the thread in the other hand.

"How can I thread the needle if I can't see the eye of the needle?"

"You will be guided by the Goddess, if she wishes to grant you her blessing. If you succeed, it will be the omen your mother is looking for."

Su Hei Looked at her mother and was struck by the dreamy expression on her face. Li Ling's eyes were closed. For once, her mother was tranquil. She had to try for her mother. Su Hei picked up the needle. The needle's aperture was not overly small. She held it above her head and with the other hand, she tried to aim the cotton. She missed. She tried again, and yet again she missed. Suddenly she felt Ah Chu's hand guiding hers. Su Hei looked at her mother who still had her eyes closed. "Is it done?" asked Li Ling, a smile still lingering on her lips.

"Perfectly," replied Ah Chu.

***

The music finished with a flourish. Ann Ee (nicknamed Annie by her Western clients) ran her fingers nimbly down the *pipa*, plucking and vibrating the strings of the lute with her right hand. She looked up demurely through her lashes at the men seated around her and smiled, her eyes engaging each of them in turn. She made everyone feel that the song was for them and them only. "This one," she said looking directly at Siew Loong before sweeping her eyes to include the other four men and returning them on Siew Loong, "is for you." Picking up the *pipa*, she began to sing; her melodious voice rose and fell. The room fell silent.

Siew Loong leaned back on the cushions, losing himself in the music that floated across the room. A girl came in, swaying gently on her bound feet, with a tray of drinks and placed it on the low table. She knelt down and from the depths of a lacquered basket took out a hot towel. The air was instantly filled with the warm scent of jasmine. She placed the towel on Siew Loong's forehead and began to massage his neck. Her long slim fingers caressed and kneaded. They moved on to his shoulders. Siew Loong could feel the knots in his back yielding to the pressure of her fingers. He inhaled deeply the scented towel; she replaced it immediately with a fresh one, moving it this time to his neck. He smiled, his eyes hooded and relaxed. For the first time that day, he felt the cares and pressures of the day lifted from him. He knew it would not last long, but for that moment he would enjoy all the pleasures afforded to him.

The music finished. He felt the brush of satin skirts on his forearm, a cheek against his. "Did you not like my song?" whispered Annie in his ear. Her breath was warm against his cheek. He could smell her perfume.

Siew Loong placed an arm around her waist and drew her closer. "Of course! Where are the others?" he asked.

"I sent them away," she pouted prettily before sitting on his lap. She waved away the girl, whose hands were still poised around Siew Loong's neck. She didn't need a rival. The maid had served her purpose. She wanted to be alone with Siew Loong. She nuzzled closer to Siew Loong and rested her head on his shoulder. "Would you like me to rub your back? Come, come to the bedroom. We would be more comfortable."

"*Ahhh!* The bedroom!"

"Are you going to refuse again? I might not invite you any more. Any of your friends tonight would have jumped at the chance. And you know I don't invite just any one to my bedroom." Annie's eyes sparkled and teased even as she scolded. Her hands caressed his face, lingering on his lips, and then his throat, and then lower. His body responded. That was what Siew Loong liked about her. She never nagged like Suet Ping or his mother. She always accepted whatever he wished to do. Her coquettish charm won more battles for her than the threats and fights waged by his mother and wife. Perhaps battle was too strong a word to use for Suet Ping. She never fought for her rights. He wished that she would. Her acquiescence annoyed him. In bed, the same submissive attitude killed his passion. He hated the injured look on her face. What Annie lacked in looks, she more than made up with her passion and her ability to sense his moods.

She got up and pulled him to his feet before swaying to the bedroom. He watched the way she sashayed, the soft rustling sound of satin against the roundness of her buttocks. She looked back, a knowing smile full of promise on her lips. He sighed and followed her in.

/ ***

Sun streamed into the bedroom through a gap in the curtains. In the spiral of light dust swirled like snowflakes. The air was heavy with the incense of the previous night and the lingering smell of sex. In the vast canopied bed, two people lay entwined. Siew Loong, deep in sleep, had one arm flung out wide, his legs spread-eagled beneath hers. His chest, smooth and bare, rose and fell. The corner of his mouth quirked; he turned to his side. His hand reached out. "Li Ling," he murmured. She appeared before him, her hair spread out like a silken curtain. She smiled and the dimples in both cheeks deepened. He reached out to touch it.

"It's me," Annie said, bending over him, her hair cascading down to his chest.

***

Li Ling looked on, eyes bright with pride. Within the space of a month, she saw her daughter transformed into a woman. Her hair was a sheen of black, her brows plucked like the wings of a phoenix and her skin, pale and smooth like a peach. Under her watchful eye, Ah Chu taught Su Hei everything she deemed essential to be a dutiful daughter-in-law. "Win your mother-in-law's heart, and you will win your husband's affection. Of course," she smirked, "other skills are also required and I have asked Hui and Huan to help out. They were masters in their trade when they were young. You, little girl," Ah Chu tapped Su Hei's head, "need all the skill you can get. You face great competition. Ann Ee is famous for her charms, a true courtesan, a *Shuyu*, adept in singing, the flute, the *pipa*, and story telling. She makes men fight for her. They court her though she does not necessarily bestow her favours on them. All this lends more spice and urgency to their quest to win her."

"Wait!" interrupted Li Ling. She did not like what she was hearing. She took Ah Chu aside. "I am not sure I want Su Hei to be competing with this Ann Ee on such a platform. Siew Loong loved me when I was an innocent young girl. He will be looking for such traits in Su Hei. It won't be another courtesan that he will be seeking."

"All men want the same thing. Believe me. A little art in love does no harm."

From the corner of the room Su Hei observed the two women in close consultation, their heads together. From time to time they looked her way. She blushed. Her mother seemed a renewed woman in the past month. She was energetic, she was loving; at times she was tearful, holding Su Hei at arms' length before clasping her to her bosom. Su Hei couldn't quite make out what was happening. Whatever it was, it was better than the mother she knew of old, the one who was lifeless and bitter. There was such hope in her mother's eyes now. She shone with excitement. Surely, Su Hei thought, I must do whatever it takes to make her happy.

Chapter 42

SHAO PENG HELD THE letter with trembling hands. She read its contents, not once, not twice, but three times. She could hardly believe it. Li Ling had sent her a letter after all these years. She had given up hope of ever hearing from Li Ling for all the letters she had sent her had been returned unread.

Jack put down the book he was reading. The rustle of paper and the silence following it intrigued him. His wife normally volunteered information and snippets from whatever she was reading. At times it was like being in a room with a running commentary. He looked at her covertly. She was breathing hard. He saw how she licked her lips. Her mouth was slightly opened and under the light of the lamp, the irises of her eyes deepened to dark chocolate.

"Bad news?" he asked.

She shook her head, eyes wide with uncertainty, for she still could not believe that it was true. "I've got a letter from Li Ling."

Jack put his book down and went over to his wife. "Really? She wrote?"

"Someone, probably a professional letter writer, wrote on her behalf. It is filled with rather flowery and stilted language. Nevertheless, it came from Li Ling."

"How wonderful!" Jack took her hand. "Aren't you glad, happy even? What does she say?"

"She is in good health and is in China. She has sent her daughter Su Hei over to Malaya. She might well be here in Kuala Lumpur or at least will be here soon. Li Ling said that Su Hei will be lodging with Ah Chu, the woman who gave her temporary shelter before she returned to China."

Jack looked blankly at her. "Ah Chu? Do we know her?"

"I do. She was the mother of the women my father was involved with when he was alive. Although I did not know it at that time, I found out later that she was also the one that Ah Sook contacted to give shelter to Li Ling when we rescued her from her husband. I suppose it is logical that Li Ling would contact Ah Chu now since she must have formed some sort of relationship with the woman."

"What was the purpose of sending her daughter here?"

"She said that she wanted Su Hei to have the education that she herself so foolishly rejected. She asked me to help her."

Jack's face fell. "You can't. At least not for long."

"Why not?"

Jack got up. He went to a cabinet and, from a drawer, took out a box. In it was a stack of photographs. He spread them out on the table. "I have been meaning to talk to you about this but we were overtaken by events. You have been so distraught these last weeks with your stepmother ill and the situation with your brother that I couldn't bring myself to talk to you about it."

Shao Peng leaned over the black and white photographs on the table. They were grainy and yellowed with age. She saw that many were pictures of houses and streets; tall brick houses, some four storeys high, with long windows overlooking narrow streets lined with trees. They had little wooden gates in front with narrow cobbled paths leading up to the front doors. In one picture, a church with tall sloping roofs and a steeple sat at a corner; adjoining it was a rambling house with the sign, *The Vicarage*. Another showed a playing field with nodding heads of daffodils at its perimeter. In yet another, a game of cricket was being played on a lawn that was as smooth as silk. Mixed in the midst of these pictures was one with a pony cart. Huge urns and crates of milk bottles sat in the middle of the cart; the milk bottles gleamed white against the black and grey in the background. At the bottom of the stack was a picture of a couple: the man had a moustache and long sideburns. On the bridge of his long nose sat a pair of round glasses. The woman had crimped dark hair drawn back from a serious pale round face.

"My mother and father, as you know, and this is me at twelve during the school holidays." He fished out of the pile yet another photograph. "I went to Yorkshire Society School at Mead Place, a school for Yorkshire-born boys before going to London University. Then as you know, I came to Malaya to join the Straits Settlements Civil Service as a junior cadet."

Shao Peng took the photographs reverently. They conveyed a picture of serenity and order, of milky grey light where the sun was dim, of cold and frost, and the incredible loveliness that had always caught her imagination when she was a young woman reading avidly the books from Uncle Grime's library in Singapore. "Why are we looking at these?" she asked.

"This would be where we would be living if we agree to return to the UK. This might be a school that James could attend, unless we decide to send him to a boarding school. The house in the centre is one I have inherited from my parents. For that reason, we can't get too involved with schooling for Li Ling's daughter."

Shao Peng's hand fluttered to her neck. She swallowed.

"We have to decide James's future and also ours. We could return to England and make a new life. The time is right. I feel that it might be better for James in terms of education. I have an opportunity to join the Civil Service in England as an old Malaya hand."

Jack took his wife's hand in his. "We have been postponing this discussion. We need to have it."

Shao Peng nodded. She realised that a decision had to be made. It was essential that James attend a proper school. Their attempt to send him to the private school run by Mrs Hurth, the wife of a coffee planter, had been a total failure. Instead he had a tutor instead and they had supplemented this by taking turns to teach him. This had to change.

Jack had broached the subject many times. Yet she grappled with the hope that it could once again be put aside. How could she pack and leave when her stepmother was ill, especially when she was the cause of it? How could she leave when her brother seemed to have thrown caution to the wind in his personal life? How could she refuse poor Li Ling? Wasn't it what she wanted for her? Yet how could she refuse Jack? How could she not leave for the sake of her son, James?

"You cannot always live the life of others," Jack said reading her thoughts.

"Is that what you would like? To leave here?" asked Shao Peng.

Jack's voice wavered. He knew his wife. She always put someone else first, before herself. He did not want to force her. He wanted her to make the right decision. He weighed his words, hoping to find the right balance. "If I am to eventually return to England," he said, "then I would like us to go now when we are not too old. If you wish us to stay and make our life permanently here, then I will. Your brother has suggested that I look into coal mining in Rawang. We are taking the railway to the north and the south of Kuala Lumpur to service the rubber estates. Soon the railway would branch off to the east coast of the peninsula. The discovery of coal in Rawang offers a good investment opportunity."

Jack saw how Shao Peng's face brightened at the latter narrative. He realised that he had over-played the positive aspect of staying and worried that she would interpret it as something that he wished. He backtracked. "The most important consideration, of course, is James's education. I think we have been leaving it rather late. He should go to a proper school."

Shao Peng grasped the lifeline he threw at her. "We have of course the Victoria Institution that we could consider," she said. "Kapitan Yap Kwan Seng, with the help of Mr. Loke Yew and Mr. Pillay, has made this a very viable and good school modelled after the Raffles Institute in Singapore. Could that not be a possible alternative? "

Jack's reservation showed in his face. He did not reply.

Shao Peng saw the flicker in his eyes. She understood. She must give way. She must not be selfish. "You are right. We should seriously consider leaving. It would be best for James. In which case, I will have to think of another way of accommodating Li Ling's wishes." She busied herself rearranging the photographs, her head bent to hide the emotion in her face. She told herself that Jack had given her so many years in Malaya. It was time she gave him back what he wanted. Jack placed an arm around her. The pressure of his fingers was reassuring. She hid her face in his shoulder. His shirt was soon wet with her tears.

***

The following morning, before the first glimmer of sun, Shao Peng was up. She slipped out of bed leaving Jack sound asleep. The house was silent except for the ticking of the clock. Thrusting both arms into a silk wrap, she made her way to the kitchen. Her feet padded silently down the short flight of steps and onto the tiled flooring in the kitchen. It was cold. The back door leading to the kitchen garden was flung open and a cool wind blew in bringing with it the damp green smell of dawn. She went swiftly to the door to close it. Ah Kew appeared at the doorway before she reached it.

"*Aiyah!* What are you doing up so early?" Ah Kew demanded. The maid shook off the wooden clogs she was wearing outside the doorway and came into the kitchen barefooted. "Are you not well?" She frowned, closing the door behind her. "I went out to get some spring onions from the garden for this morning's breakfast." She thrust the bunch in front of her; they were fresh green with the dew on them. Bits of earth clung to the roots.

"I just wanted a cup of tea. I have been up for ages."

"Sit down and I'll make you some." Ah Kew placed a big iron pot on the stove and busied herself stripping the outer leaves of the green shoots before running water over them to get rid of the dirt. "I'll get on with the porridge while we wait for the water to boil." She took a pot from the cupboard and ladled a cup of rice grains into the pot. After washing the rice, she stirred in a pinch of salt and a big spoonful of sesame oil. "I prepared the chicken broth last night and it is bubbling nicely. I'll add it to the rice now and let it boil until all the grains are broken up and the broth thickened to a lovely pouring consistency. Then it is ready for eating. The pieces of chicken meat and the thousand year old eggs," pointing to the dish of eggs the colour of black treacle at the sideboard, "go into the porridge when you are ready to eat. Would you..."

"I have news from Li Ling," Shao Peng interrupted Ah Kew's stream of chatter.

Ah Kew hit the cleaver on the wooden chopping board with a loud crunch; the knife dug deep into the board. She darted a quick look at Shao Peng. Her eyes narrowed into slits; deep creases radiated from their corners like spokes in a wheel. "What does she want?" Her voice was frosty with disapproval. The girl, she thought, was nothing but trouble.

"Aren't you going to ask how she is?" asked Shao Peng, surprised by the animosity.

"Well, how is she?" Ah Kew didn't give Shao Peng time to answer. "Don't get involved with her again. She has brought you endless problems, remember!" Ah Kew resumed the dicing of the spring onions. The cleaver went at reckless speed leaving a trail of tiny bits of green and white on the wooden board. With a flourish, she picked up the whole lot with the side of her cleaver and deposited them in a little dish. Her displeasure manifested itself in her wielding of the knife.

"Don't be too harsh on her. She was just a young girl."

"Young? Not that young! Old enough to ensnare a man. People talk. I hear things in the market."

"Don't be silly. She just wants me to help her daughter learn. What could be wrong with that?" Shao Peng regretted mentioning Li Ling's name. She hoped that she would not get the same reception when she saw Rohani later that morning. "I am going to dress now. I'll have the tea later," she said.

Ah Kew shook her head. "My mistress never learns."

Chapter 43

Rohani was propped up in bed. Her once abundant hair, now streaked with white, was left unbound. The tortoiseshell comb that held her hair lay abandoned on the table by the side of her bed alongside a glass of water and bottles of medicines. Her hands, thin like a bird's and mottled, lay lifeless on the bed cover. From time to time, she would dab at her eyes. Children's voices floated up from the garden. She looked forlornly out of the window. She saw James's kite swirling outside the window rising higher and higher until it disappeared completely from her view. Shrieks of laughter followed it. They were Fern's and Rose's.

Another tear rolled down Rohani's cheeks. Soon, James too would disappear from her life, along with Shao Peng and Jack. How could she bear it? She had as good as lost her only son, Siew Loong. After the initial days of her illness, his visits had again become few and far between. It was all her fault. She could only blame herself for the unhappiness she had caused everyone. Poor Siew Loong. Poor Suet Ping. Poor Rose and Fern. Would they ever forgive her when they grew up and learnt the truth of her actions.

Perhaps she should consider Shao Peng's proposal. She could at least put right the wrong she did to Li Ling by taking her daughter in and giving her the education she sought. It would be a start to her atonement. It would, after all, not be much of a problem. Shao Peng had promised that she would make all the arrangements for schooling before she left. If Su Hei went to the same school as Fern and Rose, then the logistics of sending her there would be simple. She must make amends for her sins. She did not realise the full scale of Li Ling's sufferings until this morning when Shao Peng told her. Poor girl.

She lifted the bed cover and placed her feet on the floor. Her legs felt shaky, as though they could not remember what they were for. She rose slowly, holding on to the bed's edge. Through the window, she saw the kite bob down before swooping up again, its colourful tail swishing through the air. How wonderful, she thought, if I were to be like the kite. She reached for her walking cane. With infinite care she walked to the window and looked out to the garden. Fern and Rose were running after James as he tugged and pulled on his kite. Soon there would be just Fern and Rose. Would Siew Loong ever return to his wife? Would he give her a grandson? If not, she was to blame for ending the family's bloodline. There would be no heir to carry the family name. Ngao would not forgive her, if he were alive.

***

"No! This would be better." Li Ling held up a garment for Ah Chu's inspection. "See here!" She fished out a grainy photograph taken when she first arrived in Malaya. Shao Peng had arranged for the picture as a memento. It showed Li Ling, Lai Ma and Jing-jing sitting in a row. Lai Ma was in the centre looking stiff and self conscious; Li Ling was on her left and Jing-jing on her right. Both were staring straight at the camera without a hint of a smile. Shao Peng, her lips slightly apart as though caught unaware, stood behind them in a loose Mandarin collared ensemble with frog buttons running down one side of the bodice.

Ah Chu peered closer at the photograph. Li Ling had on a plain looking *samfoo*. Its low stiff collar was buttoned up at the neck; the trousers, wide at the bottom, were of the same material. The dress was completely shapeless.

"Mine was pink, although you can't see the colour from this photograph. We should make a couple of these dresses for Su Hei. I want her to look like me when I was young."

Ah Chu sniffed; her nose twitched as though she had smelt something bad. She looked at the photograph again. It was true that Li Ling was very pretty despite her glum face. But it was unthinkable to make Su Hei wear those awful clothes. She pointed at the dress. "Not very flattering. It is not stylish is it? How would Su Hei compete with Ann Ee who owns a wardrobe that can fill this room. I was told Ann Ee wears only brocades and silk. Colourful clothes: gold, reds as vibrant as the hibiscus flowers in our garden or as deep as red roses; lush green that conjures up the scent of forests. How could the pink you describe do anything for Su Hei?"

"Didn't I say that we are not competing with that woman? I want Su Hei to be me when I was young." Li Ling lowered her voice and cast an anxious eye at her daughter seated within earshot. "I want him to fall in love with me all over again. Can't you see that?"

Ah Chu saw the tremble in Li Ling's lips. She sighed. "Fine! Fine! I understand." At times she wondered if Li Ling was becoming a bit crazy. She had gone along with the idea because of the grudge she bore against the Ong family. Now she wasn't sure if she had done the right thing. What started as a bit of prank seemed to be growing into something bigger.

Li Ling rushed over to Su Hei. She snatched a hairbrush from the dressing table and began brushing Su Hei's hair. She applied the brush vigorously, stroke after stroke until the hair crackled. Her eyes shone with fervour. "I think we should do something to make her hair more beautiful. Do you think we should oil it just a tiny bit?" She ran her fingers through her daughter's hair and twisted it right and left. "I had my hair braided when I was young. Su Hei should have it done the same way. Here, help me do the other side and let's see if she looks like me in the photograph."

They braided Su Hei's hair; then they dressed her in a pink *samfoo.* "There! What do you think? Li Ling stepped back and looked at Su Hei with satisfaction.

Su Hei kept still as a mouse while the two women fussed and argued around her. Her mother was looking happy. She wondered what was to become of her. Both women had assured her that they had her best interests at heart. "When I was young and foolish," said her mother, "I refused to go to school. It was a big mistake on my part. I do not wish that to happen to you. You will get a chance to learn and possibly marry a man who any girl in town would jump at the chance to marry."

"What if I don't like him?" Su Hei had asked.

Her mother had looked shocked at the suggestion. "How could you not if you were my daughter? You are my blood. You are me. Oh my beloved daughter. You will love him and he you."

Su Hei was frightened by the intensity of her mother's eyes. Her whole face seemed animated. "You will, you will," Li Ling assured Su Hei grasping her arms. Su Hei's skin tingled from the heat of her mother's hands.

***

A week later, Ah Chu brought Su Hei to the Ong's household. Shao Peng was expecting them.

"This is Su Hei, Li Ling's daughter. She has only just arrived from China and is still finding her way around." Ah Chu ushered Su Hei forward, her knuckles digging into the small of the girl's back giving her no opportunity to resist. "If you don't mind, I'll take leave now," she said to Shao Peng. "I don't want to take up too much of your time."

Su Hei turned in panic and grabbed Ah Chu's hand. "Don't leave, not yet," she pleaded.

Ah Chu gave Su Hei a look warning her not to say anymore. "You'll be all right. I'll come to see you when I can."

Turning back to Shao Peng, she explained. "She is just shy. She'll be fine. I am sorry to leave so abruptly but I have urgent matters to attend to at home." Ah Chu did not wish to stay a minute longer because she did not want to answer awkward questions. She deduced her past dealings would not endear her to the household. She especially did not want to chance seeing Rohani. She placed a folded letter in Shao Peng's hand. "Su Hei brought this with her from China. I am sure you will find all the information you need in it."

The words passed over Shao Peng's head. She stood speechless, transfixed with her hand clasping the letter and her world at a standstill. Su Hei stood silently looking down. When she finally raised her eyes, Shao Peng took a step back, almost stumbling in the process. Her hand shot up to her chest; the letter fluttered to the floor. She could feel her heart beat. "Su Hei? she asked hesitantly. There was no mistaking her for anyone but Li Ling's daughter. She was her splitting image.

"So, this is her," said Suet Ping coming into the drawing room blissfully unaware of the tense under-currents. "What a pretty girl! Come, come and meet my daughters, Fern and Rose. You will be going to the same school and they will help you out."

Suet Ping's entrance brought Shao Peng to the present. She looked at her sister-in-law. Suet Ping showed no sign of recognition. Then why should she? Li Ling was always in the kitchen and Suet Ping was a guest then and probably did not notice the servants. She must take a grip of herself and not spoil it for Suet Ping.

"Yes, let's go and see Fern and Rose," she agreed with a brightness she did not feel. "It is not I but my stepmother who is the mistress of this household. She is taking a nap and we should not disturb her." So saying, she led Su Hei to the stairway.

"Do you have any other luggage?" Suet Ping asked looking at the meagre bag in the girl's hand. Surely, she wondered, there could not be more than three garments in the whole bag.

"No," Su Hei answered, "just this."

"Come! We'll go to your room and deposit your bag. We'll check later to see what else you might need." Shao Peng glanced at Su Hei from the corner of her eye. She was troubled and could not dispel the feeling of *deja vu*. She could feel the hairs standing up on her arms. She shivered.

They went up the stairs with Suet Ping following closely. "You are in the room next to my daughters," she told Su Hei. "You will share their bathroom. It is not a big room and Fern and Rose have helped decorate it. You'll see." Suet Ping was glad to have another young person in the house. With her mother-in-law ill and Siew Loong away most of the time, the household had become even more gloomy.

Su Hei ran her hand over the banister; the wood was satin smooth under her fingers. She withdrew her hand hastily; she had left a trail of damp finger marks. Looking up, she saw lights that twinkled like diamonds. A large blue and white pot of ferns stood at the corner of the landing, their fronds lush and full, sprouting from its core. The house was very grand; it was in fact the most beautiful house she had ever seen. She felt intimidated by it all. Her stomach churned. She wished her mother was with her to see it. She could not reveal that her mother was in the country. She did not know when she would be able to see her again. She felt herself being carried along by a tide of events she had no control over. She regretted promising her mother so much.

Shao Peng, observed the flit of emotions on the girl's face and the desperate sadness in her eyes. "What's the matter?" she asked.

Su Hei shook her head. She could not speak.

They stopped in front of a door. "Here you are. I hope you like it." Shao Peng pushed open the door and stepped aside to allow Su Hei in. She looked at Suet Ping. Their eyes met. "Perhaps we should let you settle down and make yourself at home. Fern and Rose will come to you in a while. When you are ready come down. We'll talk then."

After they left, Su Hei sat on the bed. Her mother's instructions ricocheted in her head and an incredible sense of tiredness came over her. She lay on the bed and drew her knees up to her chest. She was frightened.

Chapter 44

SHAO PENG TURNED A PAGE of the book. She was listless. She could not concentrate. She kept returning to the previous page to remind herself of what she had read. With a sigh of frustration, she closed the book firmly. She could not get over the meeting with Su Hei. She found herself covertly examining the girl whenever she had a chance. Su Hei not only looked like Li Ling, she talked and moved like her. She had a habit of brushing her fringe to one side whenever she was spoken to; when she smiled, her cheeks dimpled in the disarming way that was Li Ling's. Most disconcerting of all were her eyes; she had big long eyes with thick lashes and they looked straight at you, uncompromising in their directness; just like her mother. Shao Peng had to stop herself from calling her Li Ling. She had an overwhelming desire to gather Su Hei in her arms and apologise for failing her mother. Despite everyone's assurance that Li Ling's troubles were not Shao Peng's doing, Shao Peng never forgave herself. Su Hei's sudden appearance into her life gave her a chance to make amends and she had to do it quickly before she left for England. Yet she was uneasy. She couldn't quite place what was causing it.

"Why the glumness?" asked Jack coming into the bedroom. He slipped out of his dressing gown and came to bed. "I thought you said everything was going well."

"Yes it is. Fern and Rose took to Su Hei as did Suet Ping. I was apprehensive that Rohani would find her likeness to Li Ling difficult. I was wrong. My stepmother was kindness itself. No mention was made of the past. Perhaps that was for Suet Ping's benefit. Suet Ping knows nothing about Li Ling and my stepmother's fear that my brother would fall in love with her. I think Rohani was also kind partly because she was very sorry for Li Ling's sufferings. If you remember, she literally drove Li Ling out of the house. Mind you, Su Hei helped herself a lot by her winning ways. Unlike her mother Su Hei was very solicitous towards Rohani. She asked after her health; she was polite; she was ready to fetch and carry for Rohani and anticipate her wishes."

Shao Peng looked at her husband, an amused smile on her lips for the first time that evening. "Despite my stepmother's longing to return to her *kampong* and her people, as she puts it, she has become very Chinese in her outlook. Such things seemed to matter to her more and more, day by day."

"So why then were you frowning earlier on?" Jack slid an arm around Shao Peng and drew her close. She put her head on his shoulder.

Shao Peng shrugged. "I don't know. Su Hei's resemblance to her mother, I suppose. It is uncanny. I wonder how my brother will react if he sees her."

***

Siew Loong pushed aside the papers he had just signed and got up. The lengthy quarantine of immigrant labour in Port Swettenham had held up work in his rubber plantation. The cost of these delays was fast rising. He had to find a way to stop these irrational measures. He had not believed what was said about conditions in the detention centres and had gone to see for himself. He was shocked to the core.

Thousands of men and women were cooped up in unspeakable conditions. They had literally only standing room. Each person had to himself less than five square feet of space in the closed internment area. It was foul. The place stank. There were only twenty-three latrines for the three thousand odd coolies interned in the area. Fifteen were for men and eight for women. In the past couple of months alone, several hundreds of lives had been lost under the wretched conditions. This could well exceed the lives that were intended to be saved by the quarantine. It made him angry. How could anyone think that such a quarantine would help save lives? Why weren't the Authorities more prepared?

Immediately on his return from Port Swettenham, he got together with other planters to lobby for its removal. Many of the British firms had as much to lose as he did if not more. They argued for better sanitation and health facilities. Unfortunately, not everyone gave the problem their full attention. The disunity left the lobby in disarray. Siew Loong sighed. He picked up a copy of the Penang Gazette. It would seem that what was written had more than a grain of truth; 'everybody's business had become nobody's business.'

"And now this!" He muttered angrily picking up the Malay Mail. Almost overnight, plantations were told to provide welfare and medical facilities for their workers. There were no public hospitals they could turn to. The expansion of rubber had risen by well over a hundredfold since it first started but the Government seemed not to have anticipated the problems that had arisen. So they had given the task of solving it to planters.

How could he provide such facilities? How could he, an individual, provide what should be supplied by the Government? Yet how could he not? He was legally bound to do so. If he did not, his supply of work force would dry up. They would just stop his license to bring labour in.

His mind became totally occupied with the problem of setting up and running a hospital on his estate. He had no experience in it. He didn't know where to get the right staff for a hospital. Agitated, he paced up and down the room. Maybe he should try to convene a meeting with one of the many foreign-owned plantations and work out a way to set up a hospital jointly with them. "Sime Darby or Guthries?" he asked aloud. "Which one would be more amenable?" A bigger hospital meant more economy of scale. He would be able to have better facilities, better staff. He should try to make an appointment with Dr. Galloway and Dr. Malcolm Watson, both of whom had done good work in tropical diseases. He should also consult Kapitan Yap Kwan Seng. The Tung Shin hospital he built in Sultan Street for paupers might offer him some ideas. He snatched a piece of paper and scribbled down his ideas.

"*Towkay!* Boss, shall I start to lock up now?" interrupted the porter. "The other staff have long left the office."

Siew Loong stopped in his tracks. "Yes! Lock up. I am finished here." He sat down. The thought of returning to his small empty apartment adjacent to his office left him cold. Yet he was reluctant to go to Ann Ee. She had become too clinging. Perhaps, he should go home. He had not seen his mother and his two girls for a while.

Chapter 45

SIEW LOONG SWUNG HIS LEGS out of the car. The gravel crunched under his feet. He turned, shifting his weight to close the door and stood for a moment to gaze at the house silhouetted against the fast darkening sky. Sunlight peeped from behind a cloud and lit up his mother's quarters in the west wing. It was a place where he had found solace when he was young, where cuts and hurts were tended to, a place where he had access while his sister Shao Peng had not. Now he was a reluctant visitor. Siew Loong wondered how his mother was. A servant came out; she saw him. She retraced her steps and ran inside, no doubt, he thought, to warn his mother and the kitchen. The front door opened from within by unseen hands, like a magical force that had been waiting for his return that evening. He stepped in, pausing to allow a maid to undo his shoes and help him into a pair of house slippers. "*Siew yeh*, master," she said. He mumbled a reply and thanked her.

The house was quiet. When he was a child, he imagined the house to be a breathing, living entity. The swish of curtains when the wind blew or the slam of a door were transformed in his mind into magical powers. He had loved his home.

He made his way to the stairway. Sounds of chatter and giggles floated down the stairway. He recognised them as Fern's and Rose's. He was tempted to visit them first instead of seeing his mother. He decided against it. It was best that he got it over with. The question of his duty to bring forth a son would no doubt be at the top of his mother's agenda. He mounted the steps, his heart heavy.

***

Siew Loong knocked. Voices came from within. He hesitated. He did not want to confront his mother and his wife at the same time. It would be too much. For the briefest of moment, his fist stayed suspended mid air; then he pushed open the door and went in. He could not allow himself to be intimidated in his own home.

His mother was talking animatedly to Suet Ping and another woman. Her face lit up when she saw him. She beckoned him to come to her, rising to her feet at the same time and rushing to meet him halfway. Siew Loong felt a twinge of guilt. How could he be so churlish when his mother was so happy to see him. Suet Ping too came forward. His smile faltered. His eyes shifted to the remaining figure, a slim form with slender arms and a tiny waist, that was vaguely familiar. The form took a step and turned around. His heart contracted and he could hardly breathe. "Li Ling?" he gasped.

Rohani saw the astonishment in his face. "No! It is Su Hei, Li Ling's daughter. I too was taken back by their resemblance. I'll tell you more when you have settled down."

She indicated to Su Hei that she could leave. Su Hei smiled, bobbed her head and addressed him as master and left. Siew Loong watched her go. His heartbeat quickened with each intake of breath. He was unable to concentrate on the things that his mother said to him. All he could think of was what he had just seen. Li Ling had become a reality instead of a dream that haunted him. He excused himself and hurried out of the room.

***

Siew Loong came home every day after that day. Rohani was delighted. One morning after he left for work, Rohani went in search of Suet Ping. She found her daughter-in-law in the sewing room bent over her embroidery. "What are you making?" she asked.

Suet Ping placed the tambour frame down. "A pillow case. Should you be walking? You could have called me." She got up and took Rohani's arm helping her to a chair.

"I am feeling so much better now that Siew Loong comes home every day," Rohani relinquished her walking stick, placing it against her chair. "Are you happier now that he is back? Is he treating you better?"

"Yes!" Suet Ping could not meet her mother-in-law's eyes. Siew Loong had not shared her bed in the entire week that he had been at home. She suspected that it was common knowledge in the household. Siew Loong had had a room made up for himself. It adjoined hers. She went to him thrice; each time the door was locked. She blushed in shame at the memory of his rejection.

She had placed a ear against the door and sensed his presence behind it. She had messed up her bed in the morning to pretend that his side of the bed had been slept in and had opened the adjoining door after he left his room. She feared that the servants were not fooled by her deception. The thought made her cringe.

Rohani guessed that all was not well. "*Mmmm* ... Shall I say something to him?"

Suet Ping turned a deeper red. "What can you say *ibu*?" She replied in Malay.

"Could you not go to him?"

Suet Ping hung her head. "I tried." She spread her fingers out, her knuckles white against the strain. "Please, *ibu* don't let's talk about it. My husband is not interested in me. Perhaps I should return home to my parents." She dreaded the thought of being sent home in such disgrace.

"I won't hear of it! It is my son's fault or rather mine for having landed both of you in such a situation. *Adoi! Apa yang boleh buat!* Rohani lapsed into Malay as to what she should do. "Come, wipe your face. Say no more about returning home. We'll have to work out a plan," she said with more confidence than she felt.

***

The car stopped in front of the house. Fern and Rose got out. Giggling and laughing, they ran ahead. Su Hei rose and was about to follow suit when Siew Loong stopped her. She felt his hand clasping her arm. His fingers were burning hot. She turned and smiled at him.

"Are you settling down?" he asked with his hand still on her arm. His eyes did not leave her face. She nodded. He released her, his fingers tingling from the touch, his heart beating fast. "Good," he said with a wave of his hand that she should go.

He sat behind the wheel and watched Su Hei step out of the car and turned to smile at him. He could not stop the longing and guilt in his heart. He knew he should not think of Su Hei in that way. She was too young for him. He reminded himself that Su Hei was not Li Ling and he was no longer the young Siew Loong. He was a husband and a father. Yet he could not shake off the feeling that Li Ling and Su Hei were one and the same. At times in the past week, like a moment ago, he wanted to crush her to him, to devour all of her. He wished he could wipe off all the years in between and start anew. He knew that it was not an option.

With a heavy heart he got out of the car and followed the girls into the house. Suet Ping was there to meet him. She was the last person he wanted to see. He felt guilty enough without being reminded. Suet Ping, however, seemed not to notice anything amiss.

"The girls were so excited that you went to fetch them from school. What a lovely idea and surprise for them," she said, bending down to set his house slippers on the floor.

"There is no need. I can do it myself." He wanted to jerk his feet away. Instead he took the slippers from her and slid them on. Without saying another word, he walked away.

Rebuffed, Suet Ping looked quickly around to see if anyone else noticed the exchange. She went into the dining room. Everyone was already seated around the table. She slipped into her chair and apologised for her lateness. She had to set the example of inviting her elders to eat. Rohani had adopted this practice as she did much of the etiquettes practised by Chinese families. It was what her father-in-law would have liked if he was alive.

The young were not supposed to start eating before their elders.

"*Nai-nai sik fan*," she said. She stared at Fern to prompt her. To her relief, her children needed little prompting. At least, that part went well, thought Suet Ping. She picked up her chopsticks and began choosing the best pieces of meat for Rohani.

"Your wife is such a wonderful woman," Rohani whispered to Siew Loong. "She looks after me like a daughter takes care of her mother."

Suet Ping turned her attention to her husband and began placing food on his side plate. This was what her mother had instructed her to do. "First look after your mother-in-law, then your husband," she had said.

Siew Loong grunted. "Please don't. I can do it myself. Just eat, will you? Stop fussing!"

Suet Ping swallowed. She tried hard not to mind what was again clearly a snub, this time in front of the whole family and even the attending servants. She glanced quickly at her children. Fern's eyes were like saucers and Rose's lips quivered. Siew Loong saw and was immediately contrite. He tried to make amends and told Suet Ping more kindly that she should look after herself and not worry about others.

He chided himself. It was not his wife's fault that he had little feeling for her. He should not have married her; he should not have acceded to his mother's demand. But the water was under the bridge and he should really try to be nicer. He made up his mind that he would go to her that night. Siew Loong stole a fleeting look at the far end of the table. He had tried not to look that way. He just couldn't resist it. Su Hei was seated there. She saw him look her way and smiled, the dimples deepening in her cheeks and her eyes warm as they engaged his. His heart did a double flip. He returned the smile. Rohani saw the exchange.

***

It was the weekend. Remembering what her mother and Ah Chu had instructed, Su Hei went to Rohani's room. She knocked and then, on hearing the invitation to go in, pushed open the door with her shoulder and entered.

"What do you have with you?" Rohani was surprised for Su Hei was carrying a basin, with a towel draped around her forearm. Two little wooden implements hung around her shoulder.

"Good morning. I came to ask if you would like me to attend to your feet." She had observed Rohani's discomfort when she walked. "My mother taught me how to do it. She said that it is a wonderful treatment for tired feet; it will help improve blood circulation. Would you like that?" She placed the basin down on the floor and fished out a phial from her pocket and handed it to Rohani. "I got some lovely aromatic oils from her."

Rohani took the phial and inhaled. "*Mmmm!* Wonderful. Let's try it. Shall I sit down?" She was eager to try anything to reduce the swelling in her feet and ankles.

"Yes please. I'll fill the basin with warm water."

Su Hei took the basin and pattered out to the bathroom. She was excited at her first undertaking. It was a chance to put into practice what she had been taught. She returned with the basin filled with warm water. She placed it on the floor and gently placed both of Rohani's feet in the basin. The warm steam and scent filled the room. Rohani felt her body relax; she leaned back and allowed herself to be administered to. Su Hei knelt in front of her and gently sluiced the feet, trickling the warm water between the toes. She laid a towel on her lap and placed Rohani's foot on it; then she massaged it, her thumbs working deeply into its pressure points. A small sigh of pleasure escaped from Rohani. After each foot had been washed, massaged and oiled, Su Hei took out her two little sticks with a wooden ball attached to each. "I am going to gently pummel your soles with this to help improve blood flow. Tell me if it is too hard," she said. Rohani emitted a grunt. She had nodded off; her shoulders sagged in total relaxation, her head lolled back and her lips parted.

Su Hei was pleased. Quietly she rested Rohani's feet on a foot stool and gathered her tools. She straightened up and left the room.

***

Suet Ping sat back on her chair. Outside a storm was whipping up the trees to a frenzy. The rain splattering on the roof drowned all sounds in the house. She laid down her sewing. She was on edge. The room felt like a prison, the air humid and cloying. There was nothing for her to do. Her husband was working hard in his office downstairs and would not welcome any interruption. Her mother-in-law was needing her less and less. As the days and weeks passed, Su Hei had taken over more and more of the things that Suet Ping used to do for her mother-in-law. On days like this, Suet Ping felt superfluous.

Suet Ping got up. She felt stifled. She needed to get out. Perhaps she could pop into the kitchen. Someone was bound to be there. She could talk to them and it would help fill her loneliness. Fern and Rose had gone for the day to Shao Peng. If they were in, their laughter and chatter would at least fill some of the emptiness. She went out to the stairway with the sound of rain beating in her head like a drum. Midway down the stairs she paused. She saw Su Hei heading towards the lobby with a tray in her hands. On the tray was a teapot, a teacup and a small plate of sweet mung bean biscuits, her husband's favourite. The lobby led to a set of rooms to the east wing of the house, one of which was his office. No one was allowed in when he was at work unless it was something urgent. A sudden unease came over Suet Ping. She hastened down the steps. Su Hei heard her and turned around with a wide disarming smile.

"Ah Tai asked me to take this to Master," she explained. "He had asked for tea. The kitchen is rather short-handed at the moment."

"I'll do it." Suet Ping took the tray. She watched until Su Hei could not be seen. Carefully balancing the tray, she went to Siew Loong's office. His face lit up and then froze when he saw her. Suet Ping's heart sank. She saw the guilt in his face. She realised that he was expecting Su Hei and was disappointed when it was her, his wife. She said nothing. She set the tray down and left. She could feel his eyes on her back. Outside the office, she leaned against the door. She breathed deeply to calm herself. She should have expected it. His sudden reappearance at home should have been a warning.

Chapter 46

"So you are really leaving?" asked Fern.

"Yes," said James. "I don't want to. My parents say that it is for the best. I will hate it I am sure. I will hate being in a big school. I have never been in one. My friends tell me that boarding schools are nasty." James was downcast. He had been arguing with his parents against returning to England.

"You are not going to a boarding school, James," interrupted Shao Peng, coming into the room. "Your father and I will be with you. You will be going to your father's old school. We'll make sure that you will not be bullied." Shao Peng went over to James and placed both arms around him. James struggled and broke free. He didn't want to look like a sissy in front of his cousins.

"I hate you," he shouted and ran out. He slammed the door.

Shao Peng sighed. "Both of you must come and visit us in England. James would like that very much and we too. In fact, I am sure I can arrange for you to go to school there. Perhaps I could talk to your father and mother about it, that is of course if both of you are interested. I won't say a word if you are not."

Fern looked at Rose. The thought of studying in England had never crossed their minds. It was already a wonderful thing that they went to school and studied English. Not many girls had such an opportunity. The idea of leaving home for a foreign country filled them with both apprehension and excitement. Fern clasped her sister's hand in her own. "We don't know if we are interested or not interested," she said. "Can we discuss it among ourselves?"

"You don't have to tell me now. We still have a month before we leave, so there is plenty of time. I..."

"Shao Peng!"

Shao Peng spun around at the sound of her name being called.

"Mummy! Why are you here?" asked Rose.

Shao Peng realised immediately that something was wrong. Suet Ping looked distraught. "Why don't both of you go to James and comfort him?" she asked the two girls.

"Please go," Suet Ping said.

The girls sensed that it was not the moment to protest or ask questions. Impulsively, Fern went to her mother and threw her arms around her; Rose followed suit. Then they left with a final backward glance at their sobbing mother.

***

"I came here because it was you that brought that vixen to our house."

"I don't understand what you are talking about. Surely you are not talking about Su Hei?" What has she done?"

Suet Ping, her face red with anger, shouted. "She is trying to take my place. Why didn't you tell me that my husband had a history with Su Hei's mother? I am the last one to know. I had to learn it from a servant! How could you have brought her to my house knowing full well that it could stir up old feelings in Siew Loong? To think that I trusted you! To think that I welcomed her with open arms and asked my daughters to befriend her!"

"Are you sure she is trying to lure Siew Loong away? She is only a young girl for goodness sake! And as for Siew Loong's so-called relationship with Li Ling, the mother, I wouldn't call it that. He liked and pitied her. Didn't he marry you instead?" Even as she protested, Shao Peng was beginning to doubt herself. The strange feeling she had since Su Hei's arrival had been unsettling her for weeks. She had not been able to fathom its cause. She asked herself if this was what was troubling her. Was she guilty of unwittingly burying her reservations? Had she allowed her desire to make amends blind her to what, with hindsight, seem a possible outcome?

"I don't know why he married me. It was certainly not because he loved me."

Shao Peng took a step towards her sister-in-law. She tried to take her in her arms and console her. Suet Ping pushed her away.

"Calm down! Let's speak to Rohani. I am sure it is not like what you think. Su Hei just wants to make herself useful. She is grateful to be taken in and treated so well." Inwardly, Shao Peng prayed that what she said was true. She still could not bring herself to believe that her brother would have an affair with someone so young. He was too strong and rational for that. Neither could she believe that Su Hei could be so devious.

"I want her out of my house. You understand? I won't allow you to bulldoze the issue away by bringing my mother-in-law into it. Rohani is bewitched by the girl."

Shao Peng flinched. She had never seen Suet Ping so angry before. "I will take her away. Let me talk to Siew Loong. We cannot accuse him without giving him a chance to explain himself."

Upstairs, crouching down on a step and hanging on to the banister, Fern looked at her sister. They heard it all. They asked each other if their father, their stern and upright father, could have fallen in love with Su Hei? What would become of their mother? What would become of them?

***

The house was quiet. The storm had cleared the air. Outside in the garden, an owl hooted and a cacophony of insect sounds filled the night with an urgent buzz. In the distance a dog yelped. Su Hei peered out of the window and looked up. The rain had stopped but water continued to drip from the eaves of the roof; it splattered down to the ground below, bringing sparks of bright silver into the dark. Gradually the drops grew less frequent until everything became still.

Su Hei shivered for the night air was cold. She closed the window. Dinner had been a very strained affair that evening. Suet Ping and the girls were not at the table. Ah Tai said that they had returned from Shao Peng's and would not be joining them. She wondered why.

She got into bed and pulled the sheets right up to her chin. So far she had done all that her mother had instructed. She had tried very hard to please Rohani. She was friendly to Fern and Rose and respectful to Suet Ping. She had helped the servants in whatever they wanted her to do and above all she had smiled whenever Master Siew Loong looked at her. And it would seem that he looked at her a lot. She was conscious of his eyes following her movements, so much so that she was embarrassed at times. She hoped that it was not obvious to the others. It was not hard to smile at the Master. He made her feel good.

She lifted the sheet and looked down at her chest. Her breasts stood pert, the nipples hard. She was more aware of her body than she had ever been since she moved here. Perhaps it was the Master's looking at her that prompted it. A warmth spread over her, lodging deep in her groins. She wanted to clamp her legs tight. Ah Chu's daughters had told her about what would happen between a man and a woman. It had initially filled her with horror; then fascination and curiosity followed. She let the sheets fall and slid deeper into the bed.

Her mother hoped the Master would marry her. How could that be? He was already married. Mistress Suet Ping had been so nice. Wouldn't she be hurt? Su Hei turned on her side. She was probably worried about something that would never happen. Although Master Siew Loong was always staring at her, he had said little beyond the ordinary polite questions about her well-being. She reached out and hugged the bolster to her. How would it feel if he was to hug her? She clasped the bolster even more tightly, rubbing her body against it. What if he touched her?

***

The sun was barely up when Shao Peng arrived at her brother's home. She went straight into the house and was told that Siew Loong had just finished his breakfast and was about to leave. She walked quickly towards his office and caught him leaving it with a case in his hand. He looked up in surprise.

"Why are you here?" he asked striding forward without stopping. "I don't have time to speak to you. I have to leave now; I have urgent matters to attend to in the estate. The Port Authorities have released my workers. They will be arriving at the estate in a couple of hours time. There is much paperwork to complete."

She strode alongside him, keeping pace. "I need to talk to you. It is about Su Hei."

For a split second, his pace faltered. Then he walked even more rapidly than before. Shao Peng found herself running to keep up with him.

"Nothing to talk about. I suppose it is Suet Ping who asked you to come. I expected this to happen when she came home and refused dinner."

Shao Peng grabbed hold of his forearm. "Are you having an affair with Su Hei?"

He flung her arm away. The violence of it sent her reeling. She recoiled from the fury in his face.

"It is none of your business. Go home! Pack and leave! Your intrusion into my affairs is not wanted." He did not raise his voice; the terseness of his speech and his face was enough.

"Don't you understand? It is my business. I brought her here. I will never forgive myself if my actions cause such havoc for your family. Please, please Siew Loong, listen to me." She touched his arm again, gently this time, her voice pleading.

He stopped mid-stride. He said nothing. Neither did he look at her. Silence brooded between them. Time ticked by. It was just minutes, may be even seconds; in Shao Peng's mind it seemed like hours.

"I loved Li Ling. I didn't know how much until I lost her. By then it was too late and I had married. You know that I married to please mother. I can't do it any more. Of course Su Hei brings back all my memories of Li Ling. What do you expect? When I see her, it is as though I never grew older and we are those two young people years ago. I have not touched her. Tell Suet Ping if that would make her happier. I can't, however, vouch, that I can remain celibate forever. After today, I will not stay at home. I cannot risk the temptation. Perhaps having me consort with other women outside this household is preferable. I am not heartless. I understand Suet Ping's situation."

He turned to face his elder sister. " I cannot bring myself to go near Suet Ping. I tried. I am sorry, truly sorry."

Shao Peng saw the wretchedness in his eyes. She could feel his hurt like her own. She, the elder by so many years, had been the cause of her young brother's hurt.

"What if I take Su Hei away. Would that help?"

"Why should she suffer? I'll go."

Siew Loong walked quickly away, out of the house and into the car. Shao Peng watched as the car sped away.

***

"What did he say?" Suet Ping asked even before she reached Shao Peng.

With eyes bleak with sadness, Shao Peng turned to her sister-in-law. She was torn between these two young people. They were both suffering and all for that one wrong decision, they married without love. She thanked God for her own situation; she fought for the right to choose her own husband and despite the pains she suffered when she was young, at least in her old age she had the comfort of a husband that she loved and who loved her. These two people had none of what she had. She took

Suet Ping's hands in hers. They were ice cold. "He said he never touched Su Hei."

Suet Ping's eyes lit up and her lips trembled with relief.

"He said he'll not come home any more because he cannot guarantee that he can maintain this for much longer."

The silence that followed was like a throbbing heartbeat, violent, emotive, silent. The light in Suet Ping's eyes went out. Her face aged visibly. She turned and made her way up the stairs, the stairway that she had just minutes ago descended in such a hurry, full of fear and yet still hopeful. The hope was completely gone.

Shao Peng followed her. "We'll talk to Rohani." She was seized with a sudden anger at her stepmother. She blamed her for her selfishness that drove Li Ling away, that resulted in Li Ling's sufferings and the sufferings of a brother that she loved and the suffering of a sister-in-law who by all accounts was blameless. She pounded on Rohani's door and marched in without being invited. She told Rohani what happened. By the time she finished she was breathless and drained.

"I know I am to blame," her stepmother said. "Let's not play the blame game though. If you had not brought Li Ling and if you had not brought Su Hei to this household, none of this would have happened. Of course, if I hadn't put pressure on those two young people to marry, this too perhaps would not have happened. If! If! What is the point? What do you want me to do? Kill myself?"

Rohani's face was suffused with blood as she screeched out her frustration; the veins in her temple and the tendons in her neck pulsated with a life of their own. She stood up, swayed and sat down again. Shao Peng fearing another heart attack went immediately to her stepmother. "You are right. I am sorry. I too am to blame. Take a deep breath. Try to keep calm." She snatched a glass of water from the table and held it for Rohani.

"Ask Suet Ping what she wants," said Rohani in a quieter voice. "It is not what we want that counts. Does she still want to be Siew Loong's wife? What is she prepared to do to keep him? In the end, I am afraid, that is all that which matters. If she wants a divorce, I would not stand in her way although I do not wish it. Then of course, what does Siew Loong want? What will bring him home again?"

***

Suet Ping went home to her mother. She took Fern and Rose with her. She told no one. Mayhem broke out the minute she stepped into her parents' house. Mrs Lam was shocked at her daughter's audacity in returning home without consulting her or her mother-in-law.

"Whatever happens, you owe it to your mother-in-law to tell her that you are leaving. You owe it to your father and me to tell us before making such a momentous decision. What will people think! Be assured, people will say that it is your fault; that your inability to bear a son has caused the Ong family to kick you out. You should know that is a legitimate reason for a husband to divorce a wife. Worse, people could say that you have done some terrible things like ... like adultery or failing to be filial to your mother-in-law! They will not believe that you left on your own accord. What shame for our family! Listen, I have never heard of a woman leaving her husband. Who will look after you and your daughters? Have you thought about Fern and Rose? How could you be so selfish to think only of yourself? What are their marriage prospects if people know that their mother was discarded by the husband's family?"

Suet Ping clamped her hands to her ears to shut out the accusations hurled at her. Mrs Lam pulled them away. She pushed her face close to Suet Pings. Alarmed, Fern and Rose sobbed and huddled together in shock.

Mrs. Lam Mu Lan stopped. She pulled Suet Ping into her arms. "I am sorry," she murmured into her daughter's hair. "I do not wish you to be hurt. But we women have to accept our fate." She stroked Suet Ping's hair.

"Look at Fern and Rose. Think of them."

Lam Mu Lan fished out a handkerchief and wiped her daughter's face. The tears had soaked into her own blouse and were still flowing down Suet Ping's cheeks. "Do you love Siew Loong?" she asked.

Suet Ping blew her nose and nodded.

"You told me about this girl Su Hei. Would you consider this?" She whispered in Suet Ping's ear. "Go home and think about it. Don't let on that you came home with the intention of leaving your husband. Just say that you went to see your parents for the day. Think carefully and let me know. I'll help you in whatever way I can."

***

Suet Ping returned to the Ong's household. After comforting Fern and Rose and seeing them to bed, she sat in the dark alone to think over her mother's proposition. The crying and talking had left her exhausted, yet strangely calm. It was as though a great weight had been lifted from her. Her mind was cleared. She did not want to be seen as a woman discarded by her husband. Why should she? She had done no wrong. She wanted to stay as Mrs Ong Siew Loong, the rightful first wife. Why should anyone have her place? She wanted to win Siew

Loong's love. So she should give him what he wants. If that was Su Hei, then let it be Su Hei.

Having such a young girl as the second wife was better than contending with one that was experienced and could and would fight back tooth and nail. Her mother assured her that such loves will come and go; the wife will remain. And she Suet Ping will remain. In turn Suet Ping should ask for her due in return for her acceptance of Su Hei. Her mother had explained that the practice of secondary wives and concubines was so ingrained in the Chinese culture that she was in fact surprised that Siew Loong had not taken one earlier. She had reeled off a list of men, rich men with not two, but even three, four or more wives. Suet Ping found comfort that she was not the only wife so misused.

She sat still as a dormouse in the dark letting these thoughts go through her mind. Her heart hardened. Yes, she resolved, I would have to have my dues. Su Hei's firstborn son shall be mine and mine alone. I shall name him Ming Kong. She would have to give him up completely to me to raise and love. That would be my condition for my consent that she be taken in.

***

The wedding took place one month later.

From across the street, Li Ling stood amongst the crowd to watch the procession. She caught her breath when Siew Loong came out to greet Su Hei and to take her formally into the house. She closed her eyes. It was like he had come for her. Li Ling received the look of love Siew Loong gave to Su Hei as her own. Her heart brimmed over with happiness and pride. She was not just a flash of water. She was part of Siew Loong.

The Historical Background

In writing this novel, I was inspired by real historical events in the late 1800s and early 1900s and wove them into the story.

In China, where the story begins, it was a time of the rise of warlords and social unrest. Christian missionaries flocked into China following its defeat in the Second Opium War, sparking hatred against foreign imperialism and Christianity. This was later to manifest itself in the Boxer Rebellion (1898–1900) where thousands of Chinese Christians and many foreign missionaries were killed.

In Malaya, the changes were equally dramatic. More and more Chinese women came to Malaya when China lifted the ban on their travel. Where previously there were well over ten Chinese men to one Chinese woman in the country, the disparity in numbers between the genders began to fall. Amongst the rich

Chinese, polygamy grew to become more common place. Rubber was introduced into Malaya and the crop overtook tin as the main foreign exchange earner in the country. With it came Indian and Sri Lankan migrants who supplied most of the workforce for the plantations. This second wave of mass migration into the country following the first advent of Chinese labour to work in the tin mines wrought huge social and political changes in the country, the impact of which remains today.

With the entry of these two ancient cultures, geographical segregation amongst the different ethnic groups began to materialise and solidify. In Kuala Lumpur where the story is mainly located, the Chinese congregated in Chinatown, now known as Petaling Street, or *Chee Cheong Gai*. Later they spread to Pudu. The Indians settled in rubber plantations. Within cities, however, they stayed mainly around railway depots because they provided the workforce for the construction of railway lines. Brickfields and later Sentul, both railway centres, became the hub for Indians in Kuala Lumpur. In the face of this, the British administration established Kampong Baru for the Malay people to preserve their culture. The British kept themselves apart from the local populace, occupying the hilly western part of the city to the west of the Gombak river. This segregation is often suggested as one of the main causes for division between the races.

Kuala Lumpur, situated between the confluence of the River Klang and the River Gombak, was transformed during this period from a settlement of huts to the beginnings of a modern city built of bricks and mortar. Several notable events sparked this transformation. The first were the great fires and floods of the early 1880s which swept away large parts of the town. When Frank Swettenham took over the administration of Selangor in 1882, he decreed that new buildings were to be built of brick and mortar. Two appointed Chinese leaders of the time, Kapitan Yap Ah Loy and later on Kapitan Yap Kwan Seng, rose to the challenge. Yap Ah Loy bought the land now known as Brickfields and set up a brick-building industry that was to spur on the rebuilding of Kuala Lumpur. Yap Kwan Seng, when he took over the post of Kapitan China, did the same thus aiding in the further development of the town. The floods described in the novel were inspired by the great floods that tore down much of Kuala Lumpur in 1881. The tapioca and rice mill mentioned in the story were inspired by the tapioca factory owned by Kapitan Yap Ah Loy.

A system of education gradually took root in the late 1800s. Christian missionaries played an important role, often with the philanthropic support of Chinese businessmen and the Kapitans China appointed to oversee the Chinese community. I borrowed the beginnings, though I did not keep strictly to the timeline nor the real characters, of Bukit Nanas Convent in my novel.

The *real* sisters of the Congregation of the Holy Infant Jesus who started the school in 1899 soon after they arrived were: Reverend Mother St Levine, Sisters St Sabine and St Magdalene. Any resemblance of the characters in the book to these three women is purely coincidental. The first school was in a garden shed located opposite Bukit Nanas, or Pineapple Hill so named because of the pineapples grown around an old fort. Provided by a Chinese lady, *Nyonya* Ah Yok, it inspired the one described in the book. The school later moved to Brickfields. This was made possible by its benefactor Goh Ah Ngee who helped raised funds for the purchase of a hotel (the Victoria Hotel) which was used to house the school. In 1912, the school moved back to its present location, Bukit Nanas.

Other prominent missionaries who aided the development of education in Kuala Lumpur include Betty Langland, who started the first girls' school in Kuala Lumpur. The school was first conceived in 1893 when she brought some girls together and taught them to read. It was originally called the Chinese Girls' School before acquiring its present name, Bukit Bintang Girl school, when it moved to that location. Then there was the Methodist Girl school (1896), Methodist Boy school (1897), St John's Institution (1904) and St Mary's (1912), my old school. The Victoria Institution, a boys' school mentioned in the novel, was for many years the only secular school in Kuala Lumpur. It was founded in 1893 *interalia* by my great grandfather Kapitan Yap Kwan Seng and formally opened in 1894 and named after Queen Victoria, to commemorate her golden jubilee. The Victoria Institution provided my sixth form education. Albeit a boys' school, it took in a handful of girl pupils from girl schools that did not have sixth form facilities.

Lawlessness and fights between secret societies and gangs were commonplace. Many a battle between rival clans and chieftains were fought in Bukit Nanas. In the early days, the British Administration, for the most part acting only in an advisory role, left the care of the different ethnic groups to the heads of the respective communities. Brothels, opium and gambling dens were rife. Many if not most of them were tied to secret societies and triads. In 1877, Singapore had 212 public brothels; by 1905 the numbers reached 353 housing in total some 1,150 prostitutes. Kuala Lumpur, a much smaller township in comparison, had about 53 brothels and just under a thousand prostitutes in 1906. The numbers excluded non-registered brothels and other informal arrangements for trafficking women. Conditions in these brothels were often described as horrendous. Venereal diseases were rife. Life for these women was hard.

I have given a glimpse of the historical inspiration behind the novel. But it is to be remembered that this is a book of fiction, and its characters and happenings are purely sprung from imagination.